OCEANSIDE PUBLIC LIBRARY
330 N. Coast Highway
Oceanside, CA 92054

D0056735

Also by John Saul

Suffer the Children
Punish the Sinners
Cry for the Strangers
Comes the Blind Fury
When the Wind Blows
The God Project
Nathaniel
Brainchild
Hellfire
The Unwanted
The Unloved
Creature
Second Child
Sleepwalk
Darkness
Shadows
Guardian
The Homing
Black Lightning

THE BLACKSTONE CHRONICLES

Part 1: An Eye for an Eye: The Doll
Part 2: Twist of Fate: The Locket
Part 3: Ashes to Ashes: The Dragon's Flame
Part 4: In the Shadow of Evil: The Handkerchief
Part 5: Day of Reckoning: The Stereoscope
Part 6: Asylum

The Presence
The Right Hand of Evil
Nightshade
The Manhattan Hunt Club
Midnight Voices
Black Creek Crossing
Perfect Nightmare
In the Dark of the Night

THE
Devil's Labyrinth

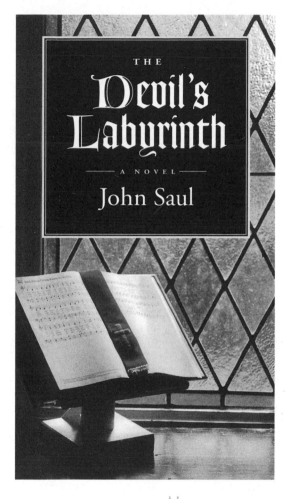

THE
Devil's Labyrinth
—— A NOVEL ——

John Saul

BALLANTINE BOOKS 📖 NEW YORK

OCEANSIDE PUBLIC LIBRARY
330 N. Coast Highway
Oceanside, CA 92054

The Devil's Labyrinth is a work of fiction. Names, characters, places, and incidents are the products of the author's imagination or are used fictitiously. Any resemblance to actual events, locales, or persons, living or dead, is entirely coincidental.

Copyright © 2007 by John Saul

All rights reserved.

Published in the United States by Ballantine Books, an imprint of The Random House Publishing Group, a division of Random House, Inc., New York.

BALLANTINE and colophon are registered trademarks of Random House, Inc.

ISBN 978-0-345-48703-2

Printed in the United States of America

www.ballantinebooks.com

2 4 6 8 9 7 5 3 1

First Edition

Text design by Laurie Jewell

3 1232 00811 9234

AUG 0 6 2007

In appreciation of
Dr. Michael Hart
and
Dr. Howard Maron
and
the crew at MD^2,
for getting us through 2006
and beyond.

THE
Devil's Labyrinth

PROLOGUE

THE OLDER BOY laid a gentle hand on the younger one's shoulder. "Ready, *Paquito?*"

The younger boy choked back his tears and nodded, determined not to let his brother see how sad he was. Avoiding his brother's gaze, he instead kept his eyes fastened on the box in his hands, the cardboard box he was clutching so hard its sides were starting to give way.

"Okay, then. Let's go." The older boy was armed with a rusty shovel from the old potting shed behind what used to be a stable, but was now a small apartment his parents rented out to vacationing *Americanos.* He led the way across the overgrown courtyard to a space between three palm trees, which hadn't yet been choked by the foliage that always seemed to grow back faster than even both brothers could cut it. "Here, okay?"

The smaller boy eyed the spot carefully, but then his gaze shifted to the small grotto that was almost invisible in the deep shadows of the farthest corner of the courtyard. "No," he said, his voice soft but certain. "Over there. Next to the Blessed Virgin."

The elder brother sighed, but headed toward the tall statue of Santa Maria. Glancing back at the house, he saw their mother standing in the doorway, her wild hair done up in a red cloth, a cleaning rag in her hand. For a moment he thought she was going to call out to them, but instead she merely shrugged, returning to her work even before he sank the shovel into the soil and lifted out the first clod of earth. "Good," he said. "The Virgin will look after Pepe."

"Do you think I should have made a *sudario*?" the smaller boy asked, his voice suddenly anxious.

"You only need a shroud for a person," his brother told him.

Barely hearing his brother, the younger boy opened the box and looked inside at the large, lifeless body of the iguana that had been his pet for more than three years. Practically as long as he could remember.

His finger trembled as he stroked the smooth skin of the lizard's leg, but now that he was dead, Pepe felt completely different than he had only yesterday.

He felt—dead.

But it was all right. Jesus would take care of him, just like the nuns said Jesus would take care of everybody. Except maybe not, because the nuns also said Jesus only took care of Catholics and everybody else went to—

Infierno.

He could barely bring himself to say the word, even to himself, and suddenly he felt himself burning with a heat even more intense than that of the Spanish summer afternoon.

Then, just as he was putting the lid back on the old shoe box that was his pet's coffin, his brother's shovel hit something.

Something hard.

But not a rock. Something different.

Something metal.

The older boy dropped to his knees.

The younger boy set the iguana in the protective shade of the courtyard wall and watched as his brother dug with his fingers, then lifted out a tarnished box with what looked like the outline of a cross on its lid.

"It's for me," the younger boy breathed. "A gift from the Virgin for giving her the body of Pepe."

The older boy smiled at his little brother. "You know what?" he asked, seeing that the boy's tears seemed finally to have dried. "I think you just might be right!" Brushing the dirt from the box, he glanced back at the house once more, just to make sure their mother wasn't watching, then carefully set the object he'd unearthed aside. "Take Pepe out of the box."

"Out of the box?" the smaller boy echoed.

"Yes, hurry, before Mama comes."

His brow furrowed, the small boy lifted the body of his pet out of the shoe box and laid him in the dirt hole his brother had dug. At the same time the other boy placed the object he'd taken from the earth into the shoe box and replaced its lid.

The older boy put his hands together and bowed his head. "*Santa Maria,*" he whispered, "look after our friend." Both boys crossed themselves, and a moment later, the hole was once again filled with soil and tamped down so the grave was nearly invisible.

"Do not tell anyone what we found in the garden," the older boy said as they stood up.

"Why not?"

"Because it's our secret, at least until we find out what's inside. Come on. You go in the kitchen door, and I'll take the box and put the shovel away, then meet you upstairs. In your room. Okay?"

Some of his grief assuaged by the excitement of this conspiracy with his brother, the boy nodded eagerly, and set off toward the house.

Their mother, humming along with the radio, stopped her youngest child at the door. She hugged him close, kissed the top of his head, then stroked his hair away from his forehead. "*Mi pequeño,*" she murmured. "You know he's gone to be with Jesus and the Holy Mother."

"*Sí,* Mama," the boy said, though he wasn't really sure she was right, at least not if what the nuns had said was true.

When she finally released him, he ran up the stone stairs to the floor above and went to his room, where his brother was already waiting for him, the object they'd dug up sitting on his bed. Where the shovel had struck the box, the boy could see a glint of silver.

Carefully, his brother worked the cover loose until he was able to lift it from the box. Inside, a wooden dowel protruded from the top of a disintegrating cloth bag.

"Be very gentle," the older boy said as his brother reached for the object, nodding, but even as his trembling fingers touched the bag, it began to fall apart.

"You do it," the little boy said, jerking his hand away.

His brother picked away the rotting threads of fabric to reveal what looked like some kind of yellowish paper wrapped around the wooden dowel.

Then, when he picked the object up, the wood crumbled to dust just as had the fabric that wrapped it.

But the scroll was of a hardier material—though it looked thin and fragile, it remained intact.

"*Piel curtido,*" he whispered. Sheepskin. He picked up the scroll and unrolled it just far enough so they could both see that it was inscribed with an ornate design.

"A treasure map," the younger boy breathed. "I bet that's what it is."

His brother opened the scroll a little farther, revealing words inside the parchment's border. "I can't read it," he said. "It's written in some other language. A different alphabet." He rolled it back up and put it back in the box. "I think it's very old."

"It's mine," the younger boy declared.

"It's ours," the older boy corrected, replacing the worn and tarnished lid on the box. "But you can keep it hidden in your closet."

† † †

Late that night, alone in his room but still awake, the younger of the brothers lay in bed, wondering at the meaning of the box and the scroll. It was certainly a gift from the Holy Mother—of that he was sure. After all, hadn't she directed him to bury Pepe where the object lay, when his brother had wanted to dig the grave in the midst of the palm trees?

The box and its mystery was his reward for listening to the Holy Mother and following her instructions.

He slipped out of bed and soundlessly opened his closet door. He retrieved the box and scurried with it back to his bed. By the light of his bedside lamp he worked the top free as he had seen his brother do.

Inside, the golden sheepskin scroll seemed almost to glow with a light from within. He carefully wiped his perspiring fingers on his pajamas and then ever so carefully lifted the scroll and unrolled it.

Symbols he didn't understand covered it in neat rows, and though some of the ancient parchment was stained, none of the ink had faded at all.

As he gazed at the indecipherable words, he realized that whatever they were, they were meant for him.

Only him.

They had been buried for a very long time—he couldn't even imagine how long—and they had been waiting for him. And when the Holy Mother had seen that he was ready, she had guided him to the place and given him this gift.

The boy replaced the scroll and the lid.

His finger traced the crucifix on the lid. Except that it wasn't really a crucifix at all—it looked more like the place where a crucifix had once been, but had been pried away, like a stone removed from its setting. He held the box closer to the light and examined it more carefully. Yes, there had once been a cross attached to the lid, but it was gone.

But where was it? Perhaps if he prayed very hard, the Holy Mother would lead him to the crucifix, too, and then he could put it back in the lid of the box, where it belonged.

"*Ave Maria,*" he whispered. Then, cradling the box, he moved to the window and gazed out at the statue in the grotto at the far end of the courtyard. The moon was full, and the face of the Holy Mother was bathed in a light as silvery as the box he held. Above her, millions of stars filled the night sky.

"I will learn to read this, Holy Mother," the boy whispered. "I will learn to read this and do whatever it is you wish me to do."

KUWAIT † 1991

Yellow.

Everything was yellow. Not just the desert; not just the sun. Everything.

The sky.

The heat itself.

All of it—yellow.

It had been bearable until a few moments ago. Until then the sky, at least, had been blue—a pale blue, not the brilliant blue of the sky at home, but at least the right color. Then, only a few moments ago, it had changed. The wind had picked up, a stain had spread across the sky, a stain the color of camel urine.

As the sandstorm raced across the desert the convoy ground to a halt, the transport trucks themselves seeming to hunker low to the ground against the howling force that swept toward them. It came at a terrifying speed. The men who couldn't see it—the ones deep at the front of the truck, where at least there was a layer of canvas to protect them from the pale yellow nightmare—even they looked as if they were trying to shrink within themselves, to withdraw their extremities as might a turtle, were it so foolish to be caught in a gathering maelstrom.

But as the yellow wall surrounded the convoy, then caved in upon it, there was a strange beauty to the storm—a beauty so rare that the man in the very back of the truck rose from his defensive crouch, his hands gripping his camera. Swinging his legs over the back of the truck, he dropped to the ground, then scuttled into its lee. The wind was blocked just enough by the truck for him to straighten up, but its force was still strong enough to tear at his face.

He ignored the pain, pressed the shutter release.

He could feel the camera vibrate slightly in his hands as the film advanced.

Twisting first one way then another, he kept his finger on the release, catching one yellow image after another. Then, in the corner of the viewfinder, he thought he saw a shape.

A man?

He turned toward it, trying to center it in his lens, but even as the image began to shift, he realized his mistake.

Realized it, and tried to rectify it.

Too late.

The force slammed into his chest as he dropped to the ground.

The camera fell from his hands, bounced, and skidded under the truck.

Peering down at his chest—which somehow didn't seem to hurt at all, despite the force of the blow—he wondered what it was that had struck him. A moment later, as a dark red stain blossomed on his khaki shirt, he knew.

He tried to speak, but his words sank in the blood that filled his mouth, and when he tried to spit, the howling wind slashed back at him, adding dust, grit, and sand to the mix of blood and saliva.

As he tried to swallow the whole grotesque mixture, fast enough at least to catch his breath, the truth of what was happening slowly sank in.

He was dying.

Dying here in the desert with the wind and sand howling around him. He cried out for help, but knew it was already far too late.

A sense of calm began to overtake him, as if the eternal tranquility of death was already embracing him.

He choked, coughed again, and struggled for the next breath.

A breath that seemed hours—an eternity—away.

Make peace.

The thought came softly to him amid the twin storms that were now raging around him, one as his organs struggled to survive, the other bent only on grinding him down into the sand that surrounded him.

Make peace.

There was no pain at all, but now his mind refused to focus. Too much of his attention was being demanded by his failing body, when already his spirit knew there were more important things at hand. His body suddenly seemed to be nothing more than an inconvenience, in-terfering with all that was truly important.

He had things to do.

He needed to pray.

He needed to make peace.

Yet this was not the way he was supposed to die.

Not so young, not with so much left to do.

But it was happening again.

He was dying like his father had died.

Like his grandfather had died.

The roar of the storm faded from his ears as his mind began turning away from his body until he finally knew that his ruined body and its discomfort were no longer of any concern to him at all. He felt a softness, a lightness of being.

Make peace.

Though almost beyond his control, his fingers made their way to his chest, to the crucifix that had been worn by all the generations of his family.

The crucifix that was supposed to have protected them.

But it had never protected any of them.

Never helped any of them to survive, to see a child grow up, a grandchild born.

With the last of his physical energy, he tore the thing from around his neck.

Then he felt hands on him, and a soldier's face was close to his, shouting over the howling wind.

But it was too late.

Far too late.

He pressed the crucifix into the soldier's hand, and felt eternal peace begin spreading through his soul.

"*Protect . . . ,*" he whispered. "*. . . son . . .*"

He closed his eyes and gave himself to death.

CHAPTER I

RYAN MCINTYRE PICKED up his cereal bowl, held it to his lips, drank down the last of the sweetened milk exactly the way he had for at least the last fourteen of his sixteen years, and pretended he didn't notice his mother's disapproving look. With a glance at the clock, he stuffed the last half of his third slice of buttered toast into his mouth then stood up and picked up his empty bowl and plate. He had just enough time to grab his books and get to the bus stop.

"Do you have any plans for after school today?" his mother asked.

Her tone instantly put Ryan on his guard. "Why?" he countered, as he put the dishes in the sink.

"Because we're going out to dinner tonight, and I'd like you to be home by five-thirty."

Ryan's eyes narrowed, and he felt his day cloud over. But maybe he was wrong. "Out to dinner?" he echoed, turning to face his mother. "Just us?"

Teri McIntyre turned to meet her son's eyes. "With Tom," she said. "He's taking us both out to dinner, and I'd like you to be home by five-thirty. Okay?" There was a tone to her final word that betrayed the knowledge that she knew it was not okay with Ryan at all. His next words confirmed that knowledge.

"I don't want to go to dinner with Tom Kelly," Ryan said, instantly hating the whiny quality he heard in his own voice. He took a deep breath and started over. "I don't like that he's always around. It's like he's trying to move in on you."

"He's not moving in on me," Teri said, her eyes pleading with her son as much as her voice. "He's just helping us through what is a very difficult time."

"He's helping *you* through *your* difficult time," Ryan shot back in a tone that made his mother flinch.

"He'd like to help you, too," Teri said, her eyes glistening.

"I don't need his help." Ryan moved toward the stairs. "And I don't need anybody trying to replace Dad, either."

"He's not trying to replace your father, Ryan," Teri said, her voice quivering. "Nobody could."

His mother's words burning in his head, Ryan ran up the stairs to his room. Damn right no one could replace his father, and especially not Tom Kelly, who seemed to be at their house all the time now, trying to be nice.

As Ryan scooped his books off his desk and dumped them in his backpack, his eyes caught on the picture of his father that always sat right next to the desk lamp, and he paused.

Something in his father's gaze seemed almost to be speaking to him. *Grow up,* his father seemed to be saying. *You're sixteen years old and you're still sucking your milk from your bowl like a two-year-old. It's time to be a man.*

His backpack clutched in his right hand, Ryan stood perfectly still, feeling his father's eyes boring into him.

Grow up. And be fair.

Be fair. The words his father had spoken more than any others. Ryan sighed, giving in to his father's silent command. If he was going to be totally fair, Tom Kelly wasn't really all that bad. In fact, he'd been a lot of help to his mother over the past six months. When the car had broken down, Tom had fixed it. When the roof had leaked, Tom had known who to call and made sure his mother didn't get cheated. And when the basement had flooded, Tom had helped move things upstairs then helped clean the place up again, and never said a word about the fact that Ryan had managed to avoid speaking to him through the whole long day.

Still, nobody could replace his dad.

It had been two years since his father's deployment and less than two years since an Iraqi roadside bomb had taken out the Humvee his father had been in. When he wasn't actually looking at his father's image, Ryan was finding it increasingly hard to remember exactly what his father's face looked like. But right now he *was* staring at that image, and he could see very clearly exactly what Captain William James McIntyre was expecting from his son.

He sank down on his bed and thought about going to dinner with his mom and Tom Kelly.

His mom kept saying that her liking Tom Kelly had nothing to do with her love for his father, but Ryan was very certain that wasn't quite true. And despite his own determination to keep his father's place open in this house—in this family—his mother might just try to fill that place with someone else.

But what if it all turned out to be a horrible mistake? What if one of these days his father walked through the front door yelling, "Honey, I'm home!"

But then, as Ryan gazed at the portrait again, he remembered what his dad said to him the day he left for Iraq. "You're the man of the house now, Ryan, so take good care of your mother. I'm not sure how long I'll be gone, but I know this is going to be harder on her than it is for me. So you be there for her, okay?"

Ryan had nodded. They'd hugged. Then his father was gone.

But his words were still there in Ryan's mind, as fresh as the day he'd spoken them. *You be there for her.*

His eyes shifting from his father's image to the mirror over his bureau, Ryan stared at his own sullen reflection.

Not good enough, he told himself. Then he repeated his father's words one more time. *Be there for her. And be fair.*

Grabbing his backpack, he ran down the stairs. His mother was still sitting at the kitchen table, cradling her coffee in both hands.

"I'll be home by five-thirty," Ryan said, and kissed her on the cheek.

The smile that came over her face told him that whatever he himself thought, he'd done exactly what his father would have wanted him to do. Kissing her one more time, just for good measure, he dashed out the front door just as the bus was pulling up to the stop at the corner. *Okay, Dad,* he thought. *I did the right thing. Now make the bus driver wait for me!*

But even as he broke into a run, he saw the bus doors close and watched helplessly as it pulled away.

† † †

The peeling walls of the second-floor classroom of Dickinson High School's main building felt like they were closing in on Ryan, and directly behind him he could almost feel Frankie Alito trying to get a peek over his shoulder at the history test the class was working on. Ryan stiffened, knowing Alito was expecting him to slump just low enough at his desk to give the other boy a clear view of his answers, and as he thought about what Alito and his friends might do to him after school if he refused to let Frankie cheat, he felt himself starting to ease his body downward. But just before Alito could get a clear look, Ryan heard his father's voice echoing in his head:

It's time to be a man.

Instantly, Ryan sat straight up, determined that for once Alito could pass or fail on his own.

Then he felt the poke in his back. He ignored it, not shifting even a fraction of an inch in his seat.

Another poke with what felt like Alito's pen, harder this time. Ryan kept his eyes focused on the test in front of him, but shrugged his shoulder away from Alito's pen point.

"Gimme a look, geek," Frankie whispered, punctuating the last word with another, harder jab.

"No way," Ryan muttered, straightening even further in his chair and hunching over his paper, trying to stay out of Frankie's reach. He glanced up at the teacher, but Mr. Thomas was busy at his desk, a stack of papers in front of him.

"Last chance," Alito said, and Ryan felt another poke. But this time it was down low, just above his belt.

This time it wasn't a pen point.

And this time his body reacted reflexively. Ryan twisted around just in time to see the flash of a blade.

The kind and size of blade that meant business.

"Now!" Alito hissed, jabbing the point of the knife hard enough to make Ryan jump.

Ryan yelped as the point dug into him and the teacher's head snapped up.

"Something wrong, McIntyre?" Mr. Thomas asked from the front of the room.

Suddenly every eye in the classroom was on Ryan.

"No, sir," Ryan said. "Sorry."

Mr. Thomas stood up and came around his desk.

"Really," Ryan said. "It wasn't anything."

The teacher advanced down the aisle, his eyes never leaving Frankie Alito, and came to a stop next to Ryan.

"Really, it was nothing, Mr. Thomas," Ryan said, praying that Alito had at least been smart enough to slip the knife back in his pocket.

"Both hands on your desk, Alito," Thomas commanded. Ryan kept facing directly forward, not wanting to see what was going to happen next.

"What's that?" He heard Mr. Thomas ask.

"Nuthin'," Alito answered.

"Hand it over," the teacher said.

Ryan could almost see Frankie Alito glowering, but then the teacher spoke one more word, snapping it out with enough force that Ryan jumped.

"Now!"

The tension in the classroom grew as Alito hesitated, but when Mr. Thomas's gaze never wavered, he finally broke and passed the switch-blade to him.

"Thank you," Thomas said softly. "And now you will go down to the office, where you will wait for me. I'll be there at the end of the period, and you will be out of school for the rest of the year, even if we decide not to press charges, which I can assure you we won't. You're through, Alito."

His face twisted with fury, Frankie Alito got to his feet, jabbing an elbow hard into Ryan's shoulder.

"I saw that, too," Mr. Thomas said. "You're only making it worse."

Alito shrugged and walked to the door, then paused before opening it. He turned his eyes, boring into Ryan, and then he smiled.

It was a smile that sank like a dart into Ryan's belly.

"Okay. Show's over," Mr. Thomas said, breaking the uneasy silence that had fallen over the room. "Back to your tests. You have only ten minutes left."

But for Ryan, the test was already over. He stared at the questions that still remained, reading them over and over again, but no matter how many times he read the words, he couldn't make sense of them.

It wasn't enough that he had to worry about his mother and Tom Kelly. Now he had to face Frankie Alito and his friends, who would no doubt jump him when he was on the way home after school.

He turned his head and looked out the window. In the distance, he could see the skyline of Boston, and though he was pretty sure it wasn't really possible, he thought he could even pick out the spire on top of St. Isaac's School.

The school his mother had talked about the last time he'd come home with a black eye after a run-in with Frankie Alito.

Except he was pretty sure it hadn't been his mother's idea at all. In fact, he'd have been willing to bet it had been Tom Kelly's idea.

But now, as he stared at his unfinished test, and knew all he had to look forward to for the rest of the day was Frankie Alito's fury, he began to wonder.

Surely St. Isaac's couldn't be any worse than where he was.

"Time's up," said Mr. Thomas.

CHAPTER 2

BROTHER FRANCIS STOOD in the doorway of the vast dining room at St. Isaac's Preparatory Academy, scanning the tables of students, searching for Kip Adamson. At least half the school's two hundred students were sitting at the long tables eating, talking, and laughing, yet despite the noise they were generating, the chamber was still far quieter than had been the much smaller cafeteria at the school Brother Francis had left only last fall. Indeed, it seemed to him as if the old stone building housing the dining hall was somehow offended by the noise, and, rather than tolerate such frivolity within its walls, had somehow found a way to absorb the noise the school's students made, muting it almost as quickly as the students generated it.

Though he was new to St. Isaac's, Brother Francis had a knack for attaching names to faces, and now he was able to greet nearly every one of the students by name as he walked between tables in search of one particular face. Kip Adamson, though, was nowhere to be seen; he'd already missed his senior math class, and Sister Mary David had sent Brother Francis to find out why. Sister Mary David's wrath was legendary; not only would nobody willingly miss her class without an ironclad excuse, but she wouldn't hesitate to vent her fury upon Brother Francis, should he prove unable to explain young Adamson's absence.

Kip must have had a good reason—at least, he'd *better* have had a good reason.

In the far corner of the dining hall, Brother Francis spotted Clay Matthews, Kip's roommate, sitting with his usual group of friends. As Brother Francis approached, he caught a glimpse of playing cards, and suddenly knew why they were all knotted up in the corner together.

"Hey, Brother Francis," Tim Kennedy said loudly enough that the young cleric was sure it was meant as a warning to Tim's friends rather than a greeting to himself. Sure enough, the other boys' heads snapped up the instant Tim spoke.

Brother Francis put on his sternest face. "I believe you're all aware that gambling is against the rules," he said. The boys glanced at each other uneasily. "Think what would have happened if it had been Sister Mary David who caught you instead of me."

As the rest of the boys paled slightly, José Alvarez did his best to look utterly innocent. "Gambling?" he asked, as if Brother Francis had spoken in some exotic language he didn't quite understand.

"We're just playing Crazy Eights," Darren Bender said.

"I see." Brother Francis held his hand out for the cards. Clay Matthews groaned, squared the cards into a deck and surrendered them to Brother Francis, who slipped them into one of the deep pockets in his cassock. "Have any of you seen Kip?" he went on. "He missed his math class."

The boys shook their heads. "He might still be in bed," Clay said. "I don't think he's been feeling good."

Brother Francis frowned, his lips pursing. "Oh? Did he go to the infirmary?"

Clay shrugged. "It wasn't like he was sick with the flu or anything. He's just been acting kind of strange for a while."

"Strange how?" Brother Francis asked, though he was fairly sure that whatever answer he got wouldn't be particularly enlightening. Sure enough, Clay only shrugged again. "Okay," Brother Francis sighed. "I'll check around. Meanwhile, if you see him, have him come to my office."

Leaving the dining hall, Brother Francis began making his way through the maze of hallways and short flights of steps that connected all the various buildings into which the school had spread over the century it had been on Beacon Hill. Even after eight months, Brother Francis was still finding areas he couldn't remember ever seeing before. There were offices and classrooms spread through dozens of buildings, not to mention the dormitories for the students and the residences of the staff. The students all seemed to know the sprawling old buildings better than he did, and had found shortcuts he knew nothing about. Still, now he was at least able to find his way from the dining room to the boys' dorm without getting lost.

At least not too lost.

He knocked on the door of room 231, but there was no answer. "Kip?" he asked, then knocked again before turning the knob and entering.

The room was kept as neatly as the school demanded, with both beds made. The items on the desks were orderly, the closet doors were closed, and the dresser top clear.

But no sign of Kip; no clue at all as to his whereabouts.

Brother Francis used his cell phone to call the infirmary, rather than walking all the way over to the other side of the school, but the nun on duty told him that Kip hadn't been there, either.

As he pocketed the phone, worry began to gnaw at his gut.

He moved to the window, looking down over Beacon Hill. From where he stood the view was unobstructed all the way to the Charles River, and Cambridge beyond. Idly, he wondered what the Puritan founders of the city would think about a Catholic school sitting atop their finest hill, the gothic architecture and spires of the school's original building towering over the lower structures that some of those Puritans had built themselves.

Turning away from the view beyond the school, Brother Francis glanced once more around the room, but nothing had changed.

Kip had not miraculously reappeared.

Not that Brother Francis had really expected him to, given that the student population of the school had a disproportionate number of high-risk kids, one of whom was none other than Kip Adamson.

The odds were that Kip had just taken off. Brother Francis had been warned that it happened; indeed it had happened once before this very school year.

But it still bothered him. Silently he offered up a prayer to Saint Aloysius Gonzaga, on the chance the patron saint of teenagers might have a spare moment for Kip Adamson, wherever he was. The prayer sent heavenward, Brother Francis started back through the narrow, winding hallways. His heavy crucifix swung from the belt on his cassock, and despite the constant chill that the cold stone walls seemed to cast over the school, perspiration began to bead on his forehead.

Wherever he was, Brother Francis's intuition was telling him, Kip Adamson wasn't anywhere within the complex of buildings that made up the school.

But worse, Brother Francis's intuition was also telling him that there was going to be an ugly outcome to this whole situation.

A very ugly outcome.

CHAPTER 3

RYAN MCINTYRE CHECKED OVER his test one last time, put his pen away, and glanced up at the clock above Mr. Thomas's desk: two minutes to four. He'd finished the test with time to spare, and he was all but certain he'd aced it. Slinging his backpack over his shoulders, he picked up the finished test and laid it in front of the teacher. "Thanks for letting me do this," he said. "I know I should have been able to—"

"Forget it," Mr. Thomas cut in, picking up a red pencil as he began scanning Ryan's test. "Nobody needs a knife poking them in the back while they're taking a test." He glanced up from the pages in front of him. "How're you getting home?"

"Same way as always," Ryan sighed. "The bus." He saw a flicker of uncertainty in the teacher's eyes, and knew exactly what he was thinking about. The same thing Ryan had been thinking about all day, or at least since lunch time.

Frankie Alito coming after him as soon as he left school.

It had started at noon, when a hush had fallen over the cafeteria the moment he'd walked in. It had taken him a minute or so to realize that nearly every eye in the room was on him, but he'd done his best to ignore it while he filled his tray with food and found a seat next to Josh Singer. "What's going on?" he asked. "How come everyone's staring at me?"

"Frankie Alito got expelled, just like Mr. Thomas said he would," Josh told him. "And everybody thinks you're either a hero or the dumbest guy on the planet."

Ryan had kept his eyes focused on his food, but he knew he wouldn't be able to eat.

"I'll be okay," he now said to Mr. Thomas. "See you Monday." Turning away, he left the room before the teacher could say anything else.

The halls were quiet and empty of students and the only sound other than his own footsteps echoing down the long corridor was the shouting coming from the gym, where the cheerleading team was practicing.

Maybe he should just stay here, where at least he was safe. After all, they'd probably grab him when he got off the bus near his house.

But then, as he realized it was an hour later than the usual time he left school, he had an idea. Maybe there was a way not to get beaten up, at least not today.

Ryan stopped at his locker on the second floor long enough to leave his history book and pick up his jacket, then pulled out his cell phone as he started once more down the corridor. He pressed the speed dial key to ask his mother to pick him up.

But all he got was her voice mail.

"Hi, Mom," he said to the machine. "I stayed after school to make up a test. I was hoping you could pick me up, but I guess you're doing something. See you when I get there."

He snapped the phone shut and was about to drop it back in his pack when the boys' restroom door suddenly slammed open and two of Frankie Alito's best buddies—Bennie Locke and Stan Wojniak—burst out and grabbed him, jerking him off balance and shoving him through the restroom door before he even had time to react. His cell phone flew out of his hand and shattered on the hard tile floor, then the door slammed shut and Ryan himself followed the ruined cell phone, his elbow smashing on the filthy floor beneath the sinks.

As pain from his elbow shot through Ryan's body, Bennie Locke grabbed him by the leg and jerked him out from under the sinks. Ryan grabbed onto one of the drainpipes and lashed out at him with his left foot, but the kick went wild as Wojniak's own shoe crashed into Ryan's jaw.

Ryan felt his hands go slack and blackness swirled around him.

"Maybe this'll teach you to do what you're told," Wojniak snarled, drawing his boot back to kick Ryan in the side.

Ryan felt his ribs crack—thought he could hear them pop. White-hot pain erupted on his left side, and for a second he thought he might pass out. "Don't," he whispered, instinctively curling up to protect himself from whatever might come next.

"Listen to him," Bennie mocked. "Beggin' like a little girl." His lips twisted into a vicious sneer. "Freakin' loser!"

Another kick landed squarely, this time on Ryan's hamstring, and another kind of agony shot through his body.

He tried to scream, but his cracked ribs prevented him from drawing a deep breath, and all that emerged from his throat was a faint whimper.

The kicks came faster after that, and all Ryan could do was close his eyes, wrap his arms around his head, and wait for it to be over. Again and again he felt the hard toes of their shoes crash into him. But then the pain began to fade, as did their taunting voices, and when the darkness surrounded him again, Ryan didn't fight it.

He embraced it.

And finally the kicks ended.

CHAPTER 4

ITH A FLASHLIGHT in one hand and the big key ring Sister Margaret had given him in his other, Brother Francis pushed open the stairwell door behind the dining room and searched the wall for the light switch.

Nothing.

No switch. Not even an overhead bulb with a string. Not that Sister Margaret hadn't warned him. "The Holy Grail itself could be down there, and no one would ever find it," she'd said when she handed him the heavy key ring and flashlight. "And if you should run across Sister Agnes Leopold, tell her she's twenty-seven years too late for her final vows." Rolling her eyes at the blank look on Brother Francis's face, she told him she was only kidding, then abruptly left him to begin his search of the basement.

Now, faced with the impenetrable blackness below, Brother Francis was suddenly transported back to the day years ago when his own brother had locked him in the basement and turned out the lights. He'd been five then, and terrified. *But I'm an adult now,* he reminded himself, *and there's nothing to be frightened of.* Swallowing hard, he turned on the flashlight and started down the darkened steps, telling himself that even if he didn't find Kip Adamson, it was time he familiarized himself with the interconnecting labyrinth of tunnels that connected all the buildings that St. Isaac's had spread through over the last century. The students, he was already well aware, used basements and sub-basements like their own private freeway system, even starting to call it the Big Dig, after the decades long project that had finally buried Boston's freeway system underground. Though he knew the subterranean maze let the students maneuver around campus quickly—and undetected—this was the first time he had ventured below the ground floor, and even as he came to the bottom of the stairs he was wondering if maybe he shouldn't just turn around and go back up into the late afternoon light. Still, before he sounded the alarm about Kip Adamson's disappearance, he needed to search the whole campus, and that certainly included the tunnels.

At the bottom of the stairs there was a large and empty chamber, with three passageways leading in as many directions. Brother Francis took the one to the left, and almost missed another short flight of stairs, stumbling before catching himself against the clammy concrete wall. He moved slowly, trying every door he came to, but all of them were locked. Then he came to another intersection, and slowly the enormity of the underground campus began to dawn on him.

There must be miles of tunnels under these buildings.

The beam of his flashlight caught a glint of brass, and a moment later he found himself looking at an ancient accordion-doored elevator, barely large enough to hold two people.

Behind another door was a storeroom where his flashlight played over two ornately carved wooden confessionals, both of them covered with cobwebs. Something glowed inside one of them, and a moment later a large rat darted out and disappeared into the shadows beyond the reach of the flashlight's beam.

He moved on through the tunnels, feeling the musty darkness closing in around him, trying to keep track of every turn he made, but knowing deep in his heart that he had no idea where he was.

The beam of his flashlight grew weaker.

Then, from down a corridor to his right, a faint glow of light!

He shined his flashlight toward it and saw a single door, heavily carved, with a small panel of stained glass set into it.

A panel in the shape of a heart.

He moved closer to the door and flicked off his light.

The heart embedded in the door seemed to throb.

He reached out to the door, tentatively at first, and as his fingers touched the wood something inside him told him to turn away.

Instead, he pushed the door open.

Beyond the door was a tiny chapel that held a confessional, two short pews, and an altar.

A single candle stood burning on the altar.

Above the altar hung an enormous crucifix—large enough to dominate a chamber ten times this size.

A bloodied Christ hung from the cross, seeming to stare Brother Francis squarely in the eye.

His own heart throbbing now, Brother Francis backed out of the chapel, reflexively crossing himself as he pulled the door closed.

Turning away, he hurried back down the corridor.

But a dozen steps later, he was no longer certain he was going in the right direction. He shone the flashlight both ways, but its rapidly yellowing beam quickly faded into darkness.

Then the flashlight faltered and faded away.

He slapped it on his palm, and for a brief moment the light flickered back on, but then went out for good.

The throbbing of his heart grew into an audible pounding and the familiar heaviness of panic began to grip his chest.

His skin began to crawl as, unbidden, his mind began to conjure what might be lurking in the corridor, creeping toward him.

The chapel! If he could find his way back to the chapel, he could take the candle from the altar!

But as quickly as the thought came, he knew it was hopeless—he had no idea which way the chapel was, and he could wander in the dark for hours without finding it.

His heart began to race, and the panic that had begun in his chest spread through his body. Despite the stale chill of the air around him, a trickle of perspiration oozed down the side of his face.

Then, from out of the darkness, a sound.

Faint, barely audible, but a sound.

"H-Hello?" Brother Francis said, his voice echoing oddly. Steeling himself, he spoke again: "Who is it? Is someone there?"

No answer.

He took a single step farther down the tunnel, but froze when the keys in his left hand jangled loudly.

You're not a child any longer, he told himself, but the words did nothing to assuage the fear of the surrounding darkness that his brother had inculcated in his mind so many years ago.

His rising panic suddenly threatening to overwhelm him, he instinctively reached for one of the walls to steady himself, and his fingers closed on a large padlock.

Again he froze, listening.

Silence.

His fingers explored the lock, finding an enormous keyhole that felt like it would need an old skeleton key. Releasing the lock, he fumbled with the key ring until he found the largest of the keys, then tried to fit it to the lock.

Too big.

He tried a second key, then a third.

The fourth one slid into the slot, turned, and the lock fell open. Brother Francis slipped the lock from its hasp, pushed the door open and groped the wall inside, silently uttering a prayer to whatever saint might watch out for things like light switches.

A moment later his prayer was answered: he found a switch, flipped it, and a dim yellow bulb illuminated a small storeroom filled with slumping cardboard boxes.

But no sign of Kip Adamson.

He stood in the doorway to the storeroom, looking both ways into the endless darkness of the tunnel. Though his heart was no longer pounding as it had been a moment ago, Brother Francis was still loath to turn off the light. He had no real idea of where he was, and just the thought of trying to find his way out in pitch darkness made him shudder.

Yet what choice was there? If he left the single dim bulb in the storeroom burning, its light would carry no farther than the end of the corridor in which he stood, and that was no more than twenty feet—thirty at the most.

Then, from somewhere off to the right, he heard a sound.

Voices.

Distinct voices.

The tendrils of panic falling away from him like leaves from a tree in the last days of fall, he reminded himself to tell Sister Margaret to have every burned-out bulb in the basements replaced, then called out into the darkness. "Hello? Who is that?"

"Brother Francis?" a familiar voice replied. "What are you doing down here?"

A moment later Clay Matthews and Darren Bender emerged out of the darkness into the faint glow spilling from the open storeroom door.

"I might ask you the same question," Brother Francis replied, hoping they couldn't read the relief in his voice.

"We're looking for Kip," Clay said.

"Shouldn't you be studying?" Brother Francis countered, glancing at his watch. "It's still an hour until dinner."

"We couldn't study," Clay told him. "We kept thinking about Kip, and I remembered him saying he'd come down here to make his confession in some kind of chapel I'd never heard of before and . . ."

As his voice trailed off, Darren Bender shook his head. "I keep telling Clay he's gone, but he wants to keep looking."

"How many of the basements have you searched?"

Darren shrugged. "Most of them. We started under the library, and went around the long way under the gym and the rectory. We figured we'd go under the auditorium on our way back to the dorm and check the rest on the way to dinner."

"He's not under the dining room," Brother Francis sighed. "I already looked there. We might as well head back to the dorm."

Fifteen minutes later, Brother Francis brushed dust and cobwebs from the shoulders of his cassock, then rapped quietly on Father Laughlin's door.

The old priest looked up from the book he was reading, and when he saw Brother Francis, a smile spread across his soft, wrinkled face. "Come in, Francis," he said. "Sit down."

Brother Francis entered the office and closed the door behind him. "Bad news, I'm afraid," he said, then perched nervously on the edge of one of a pair of carved wooden chairs with a worn velvet seat.

The old headmaster's brows rose. "Oh?"

"One of our boys—Kip Adamson—is missing. He doesn't seem to be anywhere in the school at all, and I'm afraid—" He hesitated, then decided there was no easy way of putting it. "I'm afraid he's run away."

"Kip Adamson," Father Laughlin repeated.

Brother Francis nodded. "He's one of our at-risk students. Nothing too bad—a little shoplifting—that sort of thing. But the odd thing is that he's been here two and a half years, and according to the records he's been one of our best successes. No disciplinary problems, and better than average grades. Far better, actually."

"And he's missing, you say?" Father Laughlin asked, taking off his wire-rimmed glasses and rubbing the bridge of his nose.

Something in the old priest's tone made Brother Francis wonder if Laughlin was truly grasping what he was saying, and he found himself wondering, not for the first time, if perhaps Father Laughlin was a little too old and a little too out of touch with today's youth to be running a school like St. Isaac's. The old priest seemed like a relic from a kinder and far gentler era. "He's the second one this year," Brother Francis sighed. "And I have to say, I'm feeling like I must be responsible. I feel like I must have failed these boys in some way." He paused, then finished his thought. "I'm wondering if you made a mistake bringing me here. Perhaps I'm just not cut out for this kind of school."

Father Laughlin shook his head. "This isn't your fault, Francis. It's just—"

"No child has gone missing from this school in the last five years," Brother Francis cut in. "Then I arrive, and lose two in my first year."

Brother Francis sighed heavily again. "And I'm having a very hard time trying to figure out what I'm going to say to Kip's parents."

Father Laughlin didn't respond right away, but finally put his glasses back on and looked up at the young cleric. "There's more than one reason the Cardinal sent us Father Sebastian Sloane at the same time he sent you," Laughlin said. "And one of those reasons is that Father Sebastian not only has a great deal of experience with troubled students, but with their parents as well. Let's wait until after dinner, and if the Adamson boy still hasn't turned up, you can explain the situation to Father Sebastian. Then—if it becomes necessary to talk to the boy's family, he can do it. I'm sure Father Sebastian will know exactly what to say." Laughlin reached out and gave Brother Francis's arm a reassuring squeeze. "And in the meantime, we'll all pray for Kip's safe return."

As he left the headmaster's office a few moments later, Brother Francis tried to tell himself that everything was going to turn out all right, that Kip Adamson was going to turn up. But no matter how hard he tried, he couldn't make himself believe his own words.

No, something was wrong.

Something was very wrong.

CHAPTER 5

TERI MCINTYRE ADJUSTED the belt on her skirt and checked her watch again. 5:50. She'd been annoyed when Ryan hadn't shown up as promised by 5:30, but already annoyance was dissolving into worry. Ryan, even when he was small, had been the kind of boy every mother dreams of. When he said he'd do something, he did it, even if he didn't want to, and Teri knew that even though Ryan didn't particularly want to go to dinner tonight, he had said he would. And according to his message, he'd left the school around four. So what had happened?

Why wasn't he home?

She picked up the phone and dialed Ryan's cell one more time, but clicked off when she heard his voice mail; she'd already left him two messages to call home, and a third wasn't going to accomplish a thing. She went downstairs to wait for him.

Beyond the front window the street was empty, and a bus was just pulling away from the stop at the corner. Teri perched on the arm of the sofa where she had a view of the driveway and front walk, and gnawed at a cuticle as she thought about what to do.

And what might have happened.

As if to escape her own thoughts, she left the sofa and went to the kitchen, where she dug the address book out of the catch-all drawer. Less than a minute later she dialed the school, but everyone in the office had gone home for the day, and all she got was a recorded message. She clicked off, then dialed Josh Singer's house. Maybe Ryan had stopped over there on his way home, got involved in a video game or something, and simply lost track of time.

"Hi, Melinda," she said when Josh's mother answered. "It's Teri McIntyre. Is Ryan there by any chance?"

"Hey, Teri. No, I haven't seen him. Hold on a minute. I'll get Josh."

Teri unconsciously tapped her fingernails on the Formica countertop while she waited.

"Mrs. McIntyre?"

"Hi, Josh. I'm looking for Ryan."

"He was going to make up a history test after school. He—"

"I know about the test," Teri cut in. "I thought he'd be home by now. If you see him, have him call me right away, okay?"

"Sure."

Teri hung up just as she heard a car door slam outside. Phone in hand, she hurried to the front door, thinking maybe someone had given Ryan a lift, but instead of Ryan, it was Tom Kelly coming up the walk. She glanced at the clock even though she already knew exactly what time it was. Sure enough: 6:00 on the dot.

Tom Kelly was nothing if not punctual.

She opened the door to be greeted with a smile and a kiss, but instead of returning his hug, she pulled away, her eyes going to the bus stop at the corner where two people were getting off the last bus of the afternoon.

Neither of them was Ryan.

Tom, feeling the tension in Teri's body, dropped his arms to his sides. "Something's wrong," he said.

Teri nodded. "Ryan promised to be home a half hour ago and he's not here yet."

Tom visibly relaxed and pulled her close again. "So he's late—he's sixteen. He'll get here."

"But he was going to go to dinner with us, and we'll be late for the reservation."

"Then leave him a note and some money for a pizza. He'll go with us another time." He was already reaching for his wallet.

Teri shook her head and moved back into the house. "This isn't like him. Call the restaurant and see if you can push the reservation back fifteen minutes. I'm going to call some more of his friends."

Tom smiled wryly. "Why don't you call the police department and all the hospitals while you're at it?" When Teri glared at him, he took her hand, sat on the sofa, and pulled her down next to him. "He's sixteen, Teri," he repeated. "Almost seventeen. He's allowed to assert his independence."

"No, you don't understand—"

Tom put a gentle finger to her lips, silencing her objections. "His father died barely two years ago, and you've been seeing me for almost six months. He's got to be thinking I'm trying to replace his father. You've got to give him some slack."

Suddenly this morning's fight came flooding back to her, and she realized Tom was right. Ryan had tried to act like an adult when he agreed to go to dinner, but he hadn't really wanted to.

"You've got to give him some time, Teri. He has to deal with things on his own timetable, not yours."

Teri looked beseechingly into his eyes. "Then where could he be?"

Tom shrugged. "It's Friday night. He and a couple of friends could have gone out for pizza and a movie."

"He promised he'd be home," she insisted, shaking her head. "He left school a few minutes after four—he should be here by now."

Tom squeezed her hand reassuringly. "You can't make him be what you want him to be. Somewhere along the line he just decided he didn't want to go out to dinner with me. And that's okay. You can't freak out every time he's an hour late, or you'll go insane by the time he's off to college." He kissed her cheek, then stood up, drawing her to her feet. "C'mon. Let's go have a nice dinner, and you can have a chat with him when we get home. And just a chat," he added with mock severity. "Not a tirade. Okay?"

Teri shook her head. "I just don't think I can go. I'll be worried every minute and—"

"Sorry, not going is not an option," Tom interrupted. "If you stay home, you'd miss a terrific meal, and you'll just sit here ruining your manicure."

Teri tried to scowl, but couldn't quite pull it off. "But I won't be able to enjoy the meal, or you, or anything else," she sighed.

"You'll enjoy it more than you'll enjoy just sitting here. So maybe you won't be scintillating. Who cares? Just leave him a note and have him call you on your cell when he gets home. And I promise if he's not home by the time we get back, I'll not only help you track him down, but do half the worrying, too. Okay?"

He was right—of course he was right. And if it hadn't been for the dinner date—a date Ryan hadn't really wanted to go on at all—she wouldn't even be worried. Probably all that had happened was that he'd changed his mind about having dinner with them, and hadn't called because he didn't want to let himself get talked back into it. She took the phone back to the kitchen and scribbled a note to Ryan, leaving it on the refrigerator where he couldn't miss it. Then she checked her cell phone for messages one last time, made sure it had enough charge and dropped it into her purse.

"Okay," she sighed as she returned to the living room. "I guess I'm ready." But as she slid into the car a minute later, she knew she wasn't ready at all. Despite Tom's words about enjoying the evening, she was certain that all she would do would be to worry about Ryan.

Something, she just knew, had happened to him.

She couldn't explain it, but she knew.

She knew, the way a mother always knows.

† † †

Caleb Stark filled his mop bucket with hot, soapy water from the big sink in the custodial closet, then pulled the rolling bucket behind him down the long hallway that ran the entire length of the second floor of Dickinson High.

There was new graffiti on some of the lockers in the west wing, and someone had spilled something slimy down the stairs from the second-floor landing. The goo was important—Caleb remembered that clearly—anything on the floor had to be cleaned up, especially if someone could slip and fall on it. Then, if he had time, he could work on cleaning the graffiti off the lockers.

But even before going after the slimy stuff, he had to tend to all the things he was supposed to do every day, because if he didn't tend to them in the same order every day, he'd lose track, and some things might not get done. And if *that* happened, his counselor might decide he wasn't smart enough to live on his own after all, and send him back to the halfway house.

And then his mother would be disappointed, and she might cry, and Caleb hated it when his mother cried.

Telling himself not to forget about the slimy stuff, Caleb pushed his cart down the corridor, found the big, wooden doorstop, and opened the boys' bathroom door. It was while he was sticking the doorstop under the heavy door to prop it open that he saw the dark red footprint on the linoleum. At first Caleb thought it might be some kind of mud, or maybe even paint from the art classroom down the hall, but as he followed the tracks farther into the restroom, he saw that the stuff wasn't mud or paint at all.

It was blood.

And a boy was lying in the middle of the bathroom floor, with a big puddle of blood around his head, which had oozed along the grout joints between the tiles.

"Holy Jesus," he whispered softly, his mind suddenly spinning as he tried to remember what he was supposed to do if something like this ever happened.

He stepped a little closer, trying to get a better look at the boy's face, but he was pretty sure he wouldn't recognize him even if it was some-one he knew because his face was all covered with blood.

And he looked dead, too.

But as Caleb stood staring at the boy, still trying to remember what he was supposed to do, the boy suddenly took a ragged breath and moaned.

Either the slight movement or the sound made something click in Caleb's mind, and he suddenly knew what to do. "If you're ever hurt, or really sick, find a phone," his counselor had explained to him when he was moving into his own little apartment. "Then dial 911, and tell them where you are. And someone will come to help you." The counselor's words echoing in the depths of his memory, Caleb dropped his mop and hurried from the bathroom to the faculty lounge, where he knew there was a telephone. He spoke very clearly, and told them exactly where the boy was, in the restroom on the second floor of the main building of Dickinson High.

Then he went back to the restroom to see if he could help the boy, and maybe five minutes later, a bunch of people started arriving, just like his counselor had told him would happen.

Someone was kneeling at the boy's side, and police were milling about in the hallway. Caleb watched from the doorway, nervously twisting at his forelock. "Is he going to be all right?" he asked as two men wearing some kind of jumpsuits brought in a stretcher and lifted the boy onto it.

"Hope so," one of the paramedics said, handing Caleb the boy's bloody backpack. "Here. Find out who he is and get in touch with his parents."

Caleb, uncertain what he was supposed to do, started to open the backpack, but even before he could look inside it one of the school's security guards took it away from him. "Tell you what, Caleb," the guard told him. "Why don't I do that, and you can go call the principal and tell him he better come over here." He handed Caleb a card with a telephone number on it, and steered him out the door.

Caleb, grateful for the simpler task of just calling the principal, started toward the faculty lounge for the second time, and as he passed the slimy stuff on the stairs, reminded himself to make sure he cleaned it up before he went home.

The graffiti, though, was going to have to wait for another night.

CHAPTER 6

BROTHER FRANCIS NERVOUSLY wended his way through the Boston traffic as Father Sebastian gazed silently out the side window.

"Kip's parents live in Newton," Brother Francis offered, more to break the silence than anything else. "It's a little bit west of the city, but not very far."

Father Sebastian finally turned toward him and smiled slightly, and Francis could see why the students—at least the girls—liked him so much. There was something in his face that was both gentle and intense, giving anyone who talked to him the feeling that he was not only listening to them intently, but empathized with whatever they were saying. Combined with his olive complexion, deep dark eyes, and thick, coal-black hair, he struck most people as being someone who could as easily have been a doctor as a priest. Or even a movie star, though he seemed so completely unaware of his effect on people that Brother Francis was sure he'd never even thought of such a thing.

"Not a problem," Father Sebastian said. "I can't say I'm looking forward to this any more than you are. Any idea what the Adamsons are like?"

Brother Francis pulled off the turnpike, found Centre Street, and started south. "I haven't actually met them, but I took a look at Kip's file before we left."

"So did I," Father Sebastian sighed. "And it didn't tell me as much about the parents as it did about Kip. On the other hand, there wasn't anything negative about the family, so it seems to me that our main job is to find out if they've heard anything from him without getting them too upset."

"It's their son," Brother Francis said, turning left on Beacon Street. "He's missing—they're bound to be upset." He turned right onto Greenlawn Avenue and started looking for the address. "Here it is," he said, pulling the car to a stop in front of an utterly nondescript middle-class home, which told him no more about Kip's family than the file had. He switched off the engine.

"God willing," Sebastian said, "we'll find out where Kip is."

"God willing," Francis echoed.

Together they got out of the car, walked up to the front door, and Father Sebastian pressed the bell. A middle-aged man, wearing a white polyester shirt and a slightly stained tie, which was loosened at the neck, opened the door. He stared at them blankly for a moment, but as he took in their clerical garb his eyes clouded and his expression soured.

"Mr. Adamson?" Father Sebastian asked, though he was already certain they were talking to Kip's father.

Gordy Adamson nodded curtly, held the screen door open for the men to enter, and called out to his wife. "Anne! A couple of priests are here! The brat must be in trouble again!"

Anne Adamson emerged from the kitchen, drying her hands on a dish towel, her forehead furrowing. "Kip?" she said. "What's he done? He's all right, isn't he?"

"I'm Father Sebastian, and this is Brother Francis," Father Sebastian began.

"Please sit down," Mrs. Adamson said, ushering them farther into the living room. As the two men lowered themselves to the edge of the living room sofa, she fluttered nervously next to a wing chair, then settled onto its arm.

Her husband remained standing, leaning against the wall, his arms drawn tight across his chest, his eyes narrowing with suspicion as if he was already certain his son had committed some kind of offense whose repercussions were about to come down on his own head.

"Is Kip all right?" Anne asked again.

"We have no reason to think he's not," Father Sebastian said a little too quickly.

"If you didn't think something was wrong, you wouldn't be here," Gordy Adamson announced, not moving even a fraction of an inch from his post by the kitchen door. "So why don't we just cut to what he's done, all right? It's not like we haven't heard it all before."

Father Sebastian took a deep breath, and started over again. "Kip appears to have left campus without permission this morning. We were hoping that he'd come here, or that at least you've heard from him."

"Goddammit," Gordy spat.

"Gordy!" Anne shot her husband a warning glance, then turned back to the two clerics. "We haven't heard from him."

"Aren't you people supposed to keep an eye on him?" Gordy demanded, his anger focusing on Brother Francis. "Isn't that why we sent him to St. Isaac's? To make sure things like this didn't happen?"

"I've been working pretty closely with Kip the last eight months," Father Sebastian replied as Brother Francis shrank back from Gordy Adamson's anger. "He's been doing very well—good grades and an attitude that's been improving. Aside from the usual mischief all our kids get into now and then, he hasn't been any trouble worth more than a quick confession and a couple of Hail Marys for penance." His cavalier reference to the confessional had the intended effect; Gordy Adamson's arms finally dropped to his sides and he moved closer to his wife. "Frankly, it's a mystery to me why he left," Father Sebastian finished.

"We sent him to St. Isaac's because you have a reputation for dealing with kids like that—what do you call it? 'At risk,' whatever the hell that means. So how could he just walk out?"

"St. Isaac's isn't a prison, Mr. Adamson," Father Sebastian said. "The students aren't prisoners, and we're not guards. I'm a psychologist, and I treat all our students—especially the so-called 'at risk' group—with a great deal of respect. The school has found that for the most part our students rise to our expectations, and I'm happy to be able to tell you that Kip has done exactly that, right up to this point. Which is why his disappearance is such a mystery."

"Something must have set him off," Anne Adamson said, her fingers twisting a corner of her apron. "It's what always happens. Everything seems fine, then something sets him off. It's like he just goes crazy." She seemed about to burst into tears, and Brother Francis reached out and took one of her hands in his own.

"I'm sure nothing like that happened at all," he began. He was about to say more, but fell silent as Father Sebastian shot him a warning glance.

"Perhaps there *was* something," Father Sebastian said. "But if there was, we don't know what it might have been. It's much more likely that Kip has just gone off to sort out his feelings."

"*Sort out his feelings?*" Gordy shot back, his voice edged with contempt. "What kind of psychobabble is that? You lose a kid you should be watching like a hawk and you say he went away to sort out his *feelings?*"

"Perhaps I put it badly," Father Sebastian said evenly. "The point is that he's gone off before, hasn't he? And he always came back home?"

When Gordy Adamson only glowered at the priest, his wife spoke. "He's right, Gordy." She tried to put her hand over his, but he pulled it away.

"We sent him to your damn school so he wouldn't run away anymore," Gordy said, his voice grating. "If you're just going to let him take off, what's the point? Maybe we shoulda kept him home. He coulda run away from here and it wouldn't cost us a dime!"

"Gordy, please—" Anne begged.

Gordy Adamson's expression darkened and he moved slightly away from his wife. "I'm just sayin'—"

"It's all right, Mrs. Adamson," Father Sebastian cut in quickly. "Actually, he's got a point. But the odds are Kip will be back by morning."

"And if he's not?" Gordy challenged.

"Then we'll talk about it in the morning," Father Sebastian calmly replied. "If there's one thing I've learned in dealing with kids over the last few years, it's never to borrow trouble. And so far, there's no evidence Kip is in any trouble."

"But isn't there anything we can do?" Anne fretted. "It seems like there must be something!"

Father Sebastian smiled at her. "Actually, there is. You can make a list of anyone Kip might have gotten in touch with, and start calling. I'm talking about all his friends from before he came to St. Isaac's—everyone that you can think of. And give us a copy of the list so we can follow up, too."

"And maybe we should call the police," Gordy said, his tone as challenging as the look in his eyes.

"We certainly can," Father Sebastian said, refusing to rise to Adamson's bait. "On the other hand, given that Kip has no criminal record, the police aren't likely to do anything at all for at least twenty-four hours, but if you want to spend most of the night answering questions, I'll be happy to get the ball rolling."

Brother Francis watched as Gordy Adamson visibly deflated.

Ten minutes later, the list of Kip's friends and their phone numbers in hand, the two clerics left.

"Well, we didn't learn much there," Brother Francis sighed as he started the car.

"Actually, we did," Father Sebastian replied. "We learned that Gordy Adamson is a thoroughgoing son-of-a-bitch, and that wherever Kip goes, it won't be home."

As he started back toward Boston, Brother Francis decided that he liked Father Sebastian.

He liked him a lot.

CHAPTER 7

Teri McIntyre's knees threatened to buckle when she saw Ryan's battered face, ashen beneath the swelling and bruising. Tom gripped her arm to steady her as she moved to her son's bedside. All around him was the machinery of the hospital, but blessedly he didn't seem to be attached to more than two of them—one an I.V. drip, the other monitoring his vital signs.

"Oh darling, I'm so sorry," she whispered, leaning close, not wanting to wake him if he was sleeping, but wanting to be sure he heard if he was awake. Ryan opened his eyes and gazed at her for a moment. Then his eyes shifted to Tom Kelly, and Teri thought she saw them narrow for a split second before he let them fall closed again.

Tom brought over a chair, and Teri sank into it, taking hold of her son's limp hand. "Who did this?" she asked gently. "Someone from school?"

Ryan opened his eyes again and looked at her, his swollen lips attempting a grim smile.

"Don't try to talk," Teri told him. "Just nod or shake your head if it doesn't hurt too much. Have the police talked with you?"

Ryan nodded.

"Do they know who did this?"

Ryan shook his head.

"Well, we'll find them," Teri assured him. "They won't get away with this." Her voice began to rise. "We'll send—"

She felt Tom's hand on her shoulder, squeezing gently, and took a deep breath.

Once again Ryan's eyes opened, and now he tried to form a word with his battered mouth. Teri poured a glass of water from the plastic pitcher on his nightstand, took the wrapper off a fresh straw, and held it to his lips as he sucked weakly. Still, the little water he managed seemed to help. "Just—just forget it," he whispered.

Teri stared at him. "Forget it?" she echoed.

Ryan took as deep a breath as he could, exhaling it in a rattling sigh. "It'll just make it worse for me," he said, struggling to pronounce each word clearly.

"How could anything be worse than this?" Teri asked, but even as she spoke, she knew exactly what worse could look like.

Ryan could be dead.

As if he'd read the thought in her expression, Ryan closed his eyes and sank deeper into his pillow.

Teri sat back in her chair, unconsciously smoothing her skirt. *How long had he lain in that bathroom?* she wondered. Had he been lying there unconscious in a pool of his own blood all the time she'd been sitting in the restaurant with Tom? How could she have done it? How could she have gone out on a date—a *date*!—without knowing exactly where her son was? What kind of mother was she? If only she could trade places with him; she should have been beaten up, not him.

If only Bill were here! He'd know what to do. Why did he have to die? He ought to be here helping her. Helping her, and helping Ryan! Tears welled behind her eyes, but she steeled herself against them; the last thing Ryan needed right now was to have her start crying.

The hospital room door opened and a young doctor with a stethoscope hanging around his neck strode in and offered her his hand.

"Mrs. McIntyre? I'm Dr. Barris. Your boy here seems to be a lot stronger than he looks right now. We took CAT scans of his head and torso, and he actually looks a lot worse off than he is. There's some bruising, but he'll be just fine."

Teri felt a little bit of her burden of guilt lift at the doctor's words. "When can he come home? Tonight?"

Barris shook his head. "It's bad enough to make us want to keep him overnight for observation, but if nothing worrisome develops, I'll discharge him tomorrow. Sunday at the latest."

"Well at least that's good news," Teri sighed. She gave Ryan's hand a quick squeeze. "Did you hear that?"

Ryan nodded, but didn't open his eyes.

"We've given him something for the pain," Barris went on. He should be down for the night within about ten more minutes."

"Can I stay with him?" Teri asked. "Just sit here?"

The doctor shrugged noncommittally, but Tom Kelly shook his head. "I'm not sure that's such a good idea. Just let him sleep."

"But what if he needs something?" Teri pleaded and suddenly Tom understood exactly what was really in her mind.

"He's not going to need anything, and if he does, he's got a whole nursing staff to take care of it for him. But I'll bet he'd like you to be awake tomorrow, instead of passing out whenever he tries to talk to you."

Teri looked helplessly at Ryan. His eyes were closed and he seemed to be breathing regularly and easily. Tom was right—there was nothing she could do for him tonight. "Okay," she said, rising shakily to her feet.

"I'll see you all in the morning, then," Dr. Barris said. His pager beeped, he glanced at it, then said a quick good-bye and left the room.

Teri leaned over the edge of the bed and kissed Ryan on the cheek, then smoothed his hair, which was still damp from the nurse washing the blood out of it. She looked down at her son, her chest tight. "Good night, honey," she said, brushing his cheek with her lips. "Sweet dreams."

Ryan neither opened his eyes, nor gave any acknowledgment that he'd heard her words.

† † †

In the car, Teri finally let her tears flow. Tom drove slowly and said nothing, letting her deal with her roiling emotions. But when he got to her house, he pulled into the driveway, killed the engine and turned off the lights. "I think maybe I'd better come in, at least for a while," he said softly.

Teri blew her nose, took a couple of deep breaths, and nodded.

"I don't know what to do anymore," she said a few minutes later as she started making a pot of coffee. "We should be able to press charges against whoever did this to Ryan. But I know what he means—it could just make things worse for him!"

"I have a suggestion," Tom said, taking the milk out of the refrigerator, setting it on the kitchen table, then sitting down.

"I know," Teri sighed. "St. Isaac's. But even if he agreed to go and we could get him in, I can't see how I could possibly manage the money. Bill's death benefits just weren't that much."

"St. Isaac's has to have some kind of financial aid program." He hesitated, then: "And I'm not totally broke."

Teri's eyes glistened with tears even as she shook her head. "That's incredibly sweet of you, but you know I can't take your money," she said, then held up a protesting hand as Tom opened his mouth to argue with her. "And even if I could, I don't think I want Ryan living somewhere else."

"And those kids who beat him up will be back at Dickinson High on Monday morning," Tom reminded her.

Exhaustion flowed through Teri like liquid lead. "Oh, God," she sighed as she looked around for clean coffee cups, then just pulled two from this morning out of the dishwasher.

"Listen," Tom pressed. "I know someone who works at St. Isaac's. Let me at least give him a call and see what the possibilities are. At this point we don't even know if we can get Ryan in. But let's at least find out what the options are, okay?"

"Okay," Teri agreed, too numb to argue. "And who knows? Maybe that's where he should be." She poured each of them a cup of coffee, set the pot down on the table, and sank into the chair opposite Tom, who reached across and took her hand, squeezing it as gently as she'd squeezed Ryan's a little while ago.

"Hey," he said. "You're not completely by yourself, you know. And things will get better."

She nodded her head. That was good to hear, even though she didn't believe it.

CHAPTER 8

RIP ADAMSON WAS leaning against a brick wall. The thing was, he had no idea why he was there, or how long he'd been there, or even where the wall itself was. He felt oddly paralyzed, afraid to move, afraid even to look around, as if any movement at all might cause whatever reality he was in to vanish as abruptly as it had come.

But *was* it real? Maybe he was dreaming—in fact, he *had* to be dreaming, since nothing about either his surroundings or his body felt real at all.

Then his fingers brushed against the coarse bricks behind him.

They felt real.

He looked at his hands.

They looked real.

He curled his fingers into fists, and then relaxed them.

It was all real.

He sank to the sidewalk, trying to figure out what had happened to him. Where was he? How had he gotten here? And why was he here, wherever "here" was?

He looked down the dark, deserted street. A neon bar sign was glowing halfway down the block, but other than that all he saw were the stoops in front of a series of old brownstone houses. But not nice ones like the ones on Beacon Hill or in the Back Bay.

These looked more like slums.

And it felt late. After midnight? He couldn't tell.

He rose back to his feet and moved slowly along the narrow city sidewalk, looking for landmarks—anything recognizable. But nothing looked familiar.

How could he have gotten here? He searched his memory, but the last thing he could really remember was eating pancakes for breakfast in the dining room at St. Isaac's.

And he'd felt a little dizzy. He'd headed back to his room, but . . .

The memories tumbled through his head now. *Hot!* He'd felt so hot he thought his flesh was being seared right off his bones.

And all around him, vivid colors had pulsated, colors so vivid he could not only see them, but *feel* them, every nerve in his body tingling and vibrating.

And voices! Guttural, garbled sounds in a language he didn't understand, but the meaning of which he'd understood.

Then the things—horrible, impossibly hideous creatures—had come. Even now, in the darkness of the empty street, they rose out of his subconscious to taunt him, their lips twisted, their burning eyes leered.

In the darkness of the night, he felt the same urge to flee he'd felt this morning.

Was that what had happened? Had it been some kind of nightmare that he'd tried to flee from? But if he'd been asleep, and dreaming, how had he gotten to these empty streets he'd never seen before?

Unless this was the dream, and in a minute he'd wake up, and be back in his room at school and Clay Matthews would be asleep in the other bed.

The things were back now, all around him, and he ran his hands over his face, sweating even in the cool of the night.

A drunk stumbled out of the bar and Kip shrank into a shadowed doorway, his vision suddenly blurring as if he were looking through a greasy window. He rubbed his eyes, but the blurriness remained.

Then the strange dizziness he'd felt this morning struck him again, and he clung to the brick wall, fighting the vertigo.

The man wandered toward him, singing softly to himself, and Kip watched from the shadows, a strange hunger growing inside him.

He wanted something—craved it.

But what?

The guttural voices were jabbering again, and, in the blurred periphery of his vision, Kip glimpsed the demons reaching toward him, wanting to touch him, to tear at him.

To devour him.

No!

His right hand slid into the deep front pocket of his cargo pants, his fingers closing on a hard object. A second later he was staring at a knife.

A large knife with a bone handle, into which was folded a thick blade.

He'd never seen the knife before—he was sure of it—but he knew what to do.

He pressed a small button on the knife's haft, and the blade flicked out, locking instantly into place.

He tested it with the thumb of his left hand, and watched as blood began to ooze from a deep cut.

A searing pain shot through his hand and up his arm.

The voices of the demons gurgled with pleasure.

He stepped out of the shadows and into the path of the drunk. The man slowed and looked puzzled for a moment. His bleary eyes focused on the knife, then shifted to Kip's face.

Even in the dim glow of light from the streetlamp at the corner, Kip could see the blood drain from the man's face. Seeming to sober in an instant, the man wheeled around, shambled down the sidewalk, and disappeared back into the bar.

Kip peered down at the knife, still glistening with his own blood. Clutching it tighter, he turned and started the other way. Toward the end of the block, light flooded the sidewalk as someone emerged from one of the brownstones. Then the light was gone, and a figure came down the steps from the house's stoop.

Kip slipped into the shadows, sweat flowing from his face.

The figure turned and began to walk away from him. A woman with a small dog on a leash.

Kip stepped out of the shadows and started after her, his footfalls silent in the night.

Somewhere on the edges of his consciousness he heard a sound, a soft wailing.

Like the sound the woman might make when he plunged the knife deep into her belly.

His step quickened, and, as the wailing grew louder and he closed in on the lone figure ahead of him, his fingers tightened around the handle of the knife.

The woman paused as the dog stopped to lift his leg on a fire hydrant, and suddenly sensed that she wasn't alone on the street. She turned, looking full into his face. Kip saw her eyes widen, and the blood drain from her face as it had from the drunk only a few minutes ago. Then, as the wailing grew into the screams of sirens, the woman backed away, then turned to flee.

Too late.

Kip caught up with her, his left arm snaking out, his fingers closing in on her hair. He yanked her backward and she fell against his body.

Now there was a strange red and blue glow pulsing in the darkness, and the sirens continued screaming.

A moment later, voices were howling at him, and Kip froze.

The dog's barking rose out of the melee around him, and the woman, too, began to scream.

Pulling her head back even farther, Kip's right hand rose as if from its own volition and then the blade was ripping across the woman's throat. In an instant her screams died away to nothing more than a wheezing gurgle and blood spewed from the gaping wound the blade had opened. Her knees buckled and as she sank to the sidewalk, Kip sank with her. He was on his knees now, crouching above the woman. She lay on her back, her glazing eyes staring up at him.

The sirens fell silent.

He heard the sound of car doors slamming.

Voices—real voices—shouted into the night.

Kip heard nothing as the demons in his head urged him on. He raised the knife and plunged it deep into the woman's chest.

Her body shuddered reflexively.

Kip raised the knife again.

He felt something slam into his back, and heard a loud popping sound.

The knife arced down again, sinking into the woman's belly. As the blade sliced through her stomach and intestines, another bullet slammed into Kip.

This time, though, it wasn't his back the bullet hit.

This time it was his head, and in the instant it shattered his skull and entered his brain, blackness descended over him.

He pitched forward, surrendering his soul to the demons inside him, and his body dropped on top of the woman he'd just killed.

The street—and the demons inside Kip—fell silent.

CHAPTER 9

H E WAS BACK *on the floor of the boys' restroom at Dickinson,
curled up in a fetal position, bracing himself for the next kick.
Only it wasn't just Stan Wojniak and Bennie Locke this time. Frankie Alito
was there, too, along with three other guys, and all of them were kicking
him, their shoes thudding into his sides and smashing his face. Even the
walls seemed to be closing in on him, and there was no place to hide, and
more guys were around him, and then he saw the knives.*

*First in Alito's hand, and then in Locke's, and then they all had knives,
and they were closing in on him, and his heart was pounding so hard he
could hear it, and he opened his mouth to scream but nothing came out
and—*

—and Ryan jerked awake in the darkened hospital room. Its silence
broken only by the pounding of his own heart, and the groan that escaped his lips as the pain of his convulsive awakening broke through
the narcotics and threatened to tear his chest apart.

He lay perfectly still, willing the spasm of pain to break. The beating
was over—he was safe. Safe in the hospital, and tomorrow he would go
home.

Tomorrow or Sunday.

The wave of pain finally began to recede, and he turned over onto his good side, wincing at the new pang of protest from his cracked ribs. He held still again and closed his eyes, but after the nightmare he didn't really want to go back to sleep again, at least not until the last remnants of the dream were completely gone.

Besides, he wasn't sleepy, and what he really wanted was someone to talk to. But not his mother, who would only start crying, and certainly not Tom Kelly. And he didn't want to call any of the nurses, either. They'd just give him some more pills.

The person he really wanted to talk to was his father.

His father would know what to do, would tell him how to handle Frankie Alito and all his friends when he went back to school on Monday. But his father couldn't help him, because his father was dead, and wasn't coming back, and Ryan was just going to have to figure out what to do by himself.

A single tear rolled out the corner of his eye and he quickly wiped it away. Then there was a soft knock on the door. As Ryan fumbled with the controller and found the light switch, the door opened and a dark-haired man stepped inside.

A dark-haired man who was neither a nurse nor an orderly.

Ryan gazed at him uncertainly.

"Ryan?" the man asked. "Ryan McIntyre?"

Ryan nodded.

The man stepped fully into the room and let the door close quietly behind him, and without the brighter lights of the hallway behind him, Ryan could finally see the clerical collar the man wore.

A priest.

"I'm Father Sebastian Sloane," the priest said, lowering himself onto the chair closest to the bed.

Ryan frowned. What was a priest doing here? Had his mother sent him? But maybe he was just the chaplain at the hospital or something. Before he could ask, though, the priest spoke again. "I think you know a friend of mine. Tom Kelly?"

Ryan's expression darkened. "Why'd he send you here?" he asked, making no attempt to keep the hostility out of his voice. "Is he hoping I'm going to die and wanted you to give me last rites?"

The priest didn't even flinch at the harsh words; instead he chuckled. "Not too fond of him, hunh?"

Ryan shook his head. "Why should I be?"

Father Sebastian spread his hands dismissively. "No reason that I can think of. Knowing Tom, he's probably trying to act like your father. Anyway, he sure sounded like it when he called me an hour ago." He leaned forward slightly and dropped his voice. "So how bad is he?"

Ryan shrugged. "He just keeps acting like he knows what's best for my mother and me. Like we can't take care of ourselves."

"Sounds like Tom, all right," Father Sebastian sighed. "He tries to run everyone's life. In fact, that's why I came over here tonight—it was easier to just do what he wanted me to do than try to argue with him. Although I've got to say, sometimes I'd rather just—" He cut off his words and jabbed the middle finger of his right hand high in the air. "You know what I mean?"

"Jesus," Ryan blurted out without thinking. "What kind of priest are you?"

"Actually, I'm a counselor at St. Isaac's," Father Sebastian said. He grinned, and when he spoke again his voice was tinged with sarcasm. "Is it all getting clearer now?"

Ryan groaned. "Oh, great—so he sent you here to wake me up in the middle of the night just so you could talk me into going to St. Isaac's? What'd he think—I'd be so drugged up I wouldn't know what was going on?"

"Probably," Father Sebastian agreed. "But in all fairness, you weren't asleep, and if you had been I'd have gone away quietly. Granted, getting up this late and coming over here wasn't exactly what I wanted to do tonight, but as I said, it beats arguing with Tom Kelly. So what do you think? Want to hear the pitch, or should I just go home and tell Tom you were asleep?"

"You'd really do that?" Ryan asked.

"Try me!" Father Sebastian rose to his feet. "It's almost one in the morning and this past evening wasn't really great. So just say the word, and I'm out of here and back in bed in half an hour."

"What if I want to hear the pitch?" Ryan countered.

Father Sebastian rolled his eyes. "Then I give you the short version, hope you don't have any questions, and I'm home and in bed in maybe forty minutes."

Ryan started to laugh, felt a twinge of pain in his ribs, and cut the laugh short. "Okay," he said. "I'll listen."

The priest smiled. "Beats lying here in the dark thinking about next week, doesn't it?" he asked, voicing Ryan's thoughts almost perfectly. He lowered himself back into the chair. "The main thing I've got to tell you is that things like what happened to you don't happen at St. Isaac's. We don't let them happen. If anybody there is going to give you a hard time it's going to be the nuns, not the other students. And while some of the sisters are tough as nails, I don't think they'd actually kick you." He winked at Ryan. "But don't hold me to that. I've only been there since the fall, so what do I know?"

"Tom Kelly doesn't really care that I got my butt kicked yesterday," Ryan replied. "He just wants me out of the house so he can put the make on my mother."

"From what I know of Tom, which I'll grant you isn't all that much, he's probably going to do that whether you're there or not," Father Sebastian said. "But you know, it's not such a terrible thing that he has feelings for your mother."

"It still doesn't make him my dad," Ryan insisted, and hoped his words didn't sound quite as sullen to the priest as they did to him.

"No one can replace your father," Father Sebastian. "Tom and your mom are just trying to do what's best for you. Like your dad would, if he were here. And right now, they think that the best thing is for you to get out of Dickinson High."

Ryan stared at the ceiling.

Father Sebastian put his hand on Ryan's shoulder. "It's up to you, of course. We don't tolerate the kind of stuff you're going through at Dickinson, and I can tell you that a diploma from St. Isaac's on your college applications doesn't hurt."

Ryan's attention instantly shifted back to the priest. For as long as he could remember, he'd been determined to follow his father to Princeton, but Princeton could take their pick from literally thousands of kids with 4.0-plus GPAs and perfect SATs, and after what had happened yesterday he couldn't risk blowing any more tests, let alone waste all his time watching his back.

"Any of your kids go to Princeton?" he asked, trying to sound a lot less interested than he suddenly was.

"A couple," Father Sebastian replied. "And Harvard. And M.I.T. The best of our bunch go pretty much wherever they want to go." Ryan made no reply, but Father Sebastian felt fairly sure that the message Tom wanted delivered had finally been received. "Just think about it, okay?" he said, standing up. "Now go back to sleep and get some rest."

Ryan nodded. Then, just as Father Sebastian opened the door, he spoke. "Hey."

Father Sebastian turned.

"Thanks for coming."

The priest smiled, his eyes roving quickly over the hospital room. "You seem like a pretty good kid," he said. "You deserve better than this. Think about it."

The door swung shut, and Ryan switched off the light, gazing sightlessly up at the dark ceiling. But the last remnants of the nightmare were gone, and Ryan was sure they weren't going to come back.

CHAPTER 10

ANNE ADAMSON'S EYES snapped open in the darkness of the bedroom. The first light of dawn silhouetted the big maple tree outside the window, and at first she thought the wind must have rattled its branches against the house. But there was no wind; indeed, the silence in the house seemed almost unnatural.

So what had wakened her?

She lay quietly, listening for the sound to repeat itself.

Maybe Kip was home! Maybe he'd come back!

Hope surged through her, yet still she waited.

Then she heard it again.

The doorbell!

"Gordy!" she said, shaking her husband's shoulder. "Gordy, there's someone at the door."

"Huh?" Gordy muttered, heaving himself up.

"The *door*bell, Gordy. Someone's at the door!"

"Kip," Gordy groaned, swinging his legs over the side of the bed. "Musta lost his damn key."

Anne got out of bed and reached into the closet for their bathrobes while Gordy went to the window and peered out at the street below.

An almost unintelligible curse rumbled from his throat. "Cop car out front," he said in response to Anne's inquiring look.

Anne's heart sank.

Gordy sighed. "What do you s'pose he's done now?" He took the robe Anne was holding and shrugged into it as the doorbell rang yet another time, then led his wife down the stairs, flipped on the porch light, and opened the front door.

Two police officers stood on the front porch, their faces looking sickly in the yellowish light. "Mr. Adamson?" the older of the two asked.

"Yeah," Gordy said, his eyes balefully fixing on the visitors. "Christ Almighty, if it ain't priests, it's cops." He shoved the screen door open. "Might as well come in and tell us what he's done."

The officers glanced uneasily at each other, but let themselves be ushered into the living room. "I'm Sergeant Chapman," the older police officer said. "This is Officer Haskins."

Something in his voice sent a chill through Anne's body. "What is it?" she asked. "Has something happened to Kip?"

Chapman shifted uneasily. "Perhaps you should have a seat, ma'am."

Gordy Adamson reached out and took his wife's hand. "He's dead then, isn't he?"

"Gordy!" Anne gasped, jerking her hand away. "How can you even say such a thing?" But even as she uttered the words the expression on Sergeant Chapman's face revealed the truth of her husband's words.

"I'm so sorry to have to tell you this," the sergeant said softly as Anne sank onto the edge of the sofa. "Kip was involved in a—" He hesitated, searching for the right word. "There was an altercation last night."

"What kind of 'altercation?' " Gordy challenged, his voice hard.

"The investigation isn't quite finished," Chapman went on, "but it appears your son was fatally shot by officers while in the act of—" Again he fell silent, and Gordy Adamson's eyes bored into him.

"In the act of *what*?" Adamson demanded. "Tell me what my son was doing that was so bad you had to kill him!"

Chapman took a deep breath. "I'm afraid he was in the middle of killing someone," he said. "A fifty-year-old woman who was out walking her dog."

"Killing someone?" Anne breathed. "Kip? No—you must have the wrong boy. Kip would never—"

"I'm afraid it's not a mistake, ma'am," Chapman said gently. "Your son wasn't carrying any identification, but his fingerprints are in the system and there really isn't any question about the match. But we do need one of you to come down to the morgue and make a positive identification."

Now Anne reached for Gordy's hand, but his arms were tight across his chest, his face a mask of fury. "I'm gonna sue that damn school," he said, his voice trembling with fury.

The two officers glanced uncertainly at each other. "School?" Officer Haskins asked. "What school?"

"St. Isaac's," Gordy spat. "They were supposed to keep Kip under control. What was he doing prowling the streets at night instead of sleeping in his dorm room? I ask you."

"It's got to be a mistake, honey," Anne said, not wanting—not *able*—to accept the truth of what had happened. "It wasn't Kip. It couldn't have been Kip. Kip stole a few things, that's all. But he'd never—" She clutched her bathrobe tight around her throat. "It wasn't him," she whispered.

"It was him, all right," Gordy said, his voice sounding oddly flat. "I can feel it." He shook his head tiredly. "Let me get my clothes on, and I'll go with you."

As her husband disappeared up the stairs Anne sat quietly with the two policemen, too stunned by what she'd been told to say anything more at all.

"I'm so sorry," Officer Haskins said, but Ann shook her head distractedly, as if by rejecting his sympathy she could deny the reason for it.

A few silent moments later, Gordy came back down, carrying his shoes. He dropped into a chair and put them on. "I swear, I really am suing that damned school," he muttered as he tied his laces. "You give a kid to a bunch of priests and nuns and he's supposed to be safe. But no." His voice began to crack. He tied the last knot, stood up, and took a deep breath. "Okay," he said. "Let's get this over with."

A moment later, alone in the silent house, Anne stared for a long time at the framed photograph on the mantel of Kip in his Little League uniform.

Hanging over the corner of the frame was his first rosary.

As the truth of what had happened slowly began to sink in, she rose from the chair and moved to the fireplace.

She picked up the rosary and held it to her cheek.

Silently, her eyes streaming with tears, she began to pray.

CHAPTER 11

FATHER SEBASTIAN SLOANE HURRIED along the corridor toward Father Laughlin's office, still wiping toothpaste from the corner of his mouth. Sister Margaret's tone alone had been enough to tell him that whatever Father Laughlin wanted to see him about was very serious. Which, Father Sebastian was certain, meant two things: it had to do with Kip Adamson, and it wasn't good.

He paused at the door to the headmaster's office only long enough to rap softly, then turned the knob.

Father Laughlin sat behind his desk, his lined face looking even older and more worn than usual. Sister Mary David, Brother Francis, and Sister Margaret all looked up when he came in, but none of them smiled.

The two nuns and the monk were even paler than the priest. Father Sebastian quietly took the single remaining empty chair.

Father Laughlin took a deep breath, spread his hands flat on the top of his desk, and looked straight at Father Sebastian. "Kip Adamson murdered a woman last night," he said, his voice as flat as his hands. Before Father Sebastian could even react, he spoke again. "He himself was killed by the police."

A cold numbness spread through Father Sebastian's body and he felt all the energy his body had generated during the night drain out of him. Questions tumbled through his mind, but before he could find the right words for even one of them, Father Laughlin spoke again.

"That's all we know," the old priest sighed, making the words sound like a personal defeat. "They're investigating, of course."

"Drugs?" Sebastian suggested, his eyes flitting over the little group.

Brother Francis spread his hands helplessly. "I suppose it's possible, but . . ."

As his words trailed off into helplessness, Father Sebastian remembered Anne and Gordy Adamson. She, he was certain, would be devastated at the news. But what about Kip's father? Would he even feign sorrow at his loss? Probably. But even more probably, he would start looking around for someone to blame, and St. Isaac's would undoubtedly be at the top of his list. "Has anyone spoken with Kip's parents?"

"I called their parish priest," Brother Francis said. "Kip's mother called him an hour ago, and he was already there."

Sebastian frowned. "Shouldn't Father Laughlin or I go, too?"

"That's what I thought," Brother Francis interjected. "But Father Laughlin feels it's best if their own priest handles it."

"It's just so hard to believe," Sister Mary David said, her lips compressing into a thin line as if the boy's death were a personal affront to her. "It's not as if he was doing badly here. In fact, he was doing well— his grades were up and—"

"The police will be here today," Father Laughlin cut in, garnering a dark look from Sister Mary David, who obviously had a lot more to say. "They will want to know if anyone has noticed anything about Kip. Anything unusual." His eyes roved tiredly from one face to another. "Has anyone?"

Father Sebastian glanced at the other three, none of whom seemed certain of even how to respond to Father Laughlin, let alone the police. "Nothing that I have noticed. I agree with Sister Mary David—Kip was doing well. The usual sins of a boy his age, of course." He suppressed a smile as Sister Margaret blushed and Sister Mary David scowled disapprovingly. "But I heard his confession and gave him a penance. Actually, I thought we were succeeding very well with him. At least up until yesterday."

Father Laughlin took another deep breath, and seemed to pull him-self together slightly. "Very well. If any of you should remember any-thing odd about Kip's behavior, please bring it here first. At this point there's nothing that can be done either for the Adamson boy or for the poor woman he attacked." He paused, then spoke again, his voice tak-ing on a slight edge. "I'm sure you all understand that we don't need any publicity that will reflect badly either on the school or on the Church. I think the Church has had as much of that as it can stand for the foreseeable future." His eyes moved from one face to the next. "Do I make myself clear?"

"It doesn't matter what we say," Sister Mary David said. "Some par-ents are likely to remove their children, and recruitment will be difficult for a year or so." She turned to Sister Margaret. "We ought to have a statement ready for the press."

Father Laughlin pressed his fingertips to his temples and rubbed them in small circles as if he could massage away the trouble that he was certain was about to rain down on his head.

"We'd better cancel classes for today," Father Sebastian said as Father Laughlin's silence stretched on. "We'll hold a mass for Kip, and then arrange to be in our offices and available for any of the students who want to talk about it. As for the police, the best thing we can do is an-swer all their questions as completely and honestly as possible."

As the two nuns nodded their agreement, Brother Francis raised his hand, and Father Sebastian was reminded of nothing so much as a wor-ried schoolboy who is uncertain of his lessons.

"I feel like somehow it's my fault," he said. "Was there something I missed? Some sign? Did I do something wrong? I feel as if I should have seen this coming—maybe spent more time with him, or paid more at-tention."

Sister Margaret peered at him over the rims of the half-glasses that were perpetually perched on her nose. "There are over two hundred students here," she declared. "We can only do what we can do, and for the most part, we do a very good job. None of us saw this coming, and there's no reason why we should have. We can't know everything in each student's heart at every moment."

"I just feel as if I—" Brother Francis began again, but this time Sister Margaret didn't even let him finish.

"Brother Francis, our job is to look after the children, not feel sorry for ourselves." Her eyes fixed on Brother Francis, and he instantly felt as if he was back in parochial school and about to feel the rap of a ruler across his knuckles. "Can you put your own feelings aside long enough to talk to the rest of the boys about what's happened?"

Brother Francis's face burned. "Of course I can. I'll just need a few moments to collect my thoughts."

"Which is a very good idea for all of us," Father Sebastian interjected before Sister Margaret could say anything else to Brother Francis. "And when we begin answering questions—not only from the police but from the students and their parents as well, I think we should keep in mind that this is not a time for trying to assign blame, either to Kip Adamson or to anyone else. Unfortunately, evil is insidious in the world we live in, and no one is immune. And often, it seems, the children are even less immune than anyone else."

"Still, everyone makes their choices," Sister Margaret sniffed, making no attempt to conceal her disdain for Father Sebastian's words.

"Be that as it may," Father Sebastian replied gently, "our job right now is to reassure our students and their parents that whatever caused Kip to attack that poor woman, it had nothing to do with St. Isaac's. The boy had problems when he arrived—in fact, isn't that exactly why he came here? It's not that we failed him—we simply didn't have enough time to succeed with him. Evil, unfortunately, cannot be overcome in an instant, and whatever evil inhabited Kip Adamson was obviously far stronger than any of us saw."

Father Laughlin finally stirred in his chair, and looked up. "Father Sebastian is right," he declared. "In the future, we shall all be far more vigilant."

† † †

Patrick North and Kevin Peterson had been working together long enough that neither detective had to say a word before they entered Kip Adamson's room at St. Isaac's; North would do the searching while Peterson talked to the boy's roommate. There was something about Peterson's manner that made people want to talk to him, and North had given up trying to emulate it years ago, concentrating instead on honing his already sharp eyes and innate instinct for knowing where to look for what he was trying to find. Except, of course, for his keys, which somehow still managed to elude him at least twice a day. Now he handed them over to Peterson before he pulled on a pair of surgical gloves and began his search, which he would carry out as carefully as he did all his searches, even though the disinterest of Adamson's friends had already told him the search was probably going to be futile. If there was anything to find, North figured Clay Matthews and Darren Bender would be a lot more nervous than they were.

"So you and Kip were roommates last year, too?" North heard Peterson ask Clay Matthews, scanning his notes as if he didn't already have every word of them memorized.

"Yeah," Clay said. "They stuck him with me when he first came here."

"And you requested each other as roommates again this year?"

Clay nodded. "We got along great."

Detective North pulled the sheets off Kip's bed, shook them out, and then lifted up the mattress.

A copy of *Playboy* was stashed between the mattress and the springs, which North picked up, fanned through, then tossed onto Matthews's bed.

"I'll take that," Brother Francis said, stepping forward quickly to seize the offending literature.

As Peterson shrugged sympathetically at Matthews, North turned his attention to Kip's footlocker. It was unlocked and he flipped the top open. Inside were books and photographs, a pair of sandals, and a hockey jersey autographed on the shoulder by someone from the Chicago Blackhawks.

"Has Kip ever taken off like this before?" Detective Peterson asked. Clay shook his head. "Okay, so let's get to the big question," Peterson went on. "What about drugs? Adamson ever use them?"

North looked up from the footlocker to watch the boys' reactions.

Both boys shook their heads.

"Come on," Peterson prompted them. "Not even a little pot once in a while?"

Matthews shook his head again, this time more emphatically. "I'd know. He used to do drugs before he came here, but he didn't anymore. He said he'd decided he'd gotten in enough trouble, and he was done with it."

"He thought people who did drugs were stupid," Darren Bender offered.

Peterson's gaze shifted to Bender. "And yet he grabbed a woman from behind and slit her throat," he said softly. "How do you suppose that fits with his decision to stay out of trouble?"

"How should we know?" Bender countered. "I don't even get that he could do it."

"But he did," Peterson said, sounding every bit as puzzled as Darren Bender. "So if it wasn't drugs, what could it have been? Can either of you think of anything that might have made Kip do such a thing?"

Darren and Clay looked at each other, and North saw nothing in either of their expressions that looked like they might be trying to hide something.

"Anything at all," Peterson urged. "We need some help here. Can't either of you think of anything that was different about Kip lately?"

Clay Matthews hesitated uncertainly, then: "Well . . ."

Both detectives' attention instantly focused on the Matthews boy.

"Now that I think about it, Kip has been acting a little weird," Clay said.

North's eyes narrowed. "Weird like how?" he said sharply enough that the boy actually jumped.

"I don't know, really," Clay said, his voice taking on a defensive note.

"It's okay," Peterson soothed and North, finished with his search of the footlocker, moved on to the closet. "Just tell us whatever you can. Anything at all could help."

Clay relaxed a little. "He was always kind of a loner, you know? Ever since he first came here. But lately he started to act kind of strange."

"Strange how?" Peterson asked.

Matthews shrugged. "I dunno. He sort of stopped wanting to hang out with any of us—even me. And the other day, he couldn't find a pen and he threw a regular shi—" He cut his words short, glanced guiltily toward Brother Francis, and reddened slightly. "I mean he got really mad—like throwing things! Over a lousy pen! I mean, it wasn't even like it was some kind of good pen. Just one of those cheap ones."

"How bad was it?" Peterson pressed. "The scene?"

"Really bad. His face was all red and he accused me of stealing his stuff. And he seemed like he just wanted to break things." He walked over and pointed at a black mark on the wall. "See this? He threw his shoe at me. Hard, too. Over that crummy pen, which he found five minutes later on the floor next to his bed."

"And that was unusual behavior for him?" Peterson asked.

"Definitely," Clay replied. "Kip was a loner—he was always quiet."

"How come you didn't tell me that?" Darren Bender asked. "He got that way on the basketball court, too. He missed a shot, and all of a sudden he's kicking the wall in the gym. Just because he missed a basket! I mean, it's not like he made that many in the first place—he really sucked at basketball. I thought he was going to break his foot or something."

North emerged from the closet. "And neither of you think he was doing drugs?" he asked as he started going through Kip's desk. "Like steroids, maybe?"

Clay spread his hands helplessly. "I wouldn't even know what steroids look like. And he wasn't a jock, so why would he be doing something like that anyway?"

"Okay," Detective North said as he finished with the desk and turned to Brother Francis. "There's nothing here we need. You're free to release all his belongings to his family." He turned to the boys, and decided to try prodding their memories one last time. "So that's it? There's nothing else? Nothing at all you want to tell us?"

Clay and Darren looked at each other and Clay started to shake his head. But then Darren Bender spoke. "There was one other thing. He started going to confession practically every day."

"Confession?" North echoed. "Every single day? Why?"

Now both boys spread their hands helplessly. "How would we know?" Darren asked. His eyes darted toward Brother Francis. "It's not like we get that much chance to do anything worth confessing around here."

Brother Francis's eyes rolled. "If it were up to me, you'd all be confessing three times a day, and there still wouldn't be time to get you all absolved." He turned to the detective. "Do you think it's important? About Kip's confessions, I mean?"

"Very," North replied. "So who do we talk to about what he might have been confessing?"

"You don't," Brother Francis replied. "The Church has changed a lot in the last few decades, but the sanctity of the confessional hasn't changed. It is absolute."

"Even when the person who made the confession is dead?" Kevin Peterson asked.

Brother Francis's expression hardened. "Even then," he assured them. "It is absolute, under any circumstances at all."

As they got back in their car ten minutes later, Patrick North stared up at the thick slabs of oak that were the school's front door. "What do you think?" he mused as Kevin Peterson handed him his keys. "Any way of finding out what that kid was confessing?"

Peterson shook his head. "Not a chance."

"So that's that? We're just supposed to give up?"

Peterson's expression hardened, losing all trace of the friendliness Clay and Darren had seen only a few minutes ago. "Not me," he said with a quietness that belied the steel in his words. "Something made that boy kill that woman, and I intend to find out exactly what it was."

CHAPTER 12

ERI McINTYRE PARKED HER car on the narrow lane that wound through the cemetery, decided that it didn't really matter that she'd forgotten to bring flowers for the first time in the two years she'd been coming here to visit her husband, and picked her way carefully across the grass. Coming to the headstone that marked Bill's grave, she placed her hand on the cold granite.

"Hi, honey," she said softly enough that no one would have heard her even if she hadn't been alone in the cemetery. "Well, it finally happened—I forgot to bring you flowers. Forgive me?" She decided that the unbroken silence that fell over the cemetery as she paused for a moment, implied his assent, then she slowly lowered herself down until she was sitting cross-legged on the grave. "I hope you feel like listening," she sighed, "because I sure feel like talking." She unfolded her legs and stretched them out, unconsciously falling into the same position she used to use back in the days when they would sometimes sprawl on the bed for hours at a stretch, neither sleeping nor making love, but just talking. The grass felt cool beneath her, and she ran her hand across the dark green surface, finally picking a blade as if it were a piece of lint clinging to the coverlet of their bed.

"Ryan got hurt at school on Friday—hurt pretty badly. He was beaten up by some kids, and I have to tell you, it scared me to death." She waited for a second, not really as if she were expecting Bill to say something, but just to collect her thoughts. "I've about decided to take him out of Dickinson and send him to St. Isaac's. I—well, I guess I just feel like he'll be safer, at least until he graduates." Tears blurred her eyes but she brushed them away, almost impatiently. "Don't worry," she said, determined not to give in to the grief that was threatening to overwhelm her. "I'm not going to start crying. And I know this isn't what we'd do if you were here." Now her voice started to tremble in spite of herself. "But you're *not* here, and I need to make the decision myself. She hesitated, then got to the true reason she'd come here today. "Except that I'm not making it all by myself. I—" She fell silent for a moment, then pressed on. "I've met someone, Bill. His name is Tom—Tom Kelly—and—"

And what? And she was lonely, and frightened, and miserable, and Tom Kelly had been there for her last night and helped her deal with the hospital and Ryan and the police and everything else Bill should have been there to help her with. But how could she say it? How could she say any of it without sounding cold and callous and uncaring that the only man she'd ever loved—ever intended to love—had died and left her alone to be lonely and frightened and miserable? But it was Bill that was dead, not her, and—

And she had to go on.

"Anyway, he's a good man. You'd like him." She managed a wan smile despite the bleariness in her eyes. "And Ryan will learn to—I know he will. Anyway, Tom was able to arrange a scholarship for Ryan, so it won't cost us anything. I don't like the idea of him living away at school, but it's only for a year and a half, and it's only a few miles away, so I'll see him a lot." She reached out and touched the headstone again. "And I hope it's okay with you." She fell silent again, then went on. "And I'm not talking about just Ryan, either. I'm talking about Tom, too. I hope you can understand about him, wherever you are."

She turned over onto her back and looked at the sky through the leaves in the lone tree on the hill. "He misses you," she said, a tear leaking out and sliding down the side of her face. "He keeps your picture on his desk. And I know he thinks I'm being disloyal by seeing Tom, but I hope someday he'll understand. I know you want what's best for both of us, and right now I need some help and some support." Her voice began to tremble. "The kind you can't give me anymore." She fished in her purse, found some Kleenex and wiped her eyes. In the tree overhead a bird began to sing, and suddenly Teri felt lighter and strangely unburdened. "And Ryan needs a father figure. I'm not saying that I'm going to marry Tom or anything like that, but I think he's going to be good for Ryan."

Above her, the bird sang a few more notes, and Teri decided to accept the bird's chirping as the sign she was looking for.

She smiled. "You should see Ryan, honey," she went on, the tremble in her voice steadying as her tears dried. "He's becoming a man. He's so tall—the last time you saw him, he was still a little boy. Remember how gangly he was? Well, now he's filled out, and started shaving, and every time I look at him, I see you. And he's decided he wants to go to Princeton, which is another reason to send him to St. Isaac's."

The bird chirped one last time, and flew away and Teri got to her feet. "Got to get going," she sighed, slung her purse over her shoulder, kissed her fingertips, touched them to the top of the headstone, and stepped back to stare at the name that was deeply engraved in the granite:

Captain William James McIntyre.

"Tom Kelly is a good man," Teri whispered. "But he's not you. There was only one of you, and you're still my hero. And you always will be." Tears welled in her eyes once more, but they were no longer those of the horrible, wrenching sorrow that had gripped her for most of the last two years. "I'll come back soon," she said. "No matter what happens between me and Tom, I'll come back to tell you about Ryan."

As the bird wheeled in the sky and came back to perch once more on the branch above her, Teri turned and began to retrace her footsteps on the path back to her car.

Bill had heard her, she was sure.

Heard her, and understood.

† † †

Clay Matthews watched silently as Brother Francis and two girls he didn't know—but who must have done something wrong to earn them the penance of having to help pack up Kip's belongings—finished clearing out Kip's half of the closet. The weird thing was that after complaining all last year and most of this one that Kip had too much stuff, suddenly Clay was feeling like not only the closet but the room as well was far too empty. And it wasn't that Kip's stuff would soon be gone, but that Kip himself was gone.

He was gone, and he wouldn't be back.

He was dead.

Even now the word didn't seem quite real to Clay. In fact, it felt wrong; people his age didn't die—old people did. People like his grandmother, who had died of cancer two years ago, and Mr. Endicott, who had lived across the street in Brookline, and had died last year just because he'd gotten too old.

But now Kip was dead and suddenly Clay wished he didn't have to live in this room anymore. Last night, at least, he'd been able to turn the lights on when he couldn't go to sleep, and look at Kip's stuff, and sort of pretend that maybe it was all a mistake. But even last night he hadn't really been able to make himself believe it. Somehow, in a way Clay didn't quite understand, all the stuff that had belonged to Kip had changed. It was as if just overnight it had all turned into nothing more than old clothes nobody would want, and beat-up shoes that should be thrown away, and clutter that wasn't really good for anything, but just filled up a lot of space.

And now it was all being packed up and taken away and instead of making Clay feel better it was just making him feel worse. Kip's desk looked naked without his books and CDs, and the bed, stripped of its sheets, blankets and bedspread, didn't just look bare.

It looked abandoned.

The gaping lid of Kip's footlocker—now jammed with nearly everything Kip had owned—seemed almost like the maw of some kind of beast that was swallowing up every last trace of Clay's roommate.

"Am I going to be in here by myself for the rest of the year?" he asked, doing his best to keep his voice steady.

Brother Francis shook his head. "I would be very surprised if a new student didn't arrive tomorrow."

An odd mixture of resentment and relief rippled through Clay. He didn't really want another roommate, but he didn't want to be alone, either. "Who?" he asked, even though it didn't really matter. Whoever it was, it wasn't going to be Kip.

Brother Francis shrugged. "I'm afraid that's something no one consults me about," he said. "I know there's a waiting list, and I know there are at least a dozen names·on it. If Father Laughlin hasn't already made the decision, I suspect he will have by tomorrow morning." He scanned the area around Kip's bed and desk, and then turned to the two girls. "Good job—I think you two can be excused now."

The two girls wasted no time scurrying out of the room before Brother Francis could change his mind, and after they were gone, Brother Francis laid a hand on Clay's shoulder. "Are you going to be all right?" he asked, his eyes clearly reflecting the concern in his voice.

Clay nodded halfheartedly.

"Okay. I'll go get a dolly for the footlocker. See you in a few minutes." Brother Francis left the room, glanced back at Clay, then gently closed the door.

Clay took a deep breath, his eyes fixing on the bare mattress where just a few days ago Kip had sprawled, listening to his iPod, playing air guitar and drumming on his knees. And now he'd never see Kip again.

Never hear another one of his stupid jokes.

Never play cards with him.

He was gone.

But where? Where was Kip's spirit, the *presence* of him that had always been in this room even when Kip himself was not? Was it in Heaven? Or was it in Hell, because he had killed that woman?

Or was it just gone?

Who knew what really happened to somebody's spirit after they died?

Clay flopped down onto his bed, punching up the pillow beneath his head. As he gazed over at the bare mattress on the other side of the room, his eyes suddenly fell on the seam in the wainscoting next to Kip's bed.

Detective North's questions about drugs came back to his mind.

Was it possible that Kip really had been using drugs?

If he had, he'd been lying for as long as Clay had known him. But if Kip had been using drugs, Clay knew where he would have kept them.

The one place the two detectives hadn't found, and that Clay hadn't told them about. He got up, walked around the far side of Kip's bed, and carefully removed the panel of wainscoting he and Kip had discovered no more than a month after they'd moved into the room, when Kip had become certain that the wall behind the panel was hollow. Sure enough, once they worked the panel loose they found a hole in the plaster behind the wainscoting that some previous occupant of the room must have cut in order to make a secret compartment where all the things no one would want Brother Francis—or anyone else—to find during dorm inspections could be safely stored.

Clay reached in, and his fingers found what he expected: two large plastic ziplock bags.

In his ziplock bag, Clay had five old copies of *Playboy*, half a pack of cigarettes, and an unopened pack of condoms, at least one of which he was still hoping to get to use before the end of school this year. There should have been six copies of *Playboy*, but the one Kip had borrowed was now forever gone.

The other bag was Kip's.

Clay pulled it out and dumped the contents on Kip's bare mattress.

Basically the same stuff, except that Kip's cigarettes were almost gone.

But no drugs.

For a moment Clay considered transferring the contents of Kip's bag to his own, but then changed his mind; even though Kip was gone, it didn't feel right.

It felt like stealing.

Putting both bags back into the wall, he carefully replaced the wainscoting, then went back to his bed and flopped down.

So he'd been right—Kip hadn't been doing drugs.

Then what *had* he been doing?

What the hell had happened to him?

† † †

Ryan McIntyre lay on his bed, propped up on pillows, watching his mother pack clothes into a duffel bag. But she wasn't packing nearly enough—it looked like she was packing for a weekend camping trip or something. "I'm gonna need a lot more than—" he began, but Teri didn't let him finish.

"St. Isaac's uses uniforms," she said, folding another pair of jeans and doing her best to fit them into the duffel bag without wrinkling them.

"Uniforms?" Ryan echoed. Nobody had said anything about uniforms. His jaw ached, his side hurt whenever he moved, he was getting a headache from trying to figure out what to take to St. Isaac's, and now he had to wear a *uniform*? Maybe he should just go back to Dickinson. But even as the idea formed in his mind, the memory of the beating in the boys' restroom flooded back. Whatever happened at St. Isaac's couldn't be as bad as that, so he watched silently as his mother continued folding clothes, wondering now when he was going to wear the stuff she *was* packing.

What about the rest of the stuff he was planning to take? Would he even be allowed to put posters on the walls in his room? Probably not. Now all kinds of questions were tumbling through his mind. Was he going to have a roommate? Were the nuns as mean as Father Sebastian said? How strict was everything going to be? And was he going to have to go to Mass all the time? Even worse, what if he couldn't even do the work? Private schools were supposed to be way harder than public ones, and St. Isaac's—

He cut the thought short; it was all just too much to deal with.

His eyes fell on the photograph of his father on his desk. That should have been the first thing he packed. Pain stabbed him as he got awkwardly off the bed, but he took a deep breath and pressed his side until it passed. Then he picked up the photograph. His father seemed to be looking not exactly at him, but deep into him. Ryan instantly felt the familiar pang of loneliness that always shot through him when he thought about his father, and the way his father had always been able to provide answers for his questions. Now, as he gazed at the photograph, he could almost hear his father's voice. *Grow up,* it seemed to be whispering. *Act like a man, and do the right thing.* He wrapped the photograph in a towel and handed it to his mom, who put it into the duffel.

"You don't have to take everything with you tomorrow," she said. "I can bring over anything you need."

Ryan gingerly sat back down on the bed, holding his side.

Teri looked at him anxiously. "Do you need a pain pill?"

Ryan shook his head. "I'm okay. Just nervous about tomorrow, I guess."

Teri sat next to him and smoothed his hair, then touched his swollen eye and gently traced the edge of a big bruise. As Ryan was about to brush her hand away she suddenly stood up. "There's something I want you to have," she said. "You're not as old as you're supposed to be, but I think it's time."

Intrigued, Ryan followed her through his bedroom door and down the hall to the little door that opened into the attic. They ducked in the doorway and stood up in a spacious area with a plywood floor below them and bare rafters above. Teri groped for the chain and a single hanging bulb lit the room, throwing harsh shadows across the storage space. Ryan followed her between containers of Christmas decorations, cartons of his baby clothes, and boxes of photographs, many of them so old no one even knew who they were anymore. A couple of old lamps with missing shades sat on a bent chaise lounge, and the ceramic chicken he'd painted red when he was in kindergarten sat, headless, next to the chaise on the little table that used to be in his room when he was small.

Ignoring it all, his mother crouched next to an old green trunk with a combination lock on its hasp.

A trunk Ryan couldn't remember seeing before.

His curiosity increasing, he knelt next to his mother and watched as she worked the combination, removed the lock and opened the lid.

On the top lay a sheet of tissue paper, which she pulled away to reveal his father's class-A dress uniform.

Ryan's breath caught. The last time he'd seen his father dressed in that uniform was when he received a Silver Star for Gallantry in Action, during his first tour in Iraq. It was the same uniform he wore in the photo Ryan kept on his desk. Could this be the gift?

But even before he could voice the question, his mother had lifted out the tray holding the uniform, set it aside, then removed everything below it. Finally she pried open a false bottom that was so perfectly fitted that Ryan hadn't even seen it, and took a small rosewood box from the compartment the panel had hidden. "This was with your father's things when they came back from Iraq," she told him. She turned the box so it faced Ryan and opened its hinged lid.

Inside was his father's crucifix, the one he'd worn around his neck almost as long as Ryan could remember. He picked it up gently, almost reverently. It was heavy—heavier than he'd expected. And it wasn't flat like most crucifixes. This one was thick, the body of Christ in full relief, the cross itself covered with intricately detailed carvings, each delicate etching darkened with time and tarnish.

"He was going to give it to you when you were grown," Teri said as Ryan gazed at the object in his hands. "But I think maybe you need to have it right now. He said it always helped him do the right thing."

The silver felt warm and familiar to Ryan's fingers. Despite the etching, the metal was smooth, as if it were very old, and had been worn by generations of fathers and sons. And he could almost hear his father's voice again, repeating the words he'd heard inside his head a few minutes ago. The same words his mother had just spoken.

Do the right thing.

Accepting the cross—putting the chain around his neck and feeling its weight against his heart—would mean something.

It would mean he had become a man, a grown-up.

A man his father would be proud of.

He remembered the last few days, when he'd acted like a sulking child when all his mother had wanted him to do was go out to dinner with a man she liked.

Instead, he had thought about weasling out of it. In the end, he'd thought better of it, but it had taken him too long.

And what about when those two guys had jumped him in the hall at school, and he hadn't even tried to fight back.

What kind of man would have just taken the beating he had?

Suddenly the crucifix felt like it was burning his flesh. This was something that had to be earned, not simply received.

He handed it back to his mother. "Not yet," he said.

She looked at him in surprise. "You're sure?"

Ryan nodded. "I think maybe Dad was right—maybe I'm not old enough yet."

She took the crucifix from him, kissed it so gently it almost made Ryan cry, and put it back into the box. "It's yours," she said, "and it's right here, whenever you want it. The combination to the lock is your father's birthday."

He nodded, not trusting his voice to speak. He would come back for it, but not until he had earned it.

And just now, he felt a tiny bit closer to realizing that goal.

Chapter 13

GORDY ADAMSON GLOWERED at the arthritic old priest sitting across from him. "Get this, Father, and get it good, okay?" he snarled, not even a hint of respect in his voice. "These are very simple questions, and there should be very simple answers. So tell me. Why was Kip off campus? How could he just walk away without you people knowing about it?"

"Mr. Adamson—" Father Laughlin began.

"I'll tell you why!" Adamson cut in, leaning forward and placing both hands on the priest's desk.

"Honey . . ." Anne Adamson tried to restrain her husband with a hand on his arm, but he jerked it away from her, barely pausing in his tirade.

"Because once you have your fancy tuition money to fill your church coffers, you're no better than any other school," Gordy declared, his voice starting to rise. "Any public school—any damn one of them— keeps better tabs on their students than this high-priced, ritzy-titzy place." Now he paused for a second or two, his expression transforming from belligerence to contempt. "How the hell old are you, anyway? What makes you think you know what works with today's kids?"

Father Laughlin's lips compressed to a tight line, and he looked down at his hands.

Adamson, sensing the priest's weakness like a predator sniffing out the weakest prey, bored deeper. "I bring my son here for safekeeping and a good education. So what happened?" Father Laughlin visibly flinched, which only made Gordy Adamson lean even closer. "What *exactly* happened?"

Father Laughlin shook his head and spread his hands in defeat.

"That's right," Gordy sneered. "That is exactly right! You have no idea. Well, I'm here to tell you that something happened to my boy here under this roof, and I am going to find out what it was. He was fine when he got here and two and a half years later, he's not only dead, but apparently he killed someone else, too! Which means something happened." He sat back in the chair, his eyes fixing on the priest. "Some goddamned thing happened."

Father Laughlin took a deep breath, collected his thoughts, and finally spoke. "You brought Kip to us because he was a troubled boy," he said quietly. "He'd been expelled from public school—"

"He wasn't *that* troubled," Adamson countered, leaning forward again. "He wasn't a goddamned murderer. We brought him here because we thought a little religion would do him some good." A derisive snort erupted from his throat. "Boy, were we wrong. You killed him. *You killed my son!*"

"Honey," Anne Adamson tried again. "This isn't getting us anywhere. Let's go home." As she stood up, Father Laughlin rose, too.

"Brother Francis packed Kip's things—" he said, gesturing toward Kip's footlocker, which was on the floor near the door.

But Gordy Adamson wasn't through. "I'm going to sue you. I'm going to sue you for negligence, contributing to the delinquency of a minor, and whatever else my attorney can come up with. You think your outfit is in financial trouble now? Ha! Just wait! There will be one hell of an investigation, too. You better believe it." His eyes narrowed as he prepared to deliver the coup de grâce. "And you'd damn well better hope your guys are keeping their hands off the boys!" His rage suddenly spent, Gordy Adamson collapsed back into the chair, drained. "My son," he said, more to himself than to the priest. "The only one I had."

Anne Adamson pulled on Gordy's arm until he finally hoisted himself heavily to his feet. "I'm sorry," she said to Father Laughlin as Gordy wiped moisture from his eyes with the sleeve of his shirt.

"I wish I knew what to say," Father Laughlin said. "But there seems to be no possible explanation for some of the things that happen in today's world. We can only trust in God's will, and accept that which we can neither understand nor change."

Anne nodded, and guided Gordy toward the door. He stopped at the footlocker, gazed down on it for a long moment, then bent over, picked up the trunk that held his son's effects, and moved through the door, carrying the trunk as carefully as if it were his son's coffin.

In the outer office, Sister Margaret offered a sympathetic smile, which Anne tried—and failed—to return as she opened the office door for Gordy. They made their way slowly down the hall toward the front door. Students, faculty, and clergy all moved aside to allow the grieving parents to pass.

† † †

Teri McIntyre walked up the worn granite steps that led to St. Isaac's front door, struggling with Ryan's heavy duffel bag while Ryan himself limped next to her, taking one slow step at a time, his backpack slung over his good shoulder. They were halfway up the broad flight when the front door opened, and a middle-aged man and woman came out. The man carried a heavy trunk, and carefully watched his step until he came even with Teri and Ryan.

He stopped, tipping his head toward Ryan. "This your kid?" he asked, his eyes narrow and his voice gruff.

Teri nodded.

The man's gaze fixed on the duffel bag Teri was carrying. "You leaving him here?" Teri opened her mouth to speak, but he cut her off before she could say a word. "You gotta be nuts if you leave your son here. This is not a good place for kids." He looked down at the box he carried, and when he spoke again, his voice broke. "Trust me on that."

"Excuse me?" Teri said, but before the man could say anything else, the woman took his arm and drew him away.

"Leave her alone, Gordy," the woman whispered. "Let's just go home." As Teri and Ryan watched uncertainly, the man hefted the foot-locker into the backseat of a car double-parked in front of the school, got into the driver's seat, and drove away before his wife had time to fasten her seat belt.

"Wow," Ryan breathed as the car disappeared around the corner. "What was that about?"

Teri shrugged. "I have no idea, honey," she said, trying to sound unconcerned, even though she suddenly wanted to turn right around and take her son home and keep him safe in his room.

Forever.

Which was, of course, ridiculous.

Steeling herself against the irrational thought, she led Ryan on up the steps to the impressive carved oak front doors of St. Isaac's School.

† † †

By the time Brother Francis opened the door to the boys' dormitory, Ryan McIntyre's brain felt almost as exhausted as his aching body. The mass of forms he'd had to fill out this morning had been only the beginning. Then Brother Francis had given him a tour of the school, but after the first ten minutes of making their way through the maze of hallways and staircases, Ryan had been sure he'd never be able to find his way around without a map. Then he'd had to try on one set of the school uniforms after another—which for some reason didn't seem to be marked with sizes that conformed to the ones on his regular clothes—until he found an assortment of blue blazers, sweaters, trousers, and shirts that fit, along with a tie that wasn't completely threadbare. Then there had been the schedule for his classes, along with a list of rules he was apparently supposed to memorize by tomorrow, and abide by starting today.

Everything looked old and worn, but not grubby and covered with graffiti like Dickinson High. The woodwork was all dark mahogany and walnut, every light fixture looked at least a hundred years old, and there seemed to be stained glass everywhere. But no graffiti. And no dust—not so much as a speck—which had told him even before Brother Francis enunciated the policy, that any infraction of the rules would undoubtedly lead to hours of cleaning the school.

"You're in room 231, with Clay Matthews," the monk said as they came through what Ryan hoped would be the last pair of huge oak doors he'd have to open for a while. They climbed to the second floor and walked halfway down a long corridor, where Brother Francis knocked softly on a door then turned the knob without waiting for a reply from within.

The room was empty, half of it barren.

His half.

The monk set his duffel on the floor next to the bed. "My office door is always open," he said. "I'll leave you to settle in." Then, as he headed back out the door, he turned and smiled. "Welcome to St. Isaac's."

"Thanks," Ryan said, trying to keep a sigh of resignation out of his voice. As the door closed behind Brother Francis, he set his bundle of uniforms on the empty desk and surveyed his half of the room.

At least his bed was closest to the big windows that looked out over the courtyard. He stretched out onto the bed for a minute, hoping some of the aching in his body would ease before he had to start un-packing.

A few minutes later he was just struggling to sit up again when the door opened and a boy about his own age came in, a backpack slung over his shoulder.

"Hey," the boy said. "I'm Clay—" The words died on his lips as he got a good look at Ryan's face. "Wow, man, what happened to you?"

Ryan shrugged, trying to act as if he hurt a lot less than he did, but decided there wasn't any point in telling his new roommate anything but the truth. His totally faked shrug faded away as he managed a faint grin. "I sorta got the crap kicked out of me," he admitted. "I'm Ryan McIntyre."

Clay hesitated a second, then smiled. "Clay Matthews." His eyes moved to the duffel bag that still lay where Brother Francis had left it. "You need some help putting your stuff away?"

Ryan struggled to a sitting position, then managed to stand up without wincing too much. "I can—" he began, but Clay had already swung the bag off the floor onto the bed.

Suddenly another boy appeared at the door. "Hey, Clay—" he began, then fell silent as he saw Ryan. "The new guy's already here?" he asked, coming through the door with yet another boy right behind him. "What happened to your face?"

"Nothing, compared to what he did to the other guys," Clay said before Ryan could answer the question himself. "His name's Ryan Mc-Something." He winked at Ryan. "These are Darren Bender and Tim Kennedy. They're both assholes, but at least most of the time they don't smell too bad. And don't believe Tim when he tells you Ted Kennedy's his uncle—he lies about everything."

"That is such a crock!" Tim Kennedy countered. "And it was only one time I said that. One time!" He turned to Ryan. "We were out in Hyannis last summer, and if Matthews had kept his mouth shut, we coulda gone swimming right in front of—"

"You don't even know if it was the right place," Clay cut in. "And—"

"And nobody gives a rat's ass," Darren Bender pronounced, flopping down on Clay's bed. "Father Laughlin sure doesn't waste any time, does he?" he said, deciding he didn't want to hear any more of the argument that had been going on between Clay and Tim since last summer. "Kip was here on Friday morning, and you're here on Monday morning."

"Kip?" Ryan repeated. "Is that who lived here?"

Suddenly the atmosphere in the room changed. "Yeah," Tim Kennedy said, his voice oddly hollow.

Ryan frowned slightly. "What happened to him?"

The three boys glanced uneasily at each other, each of them waiting for someone else to speak first.

"I heard it might have been drugs," Darren Bender finally said.

"It wasn't drugs!" Clay Matthews instantly countered. "Kip didn't do drugs, and you guys know it."

"Then what do *you* think happened?" Tim demanded.

Clay's eyes narrowed. "I don't know. Nobody knows."

"Nobody knows what?" Ryan asked. "What happened to him?"

Once again the other three boys glanced at each other, but this time it was Clay Matthews who broke the silence. "Kip died," he said, his voice so quiet that Ryan thought he hadn't heard the words right. But the expressions on Tim's and Darren's faces told him he had.

"What do you mean, 'died'?" he asked, his eyes flicking from Clay to Darren and Tim, then back to Clay. "You mean, like, he got sick or something?"

"He killed someone," Clay said, his voice still barely above a whisper. "Some woman. And the police shot him. But it doesn't make any sense—Kip wouldn't do anything like that."

"How does anyone know what anyone's gonna do?" Tim asked. "It's like . . ."

But Ryan was no longer listening. What kind of school was St. Isaac's? Even the worst of the kids at Dickinson had never gone out and just killed someone, at least not that he'd ever heard of. Then he remembered the people he and his mother had seen on the front steps this morning. They had to have been Kip's parents. And suddenly he remembered the last words the man had spoken:

. . . gotta be nuts if you leave your son here . . . not a good place for kids . . . trust me on that.

Trust me on that.

Welcome to St. Isaac's, Ryan thought. He hurt, he felt tired, and now it turned out he was taking the place of someone who was dead. And not just dead, but shot after he'd killed someone else.

Suddenly Ryan McIntyre just wanted to go home. There might not be the kind of threat from the Frankie Alitos of the world here, but after hearing what had happened to Kip Adamson, he wasn't sure he would be any safer here than he'd been at Dickinson High after all.

CHAPTER 14

TERI McINTYRE SIPPED HER glass of wine and finally began to relax on the couch. There had been a terrible hollowness in the house when she came home after work that afternoon—it was as if the house itself knew that not only was Ryan not home, but he wasn't coming back, at least for several weeks.

The house felt worse than empty, worse than vacant.

It felt haunted. Haunted by the memories of Ryan and Bill and all the moments the three of them had shared under this roof.

She'd called Tom, and now he was sitting in the chair on the other side of the coffee table, and though the house still didn't feel right, at least it felt a little better. "I'm trying to remember the last time I was alone here," she said. "I think it was when Ryan went to hockey camp in Toronto. He was eleven, and it was the same year Bill was sent back to Kuwait." She forced a wry smile she didn't quite feel. "I'd forgotten how much I don't like it. Always before, no matter where the army sent Bill, I still had Ryan. In ninety-one, when Bill went to Kuwait, Ryan was just a baby, but at least he was here. Now . . ." Her voice trailed off.

Tom moved from the chair to the sofa and put his arms around her.

"Let's just enjoy some quiet time together," he said, and pulled her close.

But the ghosts in the room were too real tonight. Ryan was only sixteen, and he should be living at home. She pulled away from Tom and picked up the remote from the coffee table, flicking the television on. "Let's just watch the news, okay?" she said, suddenly wondering whether calling Tom had been the best idea. His company certainly helped fill the emptiness of the house, but now she had the distinct feeling he might be expecting to spend not just the evening with her, but the night as well.

The television flashed to life, and Gordy Adamson's image filled the screen, his expression a mixture of grief and anger.

Teri gasped as she recognized the man she'd seen at St. Isaac's that morning, and turned up the volume.

"Kip was a good boy," Gordy was saying. "I know what the cops say happened, but that doesn't make any sense to me. I'm not saying Kip was perfect—he was at St. Isaac's for a reason. He was a teenager, you know? We thought sending him to St. Isaac's would help him through those years. I guess we were wrong."

Gordy's face was replaced by a shot of the front entrance of St. Isaac's Preparatory Academy, the same steps Teri and Ryan had walked up that morning.

"St. Isaac's has been accepting at-risk youths since 1906," the reporter said. "While this isn't the first violent incident that has involved one of their students, it is the first that has ever resulted in a student's death."

The shot of the front door cut to one of Father Laughlin sitting at his desk, his hands folded somberly. "We don't know why these things happen," he said. "We do our best with these troubled teens, but unfortunately we are not infallible. There is evil in this world, and it sometimes overwhelms us no matter how hard we try. All of us mourn both these tragic deaths, and it is our intention at St. Isaac's never to allow such a thing to happen again."

"No motive has been attributed to Kip Adamson's apparently random attack on Martha Kim," the reporter intoned as the camera cut away from St. Isaac's headmaster.

Feeling as if she'd just been struck by something she'd never seen coming at all, Teri snapped off the television, and turned to face Tom. "Did you know about this?" she demanded, her voice trembling.

Tom recoiled as reflexively as if she'd slapped him. "How could I know about this—I've been with you almost every minute since we got the call about Ryan being in the hospital. Neither of us have been watching the news."

Teri's eyes narrowed slightly. "You mean your friend didn't even mention it when you talked to him?" It seemed utterly impossible.

But Tom shook his head. "Not a word. All he said was that he'd do what he could, and then he called to say there was an opening. That's all I know."

Teri stared at the darkened television. How was it possible? How could Tom's friend not have told him? "A boy died to make a place for Ryan? And they didn't even tell you?"

Tom held up his hands as if to fend off her words. "Wait a minute—there might have been half a dozen openings. I don't know and you don't know."

But Teri only kept hearing the echo of Gordy Adamson's voice as he'd warned her this morning. *You gotta be nuts if you leave your son here. This is not a good place for kids.* She gazed numbly at Tom. "What have I done?" she breathed. "How could I have left Ryan there without even asking what that man was talking about?"

"Teri—" Tom began, but Teri cut him off.

"I should go pick him up right now."

"Now wait a minute," Tom said, putting a hand on her arm, but this time not letting go when she tried to pull away. "Just slow down, take a breath, and let's figure this out, all right?" When she seemed to relax just a little, he went on. "The fact that one troubled boy went out and did a bad thing—a really terrible thing—doesn't make St. Isaac's a bad place," Tom said. "You even heard that reporter say as much."

"It was still a bad decision," Teri sighed, the familiar feeling of approaching tears roughening her voice. "Bill wouldn't have—"

"Bill's not here," Tom said gently, touching his forefinger to her lips. "You have to make the decisions now, and this one was for Ryan's safety. Remember? Remember what happened to him at Dickinson?" Teri took a deep breath, exhaled. Of course she remembered. How could she ever forget what had happened? "There's no way you could have kept him at Dickinson."

She nodded—he was right, of course.

"Nothing bad is going to happen to Ryan at St. Isaac's." Tom soothed her. "He's not—" He hesitated, searching for Kip Adamson's name, then decided it didn't matter. "He's not that other boy, and what happened to that other boy isn't going to happen to Ryan." Once again Tom put his arms around her, and this time she didn't resist, falling against his strong body, feeling his fingers gently stroking her hair.

She wasn't sure if he was helping her or only making her life more complicated right now, but it didn't matter.

Bill was gone forever, and now Ryan was away, too, and she suddenly felt terribly alone.

Alone, and uncertain, and wishing Ryan were back home where he belonged. *It will be all right,* she told herself. *It will be, because it has to be.*

† † †

Sofia Capelli sat on her bed, propped against the wall with all her pillows, the open history text on her lap completely ignored, even though she needed to study for tomorrow's test. But how was she supposed to concentrate with Sister Mary David in the room, talking with her roommate as if there weren't anyone else within a hundred miles, let alone ten feet away?

As far as Sofia was concerned, Melody Hunt had been going on about Kip Adamson's death for at least a day too long, and she was pretty sure that even Sister Mary David thought it was time that she got at least a little bit past it. After all, it wasn't as if Kip had been her boyfriend, or even close. In fact, Melody hadn't even liked Kip. Why couldn't she just get on with her life like Sofia and all the rest of the girls were doing? But Melody just kept asking "Why?"

As if someone was going to find an answer, which Sofia was pretty sure wasn't going to happen.

Sofia had been just as shocked about what had happened to Kip, and had even talked with Sister Mary David about it herself. But then she'd decided there wasn't anything she could do to change what had happened. Even more important to her than what Sister Mary David had said were a few simple words her grandmother had spoken when Sofia was only five: "No sense crying over spilt milk!" And while what had happened to Kip on Friday night was a lot worse than spilt milk—a whole lot worse—the point was still the same.

There was nothing she, or anybody else, could do about it. They all, including Melody, just had to accept it.

"I have to see to the rest of the girls," Sister Mary David finally said in a tone that even Melody Hunt couldn't argue with. "Talk this over with God tonight, and perhaps He will have answers for you that I just can't provide." Melody sniffed and blew her nose, nodding uncertainly. "And don't you have a history test in the morning?" Sister Mary David added pointedly.

Melody nodded again, sniffed one last time, and put her handkerchief back in her pocket. Sofia held up her textbook as if to tell the nun that she had been trying to study for the past hour and that they'd been distracting her.

Just then, Sofia's cell phone vibrated under her thigh, and she silently thanked whoever might be the patron saint of cell phones for her having had the presence of mind to turn the ringer off.

"Then I'll leave you both to your studying," Sister Mary David said. "Good night and God bless."

"Good night, Sister," the two girls said in unison.

When the nun was gone, Melody went into the bathroom to wash her face, giving Sofia just enough time to check her cell phone.

A text message from Darren Bender asking if he could see her. She slipped the phone back under her leg just as Melody came back out of the bathroom.

"I'm going to the library," Melody said. "I'll be back in an hour."

Though Sofia was just a little bit jealous of Melody's grades, she certainly wasn't interested in spending the time required to achieve them. While Melody went to the library to study alone for at least an hour every night, in addition to doing the homework assignments in their room, Sofia had much more interesting things planned for the same hour.

Melody packed her book bag and left.

Sofia waited until she was sure Melody wasn't coming back for anything, then dug out her cell phone.

Smiling to herself, she sent Darren a quick message: *We've got an hour.*

CHAPTER 15

HE AWOKE AS *the energy around him began to change. He could feel it, almost smell it in the air.*

Someone was coming.

He sat up in the corner, and rubbed his hands over his eyes, oblivious to both the grit on his palms and the slime of broken pimples that coated his face. The important thing was to erase the last vestiges of the indolent sleep that had stolen so many hours of his time.

Time that could be far better spent than in allowing this useless body to rest.

He searched the darkness around him, but saw no more of his prison than a pinhole of light at the door.

They thought the darkness would terrify him, but they were wrong. The darkness was his friend.

The darkness gave him shelter.

The darkness made him invisible.

He knew far more than they thought; saw everything despite the darkness. He needed no eyes, no ears, nor any other senses. Merely by being still and feeling the rise and fall of energies around him, he understood his surroundings.

Now he tingled with the rising energy, as happened every day.

Or was it night?

It didn't matter.

All that mattered was that someone was coming.

Someone was coming, and bringing an opportunity for escape. If he was smart. If he did the right thing.

But so far, he had failed.

The first failure had surprised him. It should have been simple; nothing more then manipulating his own energy, focusing it on the pinhole of light that would lead to freedom. Yet when he'd made the attempt to ooze through the tiny hole like so much smoke, he'd failed.

Failed!

The human body, apparently, was a far more formidable prison than the chamber in which it dwelt.

The answer, of course, was obvious: he would simply take the human body with him.

But he had failed to manipulate the machinery of the lock on the door as miserably as he had failed to escape the human body.

Thus, he must manipulate the approaching personality.

He felt the rise in energy again, then heard footsteps through the ears of the body he inhabited.

A metallic screech erupted as the pinhole of light suddenly expanded into a blinding rectangle. The brilliance of the light slashed through the body's eyes and into its brain, and it reflexively jerked back, slamming into the wall.

"Time for dinner," a soft voice—a female voice—said.

He struggled to recover—why hadn't he guarded himself against the light?

Be human, *he told himself.* Be what she thinks you are. *He crept forward toward the slot in the door through which the female on the other side was bringing the food tray. "Hello?" he said, barely able to use the voice that was so rusted from disuse that it emerged as little more than a faint croaking sound.*

There was silence, then the human beyond the blinding rectangle spoke. "So you've decided to speak."

A toehold!

"Please," he said, searching for the words—the human words—that would make her open the door.

"Here's your dinner," she said, and slid a tray through the rectangular opening.

"I—I need something," he said softly, quietly, gently, taking the tray. What would make this human use the keys that would open his prison?

"Oh? What do you need?"

"A doctor," he said.

Again there was silence, and he could feel her indecision. Once again he tried to focus his energy, tried to reach into her mind to bend her to his will, but once again the body in which he was imprisoned held him back. Even before she spoke he knew what she would say.

"I don't think so," she sighed, with just enough uncertainty to give him hope.

"No, wait, please," he said, as she began to close the slot.

She stopped.

"I need something."

"What do you need?" she asked.

"You," he whispered. "I need to touch you. To feel you. To put my hands in your—"

She slammed the rectangle closed, and he heard her footsteps as she walked quickly away.

Furious, he hurled the tray of food across the room, then smashed his fist against the door, only barely aware of the pain that shot up the arm.

How long would it be before he got another opportunity?

Panic began to build.

He had to get out of here!

Brushing the searing pain in the wounded hand aside, as if it were no more than an annoying fly buzzing around him, he began moving his fingers over the stone walls, exploring every contour of his prison that he could reach. But he already knew every stone, knew every one of their personalities, knew the texture of every seam of the mortar that held them together. He knew the lichen that grew there—knew it all—yet once again he began going over it all once more, feeling everything, examining everything, with only the pinhole of light to help him see.

Everything he touched was exactly the same as the last time he'd touched it, and with every second his frustration grew.

When finally he was back at the point where he'd begun, he began to realize that all of it was futile.

He'd never escape.

He'd never fulfill his purpose.

He sat down and began to howl.

CHAPTER 16

Sofia Capelli felt her body responding not only to Darren Bender's kisses, but also to his touch as he fumbled with the buttons on her blouse. She should make him stop—she knew it—but it felt so good when his fingers brushed against her breasts that she just couldn't make herself pull away, and she found herself pulling his shirt up out of his pants and running her hands up the smooth skin of his back. His hand was inside her blouse now, and—

The door to her dorm room burst open, slamming hard against the wall, and Sister Mary David stood glowering in the doorway, her knuckles white as she clutched the doorframe in cold fury.

Darren leaped up, his face red, his hair mussed, tucking in his shirt as fast as he could.

"Out!" Sister Mary David commanded, her voice low but more menacing than Sofia had ever heard it before. "Father Sebastian will deal with you."

Darren dashed out without so much as a backward glance.

"You!" Sister Mary David spat, striding into the room. "Cover yourself!"

Sofia pulled her blouse together and had begun to button it when the nun grabbed her hand and yanked her up off the bed.

"You'll be lucky if we don't expel you," Sister Mary David hissed.

Expel! Fear shot through Sofia as she scrambled to button her blouse with one hand while being marched down the hall ahead of the furious nun.

"No, Sister, really—" Sofia began, frantically searching in her mind for something—anything—with which to defend herself.

But the nun wasn't listening. "We don't condone that kind of behavior here, Sofia," Sister Mary David grated. "If you want to act like a—" She groped for the right word, then found it: "—a *harlot,* then you should go to school somewhere else."

"I—I'm sorry," Sofia stammered. "I didn't want him—"

"Too late," Sister Mary David snapped, her voice cutting into Sofia like the barb at the end of a whip. "You are in charge of your actions, and you shall be responsible for the consequences." The nun guided her down a set of stairs and through another hallway. Sofia stumbled ahead, barely able to keep the pace Sister Mary David was setting.

"Wicked," the nun muttered. "Wicked, evil child!"

"No, Sister," Sofia gasped. "I'm not wicked. I'm—" Once again she searched for words that might appease the dorm supervisor. "Darren and I love each other!" she finally blurted out.

The nun stopped short and spun Sofia around to face her, her thin lips set into a harsh line. "Love does not sneak about breaking rules, Sofia. *Evil* does that."

"No, Sister—"

"Silence! I do not wish to hear another word from your sinful mouth." The nun twisted Sofia around once again and steered her down another set of stairs, then guided her so quickly through a series of narrow hallways that Sofia was at a loss as to where they were. Certainly they were somewhere she had never seen before.

What was going to happen to her? Was she really going to be expelled? Her father would kill her. He'd send her somewhere else—somewhere even more awful than St. Isaac's.

And her father would give her a beating.

"Please, Sister—" Sofia began again, trying to resist the frantic pace the nun had set, but Sister Mary David pressed relentlessly onward, the fingers of her left hand digging like talons into Sofia's shoulder, while her other hand held Sofia's right arm in an agonizing hammerlock.

Her body burning with pain and her soul with humiliation, Sofia began to cry.

The nun stopped in front of an old wooden door, unlocked it with a heavy key she took from her pocket and pushed it open to reveal a tiny chapel with an enormous carving of a crucified Christ hovering over its altar. "Stop crying and light the candle for your soul," the nun whispered.

Sofia sucked in her breath and wiped the tears from her cheeks. She picked up the single candle that lay in the box, and struck the lone match that lay next to the box. Both shook so badly in her trembling hands that she could barely touch the flame to the candle's wick, but finally it caught.

She blew out the match.

"Now get on your knees and pray to the Holy Virgin for forgiveness of your sins," Sister Mary David said.

Sofia obediently dropped to her knees on the stone floor, clutching the small candle.

"You will stay here until I return," Sister Mary David said, her voice devoid of any warmth—any mercy—at all.

Sofia nodded, her chest heaving. "Please don't expel me," she choked out. Then she crossed herself and took a deep breath. "Oh my God," she whispered. "I am heartily sorry for having offended thee and I detest all my sins, because I dread the loss of Heaven and the pains of Hell, but most of all because they offend thee, my God, who are all good and deserving of all my love. I firmly resolve, with the help of thy grace, to confess my sins, to do penance, and to amend my life."

The nun nodded once, then backed out the door.

Sofia began the prayer again.

Then she heard the ancient lock turn in the heavy oak door, and her heart lurched.

A moment later, the overhead light went out.

The chapel was completely dark, except for the tiny flame in Sofia's trembling hands. The room seemed to close in on her, and she felt as if she could no longer breathe.

"Oh my God," she began again, "I am so sorry . . . please don't expel me . . . please don't let my parents know what I did . . . I am heartily sorry for having offended thee . . ."

Sofia spoke faster and faster, trying to rid herself of the panic that was closing in on her with the darkness.

All she could see was what the flickering candle flame in her hand illuminated, and as she looked up, the visage of the tortured Christ seemed to lean closer, leering down at her as she knelt repeating her prayer of contrition. She shrank away from its ruthless gaze, doing her best to hide her shame.

But the figure on the cross held her. This being was not the Jesus who loved her and forgave her all her sins. This was an angry Christ who hated her sins. This was a terrifying Christ, looming over her, judging her.

Condemning her to an eternity in Hell.

She started the prayer yet again, careful not to breathe too hard on the flame, terrified of losing that last tiny flame that was all that held her fears at bay.

What if something happened to Sister Mary David and she never came back?

Would anybody ever know where she was?

Did anybody else even know about this chapel?

Sofia closed her eyes and took a deep breath. Now she welcomed the pain in her knees on the stone, for she knew she deserved the pain, the fear, the threat of expulsion.

She was truly contrite now, truly ashamed.

And terrified that the Christ above her might extinguish the single flame that stood between her and the darkness, until Sister Mary David returned to pronounce whatever penance she must perform. But whatever it was, she would do it. Just as long as the candle in her hands did not go out . . .

"Oh my God," she said a little louder, the sound of her voice her only company. "I am heartily sorry for having offended thee . . ."

CHAPTER 17

Darren Bender stared at the television without seeing the screen. He wasn't exactly hiding in the dorm's common room, he was just avoiding Father Sebastian. Not that it really mattered where he was; the priest would find him sooner or later.

Still, at least he would get to deal with Father Sebastian instead of Sister Mary David—he didn't even want to think about what she might be doing with Sofia.

The door to the common room opened, and Darren could tell who it was just by the expression on Clay Matthews's face. The fact that everyone else in the room sat up a little straighter only strengthened Darren's feeling that his time had come, and José Alvarez's picking up of the remote to click off the television was the final confirmation. No one ever straightened up for Brother Francis, let alone shut off the TV.

"Darren?" Father Sebastian's voice asked.

Darren's face began to burn and his heart pounded. He'd made a mistake coming to the lounge—he'd rather have this conversation in private, where at least all his friends wouldn't hear him getting chewed out. But now Father Sebastian was going to use him as an example in front of all the other guys. Just what he needed. "Yes?" he finally said,

doing his best to make the single word sound neither guilty nor frightened, and succeeding at neither.

"I hear you and Sofia Capelli were breaking a few rules this evening."

Father Sebastian didn't sound too upset, so Darren risked a slight
shrug. "I guess."

"I'm sorry?" the priest asked, his voice taking on an edge that made
Darren instantly turn to face him. "You '*guess*'?"

Darren looked up at the priest, his tongue running nervously over
his lower lip. "I mean, yes, we did, Father." He said it so quickly that a
faint snicker emerged from his roommate.

Father Sebastian silenced Tim Kennedy with nothing more than a
sidelong glare, then returned his attention to Darren. "So you think
you can just break rules whenever you feel like it?"

The sudden shift back to an easy conversational tone only served to
set Darren's nerves more on edge. "N-No, sir," he replied.

"Well, then?"

Darren took a chance. "We were just making out a little."

"That's not exactly what Sister Mary David tells me she saw," the
priest countered.

"But we weren't doing anything really *wrong*," Darren protested, immediately regretting his words as he saw Father Sebastian's expression
darken.

"Well, let's see," the priest began. "First off, you were in the girls'
dorm. That in itself is wrong, given that it's against the rules. Whether
what you were doing once you were in Sofia's room is wrong is—"

"Maybe the rules are wrong," Darren blurted out, knowing as he
spoke the words that he'd just made yet another mistake.

Father Sebastian lowered himself onto the ottoman in front of Darren's spot on the couch, his eyes boring into the boy's.

"That may be so, but it's not your decision to make. When you entered this school, you agreed to abide by the rules, whether you agreed
with them or not. And breaking that particular rule is grounds for expulsion, as I'm sure you are very well aware."

Darren heard someone gasp and felt his face start to burn with humiliation. "We—Sofia and me—we just wanted to be together."

"You can be together anywhere on campus other than the dorms. And I repeat: *you knew that.*" Darren sagged on the couch. It was actually going to happen—he was actually going to be expelled. "I want you to think about what you've done," the priest went on. "Not just in the eyes of the school, but in the eyes of God, as well." He paused, and his voice dropped slightly. "You are sixteen years old. When a boy your age stands his moral ground with an innocent young woman, God is pleased. But when he gives in to his basest urges, it pleases God not at all. It will spell trouble for both you and Sofia, and my job is to help you keep from harming yourself—or anyone else—until you're old enough to exercise your own self-control."

Darren felt a flicker of hope. Was it possible that maybe he wasn't going to be expelled after all? Was it possible that Father Sebastian intended to try to help him, and not just punish him? Then the priest stood up, and Darren, almost as if drawn by some unseen force, rose as well.

"I shall have to consider your penance carefully," Father Sebastian said. Then he looked around the room. "No one here has to study? You're all straight-A students? I'm impressed!"

Everyone but Darren scrambled to leave, and when they were alone, Darren scuffed at the floor. "I'm sorry, Father," he said, his voice trembling slightly.

"I'm sure you are," Father Sebastian replied. He laid a gentle hand on Darren's shoulder and began steering him toward the door. "I want you to go to confession before breakfast tomorrow, and then come to my office after classes."

The flicker of hope that had been burning faintly inside Darren suddenly flared. "I will," he promised. "And it won't happen again."

Father Sebastian's brows arched slightly. "I'm sure it won't."

As Father Sebastian turned to leave the dorm, Darren headed for his room. His room, and his cell phone, with which he could find out what had happened to Sofia.

His roommate, Tim Kennedy, was waiting for him, leering gleefully now that Father Sebastian was nowhere to be seen. "So you got to first base, eh?"

"Not funny," Darren shot back. He dug in his backpack for his cell phone and tapped in a quick message to Sofia: *Are you okay?*

He waited a minute, then another.

Then five more.

No response. Brushing aside Tim Kennedy's questions about what—*exactly*—had happened in Sofia's room, Darren opened his history text, but couldn't concentrate.

Sofia was being punished simply for being with him.

There was a soft knock on the door, then Clay Matthews and his new roommate stuck their heads in, Clay grinning even more lasciviously than Tim Kennedy had a few minutes earlier. "Give us the details," Clay said.

Darren shook his head. "Just go away, okay?" he said, and turned away from them.

They left.

An hour later, Tim Kennedy went to bed.

But Darren stayed up, turning pages in his history book but seeing none of the words. Every few moments he checked his phone, but it was working fine. The signal was strong, the battery was nearly full.

But no text messages had come in.

Finally giving up, Darren went to bed and turned out the light, but knew he wouldn't go to sleep.

What had happened?

Was Sofia all right? He never should have run away like a scared jackrabbit—he should have stayed, and explained to Sister Mary David that it was all his fault. He could have told her he'd pushed his way into Sofia's room, and she'd wanted him to leave but he wouldn't, and—

—and now she was probably in more trouble than he was, and would never even talk to him again, let alone let him kiss her, or touch her, or—

Rolling over and pulling the covers over his head, Darren put the phone under his pillow and tried to sleep.

Maybe tomorrow he'd figure out how to make it up to her.

Assuming she was even still here tomorrow. Knowing Sister Mary

David, Sofia's parents might have had to come and get her this very night.

Darren Bender rolled over again, punched his pillow, and tried to get comfortable. But even as he closed his eyes again, he knew it was futile. No matter what he did, he wasn't going to go to sleep tonight.

Not with the guilt gnawing at his gut that Father Sebastian had instilled in him.

How could he have been such an idiot?

CHAPTER 18

FATHER LAUGHLIN MOUNTED the steps to the diocesan rectory slowly, feeling the weight not only of the problem at hand, which he was certain had to do with Kip Adamson's death, but of his age as well. When the summons had come from the Archbishop's office so late in the day, Laughlin had hurried to shave, change into a fresh collar and shirt, and get into a taxi, yet there had been none of the excitement that years ago had invariably accompanied a summons to see the Cardinal. Of course, the Cardinal was gone now and while Archbishop Jonathan Rand was certainly a competent administrator, it simply wasn't the same. A Cardinal was a Cardinal, and an Archbishop an Archbishop, and that was that. But it wasn't just the man at the top that had changed; in the last few years everything in the Boston Archdiocese had changed.

Laughlin hesitated to catch his breath and wipe a handkerchief across his forehead before pressing the bell next to the rectory's simple front door. Something else that had changed. This was nothing like the Cardinal's mansion Laughlin used to enjoy visiting. That mansion had been sold off to pay restitution in the unending lawsuits the Boston diocese had incurred, and this far simpler house seemed to Father Laughlin far too humble even for an Archbishop.

He pressed the doorbell and a few seconds later the door was opened by a young seminar student, who immediately ushered him into Archbishop Rand's office.

An office with none of the luxury the Cardinal had enjoyed. True poverty, it seemed, had finally come to the priesthood, at least in Boston.

"Good evening, Ernest," the Archbishop said, rising to his feet and coming around his desk to shake the old priest's hand. "I am so sorry to have called you out so late in the day."

"Always a pleasure," Father Laughlin sighed, sinking gratefully into the nearest chair and hoping the words sounded more genuine than they felt.

Archbishop Rand returned to his seat behind the desk. "I wish I could say the same, but just now there seems to be precious little pleasure in this job." His eyes fixed darkly on Laughlin. "In fact, since Saturday I've found no pleasure in it at all." Father Laughlin nervously folded his handkerchief to a fresh side and wiped his face as the temperature in the office seemed to go up five degrees. "And I must tell you, Ernest," the Archbishop pressed. "There is more Church business to which I must attend than acting as apologist for your school."

Father Laughlin shifted uneasily as the temperature seemed to go up again. He was just beginning to formulate a reply to the Archbishop's words when Rand leaned back and folded his hands together across his chest. "You are as aware as I am how restless the flock in Boston has become the last few years. What you might not be aware of is how hard I have been working to calm the flock. And then along comes the Adamson boy, and in a single evening nearly wipes out the effectiveness of what I have been trying to do for several years. What little time I've had not placating people, I've been spending in prayer." He leaned forward, his eyes once more boring into Laughlin, his voice dropping. "Praying, and asking for guidance."

"Oh, dear," Father Laughlin began. "Everyone at St. Isaac's—"

"Ah, yes," the Archbishop cut in, leaning even farther forward. "St. Isaac's. That brings us directly to the point, doesn't it, Ernest?" The

Archbishop's voice took on a sharp edge. "St. Isaac's mission is to heal the children and ignite the light of the Church within them. Am I correct?"

"Of course that's one of our goals," Father Laughlin said a little too quickly as a trickle of perspiration made its way slowly down his cheek. "And I'm sure you understand that we do our best. No one understands what caused the Adamson boy to do this terrible thing. Father Sebastian had been working with him and—"

"Father Sebastian was brought here specifically to make certain that things like this don't happen," Rand cut in.

"And he's doing a wonderful job with the students," Father Laughlin said, unconsciously shrinking away from the Archbishop's accusatory tone. "But these things take time. Father Sebastian has only been with us since the fall—"

"We don't have 'time,' Father Laughlin," the Archbishop shot back. "Rome sent me here to clean up the mess this Archdiocese found itself in. The Vatican has its eye on us at every moment. They are watching me, and they are watching you, and what they see does not please them." The Archbishop fixed Father Laughlin with a cold stare. "Father Sebastian has a reputation for dealing with evil. I sent him to St. Isaac's for *that express purpose.*" He punctuated the last three words by dropping his fist to the desktop with enough force to make Father Laughlin jump. "I suggest you see to it that Father Sebastian does his job, or we will be forced not only to replace him, but you as well."

Father Laughlin's heart began to pound and his breath caught in his chest. Was it possible that he was about to be dismissed after forty-six years of dedicated service without so much as a single blemish on his record? The room felt hotter than ever, and he ran a finger around his collar in a futile attempt to loosen it. The Archbishop continued to talk, but Father Laughlin could no longer follow his words. He felt ill—dizzy—as if he might faint and, as his heart continued to throb, waited for the heaviness in his chest that always came just before one of his angina attacks. He slid his hand into the pocket of his cassock, failed to find the medicine, and remembered he'd left it on his nightstand. *Stay calm,* he told himself. *Just breathe.* After a moment the pounding of his heart began to ease slightly, and with it the pressure in his chest. He turned his attention back to the Archbishop just as his superior was finishing.

"Do I make myself clear?" Archbishop Rand asked.

"Yes, yes, of course," Father Laughlin said, though he had missed at least half of the tirade. "Perfectly clear." He took one more deep breath and wiped his handkerchief across his upper lip with a trembling hand. "I shall speak with Father Sebastian in the morning as soon as I return and I assure you we shall take measures." He looked up to gauge his effect on the other man, but the Archbishop's expression was unreadable. "*Stringent* measures," he said. "Nothing like this will ever happen again." He took a breath.

"Good," the Archbishop said, leaning back in his chair once more and finally smiling. "We all pray for a healing in this community. Especially at St. Isaac's."

Father Laughlin did his best to return the smile. "Thank you, Archbishop. You have nothing to worry about—you have my word on that."

Archbishop Rand's smile compressed to a thin line, and his brows arched slightly. "Brother Simon will see you out."

As if in response to some unseen cue, the office door opened and the young seminarian stepped in, extending his hand to help Father Laughlin out of the chair, and two minutes later Father Ernest Laughlin was on his way back to St. Isaac's, wondering whether he would soon be as summarily ejected from his school as he had been from the rectory.

No, he decided. *Whatever I have to do, I will do. But I will not leave St. Isaac's.*

† † †

Sofia Capelli stared numbly at the last inch of the candle, willing it to burn more slowly. She was clutching it so hard that her fingers actually ached, but far worse than the pain in her fingers was the agony in her legs. It felt like she'd been on her knees for hours, silently repeating her prayers over and over again, certain that at any moment the door would open and Father Sebastian would come in and end her vigil in front of the altar. But the door hadn't opened, and Father Sebastian hadn't appeared. With every passing minute the pain in her knees grew worse until now there was nothing but a horrible cold, throbbing ache, punctuated with even the slightest movement by the sensation of a thousand needles jabbing into her legs. She wasn't even praying anymore.

Instead, she was listening to the sound of her own heart, which seemed to be getting louder and louder as each moment passed.

She was tired—more tired than she'd ever been in her life. Her eyes felt heavy, and all she really wanted to do was stretch out on the floor, let the candle burn out, and go to sleep. But what if Sister Mary David came in? That would be even worse than if Father Sebastian caught her.

At least Father Sebastian's eyes were always kind.

Sister Mary David's were hard; she could make you feel like you'd been slapped just by looking at you.

How long should she stay here? Had Sister Mary David really meant for her to stay on her knees for hours? And what would happen when the candle finally burned out?

The dark.

She would be trapped in the dark with the door locked and nobody except Sister Mary David knowing where she was.

She waited, the candle growing shorter, the agony in her body building with each beat of her heart.

Then, just as the candle burned short enough that she could feel its flame starting to sear her fingers, a faint sound came to her ears.

Hope surged in her heart, and now she prayed—truly prayed—that at last someone had come to release her from this prison.

The sound of the lock clicking open answered her prayers, and tears of gratitude sprang to Sofia's eyes.

The door opened, and out of the corner of her eye, she saw Father Sebastian slip in and go into a tiny carved confessional she hadn't even noticed in the heavy gloom of the chapel. The priest disappeared, and a moment later a yellowish light behind the little booth began to brighten, casting golden highlights onto the tortured face of Christ.

The Savior's enormous hollowed eyes seemed to be boring into her from a hideously jaundiced face.

Sofia flinched away from that condemning visage, blew the candle out as the heat of its flame threatened to char the flesh of her fingers and struggled to her feet to go into the confessional. Her legs screamed in protest as she forced first one foot, then the other. A wave of dizziness broke over her.

As her knees started to give way she suddenly realized that there was someone else in the chapel—a black-clad figure silhouetted in the doorway.

Sister Mary David, savoring every moment of Sofia's agony.

No, she commanded herself. *Don't give her the satisfaction.*

She hobbled over to the confessional, pulled the musty curtain closed, and eased herself down onto the hard bench, sighing as a little of the pain in her legs began to ease.

The small partition between the booth's two compartments opened and Sofia saw the screen, which normally hid her from the priest, was missing.

She was staring directly into the deep warm eyes of Father Sebastian.

His eyes held hers, and for the first time in her life, she found herself confessing directly to the priest, unafraid, and truly contrite. "Bless me, Father," she whispered, "for I have sinned. It has been six days since my last confession."

"Yes, my child?"

Father Sebastian's voice was as soothing as the warm milk her mother had given her when she had awakened from nightmares when she was a little girl, and she knew that no matter what she told him, Father Sebastian would understand. "I have had impure thoughts, Father. I have had lustful thoughts about my boyfriend, and resentful thoughts against Sister Mary David, who caught us kissing."

"And?" the priest gently prompted, his eyes still holding her gaze.

"In my room."

"Go on."

The words poured easily from Sofia's lips. "And I let him touch my breasts."

The priest nodded slightly. "Is that all?"

"That is all," Sofia replied, feeling the burden of guilt lift slightly from her spirit.

"These are grave offenses, Sofia," the priest said softly. "I shall have to give your penance some thought."

Sofia's eyes widened slightly. Had she heard right? He wasn't going to assign her punishment right now? She looked into his eyes. What did it mean? What might he do? "I'm sorry, Father," she whispered. "It won't happen again."

"I'm sure it won't, Sofia," Father Sebastian replied. "For now, I want you to say six Hail Marys before bed tonight, and six more before breakfast tomorrow. Then I want you to meet me back here tomorrow before dinner."

"Back here?" Sofia echoed, her skin crawling at the thought of returning to this strange chapel. "No, Father, please—"

Father Sebastian raised a single finger, silencing her. "You may go."

Sofia's head whirled. This wasn't right—this wasn't how it was supposed to happen. After she confessed she was supposed to get absolution and penance, and then it was supposed to be over! "Aren't—aren't you going to absolve me?" she stammered.

"Tomorrow," the priest replied, smiling gently. "But don't worry, Sofia. It's going to be all right."

The little partition slid closed, and Sofia was suddenly alone.

She sat silently in the gloom of the booth for a moment, feeling none of the sense of relief that making her confession had always brought. Why had Father Sebastian withheld absolution? But even as she silently asked the question, she knew the answer: he wanted her to think about what she'd done. If he'd simply given her the usual Hail Marys and Our Fathers, she would have forgotten all about it by tomorrow morning.

Father Sebastian was simply making her live with her sin until tomorrow, so she'd think harder next time.

He was simply doing his job, tending to her soul.

After a moment, Sofia crossed herself one last time and pulled back the dusty curtain.

There stood Sister Mary David. Startled, Sofia gasped and almost slipped on the worn wooden step.

The nun, her lips pressed together and her eyes nothing more than accusing slits, held her ground, and Sofia had to grasp at the confessional door to recover her balance.

Silently, Sister Mary David walked to the chapel door, turned, and beckoned Sofia to follow her.

As she left the chapel, Sofia wasn't sure which was worse—Sister Mary David's cold silence, or the feeling that from the crucifix behind her, Christ Himself was glaring down upon her, condemning her for her unforgiven sins.

CHAPTER 19

I'M SLEEPING IN *a dead guy's bed!*

Ryan knew the sheets were fresh, because he'd put them on himself, and his sore jaw was cradled in the pillow he'd brought from home, but no matter which way he turned, or what else he tried to think about, he couldn't get past the idea that he was sleeping—or at least trying to sleep—in Kip Adamson's bed.

Kip Adamson.

The guy who'd gone crazy, slit a woman's throat, and been shot by cops.

Ryan stared unseeingly at the pattern of shadows cast on the ceiling from the streetlight outside. The day he had thought would never end finally had, and as he tried to go to sleep his mind ached with almost as much exhaustion as his body. His injured jaw still throbbed, and every time he tried to change position in his new bed, his ribs felt like they were puncturing right through his lungs.

He tried to lie still.

And failed.

Clay Matthews snored in the bed on the other side of the small room, but with every breath, the snoring seemed to grow louder. Was this what having a roommate was going to be like? How was he ever supposed to get to sleep? Still, everybody here had a roommate, and Clay couldn't possibly be the only one who snored, so he'd just have to get used to it.

Like he'd have to get used to everything else.

He turned over again, ignoring the pain from his cracked ribs, and tried to convince himself that being here was the right thing. As the day had gone on, and he'd found out more and more about how St. Isaac's worked, he'd also felt more and more that he would never fit in, never get used to all the rules and rituals, never get used to wearing the same clothes day after day. And it wasn't just the rules and the clothes, either. The whole place was old—*ancient*—and smelled musty and it seemed like there were priests and nuns and monks everywhere.

And the food was even worse than the stuff they'd served at Dickinson, which he hadn't actually thought was possible.

How was he going to make it through the rest of the week, let alone the rest of the year, and next year, too? But it was too late to change his mind now. He'd agreed to come here, and his mother had jumped through a lot of hoops to get him in, so no matter how he felt right now, he had to at least try.

Nor was he about to let Tom Kelly accuse him of being some kind of whining quitter who couldn't stand being away from home, even if it might be true.

Wincing at the pain in his ribs, Ryan eased back onto his good side and stared at the ugly white net curtains that seemed almost to glow in the faint light from outside.

A breeze suddenly caught them, and they billowed toward him.

Like shrouds searching for a body to wrap.

Ryan closed his eyes. Tomorrow would be better—he'd start classes, and he already knew a few kids, so he'd have some people to sit with at meal times.

He'd be okay.

But he still couldn't get Kip Adamson out of his mind.

He punched up his pillow and twisted his head to take the pressure off his sore jaw. A moment later he shifted position yet again, but no matter what he did, the bed just wasn't right.

And the last person who had slept in it had gone out and killed somebody and then gotten killed himself.

A shiver passed through him, and he pulled the blanket closer around him, closed his eyes and tried to concentrate on thinking about something else.

Anything else.

His father.

He would think about his father.

Except that the only thought that came to his mind was the memory of the night he and his mother heard about what had happened to his father. Unable even to turn off the light in his own room, Ryan had gone into his parents' room, and lay down next to his sobbing mother. He had put his arms around her, and she had put hers around him, and they had both cried themselves to sleep.

So this really wasn't the first time he'd slept in a dead guy's bed.

He tried to force the thought out of his mind, and concentrated instead on the image of his father's face that was as fresh in his mind as if he'd seen him only yesterday. "Good night, Dad," he whispered softly into his pillow. From deep in his memory, he could almost hear his father's voice saying good night back to him.

And then, just as he was finally easing into the beginnings of sleep, he heard something.

A high-pitched keening sound.

At first it seemed to come from somewhere outside the building— maybe the street—but when he got out of bed and moved silently to the window, he knew he was wrong.

It was coming from somewhere inside the building.

Somewhere below him.

The sound came again, strengthening until it was a full-throated scream.

Ryan's heart began to pound, and the pain in his chest almost made him utter a scream of his own as he shook Clay Matthews awake. "Clay! Wake up! Did you hear that?"

Clay instinctively recoiled from Ryan's touch, then rolled over and opened his eyes slightly, squinted at Ryan. "Hear what?" he asked, his voice thick with sleep.

"That scream. Just now."

Clay looked at him blankly. "I didn't hear anything." Ryan's eyes narrowed. How was it possible? Clay *must* have heard it. Then Clay propped himself up on one elbow. "It was probably a ghost," he said, his voice sounding perfectly serious despite the words he was speaking. As if he read Ryan's mind, Clay shrugged. "Hey, we have ghosts—what can I tell you? Just don't pay any attention to them."

Ryan's eyes rolled. "Ghosts. Yeah, right. How could I have been so stupid?"

Clay dropped back down onto his pillow. "Hey, I don't care if you believe me or not." He turned his head and looked at the digital clock on his desk. "Oh man," he said, "it's late and there's a history test in the morning. Good night."

Ryan eyed Clay suspiciously, trying to decide whether his roommate actually believed the words he'd just spoken, or was just pulling his leg. But Clay had already gone back to sleep, a light snore drifting from his lips. Ryan went back to his own bed, slid stiffly under the covers, and lay perfectly still.

Silence had fallen over the room. But it wasn't just the room.

There was silence everywhere now. No sounds of traffic from the street outside, no scratching of mice from within the walls themselves.

Nothing.

Ryan pulled the covers up to his chin and tried to relax, but even as his body begged for rest he knew he would get no sleep tonight.

Not in a dead guy's bed.

CHAPTER 20

RYAN SAT IN the darkened classroom the next morning, gazing mutely at the image on the screen. It was a woman, bound to a thick stake with thick ropes, her breasts bare, flames licking at her feet. The image was of an ancient woodcut, and its stark black and white seemed only to accentuate the expression of terror and agony that twisted the woman's face. In his mind, Ryan heard an echo of the scream from last night, but now it was coming from the mouth of the woman at the stake.

Father Sebastian clicked the remote control and the woodblock was replaced by a vividly painted image of a man tied to a post in a harbor, gray seas behind him, howling in terror as the tide came in to drown him.

Ryan's gaze shifted to the empty notebook on his desk. He'd heard at breakfast that since Father Sebastian had started teaching it, Catholic History was one of the most popular courses at the school, and now he knew why. The images of the Inquisition that he'd just seen had seared Father Sebastian's accompanying words in his memory with no need for any notes at all.

"Historians have said that the Inquisition was about persecuting

Jews and Muslims," Father Sebastian said. "But that is not the case at all. The Jews and Muslims had already been exiled by the secular Spanish government. What made the Inquisition necessary was that not all of them left. Some stayed, pretending to have converted to Christianity." The image on the screen changed again. Now Ryan was looking at a highly realistic picture of a man in a tall red hat decorated with an ornately embroidered cross, who was sitting on some kind of throne while an executioner ran a sword through a peasant's throat.

Ryan felt his throat constrict as he gazed at the dying man.

"The purpose of the Inquisition was not to persecute Jews and Muslims, but rather to root out and expel those who found it suddenly convenient to become Catholic. The subjects of the Inquisition were the hypocrites who professed our faith only to protect their worldly assets." He paused, his eyes sweeping the small classroom as the screen went blank. "Questions?"

Almost to his own surprise, Ryan found his hand going up.

"Ryan?"

"I—I was just wondering—" he stammered.

Father Sebastian cut off his words with an uplifted arm. "This is St. Isaac's," he said, smiling almost ruefully. "I'm afraid we're not like public school. Here we stand when we speak."

Ryan felt his face burn. He wasn't even quite sure how to ask his question, but he got to his feet and cleared his throat. "I guess I was just wondering how they thought they could tell if a person was lying about converting? I mean, won't people say anything at all if you torture them enough?"

"Of course they will," Father Sebastian said, as Ryan sank back to his seat. "As many of the inquisitors quickly came to understand. But we're not talking about the efficacy of the methods here; merely the purity of the motivation."

Another hand went up. Father Sebastian nodded at a stocky red-haired boy. "Sam?"

The boy stood as Ryan sank back into his chair. "But it doesn't matter what the motivations were, does it? In the end, didn't the Inquisition make the Muslims and Jews think that the Christians were out to exterminate them? Isn't that one of the reasons they still think that?"

Father Sebastian nodded. "Absolutely right. It's unfortunate that the Church is still feeling the fallout of the Inquisition, especially considering how long ago it ended. Even worse, its true purpose has been all but lost to secular historians, who always seem to unfairly ascribe the darkest motives to any actions motivated by religion." As the bell signaled the end of class, Father Sebastian stepped back behind his desk. "Read pages 147 to 176 and remember the test on Friday."

Ryan stared at the priest. A test on Friday? Even if he could read the whole textbook by then—which he was pretty sure he couldn't—he still wouldn't be ready for a test on Friday. It wouldn't be fair—he'd only started the class this very day. Then he remembered Father Sebastian's words about historian's "unfairly" ascribing the worst motives to the Inquisition. The hollowness in his belly was suddenly replaced by hope. He closed his notebook, waited for most of the class to file out, then approached the priest as he was starting to put the projector away.

"Father Sebastian?"

The priest looked up, and Ryan instantly remembered the night Father Sebastian had come to see him in the hospital. There was a kindness in the priest's eyes that Ryan had experienced from only one other person.

His father.

"Hey, Ryan," Father Sebastian said. "What can I do for you?"

"I—well, I was wondering if I have to take the test on Friday? I mean, I haven't even opened the textbook yet."

The priest seemed to think for a moment, but then shook his head. "Everyone takes the test, Ryan. If you study, you'll do fine. It's not going to be that hard." Father Sebastian scanned the emptying room, and he suddenly smiled. "How about if I give you a little extra edge?" Before Ryan could say anything, the priest raised his voice slightly. "Melody?"

A pretty blond girl looked up from the book bag she was packing, and Father Sebastian crooked his finger at her. She glanced quickly behind her as if to make sure it was really she the priest wanted, then picked up her books and purse, and walked up to the front.

"Melody Hunt, meet Ryan McIntyre. He's a transfer student, and this is his first day of classes here. How about if you tutor him for this Friday's test, and then maybe for another week or two, at least until he gets up to speed. Okay?" He turned back to Ryan. "Melody's a fanatic note-taker. I have a feeling she knows more about this stuff than the guy who wrote the textbook."

Melody blushed slightly, then smiled uncertainly at Ryan. "I'll try."

"That's all any of us can do," Father Sebastian said as he went back to the projector.

† † †

As soon as they were out of the classroom, Melody's smile faded, and she shuddered. "Those pictures were just horrible," she said. "Why did he even show them to us?"

Ryan barely heard her words. Instead he was focusing on the tiny pearl earrings and faint lip gloss that were just enough to make Melody look completely different from any of the other girls he'd seen so far. It was hard to look different from everybody else when everyone wore a uniform, but Melody had pulled it off. Suddenly he realized he was staring at her, and she knew he was staring at her, and he mentally scrambled to remember what she'd just said. "They were gross," he agreed, feeling a flush rising in his cheeks. "They'd never show us anything like that in public school."

"Lucky you," Melody sighed. "I've been stuck here since ninth grade. And my parents aren't even very religious. They just think this is safer than public school. Want to go get lunch?"

As Melody started down the corridor in exactly the opposite direction Ryan would have gone, he fell in beside her. "What about that guy Kip? Kip Adamson?"

Melody stopped short and looked at Ryan. "What do you know about him?"

"Not much," Ryan replied. "Even though everyone in my dorm is talking about him, nobody knows what happened. And I'm in his room."

Melody's face paled. "I don't think I could do that," she breathed. "I mean, how could you even sleep?"

"I almost didn't," Ryan admitted. "So, did you know him?"

Melody started down the hallway again. "Not really," she began. "I mean, I sort of thought I knew him until he started getting weird. It was like he turned into some kind of lost soul. You know what I mean?"

Ryan nodded, even though he wasn't sure he did know what she meant, and once more fell in beside her. "So what happened to him?"

"I don't know, and I think I must have asked everybody in school," Melody replied, her voice hollow. "In fact, my roommate's getting really tired of me talking about him all the time."

Ryan offered her a lopsided grin. "So talk to me about him. I promise I won't get tired of hearing you."

Melody flushed slightly, but didn't turn away. "At first I thought he'd just left school, like Jeffrey Holmes."

Now it was Ryan who stopped short. "Jeffrey Holmes?" he repeated. "Who's he?"

"A guy who left in November. But he wasn't like Kip. He hated it here, and after Thanksgiving he never came back." Her eyes clouded, and Ryan wondered exactly what it was she was remembering, but the moment passed before he could ask. "Anyway, we all thought that was what happened to Kip, too. We all figured he'd just taken off. Even Clay thought so."

They walked along in silence for a moment, and suddenly Ryan found himself asking Melody the same question he'd asked Clay late last night. "Did you hear anything last night? Like around midnight?"

Melody glanced at him. "Hear what?"

Ryan hesitated, but then blurted it out. "A scream." He waited for her to laugh, but she didn't.

Instead, she rolled her eyes. "That's just a stupid stunt," she said. "Someone does it to every new student. They sneak far enough away from the dorm so they can barely be heard, then scream. The new person wants to know what it is, and is told that we have ghosts. Dumb, hunh?" Ryan nodded, glad he'd asked Melody instead of giving Clay and his friends an opportunity to elaborate on the joke at lunchtime. But then Melody's expression turned serious. "But the weird thing is," she went on, "every now and then you hear something like that and there aren't any new students. And some of these buildings are hundreds of years old, and there are all kinds of stories about what they used to be used for."

The images from the Inquisition lecture immediately rose out of Ryan's memory.

Melody laughed. "There's also supposed to be the ghost of some old nun that wanders around the school at night."

"Have you ever seen it?"

Melody shook her head. "Of course not! Nobody I know has actually seen it themselves—everyone just knows someone who knows someone who saw it. Personally, I don't think it's a ghost at all. I think it's Sister Mary David—God knows she's old enough that she *should* be a ghost by now." She giggled for a second, but then her expression clouded over again. "But who knows? Who really knows anything? I mean, we don't even really know what happened to Jeffrey Holmes, do we?"

"Or Kip," Ryan added softly.

Melody looked up at him, and he had the uncanny feeling he could fall right into the depths of her blue eyes. She nodded slowly. "Or Kip," she agreed. "Who really knows what happened to either one of them?"

CHAPTER 21

DETECTIVE PATRICK NORTH strode down the long, sterile hallway, looking neither to the right nor to the left. He'd spent plenty of time in both the morgue and the medical examiner's office over the years, but he'd never quite become inured to the aura of death—unnatural death—that hung over the place.

Today, though, he had a mystery on his hands, and if he was going to solve it, he had to start here.

He stopped in front of a nondescript door with an engraved brown Formica plaque with lettering every bit as nondescript as the material upon which it was printed:

BENJAMIN BREEN, M.D.
DISTRICT MEDICAL EXAMINER

The door was ajar, and North heard a low monologue from inside. He tapped lightly on the door, then pushed the door all the way open and walked in.

Ben Breen's office barely contained the man, not to mention the stacks of paper, the overfull bookcase, the boxes filled with evidence envelopes, and all the detritus that littered the desk, and had spilled over onto the floor. Even the two plastic chairs that were ostensibly there for visitors had been pressed into service to help support the Medical Examiner's vast collection of cases, reference material, coffee mugs, snack wrappers, and just plain junk. Breen also had a penchant for medical oddities and dark jokes: a skull served as his penholder and a dusty skeleton hung in one corner with a small teddy bear inside its chest. North had never asked the significance of the teddy bear, and never would.

Breen clicked off his recorder and frowned as he tried to place the face before him, but his mind was on the report he'd been dictating.

"Patrick North," the detective sighed, resigning himself to having to introduce himself to Breen yet again. You'd think after ten years the man could at least remember his name. "Detective?" Breen still looked faintly puzzled, so North offered him another piece. "The Kip Adamson case?"

Breen brightened. "Ah, yes," he said, pulling himself up to his full six-foot-five-inch height, and then beginning a search through a file box on top of the file cabinet. "Thanks for coming down."

"No problem," North said, wondering if the M.E. was even going to be able to find the report. "Thanks for calling."

"Here it is," Breen said triumphantly, looking almost as surprised as North by how quickly he'd found what he was looking for. He opened the folder and sat back down at his desk. "Just move that crap onto the floor," he said, waving vaguely at one of the chairs. "Sit yourself down."

North set a stack of papers by the door, making a mental note to return them to the chair when he left. Apparently Breen was one of those people who lived amid chaos but knew exactly where to look for any given thing.

Breen flipped through several pages of typewritten notes and lab reports, then found the page he wanted. "Here it is," he said. "Tox screen was negative." He peered up at North. "No drugs, no alcohol. Death by close-range gunshot to the head." He handed North a sheet of paper.

"No drugs?" North pressed. It hardly seemed possible. He glanced at the copy of the official coroner's report, but didn't take the time to try to sort out all the technical language. "Did you test for all the new designer drugs? Is there something you could have missed?" Breen's left eyebrow rose a fraction of an inch, a sure sign that he was not pleased at having his judgment questioned. "I mean, the thing is that this kid's behavior was just so totally out of character. He'd gotten in trouble a couple of times, but as far as I can tell he was never violent. So unless he'd started using drugs, nothing makes sense at all. Can you run those tests again?"

Breen dropped the file to the desktop, folded his hands on top of it, and looked directly at Detective North. "We've run the screens three times. We test for every known substance. The kid hadn't eaten in probably twelve hours, but that's all. Whatever was going on inside his mind, his body was squeaky clean when he attacked that woman."

North leaned forward slightly. "Then what the hell happened?"

"Well, some people get a bit cranky when they're hungry," Breen observed. Then his tone changed, and he spread his hands helplessly. "Okay, I doubt it was the low blood sugar. Frankly, it looks to me like he just flipped out. It happens. Have you checked with his family doctor? Did he have a shrink?" He opened the file again to the front page. "He was at St. Isaac's. Have you talked to his priest?"

"No prior history, no shrink, priests won't say much," North said.

Breen returned the file to the stack on his desk and leaned back in his chair, a sure sign that the interview was coming to an end. "Whatever happened to this boy stemmed from a disease of the mind, not the body," Breen said. "Sorry I can't be of more help."

North rose to his feet and shook hands with Breen across the desk, then left the office. He could hear the Medical Examiner resume dictating even before he'd closed the door, and remembered too late that he'd forgotten to replace the stack of papers on the chair. He paused for a moment, then continued down the hall, unwilling to have to reintroduce himself to Breen twice within ten minutes. Let him find his own damn files.

As soon as he was back in his car, North called Kevin Peterson. "Well, so much for that," he said when his partner came on the line. "No drugs—nothing. Which means we're back to square one."

North hated square one.

CHAPTER 22

ABDUL KAHADIJA CLOSED and locked the door behind him. The simple act of escaping his daily ritual, setting aside this time for prayer, filled his heart with peace.

He pulled down the window shade against the afternoon sun, and drew the heavy curtains, shutting out much of the city noise.

Yes. Better.

Much better.

Quiet. Peaceful.

He opened the closet, retrieved a box from the top shelf and set it on his bed. Slowly, reverently, he unpacked his *kufi* and *thobe,* laying them out on the bed, then carefully put the ancient prayer rug on the floor, orienting it precisely toward Mecca.

Next, he stripped off his clothes and entered the bathroom. With no time to bathe again completely, he began the cleansing ritual he followed five times each day.

"In the name of Allah," he said, then ran warm water over his hands.

When cleansed three times from head to foot, he slipped into the gray, floor-length *thobe* and settled the white knit *kufi* on his head.

He stood for a moment, facing Mecca, ready to offer his prayers to Allah. But he must still his mind first.

The mission—the mission of ultimate vengeance—was at last approaching fruition, and the excitement of it interfered with his concentration.

But it must not interfere with his prayers.

He must not risk angering Allah, for this week at the mosque he would ask Allah to guide him to the one who could provide the last bit of information he required.

His heart rate increased as he visualized it, standing silently, eyes closed. This quest was his: only he understood all the myriad details that made the plan possible.

He must be infinitely careful, make not even the slightest mistake. Just one inappropriate word, a single glance or gesture, and years of planning would go to waste.

That could not happen.

He would not let that happen.

Abdul's left hand began to curl into a fist.

He relaxed his hand. The moment for retribution had yet to come.

This was the time for prayer and worship.

This was the time to escape from the pain of life and sink into the arms of Allah and the blissful anticipation of all that Allah promises to the faithful.

Taking a deep breath and putting all worldly matters aside, Abdul began. "I intend to offer two *Rikat* of *Faird, Fajr* prayer for Allah."

He assumed the *qiyam* posture, hands to his ears, and all thought vanished except the all-encompassing, fierce love for his god.

"Allah u Akbar," he whispered.

Allah is the greatest.

Chapter 23

THE FIRST THING Darren Bender saw as he opened the door to the library was Sofia rising to her feet, her gaze fixed on him, and no hint of any kind of smile either in her eyes or on her lips. Still, there was no doubt that she'd been waiting for him, and even before the door had closed behind him, she cocked her head toward the farthest corner of the room and walked toward the stacks.

Darren put his books down on a table and followed, using a different aisle but catching up with her by the windows. Taking her arm he turned her around, and whatever faint hopes he'd been nursing for a quick kiss instantly evaporated as he saw her eyes, red and puffy from crying.

"Hey," he whispered. "What's wrong? Where have you been? I've been calling."

Sofia ignored his questions. "What did Father Sebastian do to you?" The words came more as a challenge than anything else.

Darren recoiled a step back, almost as if he'd been struck. "Nothing! He talked to me and I have to go see him again tonight after school, but there was nothing special."

"Nothing?" Sofia echoed, her voice starting to rise. "You're kidding me, right?"

"Shhh!" Darren took a quick look behind him to be sure the librarian wasn't anywhere around, then moved closer to Sofia, and lowered his voice. "What happened?"

Sofia shook her head almost as if she was trying to rid herself of the memory. "Sister Mary David locked me in a chapel and made me pray on my knees for—" Her voice suddenly faltered. How long had she been praying? She couldn't quite remember. It had seemed like forever, but how long had it really been? And suddenly she couldn't even remember what the chapel had looked like! It had looked strange, and scary, but . . .

But she couldn't remember any of the details.

Only how frightened she'd been, and how much her knees had hurt, and her body had ached.

She looked up at Darren, and he could see tears pooling again in her lower lids. "It must have been hours," she went on, her voice breaking. "And then I had to go to confession, but Father Sebastian wouldn't absolve me."

Darren took one of her hands and held it in his own. What was she talking about? The priests always absolved you after confession. That was supposed to be the whole point, wasn't it? "What do you mean, he wouldn't absolve you?"

Sofia spread her hands helplessly. "Just that! He wouldn't do it. And I have to go back there again tonight."

An uncertain frown furrowed Darren's brow. "But what we did wasn't that bad," he began.

"It's not fair!" Sofia cut in, a tear dripping off her lower lashes and sliding down her cheek. "You don't have to do any penance at all? I don't believe it!"

"I don't know yet," Darren said. "Father Sebastian said he was going to think about it." He gently wiped the tear from her cheek with his thumb. "I'm really sorry—"

"Everybody's easier on boys!" Sofia broke in. "You guys get away with everything."

Though Darren knew Sofia's words weren't quite true, he also knew better than to argue, at least right now. "Don't worry," he said. "Father Sebastian's cool."

Sofia bit her lip as she struggled to stop crying. "I thought so, too," she sniffled. "But I don't want to have to go back to that place Sister Mary David took—"

As the words died on Sofia's lips, Darren could suddenly feel someone right behind him. He dropped Sofia's hand as he felt a tap on his shoulder and whirled around to find Sister Cecelia standing behind him. The librarian held her finger to her lips and glowered at him. "Quiet," she said, the single word stinging like the lash of a whip even though she'd barely whispered it. "This is a study period."

Darren nodded, his gaze going to the floor.

"And you," the nun pressed, shifting her gaze to Sofia. "You need to be studying, not flirting."

"But I wasn't—"

The nun's nostrils flared. "Three rosaries for talking back," she pronounced. "And I suggest you go back to your seats." When neither Darren nor Sofia moved, she spoke one more word: "Now."

"No," Sofia said, her voice suddenly rising. Darren put his hand on her arm, but it was too late. "I get three rosaries for talking back? All I was doing—"

The nun turned and fixed her with a steady gaze. "All you were doing was flirting," she said.

"But it wasn't just me!"

"Sofia," Darren whispered, trying to warn her off as he saw the nun's countenance freeze into a mask of anger.

Too late.

"All I'm saying is that I shouldn't be the only one who's punished for something both of us were doing."

"Insolence earns you two more rosaries," the nun decreed, her gaze unwavering. "Now are you going back to your seat, or shall we go see Father Sebastian?"

"We're going back to our seats," Darren said before Sofia could make things any worse. "And we apologize. We're really sorry—"

Sister Cecelia silenced him with a glance, turned around, and stalked back between the rows of bookshelves to her station. Darren put a hand on the small of Sofia's back and guided her to follow the nun back to the study area.

"*I* don't apologize," he heard her whisper fiercely over her shoulder.

Darren's eyes flashed toward the librarian, certain they were about to get in trouble all over again, but Sister Cecelia was already talking to someone else, and from the look on the girl's face, Darren was pretty sure she was getting a few Hail Marys, too.

Then he remembered what Sofia had said about Father Sebastian not giving her absolution. What was that about? Was he, too, going to be locked into a chapel and forced to pray on his knees for hours and then go to confession?

And what about Sofia? Why would she have to go to confession again? Wasn't once enough?

Then, out of nowhere, the words he'd spoken to the detective about Kip Adamson rose unbidden from his memory:

. . . he started going to confession practically every day . . .

Darren's stomach suddenly felt hollow.

† † †

Father Sebastian opened the closet in the small vestry and took the white linen surplice—the only garment still inside—from its hanger. He slipped it on over his cassock, and adjusted it so that it fell smoothly to midthigh, and the open sleeves hung exactly as they should.

Satisfied with the surplice, he picked up the purple stole—perfect for the sacrament he was about to perform, kissed it reverently, and slipped it around his neck.

As he moved to close the closet door, he saw a flicker of a reflection in the small mirror hanging on the inside of the door.

His father!

But of course it wasn't his father—it couldn't have been. It was only himself, catching his own reflection in half-profile, the silver of his temples becoming more prominent every day, just as had that of his father's so many years ago.

Father Sebastian turned and looked directly into the mirror, gazing deeply into his own eyes, then abruptly closed the door.

Vanity had no place in his life—not now, not ever.

As the bells in the main chapel began to chime faintly, he quickly placed around his neck the chain holding the silver cross his mother had given him on the day he was ordained, poured wine into the chalice, and picked up the small leather box that held the host.

He stepped through the vestry door into the tiny chapel in which he'd heard Sofia Capelli's confession less than twenty-four hours earlier.

It was still empty.

He lit two candles, one on either side of the altar, then turned the lights down until only the glow of the candles was left, casting flickering shadows around the chamber. As he laid the chalice and the host on the altar, he heard the chapel door open behind him.

† † †

Even as she pushed open the door in front of her, Sofia Capelli had no clear memory of what lay beyond it. It seemed as if it had taken hours to drag herself here, moving through the maze of corridors as if guided by an unseen hand, never certain where she was, nor whether she was going in the right direction. Yet here she was, standing in the near darkness, the oaken door swinging slowly open to reveal a chapel lit only by two flames. As she stepped inside, it all came back to her.

Father Sebastian stood at the altar, praying. The confessional stood dark and empty at one end of the room, the giant tortured Christ loomed over everything else.

She tried not to look at the twisted face of the crucified Savior, but the gaze of the Christ seemed to command her own, and for a long moment she stood transfixed at the door, her hand clutching her sweater tight around her neck as if its thin material could protect her from the chill that was spreading through her body.

Father Sebastian turned. "Hello, Sofia. Please come in."

His voice was soft and welcoming, and without even thinking about it, Sofia took a tentative step forward.

"Don't be afraid, my child. There is nothing to fear here in God's house." As his warm voice dispelled some of the cold that had seized her body, he offered her a gentle smile. "Come. Let us complete your penance and absolution. Together we shall banish even the impulse to sin."

His voice washed over her like a cleansing bath and as he held out his hand to her she approached the altar.

Her fingers touched his.

"We shall pray together, Sofia," the priest said, his kind brown eyes gentle in the candlelight. "Then I will ask you to prostrate yourself on the floor in front of Christ while I give you absolution. We shall finish with the sacrament of the Eucharist."

Sofia said nothing, knowing no response was expected.

"Tonight we are dealing with the evil that dwells within you," Father Sebastian said.

Evil? What was he talking about? All she and Darren had done was make out a little bit. But, so what? It wasn't like they'd actually been having sex, or had done something really wrong. What kind of evil was he talking about? Even if what she and Darren had done was some kind of sin—which she supposed it probably was—that still didn't make her evil, did it? On the other hand, Sofia had learned long ago not to argue with priests, so when Father Sebastian indicated that it was time for her to lie on the stone floor, she did as she was told.

The floor instantly brought back the chill that had come over her the moment she opened the door to the chapel, its cold reaching right into her bones.

Father Sebastian paced slowly in front of the altar, murmuring softly, but Sofia was barely listening, concentrating instead on holding the ache in her bones, the cold in her body, and the fear in her soul at bay. Soon it would be over. Soon it would *have* to be over.

Soon she would hear the words of absolution.

Father Sebastian's voice droned on, and Sofia's mind began to drift until all of it—the pain in her body, the flickering light of the candles, even the priest's whispering voice and time itself—began to blend into a single strange sensation. It was as if she was floating, borne aloft on unseen wings . . .

† † †

"Rise to your knees," Father Sebastian commanded.

All the cold and aching and fear from which Sofia thought she had been released came flooding back, and as she struggled to get up she thought she might pass out. Finally, though, she was on her knees and crossing herself, bowing her head low.

Father Sebastian opened the pyx and took a single wafer. "On the night of his arrest, Jesus took bread, and after giving thanks to God, broke it and said, 'This is my body which is for you; do this remembering me.' "

Tipping her head back, Sofia opened her mouth and the priest placed the wafer on her tongue.

"After supper," Father Sebastian continued, "Jesus took the cup and said, 'This cup is the new covenant sealed in my blood; whenever you drink it, do this remembering me.' " He handed Sofia the chalice, and she sipped the wine, then bowed her head once more, waiting for the benediction.

But Father Sebastian didn't begin the benediction. Instead, he began to speak in Latin, his voice intoning cadences she'd never heard before.

She tried to concentrate, to understand what he was saying, but she recognized none of the words at all.

The ache in her bones and the cold suffusing her body was even worse now, and once again she felt as if time itself was warping, and she would never be released from this penance.

She blinked, then squinted her eyes. The stones on the floor seemed to have fuzzy edges.

Then they began to slide around, their shapes moving in strange patterns her eyes could barely follow.

Suddenly dizzy and feeling totally disoriented, Sofia reached for Father Sebastian's cassock to steady her, but her arms had become too heavy even to lift. "I'm going to be sick," she started to whisper, but even before she could make her lips move, dark clouds began to swirl around her mind.

For an instant—just an instant—Sofia tried to fight the darkness that was closing in around her, but a moment later it was too late. She gave herself over to the clouds and the darkness and silently begged to be once more borne aloft, away from the dark chapel with its cold stone floor.

The darkness closed around her. . . .

† † †

Father Sebastian heard Sofia's tiny cry and turned just in time to see her collapse onto the stone floor.

He dropped instantly to his knees, his fingers closing on her limp wrist.

Her pulse was strong and steady.

The chapel door opened, and Father Sebastian looked up to see Father Laughlin and Sister Mary David stepping over the threshold.

"Oh, my goodness," Father Laughlin gasped as he saw Sofia's body sprawled on the ground. "Is she all right?"

"Of course she's not all right," Father Sebastian snapped. "If she were all right, would she be here at all?" He glanced up at the old priest, whose face had visibly paled even in the flickering yellowish candlelight. "But I believe she may be in far more trouble than I thought. Fainting is often the result of feeding the flesh and blood of Christ to someone who is possessed by evil."

Both Father Laughlin and Sister Mary David crossed themselves.

Father Sebastian lifted Sofia from the cold floor. "But she *will* be all right," he said softly, adjusting his arms to cradle Sofia's head. "If we do our job correctly, our faith will cleanse her."

Father Laughlin hurried to open the door to the vestry, and Father Sebastian carried the girl through.

Sister Mary David followed, pulling the vestry door closed behind her.

The two candles that provided the only illumination in the chapel flickered, then went out.

The chapel plunged into the same darkness that had swallowed up Sofia Capelli's soul a few moments earlier.

† † †

Ryan McIntyre searched St. Isaac's cavernous dining room for a familiar face among the churning sea of students, saw no one he recognized, and got in line to fill his tray. As he picked up a napkin rolled around some silverware, he scanned the room once more.

A hand popped up and waved at him.

Melody Hunt.

And she was now signaling that she'd saved him the seat next to her own.

Praying that she wasn't simply seizing an opportunity to talk about Catholic History, Ryan threaded his way down the narrow gap between the long rows of chairs that flanked the tables, nearly tripping twice, recovering himself, but still managing to slop a quarter of his Coke onto the plate of meatloaf, mashed potatoes and gravy that made up the dinner.

It didn't really look like the Coke was going to make much difference.

He set his tray in the empty space next to Melody, and squirmed onto the chair. "Hi." He sighed as he unrolled the napkin from around the silver.

Melody eyed his plate, then grinned at him. "Coke on mashed potatoes? Maybe I should have let you find somewhere else to sit."

"Wouldn't have mattered," Ryan said, sweeping the room with his eyes. "There isn't any other place. But who knows? Maybe Coke on potatoes is really good." He looked around and saw that most of the people he knew were already there. Across from Melody sat Clay Matthews, flanked by Stacy Lowell and Darren Bender. José and Tim sat on the other side of Melody, and even though it was only his second day at St. Isaac's, he seemed to have become a member of the group.

Maybe it wasn't going to be so bad after all.

"Where's Sofia?" he heard Clay ask Darren.

Darren rolled his eyes. "Doing penance."

"For what *you* did?" Stacy asked. "You gotta be kidding."

"Maybe we don't know all they did," Tim Kennedy said, trying—and failing—to leer suggestively.

"Well, they must have done something to get that kind of punishment," José offered.

"So?" Clay asked, digging his elbow into Darren's side. "Are you holding out on us? Come on—give!"

"Stop it," Darren said. "What we did was nothing."

Ryan started to pick up his fork, but Melody instantly put her hand on his wrist and nodded toward the nun who stood at the head of their table.

The room fell silent.

Clay leaned over toward Darren. "Where's Father Laughlin?" he whispered, his lips barely moving.

"Silence!" the nun commanded.

Every head in the room suddenly bowed, and the boy next to Ryan held out his hand.

Confused, Ryan looked at it, then looked around and realized that everyone in the room was holding hands. He took the boy's fingers uncertainly, but when Melody slipped her hand into his other one, he decided maybe this wasn't such a bad idea after all. He'd just have to remember not to squeeze the wrong hand.

If he could work up the nerve to squeeze any hand at all.

Then, as the nun began the blessing, Ryan felt just the tiniest amount of pressure on the fingers Melody was holding.

Ever so slightly, he tilted his head to look at her out of the corner of his eye.

She had her head bowed, and her eyes were closed.

But she was smiling.

Ryan closed his eyes, too, but there was now no way he could concentrate on the blessing. Instead, he returned the little squeeze Melody had given him, and when the chorus of students said "Amen," he opened his eyes and turned to look at her.

She was blushing.

And he was grinning.

And everybody else was staring at both of them.

Ryan decided he didn't care.

Things at St. Isaac's were, indeed, looking better and better.

Chapter 24

FALLING!

Sofia Capelli was falling through a darkness so black it was almost palpable. She could see nothing, feel only the sensation of the aching cold, and the dizzying effect of the endless fall.

Cold.

Dizzy.

Then an acrid stench scorched her nostrils and she jerked awake.

She wasn't falling, but she was still cold.

Her back was freezing; her bones still ached.

She lay silent, searching for the memory of what had happened to her, but all she found was an overwhelming feeling of dread.

Dread, and the awful sensation of falling.

Once again the sharp smell of smoke choked her and now she opened her eyes, looking up to see Father Sebastian, Father Laughlin and Sister Mary David, all gazing down on her.

And looking worried.

She must have fainted.

Sister Mary David swung a censer filled with burning incense over her, and Sofia flinched away from the curling spiral of smoke that drifted toward her nose.

She tried to sit up, but her arms and legs didn't work. She was too weak. *What was happening?*

"She is with us again," Father Sebastian said so softly that Sofia could barely hear him.

She opened her mouth to speak, formed the words in her mind, but nothing emerged from her lips. Nothing, anyway, but an unintelligible sound that was little more than a faint moan. She wanted to rub her eyes, to rub away the dizziness from her mind, erase the fog from her vision. But something was holding her back.

Something on her wrists.

A rope!

She twisted her head around and caught a glimpse of the thick, black velvet cord that ran through iron rings and held each wrist and each ankle firmly to—

A table! A cold, hard table made of solid stone!

Why?

What had she done that they had to tie her down?

Once again she struggled to speak; once again only a garbled, rasping sound emerged from her lips.

"Do not speak," Father Sebastian said. "Do not give voice to the demon."

Demon?

Sofia looked around frantically. What was he talking about? Where was she? What had happened to her?

Again she struggled against her bonds, but they felt more like they were made of steel than of velvet.

She tried once more to speak, focusing her eyes on Father Laughlin's kind old face and concentrating on forming the first syllable of his name, but when she finally opened her mouth, only a stammering "F-F-F . . ." sound came out.

And Father Laughlin turned his face away.

Her chest heaving with fear, her eyes blurred with unshed tears, Sofia stopped struggling and lay still on the table. She tried to think, tried to cut through the fog that muddled her mind, tried to remember.

Then she saw it.

A giant cross suspended upside down, just above her.

The top of the cross had been sharpened to a point—a glittering point of gold—and it seemed to be directly above her heart.

What were they going to do to her?

Sofia's eyes found Sister Mary David, but this time when she tried to speak all that came out of her mouth was a sibilant hiss.

A dream!

It had to be some kind of terrible dream.

It couldn't be real.

Sister Mary David recoiled from Sofia's strange hiss, crossed herself, and continued to swing the censer.

"Let us now confront the evil in this child's soul," Father Sebastian intoned, "that we may then drive it from her forever."

As the priest's right arm came up and he extended his fingers toward her, Sofia felt a terrible nausea rising in her belly. She howled again, terrified that he was about to touch her, and whipped her head back and forth.

What was happening?

Why was she terrified of him?

Why did she feel so sick?

And if it was a dream, why wasn't she waking up?

"Silence, demon." Father Sebastian was looming over her now, and suddenly she could see something in his eyes she'd never seen before.

Hatred.

Pure, furious, hatred.

Sofia cringed, tears leaking from the corners of her eyes.

Father Sebastian began speaking in Latin, but again they were words Sofia had never heard before, in an unfamiliar rhythm.

Then he was making signs with his hands, and moving around her as the cadence of his chant increased.

The room began to spin as Father Sebastian circled her, and now her nausea threatened to overwhelm her. Her stomach lurched, and she struggled hard not to throw up.

Is this really happening?

"The blood of the goat," Father Sebastian demanded, and Father Laughlin quickly handed him a small, dark bottle.

Sofia shrank from Father Sebastian as if he held an asp in his grip.

Forcing the fingers of her left hand open, the priest tipped the vial so the blood ran onto her palm, then did the same with the other hand.

A terrible stench began to rise from Sofia's hands and the blood oozed across her palms and began to drizzle between her fingers.

Father Sebastian circled around her, his deep voice chanting, his hands etching patterns in the air above her.

Sofia's palms began to burn.

She craned her neck to look at her hands, which now had smoke curling up from what looked like charred flesh. "Burning!" she screamed, finding her voice at last.

"Silence the demon!" Father Sebastian commanded.

Sister Mary David instantly forced a washcloth into Sofia's mouth, binding it in place by wrapping some kind of scarf tightly around her head, completely covering her mouth and barely leaving any room for her to suck air in through her nostrils.

Panic began to rise in Sofia—she couldn't get enough air through her nose, and her hands were on fire!

She squeezed her eyes shut as if blinding herself might make it stop happening.

What kind of nightmare is this?

Then she felt fingers beginning to unbutton her blouse.

Her eyes flicked open and she found herself gazing into Father Sebastian's eyes.

She wanted to fight him, but her hands were burning and all her energy was being drained by the struggle merely to keep breathing.

Father Sebastian spread her blouse wide, then unhooked her bra, exposing her naked breasts.

As her terror rose, Sofia's breath threatened to fail completely. Father Sebastian turned his back to her, and she felt a brief instant of hope, but then he turned back, holding a bloody mass of pulp in his hands. Gently—reverently—he laid the thing on her chest, and a terrible chill ran through her body as if the bloody thing itself were sucking the warmth out of her.

Father Sebastian began chanting again, and Father Laughlin lowered the crucifix hanging above her until its glittering point touched the thing on her chest.

The mass of pulp suddenly began to throb, and Sofia instantly knew what it was: the bleeding heart of whatever creature it was whose blood had burned the palms of her hands.

Now she felt something growing inside her, as if some terrible presence was awakening, crowding her out, pushing her aside with every beat of the evil heart that lay over her own.

Sister Mary David helped Father Sebastian off with his stole, then his surplice, and finally he pulled his cassock over his head.

He stood above Sofia, clad only in a gray hair shirt, which hung to his knees.

Sister Mary David untied the string that held it closed at the back of his neck and opened it wide.

Father Laughlin handed Father Sebastian a short whip that ended in a profusion of metal-barbed leather thongs. As Sofia watched in horror, Father Sebastian held the whip to his lips, murmured some unintelligible words, then raised the lash high.

Sofia shrank against the stone, trying to steel herself against the agony to come, and watched helplessly as the whip began its arc.

But instead of slashing down on her, it whipped across Father Sebastian's head and shoulders, cutting not into Sofia's flesh, but that of his own back.

Yet even as Sofia watched each stroke of the flagellum as it slashed into the priest's flesh, she felt exactly as if each lash were biting into her own body.

Felt it as surely as if he were whipping her rather than himself.

She thrashed against her bonds now, trying to scream, feeling the flesh stripping off her back every time Father Sebastian took the whip to his own skin.

And the presence that had awakened within her began to grow angry. She felt it, hot and vibrant inside her chest.

Inside her mind.

She felt it trampling her own thoughts and emotions, shoving them aside to make more room for its own fury.

Blood spattered her face as Father Sebastian slashed his back over and over again. Sofia's tongue tried to work its way past the wad of cloth that filled her mouth to taste the priest's blood.

At last Father Sebastian stopped his flagellation, reached back, and gathered a handful of ruined flesh and skin from his back. He looked down on Sofia, so close she could feel the heat of his heaving breath on her face.

He drew something on her forehead with a bloody forefinger. The heart on her chest gave one more mighty heave, then exploded in a fountain of gore as the cross above her burst into flames.

The beast within her roared, erupting with rage.

Sofia sat up, breaking the velvet ropes as if they were nothing but threads, and hurled the flaming cross aside.

Father Laughlin and Sister Mary David backed away, their eyes wide with terror, but Father Sebastian stood his ground and met Sofia's furious gaze with no sign of any fear at all.

He raised his right hand, and suddenly his voice filled the chamber. "It is through my blood that you exist and you are bound to my bidding," he declared. "I command you to submit!"

Sofia felt the presence inside her gathering to lash out at the priest, but suddenly Father Sebastian placed his broad right hand over her face.

He squeezed.

"Submit!"

As the single word echoed off the chamber's stone walls, all the strength drained out of Sofia, and she sagged back on the pallet.

Father Laughlin doused the burning cross with holy water, then righted it and replaced it on the wall as Sister Mary David removed Sofia's gag, refastened her bloody bra and buttoned her ruined blouse.

Sofia lay limp while she was being ministered to. She had no energy, but no more fear either.

It was over.

Yet the presence inside her still remained. It had been calmed, but not banished.

Sofia curled up on the cold stone, wrapping her arms around her knees as Sister Mary David cleansed Father Sebastian's wounds, then helped him on with his vestments.

When he was once again fully dressed, Father Sebastian leaned against the table, his chest still heaving from his exertions. "Give me a few moments," he said softly. "Then we shall finish it."

CHAPTER 25

RYAN FINISHED THE last of the algebra problems, closed his
math book, and stretched his cramped muscles. If he were
still at home, he'd go out and run a few blocks before he went to bed,
but a glance at the clock told him it was only twenty minutes until
lights out. But even if there was enough time, he didn't really want to
run up and down Beacon Hill, at least not just before going to bed.
Sighing, he picked up the Catholic History text and flipped to the first
of the pages that Melody had flagged for him after dinner.

He could feel his eyes getting heavy with just the first paragraph
but steeled himself to keep going. *You don't get into Princeton with
anything less than A's,* he reminded himself. But in Catholic History?
What was that about? Wasn't it the same as real history? Not that it
made any difference—in this case, at least, it was only the grade that
counted. Besides, there wasn't anything else to do until Clay came out
of the bathroom and he'd have his turn to shower.

Taking a deep breath he finished the first of the highlighted para-
graphs—which seemed to be trying to defend the Spanish Inquisition
the same way Father Sebastian had this morning—and turned to the
next section, which looked like it was going to have something to do

with satanism. When his cell phone vibrated and he saw Melody Hunt's name on the caller ID, he happily pushed the book aside.

"Well, speak of the devil," he said.

If Melody got his attempt at humor, she ignored it. "Ryan, Sofia's not back in our room yet," she said, and even over the bad cellular connection, Ryan could hear the worry in her voice. "I went looking for Sister Mary David but couldn't find her. And the nun in the admin office said that Sofia was in the infirmary."

"The infirmary?" Ryan echoed.

"Yes! But when I asked what was wrong with her, the nun told me it was none of my concern, and when I called the infirmary, nobody even answered!"

"What do you mean, they didn't answer?"

"Just that! There wasn't anybody there!"

"Maybe they were taking care of Sofia," Ryan suggested. "If she's sick, or cut herself or something, they might just be too busy to answer the phone."

"But I'm worried!" Melody insisted, her voice trembling.

"Can't you just go to the infirmary and ask to see her?"

"No," Melody wailed. "They have rules about visitors, and even if they didn't, it's almost lights out."

Ryan thought for a moment, fingering the edges of the textbook he didn't really want to read. "How about if I go? Even if I don't make it back in time and get caught, I can pretend I was coming back from the library, and got lost."

"Would you really do that?" Melody asked.

"Why not?" Ryan countered, putting more bravado into his voice than he was really feeling. "I mean, what are they going to do, kick me out?" Melody's silence was enough to tell him that she thought that might very well be exactly what they'd do. "Besides," he went on. "I'm not going to get caught." Before Melody could try to talk him out of it, Ryan snapped his phone closed, stuck his head in the bathroom to tell Clay he'd be back before lights out, and stuffed his map of the school into his pocket.

† † †

Less than two minutes later he was at the door to the infirmary, which occupied half of the second floor of a building that looked like it might once have been a private home, but had been absorbed by the school so long ago that most of its original rooms had long since vanished. And all Ryan found at the top of the main staircase was a door.

A locked door, with a frosted glass panel.

And no light behind the panel.

Black-edged gold letters informed him that the infirmary was open daily from 7 AM to 3 PM. There was also an emergency phone number, which Ryan wasn't about to dial.

Instead he called Melody back.

"There's nobody here," he said as soon as she answered. "The door's locked and all the lights are off."

"There has to be somebody there. If Sofia's there, somebody has to be there," Melody protested. "If Sofia's sick, or got hurt or something, they wouldn't just turn the lights out and leave her by herself!"

"Well, unless there's some other way in besides the front door—"

"There *is* another way in!" Melody broke in. "Oh, God, why didn't I think of it before? The back way!"

"Back way?" Ryan repeated. "What are you talking about? There aren't any other doors here, and there aren't any on the main floor, either."

"You have to go though the basements," Melody told him. "Can you make it to the dining hall without getting caught?"

"Yeah."

"Then meet me there," Melody told him. "Right across the hall from the big dining room there's a door that leads to the stairs to the basements. I'll be there in a couple of minutes."

This time it was Melody who broke the connection, and for an instant Ryan was tempted to call her back and tell her it was too dangerous—she was sure to get caught. But even as the thought came to him, he rejected it, certain that Melody was already on her way and that no matter what he said, she was going to finish what he'd begun. Putting the phone back in his pocket, he started toward the dining hall. If he hurried, he'd barely make it before lights out.

After that, they'd just have to take their chances.

† † †

Melody was already waiting when Ryan got to the dining hall, holding the door ajar. As he slipped through and she pulled the door closed behind him, he checked the faintly glowing hands of his watch. They were now officially breaking the rules, and if they got caught, he might be able to plead ignorance, but Melody would be in serious trouble. "Maybe we ought to just go back to the dorms," Ryan said. "What if the nun didn't know what she was talking about?"

Melody shook her head. "She knew. And if they'd taken Sofia to the hospital, why wouldn't she tell me?"

"Maybe she just got it wrong," Ryan suggested.

Melody shook her head again. "Not Sister Frances. She never gets anything wrong—she's the only reason Father Laughlin can keep his job. She keeps track of everything for him." She started down the stairs. "Have you been down in the tunnels yet?" Now it was Ryan who shook his head. "There's hardly any light, so watch your step. But once you get to know them, the tunnels are the fastest way to get around the school, especially if you're going somewhere you're not supposed to.

"C'mon," Melody told him, glancing back over her shoulder. "It's not far. Down these steps, under the administration building and then the infirmary. All we have to do is go up the old back stairs that nobody ever uses anymore. I don't think anyone but the kids even knows they're there." She headed on down the stairs, and after only a second or two of hesitation, Ryan gripped the handrail and followed.

At the foot of the stairs a tunnel led off in either direction. A dim light glowed off to the left, but Melody turned to the right, where it seemed to Ryan that there was nothing but blackness.

She took his hand and led him forward. "Don't worry," she whispered. "I know exactly where we are, and I know exactly how far we have to go."

Ryan's heart started beating a little faster as she led him away from the light, but he told himself it was the excitement of holding her hand that was making his pulse speed up, not any kind of discomfort with the darkness.

They moved straight down the narrow corridor for several yards, then came to a second corridor, and Melody turned left. A few moments later she turned right again, and then, as the darkness started to make Ryan feel almost dizzy, he lost track of the next turns and didn't even try to keep track of how many steps he'd taken. If he lost his hold on Melody's hand, or if it turned out she didn't really know where they were going—

He put the thought out of his mind, not even wanting to think about the possibility of being lost down here in the tangle of dark corridors that seemed to lead nowhere. His heart was pounding now, and it seemed like it was getting harder and harder to breathe.

Then, as tendrils of panic were starting to twist around Ryan, Melody suddenly spoke.

"We're almost there."

"So far, so good," Ryan muttered, hoping his near-panic wouldn't show in his voice. "Is it really stuffy down here or—" he began, but Melody stopped so quickly he ran right into her.

"Shh!" she hissed, her fingers tightening on his hand.

Ryan leaned close so he was whispering into her ear. "What is it?"

"I heard—" Melody began, but then fell instantly silent.

This time, Ryan heard it, too.

A faint scraping sound, as if a door were brushing against the stone floor.

But was it opening, or closing?

And where was it?

Ryan strained his ears, but couldn't tell if it came from in front of or behind them.

"What should we do?" Ryan whispered.

"Shh," Melody repeated. "Listen."

Ryan stood absolutely still, trying not to breathe at all, ears straining, but heard nothing. Now, though, it wasn't just the darkness that felt like it was closing in on him, but the walls themselves.

He shivered involuntarily as his whole body suddenly broke out in a cold sweat.

All he wanted to do was run.

Run, and find the closest stairs that would lead him up and out of this labyrinth, into the clear, cool night air.

Melody was moving again, and Ryan forced his panic down once more, following her down what now felt like an endless corridor.

Endless, and closing further in on him with every second that passed.

It went on for what seemed like hours, the darkness so absolute that Ryan began to see things he knew couldn't be there at all.

Tiny lights winked at him, always vanishing as he turned to look at them.

He felt things close to him in the darkness, things he didn't want to imagine, let alone see.

His panic was once more building toward the breaking point when Melody suddenly stopped again.

"Okay," she whispered. "We're here. There are some stairs just to the left, and the infirmary is at the top of them."

Ryan wanted to push his way past her and run up the stairs, but held his growing terror of the darkness in check, letting her lead him to the foot of the stairs.

Then, just as he raised his foot to take that first step up, they heard another sound.

A footstep!

Then another!

Then more. And not just one person, either, but at least two.

And they were coming toward them, every step echoing louder.

Melody froze for an instant, then moved closer to Ryan until her lips were at his ear. "Follow me, and press against the wall." She said it so softly he barely heard her. A second later he felt her pulling him past the stairs, deeper into the darkness. His heart thundering, he held his breath as if any movement, even of his lungs, might betray them. He pressed himself against the wall, Melody beside him, her hand clinging to his.

They waited.

The footsteps drew nearer until Ryan was certain that whoever was there was not only coming directly toward them, but was about to run right into them.

The steps grew louder, and now Ryan could almost feel the presence of whoever was hidden in the blackness.

He steeled himself, waiting.

And then, at the last possible instant, the steps paused.

Ryan held perfectly still. Had they been heard? Had some tiny noise betrayed them? He waited, certain that at any second a flashlight would come on, blinding him as certainly as the darkness blinded him, but exposing him as well.

Exposing him, and Melody, too.

They would be caught.

And there was nothing he could do.

Silently, Ryan began to pray.

And the steps began again.

But no longer coming toward them. No! Now the steps were going up, climbing the stairs they had been about to climb themselves!

His heart still pounding, Ryan slowly exhaled. A moment later a glow of light emerged from the stairwell. Like a June bug drawn to light, Ryan moved toward the base of the stairs. Melody, still gripping his hand in her own, stayed so close behind him that he could feel the warmth of her breath on the back of his neck.

Stopping just short of the doorway to the staircase, Ryan listened. The footsteps were still audible, but sounded muffled, and when he finally risked a quick look up the stairs, he understood why. The stairs were built around a well, and whoever was climbing them had already made at least one turn.

Ryan's mind raced. Either they could go back the way they'd come, groping through the suffocating darkness, or they could sneak up the stairs, where there would be a way out that didn't involve having to pick their way through the maze of subterranean tunnels.

And there was the chance of finding out who else had been down here tonight.

The thought of the darkness—and the terrible claustrophobia that had gripped him—was enough to make up his mind for him. As the footsteps above grew fainter, Ryan started up the stairs, with Melody silently following.

After two turns they came to the first floor landing. A door—unlocked—led into a broad hallway at the end of which was a pair of old-fashioned double doors with panic bars—the kind that could only be locked from outside. And even from where they were, Ryan could see the school's huge interior courtyard through the glass of the double doors.

They were safe.

But above them, the footsteps had stopped, and now Ryan could hear muffled voices. The words themselves were inaudible, but one of the voices sounded worried, another impatient.

And Melody, her back to the wall so she was almost perfectly invisible from the well above, unless someone leaned over and looked straight down, had moved past him, and was sidling rapidly up toward the next turn. Ryan caught up with her just as she came to the intermediate landing, where she stopped. Pointing upward, she silently mouthed a single word: "Infirmary!"

Ryan peered upward to see the shape of a man, his shoulders draped in the cassock and stole of a priest, standing with his back to the railing around the stairwell.

Then, as they watched, the area above brightened as a light—apparently inside the infirmary—went on. The man turned, and for a terrible moment Ryan was sure he was going to look down. But instead, another shape appeared.

Another head, this one belonging to someone the man was carrying in his arms—someone who was unconscious. And though they got no more than a glimpse of the person the man was carrying, both Ryan and Melody knew instantly who it was.

Sofia.

Melody had been right.

Something was terribly wrong.

And there was nobody they could talk to about it.

CHAPTER 26

ARCHBISHOP JONATHAN RAND closed his office door behind the last member of the diocesan committee for the protection of children, returned to his desk, and slumped back into his chair. He had known that putting the Boston Archdiocese back together was going to be a long-term task, but he hadn't anticipated just how difficult and uncooperative his committee members were going to be. It seemed as if all they wanted to do was fight him on every point with endless, circuitous debate that ultimately resolved nothing. Indeed, every item on today's agenda had been tabled until next month amid claims that all of it needed additional research and further extrapolations. It was as if they hoped that simply by stalling, they could make the whole mess go away.

Rand was sick of it. He just wanted to make some headway, somewhere, in some area that mattered.

There was a soft knock on his office door, and the Archbishop glanced at the clock. Not even nine in the morning, and he felt as if he'd already put in an entire day's worth of very hard work. He sighed heavily, needing no one to tell him that ignoring whatever his assistant was bringing him wasn't going to go away.

The door opened and the seminarian appeared. "Father Laughlin from St. Isaac's, to see you."

The Archbishop nodded. "Give me five minutes, please, and then send him in, along with a cup of tea."

The seminarian nodded and backed out, silently closing the door behind him.

The Archbishop closed his eyes and systematically relaxed his body, beginning with his feet. He visualized soothing blue light going up his legs, infusing his hips, then moving up his spine to that place at the base of his skull where all the tension in both his mind and body seemed to come together, creating a painful knot. Using a technique he had learned from a Cardinal from India, he focused the visualized light on the knot, then concentrated on letting the knot itself dissolve and flow down his arms and drain out his fingers. Though he didn't profess to understand how the exercise worked, Rand had found that it never failed to revitalize him.

Faith, he knew, worked in a lot of ways.

When the seminarian again knocked, then opened the door bearing a steaming cup of tea and leading Father Laughlin in, the Archbishop was ready to meet the next challenge, his strength fully renewed.

"We have finally had a success," Father Laughlin announced as soon as they were alone.

The Archbishop lifted a skeptical brow. "Really?"

Father Laughlin's head bobbed, and when he picked up his cup of tea his hand trembled, though Rand wasn't sure it was from excitement or merely age. "I witnessed it myself," the priest said, leaning forward in his chair to lay a manila envelope on the Archbishop's desk. "Here is my report, though I'm afraid I am utterly unable to convey the magnitude of what happened last night. It was amazing to witness—absolutely astonishing. Truly, Father Sebastian has a gift!"

The Archbishop eyed the envelope warily. He knew about the work that had been going on at St. Isaac's, of course. Indeed, he'd been instrumental in bringing Father Sebastian to Boston after all his work at Notre Dame. Nor was he completely skeptical of the value of the work, for the rite of exorcism, he knew, could be a valuable tool. Though he himself had never been convinced that "demons" were the cause of psychological disturbances in people, he was also aware that if someone believed something was going to make them better, it often did.

It was simply another demonstration of the power of faith.

But still, he couldn't help but be somewhat skeptical of this remarkable statement from a man who had been a priest too long. On the other hand, it had been a long time since he'd had any good news at all to report to the Vatican, and something—anything—was better than nothing. "You saw this?" he asked cautiously. "You actually witnessed it yourself?"

Father Laughlin nodded and began to recount exactly what had happened last night in the tiny chapel beneath the school.

"What is the girl's condition this morning?" the Archbishop asked when Father Laughlin was finished. "Is she aware? Does she know what happened to her?"

"She's understandably tired this morning," the elderly priest replied. "She's calm and cooperative, and resting comfortably. She doesn't seem to have much memory of the event, but I shall never forget it. It was unquestionably one of the most remarkable things I've ever seen."

The Archbishop picked up the report and placed it on the stack of papers in his "In" box.

"And there is other good news," Father Laughlin said quickly, sensing that he was about to be dismissed.

Rand looked at him inquiringly. "Go on."

Father Laughlin was now fairly beaming. "I'm happy to say that absolutely no drugs were found in the Adamson boy's system."

The Archbishop lowered his head and gazed at the old man. "And how is that good news for us? If drugs were not the impetus for his irrational behavior, Ernest, then what was it?"

Father Laughlin cleared his throat. "Father Sebastian believes it was a manifestation of the evil that dwelt within the boy. An evil which he was unfortunately not successful in driving out."

Archbishop Rand's brief hope of being able to send good news to the Vatican evaporated; there was just no credibility here. "Is this in your report?"

Father Laughlin nodded. "Father Sebastian and I agreed we couldn't—and shouldn't—hide our failures. Certainly not from the Vatican. But both of us feel that the success last night far outweighs the earlier failure. It is of great significance. Possibly even global significance."

The Archbishop paused, but finally nodded, and then stood, signaling the end of the meeting. Father Laughlin struggled to his feet, and shook the Archbishop's outstretched hand.

"I shall forward your report to Cardinal Morisco," Rand said, "and I shall, of course, advise you of whatever response the Vatican may have."

Only when the elderly priest was gone did the Archbishop finally open the envelope and glance through the headmaster's report.

A successful exorcism, he decided, was possible.

But highly unlikely.

Still, he rang for the seminarian, and when he arrived, handed him the envelope. "Scan this into the St. Isaac school file, please, and fax a copy to Cardinal Morisco at the Vatican."

The young man took the envelope and left the office.

Archbishop Rand glanced through his daily calendar. More meetings. More wheel-spinning. More make-work without concrete results.

Is this what God had in mind when He had issued the call for young Jonathan Rand?

Apparently so.

The Archbishop allowed himself a moment of self-indulgent frustration, then sipped his tea and began to prepare for his next meeting, as, in the next room, the fax machine began transmitting Father Laughlin's report to Rome.

† † †

Melody Hunt stood just outside the main door to the infirmary, struggling to control her racing heart, to banish the tight knot of fear that had grown larger in her belly with every step she'd taken as she climbed the stairs. She composed her face into what she hoped was a concerned, but—most important—innocent, expression. The problem was that Melody's mother always knew when she was hiding something, and Melody was absolutely certain that the nun in the infirmary would be at least as able as her mother to read the guilt on her face the moment she walked through the door.

But despite her best efforts, her face had an awful wooden feel, exactly as it always did when she was trying to hide something.

Maybe she should just turn away from the infirmary and go back to her room. But she needed to see Sofia, no matter what the nuns might read on her face, and besides, wouldn't walking away seem even more suspicious than anything that might show in her expression?

Taking one final deep breath, Melody pushed her way through the door and saw two students, their faces pale and their eyes bloodshot, sitting unhappily in the anteroom, waiting to see the nurse.

Ignoring the sign-in sheet, Melody stood at the front desk, nervously shifting her weight from one foot to the other as she waited for one of the nurses to appear.

A moment later, the curtain separating the waiting area from the rest of the infirmary swished open, and Sister Ignatius, dressed in the white habit of a nurse, appeared, deftly closing the privacy curtain behind her. "Melody!" she said, automatically assessing the girl's condition with her practiced eye. "What are you doing here? I do hope there isn't a bug going around."

Melody relaxed slightly—at least she didn't appear nearly as nervous as she felt. "I just wanted to find out about my roommate. Sofia Capelli?"

The nurse visibly brightened. "Aren't you nice! But you could have just called us." She cast a sidelong glance toward the two students in the waiting area. "This isn't always the healthiest place to be," she went on. "Anyway, we would have told you that Sofia was doing fine. She just fainted. Low blood sugar, I imagine. Sometimes you girls simply don't eat right—there's nothing wrong with a little meat on your bones, you know."

As if the food would let anyone at St. Isaac's lose weight, Melody thought darkly, hoping Sister Ignatius wasn't about to go off on one of her famous rants about "maintaining a healthy weight," which, Melody thought, was at least forty pounds more than she herself ever intended to weigh. But to her immense relief, for once in her life, Sister Ignatius decided not to push her point. "Would you like to see her?"

"May I?" Melody replied, suddenly feeling a little better. If they were going to actually let her see Sofia, whatever was wrong couldn't be too bad, could it?

Sister Ignatius drew the curtain far enough aside for Melody to enter the examination room, and led her through to the small ward, where Sofia lay sleeping in one of the dozen beds that made up the infirmary. She wore a green hospital gown, her clothes neatly folded on the chair next to the bed.

Though she was asleep, her face had far more color than those of the students in the waiting area; in fact, Sofia didn't look much different than she always did in the morning.

Not wanting to waken her, but wanting even more to know exactly what had happened last night, Melody quietly approached the bed.

Sofia's eyes opened as she drew near.

"Hey," Melody said.

"Hey, yourself," Sofia replied.

"You okay?"

Sofia nodded, and Melody moved her clothes from the chair to the next bed and sat down as Sister Ignatius disappeared back through the curtains to start tending to her two new patients. "What happened?"

Sofia barely even glanced at her. "I don't know," she sighed. "I was in that chapel—the one I told you about—and Father Sebastian was giving me absolution, and the next thing I knew, I woke up here."

"You mean, like, you just fainted?" Melody was sure there had to be more to the story than Sister Ignatius had told her.

Sofia shrugged. "I guess so. Doctor Conover is going to come see me, and if everything's okay, they'll let me out this morning."

Melody's brows creased uncertainly. "Weird."

Sofia spread her hands dismissively. "I guess."

Melody wanted to tell Sofia what she and Ryan had done last night, slipping into the tunnels after lights out, and seeing her being carried up the back stairs, but with nothing separating them from Sister Ignatius, she couldn't take the risk. "I prayed for you this morning at matins," she said loudly enough to make certain the nun would hear. She was also sure the words would elicit at least a rolling of the eyes from Sofia, if not some kind of sarcastic remark, but all the other girl did was close her eyes.

"That's nice," Sofia said sleepily.

Melody cocked her head, her lips pursing slightly as she gazed at her roommate. "Sofia?" she finally said, touching Sofia's arm.

"Hmm?" Sofia didn't open her eyes, but pulled her arm away.

"I'm worried about you."

"I'm fine," Sofia said.

"Melody?" Sister Ignatius peeked through the curtain. "If you don't hurry, you'll be late for class."

"Okay," Melody replied, her eyes still on Sofia. "You need anything?"

Sofia shook her head.

"Okay, then," Melody said, standing up from the chair. "I'll see you later."

No response from Sofia.

Had they given her a sedative or something?

Melody put Sofia's clothes back on the chair, and smoothed their imprint from the sheet on the next bed.

"Bye," she whispered.

Sofia gave no indication that she'd heard.

Melody slipped past the nun, who was now taking the temperatures of the sick students, waved a thank you, and a few moments later joined the throng of students heading for their first period classes.

But she was still thinking about Sofia.

Sofia, who had said she was fine.

But she sure hadn't acted fine.

In fact, it was almost like Sofia wasn't there at all. The Sofia she had always known would have told Melody every detail about last night and recounted every feeling she'd had before she fainted. But even more than that, Sofia wasn't the kind of girl who ever even got sick, let alone fainted, and had always hated the whole idea of the infirmary so much that when Melody herself had been there last year, Sofia hadn't even been able to bring herself to come and visit. So, if she was "fine," why wasn't she demanding to know why she couldn't get out of the infirmary right now?

Why was she just lying there?

Maybe she should call Sofia's father. But what good would that do? According to Sofia, all her father ever did was drink, at least since her mother had taken off three years ago.

No, better to just wait until lunch, when she'd be able to talk with Sofia. She and Ryan would tell her what they'd seen last night and Melody would watch Sofia's reaction to the story.

She would watch it very carefully.

CHAPTER 27

CARDINAL GUILLERMO MORISCO'S stomach grumbled loudly
as he made the final entry in his personal log for the day, closed
the leather-bound volume, and slipped it into its slot next to the marble bookend. The thin slats of daylight that crossed his desk toward the
end of day had vanished hours ago, leaving only the glow of the evening
lights of Rome beyond the window. The Vatican had emptied of visitors and most of its employees; all that remained were those who
worked too late too often—among whom Cardinal Morisco had been
preeminent for decades—and the custodial staff, whose hours might be
late but weren't nearly as long as the Cardinal's. Still, Morisco enjoyed
being in the office after hours, when the quiet allowed him to accomplish far more than did the hum of the day.

But enough was enough, as his stomach had been reminding him for
the last hour. Indeed, he could almost taste his favorite wine, Sangrantino di Montefalco, from near his boyhood home in Umbria. This
evening he would order a light caprese salad and a grilled bruschetta
with a spicy olive tapenade, and go to bed early. It had been a long day.

He was just locking the desk drawer when the fax machine in his assistant's office whirred to life.

If he ignored it, he could be at Gianni's within moments.

If he responded to it, he may well be here for another hour.

He heard four pages drop before the machine paused and told him-self to leave it until morning even as he found himself drawn to the pages like a moth to a flame.

After all, one quick glance couldn't hurt, could it? If it were urgent, his phone would have rung. He tried to ignore the image that popped into his mind of a moth burning in the flame that had drawn it, but it was too late.

Then, as he picked the four sheets of paper from the fax machine, the computer on his desk pinged, announcing the arrival of an e-mail.

Certain the messages the two machines had brought were related, Morisco sighed heavily and tried to forget about the Sangrantino. This was how he ended up at the office so late, night after night, and as he carried the pages back to his office he vowed—again—to learn to leave at a reasonable time.

Tomorrow.

The cover page of the fax indicated it was from Archbishop Rand in Boston.

Cardinal Morisco sank onto his chair and began to read a report from someone named Father Ernest Laughlin, apparently having some-thing to do with a successful exorcism at a private school. This Father Laughlin certainly had a turgid way with his prose, he thought as he ploughed his way through the report.

"Never before have I seen the face of evil incarnate," the priest wrote. "Not only did I see its beastly, demonic face emerge from the features of this girl, who is little more than a child, but I witnessed Father Se-bastian Sloane bring it to submission and banish it from the girl's body, leaving her soul in peace."

Cardinal Morisco pensively tapped his fingers on the desk as he quickly reread the report. It wasn't much different from all of the simi-lar ones he'd seen over the years, each sent by some minor priest hoping to further his career. Only as he read the last sentence did he realize that this report had two differences.

The first, of course, was that Sebastian Sloane was a party to it, and

Sloane was a man the Vatican had been watching for several years already, each year bringing the young priest respect from ever-higher levels.

The second was the witness's assurance that he had seen the actual face of the demon.

That was important.

Cardinal Morisco laid the pages on his desk and leaned back in his chair. It would mean a great deal if Sloane had achieved such an accomplishment, especially in Boston, from whence good news had been a scarce commodity for years.

He would advise His Holiness of this event in the morning.

For now, though, a glass of wine awaited him at Gianni's.

Except that now the e-mail in-box on his computer had turned into the hypnotic flame, and he was no more able to resist its lure than he had the fax machine's a few minutes earlier.

He clicked open the file. Nothing in the subject line; nothing in the FROM box.

Just a video file.

Cardinal Morisco clicked on the icon, the media player opened, and the video began.

Morisco watched in fascinated silence as the ritual that had taken place in the chamber beneath St. Isaac's School played out before his eyes. Struggling to understand the words Father Sebastian Sloane was speaking over the girl bound to the stone slab, the Cardinal fiddled with the volume control, but it didn't really help.

Then the girl suddenly sat straight up, breaking the bonds that held her. One of the priests and the nun shrank back in fear, but Sloane faced the fury of the girl straight on.

Then the girl turned and looked directly into the camera.

Directly into Cardinal Morisco's eyes.

It was as if evil itself were hurtling out of the screen at him. Cold terror flooded through the Cardinal's body, and he shrank away from his computer exactly as the priest and nun had turned away from the girl herself.

Morisco gripped the arms of his chair, telling himself that nothing was happening.

Nothing at all.

It was only a video clip.

As the Cardinal watched, Sloane took the girl's face in his hands, shouted unintelligibly, and a moment later the girl sank into what appeared to be unconsciousness.

The file ended.

His heart racing, the Cardinal reached for the mouse to replay the video clip, but as the arrow hovered over the icon, he hesitated, part of him wanting to watch the video again, to try to understand what he'd seen. The other part—the stronger part—was still held in the grip of the terror that had reached right out of the computer screen to seize him.

He couldn't watch it again, at least not right now.

And not alone.

But neither could he simply turn off the computer, close his office, and go to Gianni's to enjoy a glass of wine and a light supper.

Cardinal Morisco looked up at the clock on the wall.

His Holiness would still be awake—he had always kept even longer hours than himself.

Making up his mind before he could change it, the Cardinal gathered the fax into a file folder, picked up his laptop, and headed for the Papal apartment, all thoughts of dinner extinguished.

He hoped—he prayed—that His Holiness would be able to tell him that what he had seen was merely an illusion.

But even as he silently formed the words of his prayers, he was all but certain that they would go unanswered.

Like Father Laughlin, Cardinal Morisco was certain that he had just looked into the face of evil, that it would haunt him every day of his life.

CHAPTER 28

SOFIA CAPELLI STOOD FROZEN at the dining room door, the din of two hundred teenagers talking and eating crashed over her like the surf pounding at a jetty. The racket sounded louder than usual, pummeling her with enough force that she felt oddly disoriented, as if she'd never been here before.

She peered around, and slowly things came into focus: the steam tables were off to the left, the trays and silverware were on a rack at the near end of the counter. As she started toward the rack, a girl across the room stood up and waved at her, then pointed to an empty seat. Though the girl looked familiar, Sofia couldn't quite remember her name.

And the people she was sitting with looked familiar, too.

But who were they? What was happening to her? Why couldn't she re—

Before she'd even finished the thought, Sofia's mind suddenly cleared, as if some kind of wall had simply dissolved.

Melody! That was it—the girl's name was Melody. They were roommates, and she'd come to visit her in the infirmary this morning.

Was it just this morning? But it seemed so long ago!

She picked up a tray and began filling it, first with silverware, then with food, even though she wasn't very hungry.

In fact, she wasn't hungry at all. Still, she took a few vegetables and a wilted-looking salad, drizzling a little dressing over the latter.

What was she even doing here? Why not go to her room and lie down and go to sleep?

Do what you're supposed to do.

The voice was so clear it made Sofia jump slightly, and she barely managed not to drop her tray. Regaining her balance, she glanced around, but there was no one—*nobody at all*—close enough to her to have spoken the words.

She reached for a glass of iced tea, saw her hand trembling, consciously steadied it, and added the tea to her tray.

As she picked up the tray, the strange words echoed in her mind: *Do what you're supposed to do.* But what was she supposed to do?

Eat lunch.

She looked around, saw an empty table in the far corner, and started toward it, ignoring Melody, who was once more waving at her.

She drank the iced tea straight down, wishing she'd taken two glasses.

She gazed at the food, which still held no interest for her at all.

"Hey!"

The voice behind her made Sofia jump, and she looked around to see a boy standing behind her. A boy whose face seemed familiar—*a boy she knew she knew!* But what was his name?

"Okay if I sit down?"

Darren! His name was Darren Bender, and he was—

Without waiting for her to reply, Darren put his tray on the table and dropped onto the chair across from her. "How come you didn't sit with us? Melody saved you a seat."

Sofia gazed uncertainly across the table. "Was I supposed to?"

Darren's head cocked slightly as he gazed quizzically at her. "You always do."

Sofia looked down at her salad and began to pick at it. If she always sat with Melody, why hadn't she done it today? *Because she hadn't remembered.*

"Are you okay?" Darren asked.

No, she wasn't okay. She wasn't okay at all. It was as if there were some kind of weird fog in her head that was hiding things from her.

"Sofia?"

She looked up at Darren, trying to figure out how to tell him what was happening, but no words came, and she felt tears of frustration begin to fill her eyes.

Darren leaned across the table, his voice dropping. "What did Father Sebastian do to you? All I got were four Hail Marys and four Our Fathers, and that was it. The whole thing took maybe five minutes."

Sofia gazed blankly at him. What was he talking about? And then, very slowly, it started to come back to her. Darren wasn't just someone she knew—he was her boyfriend.

But now, as she gazed across the table at him, she had a sudden urge to do something to him.

To hurt him.

He was looking at her again, his eyes fixed on her as if he knew what she was thinking. "What's going on?" he asked. "What did Father Sebastian do to you last night?"

Father Sebastian. A face floated up from Sofia's memory—a kindly face of a man with a soothing voice.

Father Sebastian?

"Nothing."

"Well, something sure happened to put you in the infirmary," Darren said.

"I don't know," Sofia said, struggling against the threat of her unshed tears. "I can't remember."

"You want me to take you back?" Darren asked. "If something's wrong—"

"No!" Sofia cut in. "I just need—" She frantically looked around the dining room as if searching for something—anything—that would help her, but there was nothing.

Then she saw the crucifix over the door, and a sharp pain stabbed through her abdomen. Her fingers automatically closed around the cross that hung from the string of rosary beads she always wore around her neck.

Impossibly, it seemed to writhe in her hand, squirming at her touch.

Her hand jerked away as if she had touched a hot iron, but her fore-finger caught on the string of beads. Instantly broken, it tumbled onto the table.

Sofia stared at it in mute horror. What had she done? The beads had been given to her by her grandmother, who had had them all her life!

"What's wrong?" Darren asked as he quickly began gathering the beads together before they could roll off onto the floor. "What's going on with you?"

Sofia said nothing, but held out her hand for the beads.

Hesitating only a moment, Darren dropped them into her open palm.

She felt the rosary begin to move the instant it touched her skin and stared at it in horror as it began to writhe like a handful of snakes.

Red hot snakes.

She rose to her feet as her nostrils filled with the sickly odor of burn-ing flesh, and a single word erupted from her throat. "Noooo!" she howled, hurling the beads and crucifix against the wall, where the decades of the rosary exploded and scattered across the floor.

Without so much as a glance toward Darren Bender or anyone else, Sofia Capelli fled.

Chapter 29

Six months into his Papacy, His Holiness Innocent XIV was no more used to the splendor of his changed surroundings than he was to his changed name. When he had first come to the Vatican forty years ago and met John XXIII in these same rooms, it had never occurred to him that he himself might one day occupy them. Indeed, the thought hadn't truly crossed his mind until the sixth vote of the last conclave, when he'd thought it must be a mistake when his name was read out as having received a single vote. On the seventh ballot, he'd received more than fifty votes, and had been elected on the tenth, an event that had stunned him even more than the world beyond the confines of the Sistine Chapel.

In his own mind he was still Pietro Vitali, from the Tuscan hills north of Rome.

And he still enjoyed eating a small and simple supper alone at his desk while he tried to complete the day's work, even though that desk was now in the Papal apartment. The moment he put his fork down on the empty plate, both plate and fork were whisked away by an attendant who seemed to appear out of nowhere by the kind of magic of which the Church thoroughly disapproved. As the servant disappeared as silently as he'd appeared, the Pope sipped his tea and spent a quiet moment enjoying the exquisite art that decorated the walls.

As he was reflecting on the poverty of the priesthood, a soft rap at the door announced the arrival of his final appointment of the day.

"Cardinal Morisco to see you, Your Holiness," the young Swiss priest, who served as his secretary, said as he opened the door.

With a sigh, the Pope rose from his desk chair. He didn't especially want to see Morisco this evening; he was tired and had an enormous amount of reading still to do before retiring, but the Cardinal had been insistent and tomorrow's schedule held no opportunities. He nodded his readiness to the secretary, and was already moving toward the door when Morisco appeared. The Cardinal kneeled to kiss the gold Fisherman's ring on his hand, but the Pope waved him back to his feet as the secretary vanished as silently as had the servant before him. "No need for that this late in the day, Guillermo. What is so important that you gave up your supper at Gianni's just to see the likes of me?" The Pope settled into a chair that had been especially built for his diminutive stature, and indicated that Morisco sit across from him.

"Seeing you is always a pleasure, Holiness," Morisco began, but once again the Pope brushed the formality aside.

"Why don't we just get to the point, so you can get to Gianni's and I—since I can no longer go to Gianni's with you—can get to my reading?"

"After you see what I've just seen," Morisco replied, dropping back into the easy familiarity he and Pietro Vitali had enjoyed for the last twenty years, "you might just want to go to Gianni's with me, or at least have a bottle of his best Sangrantino sent up here." As the Pope raised a skeptical brow, Morisco handed him the fax of Father Laughlin's report to Cardinal Rand in Boston.

The Pontiff scanned the document for no more than a few seconds. "Another exorcism?" he asked, groaning silently. When he had been established for a year or two, he would be able to brush off some of these things. But for now he'd do better to give up twenty minutes listening to Morisco than to spend those same twenty minutes arguing that he knew far too much about all the ancient rites to be impressed by yet another in what seemed to be a growing flood of reports on exorcisms that invariably proved to be nothing more than the fancies of some priest's overactive imagination.

Morisco shook his head. "I think this is something different." The Cardinal queued up the video clip and set the computer on the table next to the Pope's chair, then returned to his own seat.

A moment later, an image appeared, and the Pontiff watched as the ritual unfolded, turning up the sound.

"I'm afraid it's rather badly garb—" Morisco began, but the Pope held up a silencing hand, his eyes never leaving the computer screen.

As the rite proceeded, the Pope instantly recognized some of its elements, even though he'd never actually witnessed them before. As soon as the clip was over, he played it again, this time concentrating on the priest who was performing the rite.

The man worked with confidence.

He knew what he was doing.

He'd done it before.

When the video ended, the Pope tented his fingers, resting his chin on them, then straightened in his chair. "This is very interesting, Guillermo. You were right to bring it to me." The Cardinal visibly relaxed. "Tell me, who is behind this?"

"His name is Father Sebastian Sloane," Morisco replied, and the Pope felt his pulse quicken. "Until recently, he was a professor at Notre Dame."

"I know of him," the Pope said. "His doctoral dissertation was a study of our rites in the Dark Ages."

"Which, of course, you've read," Morisco dryly observed. "Why does that not surprise me?"

"After the results of the last conclave, I should think nothing would ever surprise you again, Guillermo," the Pope replied, a small grin playing around the corners of his mouth. "And don't pretend you didn't assume I'd read Sloane's dissertation—I believe I remember talking to you about it a year ago." He smiled wistfully. "At Gianni's, as I recall." His smile faded. "Where is Sloane now?"

"A small school in Boston."

"Boston?" the Pope echoed. "This took place in Boston?"

Morisco nodded, but said nothing.

"I want you to reply to Boston, Guillermo. Tell them that if Father Sloane can duplicate what I've seen here tonight, I will rearrange my post-Easter trip to include a visit to Boston."

"A visit?" Cardinal Morisco repeated, visibly shaken by the specter of rearranging at this late date what was already a complex schedule. "Your Holiness," he said, unconsciously retreating from the easy familiarity he'd shared with his old friend for so many years. "The agenda is set. We leave in a couple of weeks! To add another stop at this late—"

"Come now, Guillermo," the Pope said, holding up his hand so that the ring of St. Peter glittered in the light of the chandelier. "No plan of man's is ever set in stone. We must keep in mind that Boston is a failing Archdiocese, and that a visit from us might resuscitate its spirit." His deliberate use of the Papal "we," combined with his equally deliberate display of the golden symbol of his authority had exactly the effect the Pontiff had intended, and he could see Morisco beginning to calculate the logistics of effecting a change in the schedule. "If Father Sloane can re-create this, have him send us the proof. What we have seen could be illusory—a mere fluke. But if he can do it twice, then we will go to Boston and witness this ourselves."

"As you wish," Morisco said, though his expression clearly belied the calmness of his words.

"I am certain he will be able to do what we ask," the Pope said, rising to his feet. "So please plan accordingly."

Morisco rose as well. "I am your humble servant."

"We are all God's humble servants," the Pope observed. As they moved toward the door, he laid a hand on Morisco's shoulder. "Some of us, of course, are more humble than others." As they approached the door, it once again opened as if by magic, and his secretary appeared, ready to escort the Cardinal out of the apartment. As he watched Morisco go, Pope Innocent XIV found himself reflecting on the power of his new position, which allowed him to change even such a vast undertaking as a Papal tour simply by uttering a few words.

He must be very careful with such power; he must pray tonight for divine guidance so that he could use that power more wisely than certain of his predecessors.

And if Father Sloane had truly done what the Pope thought he had done, then far more power was about to come into his hands than any pope had even dreamed of for at least five hundred years.

CHAPTER 30

THE LAST PLACE Sofia Capelli wanted to be was exactly where she was. But she had no choice; Sister Mary David had made that very clear when Sofia had made the mistake of telling the nun that she wasn't going to Kip Adamson's funeral. So now she stood in the foyer as the entire student body and faculty of St. Isaac's filed into the chapel, and despite what Sister Mary David had told her, Sofia still did not want to go, and was planning to slip out the door unnoticed as soon as everyone was in the sanctuary.

The moment came, and Sofia turned to make her escape. But even before she could take the first step, Sister Mary David emerged from the dark shadows of the corner to the left of the door, her eyes boring into Sofia. Sofia felt a flash of cold fury and for just an instant imagined blood gushing from the nun's neck as if Kip Adamson had slashed her rather than the woman he'd actually killed. But the vision faded as quickly as it had come, and, accepting defeat at least for now, Sofia turned to follow the crowd into the chapel, the nun close behind her.

Then, just as she crossed the threshold, it hit her. A wave of nausea that twisted her gut and threatened to overwhelm her before she could even fight it. She sank onto the end of the back pew, barely inside the door, then closed her eyes and tried to quell a growing sickness, but it only increased as the doors were closed and the mass began.

She was trapped.

She felt an overwhelming urge to bolt from the pew and burst through the door to suck in the fresh air outside, but Sister Mary David was standing sentry, her only apparent purpose being to make certain Sofia stayed for the funeral.

As Father Laughlin stood in the pulpit above Kip's flowered casket and began to pray, Sofia bowed her head like everyone else, but instead of praying for Kip's soul, she prayed that she'd be able to endure the service to the end without either becoming ill or fainting.

Or both.

† † †

Melody Hunt sat in the fourth pew with Clay Matthews on one side of her and Ryan McIntyre on the other. Darren Bender was at the end nearest the aisle, and still trying to save enough space so that Sofia could sit next to him if she showed up. As the organ played softly, Melody leaned across Ryan and touched Darren's shirtsleeve. "Why isn't Sofia with us? Did something happen at lunch that you didn't tell us about?"

Darren shook his head and shrugged helplessly. "You saw what happened, for God's sake," he whispered a little too loudly, earning a dark glare from someone in the pew behind him. "She just freaked out. I don't know what's going on—I couldn't talk to her!"

Melody sat still in her seat trying not to look like she was searching the rows of students and faculty for Sofia. Kip's parents were sitting with Father Sebastian in the front row, along with some people she thought must be his grandparents, and she recognized practically everyone else she knew scattered all over the packed chapel. But there was no sign of Sofia at all.

Finally she twisted around and scanned the crowd behind her, and there was Sofia, her face ashen, sitting in the very last pew with her arms crossed tightly over her chest. "There she is," she whispered as loudly as she dared.

The three boys all turned to look. "Where?"

"Back row by the door." She nudged Ryan. "Let me out. I'm going to go talk to her."

Ryan put his hand on her arm. "You can't go talk to her now—the mass is starting!"

Melody reluctantly turned back to face the front and slipped her hand into Ryan's.

Ryan squeezed it quickly, then spoke, his eyes on the casket, his voice barely audible. "The last funeral I went to was my dad's."

Melody searched her mind for something to say, then settled on just holding his hand even tighter. As if understanding what she meant, his grip tightened, too.

"It's okay," Ryan said, his voice sounding nowhere near as certain as his words. "It was two years ago."

As Melody once more searched for the right words, Father Laughlin signaled the beginning of a hymn, and the entire crowd rose to their feet.

The entire crowd, save one.

Sofia Capelli still sat huddled in her place in the last pew, struggling against the terrible urge to vomit.

† † †

As the service wore on, Sofia felt her nausea fade slowly away, to be replaced with a strange vibration. It seemed to emanate from the floor beneath her feet, coming right up through her shoes and into her bones.

What was happening? She looked around, but nobody else seemed to have noticed.

She leaned forward and grasped the back of the pew in front of her.

It, too, vibrated.

Could it be an earthquake?

But it didn't *feel* like an earthquake. It felt more like some kind of energy, flowing into her through her feet—and now her fingers—making her whole body hum. But what could it be? And why wasn't it happening to anybody else? But as she looked around again she realized that everyone else in the chapel looked so intent on listening to every word Father Laughlin was saying that Sofia thought a bomb could go off and they wouldn't notice.

Suddenly the people in the front pew stood up and Sofia felt a brief wave of relief—they must be feeling it, too! But no—they were just going toward the altar to file past Kip's open casket to say a last good-bye before walking slowly up the aisle and out of the chapel.

There was no way Sofia was going to do that—the last thing she felt like doing was looking at a body.

The humming inside her flared, and for a second her vision faded and the whole chapel seemed to be illuminated by red light.

Blood-red light.

Sofia sat frozen in her place as the strength and power of the hum kept building. She closed her eyes to shut out the red glow, but without the light to distract her, the humming seemed even louder.

Louder, and somehow soothing.

It filled her chest, almost as if it could supplant her heartbeat. And not just her heartbeat, but her breathing as well.

It was as if the humming would supply all the energy she could ever need. She kept her eyes closed as a strength she'd never felt before flooded into her.

When she opened her eyes, she was alone in the chapel.

Had she fallen asleep? How could everyone else have left without her even noticing? But it didn't matter. She was alone, and free to go. Except that when she stood up, the vibration only grew stronger, the humming intensifying.

Instead of moving through the doors, Sofia felt herself being drawn toward the front of the chapel.

Drawn toward the altar.

Without thinking, she moved silently down the aisle, never hesitating, never faltering, until she stood in front of Kip Adamson's casket.

The vibration—the humming, the pure energy—was swirling all around her now, and as she gazed down into the open casket, she knew.

This was the source.

Kip Adamson's body.

Sofia looked down upon his face, made up so skillfully that he looked as if he was only sleeping, and any touch might awaken him.

Any touch . . .

The vibration grew and swelled until every nerve in her body was tingling. Now she could almost pick out separate tones within the humming. Suddenly it sounded as if there were a voice deep within the sound.

A human voice.

Kip Adamson's voice?

"What?" she whispered, her voice barely audible. "What is it?"

Her hand, as if of its own volition, moved down and touched Kip's right hand, avoiding the rosary that was wound between his fingers.

A surge of something—something dark, something dangerous—flowed through her fingers, up her arm and settled in her chest.

Something from Kip.

Something that had resided deep inside of him.

Something that now resided just as deep inside of her.

With the strange new energy flowing through her, Sofia turned to leave the chapel.

Standing at the doorway, watching her, were Melody Hunt, Darren Bender and Ryan McIntyre.

Sofia found the muscles of her face, willed them to smile, and walked up the aisle toward them.

† † †

The afternoon sun almost blinded Ryan as he emerged from the chapel into the late afternoon sun, but even in the glare he recognized his mother.

And not just his mother, either. Tom Kelly was there, too, talking to Father Sebastian.

Why were they here? Had they actually come to the funeral mass?

And why was his mother's hand tucked through Tom Kelly's arm exactly the way she used to tuck it through his father's? Then he saw her spot him and pull her hand away from Tom Kelly to wave to him. But she pulled it away too quickly, which was as good as telling Ryan she was feeling guilty about something. But what? Bringing Tom Kelly here? Or holding his arm the way she used to hold his father's. Wishing he could just turn around and head for the dorm, but knowing he couldn't, he started toward her. "There's my mom," he told Melody. "And the guy she's dating, who's buddies with Father Sebastian."

"You're kidding," Melody whispered, keeping in step with Ryan. "You'll never be able to get away with anything!"

"Tell me," Ryan muttered as he managed a smile for his mother.

"Hi, honey," she said, opening her arms to give him a hug—which he barely managed to sidestep—and a kiss on the cheek, which he had no chance of avoiding at all.

"What are you doing here?" he asked. "You didn't even know Kip Adamson, did you?"

His mother reddened slightly. "Actually, it was more an excuse to see you," she said, and now Ryan felt himself flushing.

"Hi," Melody said, smiling at his mother while trying not to stare at Tom Kelly.

"This is Melody Hunt," Ryan said. "She's tutoring me in Catholic History."

"My pal's specialty," Tom Kelly said, clapping Father Sebastian on the shoulder and grinning at him. "How's our boy doing?"

Our boy? Ryan thought. I'm not your boy, and I never will be.

"You look good," Tom said, appraising Ryan in his school uniform. "How's life at St. Isaac's?"

"Fine," Ryan said, keeping his smile carefully in place and reminding himself that his mother had a right to see whoever she wanted, and there was no point in being a brat about it. He didn't have to like Tom Kelly, but he didn't have to try to make his mother miserable, no matter how much he might feel like it.

"Of course it's only his first week," Melody said. "So he doesn't really know what it's like yet."

"I gather you've been here a while?" Teri asked.

"Since ninth grade," Melody replied.

"And if we're late for class, they'll put us both back in ninth grade,"

Ryan said. "And didn't you say you needed to get your geometry book?" he added, silently praying she'd get the message that even though they still had fifteen minutes, he wanted to get out of here now.

She did. Managing to affect a look of utterly genuine horror, she offered her hand to Teri McIntyre. "We've got to run. It was nice to meet you."

"Nice to meet you, Melody," Teri said, taking the girl's hand warmly.

"I'll catch up in a minute," Ryan told her as she headed toward the dorms. "I gotta say good-bye to my mom." Then, as Melody disappeared and Ryan looked at the ground, an awkward silence hung in the air.

"Cute girl," Tom said.

Ryan shrugged, but made no reply at all.

"She seems very nice," Teri said.

"She is."

"So it's all going well?" his mom asked.

Ryan shrugged again. "It's fine," he said. "I told you it was." He wasn't about to tell her about all the strange stuff that seemed to be going on, and at least if he was here he didn't have to watch Tom Kelly putting moves on his mother.

"We'll see you this weekend, right?" Teri asked. "I'll pick you up on Saturday and you'll stay through Sunday?"

Ryan shifted his weight uncomfortably. "Yeah, I guess." Another pause, this one even more uncomfortable, and he looked up just in time to see a look pass between his mother and Tom Kelly; the kind of look that told him there was something they weren't telling him. And something he wasn't going to like once he did hear it.

"Listen, I've got to get to class," he said, cutting his mother off just as she seemed on the verge of speaking.

She hesitated, then let her breath out like a deflating balloon. "I know, honey," she said softly. "I won't keep you—I've just been missing you, that's all."

"And I miss you, too," Ryan said. "Look, I've really got to go before I get in trouble."

Once again his mother looked like she wanted to say something, but once again she seemed to change her mind at the last instant. "Okay," she said, taking a step back, and Ryan was sure she wasn't just backing away from him, but from what she'd been about to say as well. "It's been good to see you, even if just for a few minutes."

"Be good, Sport," Tom Kelly said, and held out his hand.

"Sport?" What was Tom Kelly doing, calling him "Sport?" Only his father had ever called him that. Ignoring Kelly's outstretched hand, Ryan kissed his mother's cheek. "I'll call you about this weekend."

"Okay, honey. Love you."

"Love you, too," he said. Finally relenting enough to give Tom Kelly a curt nod, he hurried after Melody, hoping she was waiting just around the corner of the administration building.

What was it about Tom Kelly that rubbed him the wrong way? He seemed like a nice guy, and he seemed to make his mom happy.

So what was the problem?

But of course he knew what the problem was: *Tom Kelly was not his father, and never would be.*

He turned the corner, and sure enough, there was Melody, waiting for him, and suddenly all thoughts of Tom Kelly—and his resentment of the man—vanished.

CHAPTER 31

MELODY CLOSED HER textbook and pushed it to the back of her desk—what was the point of even trying to concentrate on it when she'd just read the same page three times and still didn't know what it said.

No matter how hard she tried, right now all she could think about was Sofia, who lay motionless on her bed, staring at the ceiling.

Exactly as she'd been doing for the last two hours.

But the Sofia that Melody knew hated just sitting around the dorm room in the evenings. She was always the one who'd rush through her homework, and always had a scheme to go do something fun, which always seemed to involve both boys and at least bending—if not outright breaking—the school's rules.

It had always been Melody herself who had been the quiet, studious, well-behaved one.

Yet now there was this new Sofia, who just lay there, not studying, not even talking. Melody turned her chair around so she was fully facing Sofia. "I've got an idea," she said, leaning eagerly toward Sofia and doing her best to make her voice sound as excited as Sofia's always did when she was about to set out on some new adventure. "Let's call Ryan and Darren and see if they want to sneak out for a Coke."

Instead of instantly seizing on the idea, as she would have on any other day Melody could remember, Sofia only shook her head. "No, thanks."

Melody let the smile on her face dissolve into the worry that was a genuine reflection of her feelings. "Do you feel all right?"

"I'm fine," Sofia replied, but with a flatness in her voice that belied the words.

Melody moved from the chair to the edge of her roommate's bed, but Sofia didn't even look at her. She just kept staring at the ceiling, though Melody was certain she wasn't really looking at it any more than herself. She tried again, choosing her words carefully. "If something happened to you last night—I mean, something that your parents or . . . well, something the police ought to know about—"

Sofia's eyes flicked away from the ceiling and fastened on Melody for a second, and in the light from the fixture overhead they almost looked like they were glittering like a snake's. "I told you, I'm fine!" she said, spitting the words hard enough to make Melody flinch.

Flinch, but not give up. "If you're so fine, then tell me what's going on with you!" she demanded. "First you didn't sit with us at lunch, which was good considering what you did with your food. Then you didn't sit with us in the chapel, either. You sat in back like you were afraid of the place. But after the service you went up to Kip's body, and did that weird thing."

Now Sofia's eyes locked onto Melody's. "What weird thing?" she demanded.

"T-Talking to him," Melody stammered. Sofia's eyes were boring into her so hard she could actually feel them, but she didn't stop. "And not just talking to him. You were touching him. Touching his dead body! It creeped me out—it creeped everybody out."

Sofia's gaze never wavered, and her eyes seemed to be glowing with a light from within, like those of an animal stalking its prey in the dark of the night.

Melody shrank away. "I'm sorry," she whispered. "I didn't mean to yell at you. You're—You're just so different, and I'm scared."

In a flash, Sofia's eyes dilated until the irises vanished and Melody had the feeling she was staring into a vast dark emptiness. "Just leave me alone," Sofia said, her voice little more than a rasp.

"No!" Melody shot back, even though her heart was suddenly pounding with a strange panic. "You're my best friend, and if you won't tell me what's going on, I'm going to call Brother Francis, and then I'm going to call Father Laughlin, and if I have to I'll even call your parents. Something's wrong with you!"

Sofia rose up on the bed, and as her face drew closer to Melody's, her eyes glittered and her features seemed to warp and twist, her lips curling back from sharply pointed teeth. Melody recoiled from the hideous visage, springing from the bed and backing away a step or two. But as quickly as it had come, the evil mask was gone and Sofia looked once more as she always had.

And now she was smiling. "I keep telling you, I'm fine. Nothing happened to me, and nothing is wrong." She flopped down onto the bed, and sighed heavily. "Actually, I feel really, really good!"

Melody, heart pounding, stared at Sofia. What had she just seen? But even as the memory of Sofia's contorted face rose in her mind, she wondered if she'd actually seen it at all. It had all happened so quickly—maybe it was just a trick of the light. Or maybe she'd only imagined the whole thing.

"All right," she said softly. "If you're okay, you're okay. I was just worried about you, that's all."

But as she went back to her desk and tried yet again to focus on the textbook she'd cast aside, she wondered if she'd ever be able to sleep in the same room with Sofia again.

† † †

Sister Mary David had put her ear to Sofia Capelli's dorm room door just in time to hear her final words: *I'm fine. Nothing happened to me, and nothing is wrong . . . actually, I feel really, really good!*

The old nun crossed herself, and silently offered a prayer of thanks to the Holy Mother for Sofia's salvation.

All day, she'd been watching Sofia, and all day she'd been worried about the girl.

But now, reassured by the voice of Sofia herself, Sister Mary David knew everything would be all right.

Lifting her habit so its hem wouldn't drag on the floor, Sister Mary David walked as lightly down the long dormitory hallway as she had almost fifty years ago, when she herself had lived in this dormitory. Until this evening, she had been feeling the weight of that half century, especially this year. After the loss of Jeffrey Holmes and the terrible death of Kip Adamson, she had actually been feeling old.

But tonight, after hearing Sofia Capelli's words, Sister Mary David felt much better.

Tonight, she would be able to sleep undisturbed.

Things, she was sure, were getting back to normal.

CHAPTER 32

FATHER SEBASTIAN DISCREETLY held Father Laughlin's arm to steady him as the old priest eased himself down into the only padded chair in Archbishop Rand's austere office, then took his own seat at the same time the Archbishop squeaked into the chair behind his desk.

"Thank you for coming on such short notice," Rand began.

"Is this about my report?" Laughlin asked, his rheumy eyes sparkling uncharacteristically in his eagerness to hear what the Vatican might have said. Father Sebastian felt certain that there must have been a time when the old priest had been a man whose bearing befitted his height. But his mind seemed to have shrunk as much as his body, and now there was an oddly childlike quality to him. Perhaps the Archbishop would see that it was time for Laughlin to be retired, from the school at least, if not the priesthood itself.

Rand peered over the top of his half-glasses, his gaze no less sharp for his slight loss of ocular focus. Unlike Laughlin's, the Archbishop's mind was easily outpacing his body. "Your report has certainly generated interest from the Vatican," he said carefully.

While Sloane clearly understood the Archbishop's guarded tone, Father Laughlin fairly beamed. "I knew it!" he said. "I knew they'd be impressed!"

"They were," Rand agreed. "And there is something else."

"Else?" Laughlin echoed, his eyes blinking nervously. "What else?"

Father Sebastian straightened slightly, hearing something in the Archbishop's voice that told him to make absolutely certain he understood every nuance of whatever he was about to say.

"There is a possibility—and I stress that this is *only* a possibility—that our new Pope may visit Boston."

Laughlin's mouth dropped open in stunned amazement. "Here? Really?"

"Again," the Archbishop reiterated, "it is only a possibility, and as his North American tour begins in less than two weeks, I would submit that the possibility is a slim one. A very, very slim one."

"Still," Laughlin said, clutching at the idea of a papal visit like a child clinging to a bag of candy. "This is remarkable news!"

The Archbishop tipped his head a fraction of an inch. "Your report, it seems, has intrigued His Holiness. As I'm sure you're both aware, the Archdiocese has asked repeatedly for a papal visit, but until now it has been consistently refused." His gaze moved from Laughlin to Sebastian Sloane. "For obvious reasons, given the problems we've had in Boston. But apparently your work at St. Isaac's has made a difference in Rome." The Archbishop paused while Father Laughlin took a handkerchief from his pocket and dabbed at the perspiration that had broken out on his forehead. Only when he was certain the old priest wasn't going to actually faint from excitement did he finally continue, this time addressing himself to Laughlin. "Let me remind you, Ernest, that nothing is confirmed. For now, this information needs to remain strictly within the confines of this office, except for the very highest ranking members of your staff."

"My staff?" Laughlin echoed.

The Archbishop nodded. "Yes, Ernest, your staff. After all, if he comes to Boston, it is St. Isaac's that His Holiness will want to visit, and it must be ready."

"And what can we do to convince the Pope that he must come to Boston?" Father Sebastian asked.

Archbishop Rand leaned back in his chair, tenting his fingers thoughtfully, his eyes fixing on Sloane. "In the end, the Pope will of course do whatever God tells him to do, but it has been suggested that another success—another *documented* success—in your work could perhaps weigh in the decision."

Father Sebastian's heart began to beat a little faster. Like Laughlin, meeting the Pope had been a lifelong dream, and when Rand spoke again, his own excitement grew.

"The Pope, like you, has a very strong background in the ancient rites of the Church, and my sources at the Vatican say he was quite taken with what you're doing."

Sebastian took a deep breath, already anticipating what was coming. "I see," he said softly.

"I hope you do," Rand replied. "We all want a papal visit, Father Sebastian. We need one. And we are counting on you." He rose from his chair, Father Sebastian immediately following his lead, then helping Father Laughlin to his feet. As he came around the desk to see his visitors out, he spoke once more, and Father Sebastian knew his entire future rested on his ability to comply with the Archbishop's order.

† † †

They were barely down the steps of the rectory and onto the sidewalk before Father Laughlin had his cell phone in hand, dialing Sister Margaret.

Father Sebastian hailed a cab, then held the car door open for him, but instead of getting into the cab, the elder priest spoke excitedly to his secretary. "Schedule a staff meeting immediately, Sister. We have wonderful news!" Father Sebastian shot him a warning look. "It's the Pope," Laughlin exulted far too loudly. "The Pope is coming to Boston!"

His stomach dropping at the words, Father Sebastian quickly scanned the crowded sidewalk, praying that the words had gone unheard. But already at least a dozen people had stopped and turned to stare at the old priest.

Sloane unceremoniously hustled Father Laughlin into the cab, then pushed in behind him. But it was too late.

By the time the cab pulled away from the curb, several passersby were already dialing their cell phones and starting to talk.

CHAPTER 33

FATHER LAUGHLIN LEANED back against his desk and listened to the excited buzz from his staff as they whispered among themselves about the possibility of a visit from Pope Innocent XIV.

Sister Margaret had taken more notes than he would have thought possible during the meeting, and had enough suggestions from the staff to keep everyone busy for far more than the two weeks they had: the hallways should be painted, the roses trimmed, the landscaping in front of the main entrance needed to be completely replanted.

The stained glass in the chapel must be cleaned, and every cobweb in the rafters made to vanish.

Now, as Brother Donovan's voice rose above the others demanding a new floor in the dining room, Father Laughlin held up his hand and cleared his throat.

Remarkably, they all fell instantly silent.

"Unfortunately, even the prospect of welcoming the Pope to our school doesn't change our budget."

"But it will," Sister Cecelia said. "When we tell our parents' group about it, surely—"

Father Laughlin silenced her with a look. Though everybody hoped that the Pope's visit to Boston would rejuvenate the parochial schools—or at least St. Isaac's—no magic money tap was about to be opened. "We shall do what we can," he said. "But let us keep in mind that our priority remains with the children. Needless to say, a papal visit would be one of the most important things ever to happen in our lives, but we must not lose sight of our priorities." He nodded toward Brother Francis. "I am asking the dormitory supervisors to keep an especially close eye on the children. We certainly do not want anything to jeopardize the arrival of—" Dare he even mention His Holiness again, or would that jinx it. Instantly chiding himself for falling into superstition, he nevertheless hewed to its strictures. "—of our *guest,*" he went on, stressing the single word just enough to let everyone know exactly what he meant. "If any of our charges show any signs of—" He paused again, then found exactly the right word. "—of *trouble,* I shall expect you to bring it to my attention immediately."

Father Sebastian rose from his seat at the back of the crowded room. "And please, do not forget that this visit is not yet confirmed. It is imperative that we keep this news to ourselves until we know for certain."

"Are there any questions?" Father Laughlin asked in a tone that told his staff he wasn't about to answer any.

As he had intended, no one raised their hand.

"Then thank you," Father Laughlin said in dismissal. "Go with God."

The buzz began again as everyone filed out of the small office, but Sister Mary David stayed in her seat until everyone had left, only approaching Father Laughlin when they were alone. "May I have a word, Father?"

"Of course," Laughlin said, as he sank back into his chair.

"Sofia Capelli seems to be doing very well," the nun began. "But since the incident with Kip Adamson, I've heard the students talking about Jeffrey Holmes again. Is there anything I should be telling them?"

Laughlin tented his fingers in unconscious imitation of Archbishop

Rand. "Tell them the truth, exactly as we've always told them," he replied. "Jeffrey is no longer with us, and we don't know exactly what happened to him."

"But it's such a sensitive time," Sister Mary David fretted, "I just wish there were something more—"

"There *is* nothing more, Sister Mary David."

Sister Mary David fingered the large silver cross that hung from her belt. "I suppose not," she said with a sigh. "I only wish there was something we could do."

"We are trying," Father Laughlin said. "As you know. We are doing our best."

Sister Mary David gave an unconvinced nod, then put on a smile. "Thank you, Father. And congratulations on the wonderful news about the Holy—" she cut her words off abruptly as the old priest held up a hand to silence her.

"Good *night,* Sister."

"Good night, Father."

Sister Mary David scurried out, closing the office door behind her, and Father Laughlin ran his hands over his tired face. It had been a long day, and now Jeffrey Holmes was again at the top of his priority list.

Not only was the boy a potential stain on the school's record, but he weighed heavily on the old priest's soul as well.

Then, as he remembered what Sister Mary David had told him about Sofia Capelli, a tiny seed of hope sprouted in his heart.

Perhaps he should try one more time.

Yes, of course!

He *should* try. He *would* try! He could do it, he knew he could.

And if he succeeded, it wouldn't be Jeffrey Holmes's soul he had redeemed.

It would be his own.

CHAPTER 34

As the summons sounded, Abdul Kahadija filed into the prayer room along with the rest of the men who had finished their ablutions and were milling about in the mosque courtyard.

He knew he should center his thoughts on God and the praise he was about to bestow, but he was here, at this *salah,* for a dual purpose, and until he found the face that he sought in the crowd, he would not be able to concentrate.

Inside the cavernous prayer room, all the men lined up in rows in front of the imam, and as Abdul looked to his left, he spotted the man he came to find.

Peace flooded through him. Allah knew his mission, and as always, would show him the way.

Abdul stood straight and strong, the validity of his mission confirmed by the very presence of the worshipper to his left. He closed his eyes and let his adoration of Allah consume him.

When the morning prayers had finished, Abdul maneuvered through the crowd until he neared the man with whom he intended to speak after they had all filed silently out of the prayer room.

His heart hammered and his palms grew greasy with sweat as he rehearsed yet again what he would say. If he came across too strong or if his demeanor or appearance was anything other than that which Allah demanded of him, he would be refused.

The stakes were enormously high.

Abdul followed the man into the crowded courtyard, where the silence of the prayer room gave way to the boisterous noise of friends greeting friends.

The man left the mosque, Abdul close behind. In the parking lot, Abdul, keeping a respectful distance, finally spoke. "Excuse me, my brother," he said.

The man stopped, and Abdul found himself facing a stocky man in his early sixties, with graying hair and a square jaw.

Abdul's breath left him, his mouth became dry and he found it difficult to talk. He cleared his throat and began. "I am Abdul Kahadija, and I am new to the Boston area." He paused, then asked the question he had mulled for weeks. "I wonder if you can tell me where I could buy some weed killer for my garden?"

The man's face remained expressionless, but his brown eyes bored deep into Abdul's, who tried not to flinch under the probing gaze. "Weed killer," the man spoke slowly. "Or is it a pesticide that you need?"

Abdul inwardly rejoiced. The man had understood his question! "Perhaps a pesticide would better solve my gardening problems."

"Where is this garden?" the man asked quietly.

"I toil in the garden of Allah," Abdul responded.

"Then you must see Nameer," the man said. "He cultivates a similar garden path."

"Thank you, friend," Abdul said. "Where might I find Nameer?"

"He owns a nursery on the south side. If your quest is pure, you shall find him."

"May the blessings of Allah be on you and on your family," Abdul said.

"And on yours," the older man said as he pulled the white crocheted *kufi* off his head and beeped his car unlocked. "Tell me what you grow in this garden of yours."

Abdul's face flushed hot. This was a question he had not anticipated, but an answer came to him in a flash. "Easter lilies," he declared.

The man considered this, then smiled broadly, showing straight white teeth in a pleasant face.

Abdul's nervousness dissolved, and he felt his own smile take its place. "Great big Roman Easter lilies," he said again, and they both laughed.

"*Insha-allah,*" the man said.

"*Insha-allah,*" Abdul replied.

Chapter 35

RYAN EMERGED FROM the boys' dormitory, into a warm spring afternoon without a cloud in the sky, made even more perfect by the fact that it was Saturday.

He'd survived his first week of classes at St. Isaac's.

And even better, Melody Hunt was waiting for him, just as he'd hoped she would. He set his overnight bag down and dropped onto the bench next to her. All around them were people Ryan was starting to recognize, but this morning they all looked different, clad in their regular clothes rather than the blue-and-white uniforms he'd already grown used to seeing, and when one of his classmates suddenly appeared in exactly the kind of low-slung baggy pants and oversize shirt that Frankie Alito always wore, he felt a twinge of panic and had to remind himself that he was still at St. Isaac's, and not back at Dickinson.

"Aren't you going to take all your laundry for your mom to do?" Melody asked, eyeing the overnight bag that was far too small to contain anything more than a change of clothes.

"Nah. I'll do it Sunday night," Ryan replied, then cocked his head and eyed her with a look he hoped was seductive. "And while they're drying, you can teach me more Catholic History."

"You didn't get an 'A' from Father Sebastian just because of me," Melody said, blushing slightly, but not moving away at all. "You're the one who did the studying."

"And you're the one who told me what to study."

Melody scuffed her tennis shoe against the cement pathway as if not quite sure how to respond, then settled for just changing the subject. "So what do you think of St. Isaac's, now that you've been here almost a week?"

"Not too bad," Ryan said, giving up the attempt at a seductive look in favor of a wry grin. "At least I haven't been beaten up yet."

"And your face looks a lot better than it did on Monday." She hesitated, then: "Not that it looked that bad even then."

Ryan tried to fight the blush he felt rising in his cheeks. Maybe the seductive look had worked after all. "And my ribs are healing, too."

Melody looked around the rapidly emptying courtyard, with more kids leaving every second. "It's going to be boring around here all weekend with you gone," she said with a wistful tone that made Ryan's heart beat a little faster.

"Why don't you go home, too?" Ryan asked.

"My family lives too far west." Melody shrugged, but Ryan could see she wasn't as nonchalant as she was trying to sound. "But at least they'd like me to come home. Sofia's mom lives right here in Boston, like a mile away or something. But she married some rich guy who doesn't want Sofia around, so she can't go home, either."

"Ouch."

"Yeah, she only goes home on Christmas Day. Seems like the only ones who have to stay here are either troublemakers or inconveniences."

Ryan told himself he didn't fit into either category, but even as he tried to convince himself of the truth of his thought, it didn't quite ring true. But why not? The fight—if you could even call getting beaten up a "fight"—hadn't been his fault, and if his mother didn't want him at home for the weekend, why was she coming to pick him up? But, of course, he knew why he was wondering if maybe he at least fit into the "inconvenient" category.

Tom Kelly.

Who Ryan hoped wouldn't be with his mother when she came to pick him up in—he glanced at his watch—two minutes. "Uh-oh," he said, suddenly wishing he had another hour or two with Melody. "Gotta go or I'm going to be late to meet my mom."

"Okay," Melody said, and once more Ryan heard that wistful note. "Call me when you get back, okay?"

"Okay," he said, tapping her back. "See you tomorrow."

† † †

An elderly, bent woman with a wrapped birthday present in the basket of her walker was fumbling with the door to Father Laughlin's outer office when Ryan got there, and he held it open for her as she slowly made her way through.

His mother was already inside, talking to Father Laughlin, and she smiled happily when she saw him.

"Hi, honey," she said, putting her arm around him. "Father Laughlin was just telling me how well you're doing, and I was just telling him that we're going out to dinner to celebrate your first week here."

"Have a good time, Ryan," Father Laughlin said. "Just don't forget to come back tomorrow."

Before Ryan could say anything at all, the old woman with the walker suddenly spoke. "Where's Jeffrey?"

"Mrs. Holmes?" Father Laughlin began. "How nice to—"

"I want to see my grandson," the old woman broke in. "It's his birthday!"

Father Laughlin glanced at Teri, one of his eyebrows lifting slightly as he took one of the old woman's hands in his. "Why don't you come into my office?" he suggested, gently trying to guide the old woman through the inner door.

Mrs. Holmes jerked her hand away from the priest and peered up at him suspiciously. "Do I know you? I just want to see my grandson."

Father Laughlin tilted his head closer to hers and laid a reassuring hand on her shoulder. "Do you remember coming to talk with us about Jeffrey after Thanksgiving?" he asked, his voice soft.

The old woman pulled away once more, backing up slightly, then glared up at Father Laughlin. "I want to see my grandson!" she demanded.

With a deep breath and another helpless glance toward Teri McIntyre, Father Laughlin gently but firmly took the old woman's elbow and ushered her into his office. "Let's talk in here, Mrs. Holmes, all right?"

It was as if she hadn't even heard him. "Why isn't he here?" she shrilled. "Where is he? *What have you done with him?*"

Father Laughlin's response was lost as he smiled sadly at Teri and Ryan, spread his hands in supplication of their understanding of the situation, and quietly closed his office door.

Teri stood transfixed, staring at Father Laughlin's closed door.

"C'mon, Mom," Ryan coaxed, but even as he spoke, he knew she wasn't listening to him. Indeed, he could almost hear her thinking about Monday morning, when they'd met Kip Adamson's parents on the front steps of St. Isaac's.

Finally, though, she turned, her brow furrowed deeply, and followed him outside.

The car was parked in the loading zone at the bottom of the steps.

And Tom Kelly was in the driver's seat.

Suddenly, the rest of the afternoon was going to be a chore, and now, instead of having dinner in St. Isaac's dining hall with Melody Hunt, he was going to have to sit in some restaurant with Tom Kelly.

Still, it was just dinner, and then he and his mother would go home and he'd have the rest of the evening and most of tomorrow with his mother.

He could tolerate an afternoon and one dinner with Tom.

He opened the front passenger door for his mother, but before getting in, she took a last look at the old gothic building behind them, and drew her sweater closer around her neck even though the afternoon was warm. She laid a light hand on Ryan's arm. "What happened to that woman's grandson?" she asked, her eyes searching his own.

Ryan glanced up at the front door, and for just a moment he remembered the screams he'd thought he heard on Monday night. Then he shrugged off both the memory and his mother's hand.

"I don't know," he said. "Nobody knows."

CHAPTER 36

SOFIA CAPELLI WAS in the science laboratory, finishing her regular Saturday job of cleaning out all the cages where the frogs and rats and rabbits—all the animals that were used for lab experiments—were kept. It never took more than an hour, and Sofia didn't really mind it, except for the frogs, whose skin always felt slimy. Today, though, even the frogs didn't bother her. She was actually holding one of them in the palm of her hand, cupping her fingers around it. The frog sat absolutely still, as if it knew that she could kill it in an instant. It stared up at her, and Sofia fixed her eyes on those of the small creature in her hand, and as their gazes held, Sofia suddenly felt as if the frog knew her—knew what was in her mind.

And didn't just know her.

It hated her, too.

And she knew why.

It had been watching.

For weeks, it—and all the other frogs in the terrarium—had been watching as every day someone came and snatched one of them from its home and took it to a lab table and jabbed a slim blade into the base of its spinal cord before cutting its skin open to examine and toy with the organs inside.

It didn't hurt them, of course. Or at least that's what Sister Agnes had said.

But now Sofia knew that the frog in her hand had been watching, and as she gazed down at it she felt its hatred radiating outward like a million tiny needles, jabbing at her as painfully as the blades that had been used on the others of its kind.

Kill it, a voice inside her instructed. *Kill it before it kills you.*

Obeying the voice—and not even aware of what she was doing— Sofia closed her fingers, and the frog's fragile bones snapped under their pressure. Its guts swirled inside its skin, then spewed out through both its mouth and its anus.

The voice inside her sighed contentedly.

Sofia opened her hand and stared at the shapeless mass that now lay where only moments ago a living frog had been, then she dropped it into the wastebasket.

What had she done?

And why?

Feeling suddenly nauseated, Sofia turned away from the terrarium, cleaned out the rat cages, then turned her attention to the rabbits. Two fully grown ones, one black and one white, were lying side by side, sleeping as their litter nursed on the white one's teats. There were six in the litter, one black, one white, the rest in various patterns of both black and white.

Just as Sister Agnes had predicted when she'd first brought in the adult pair.

And now there they were, all nursing contentedly on their mother's teats.

All of them except one.

The little white one, who was staring through the mesh of the cage, its tiny pink eyes fixed on Sofia.

Sofia opened the cage, grasped the baby rabbit by its ears, and took it out. "Don't do that," she whispered as she left the science lab and started back toward her room. "Don't stare at me that way."

The tiny rabbit, as if sensing exactly what was to come, trembled in her hands with terror, and its very trembling made the voice in Sofia's head sigh in anticipation.

† † †

The dark cloud of depression that had gathered over Melody got darker by the moment. The weekend loomed interminably long with Ryan gone, which was ridiculous, considering that only a week ago she hadn't even known him. And now, here she was, missing him terribly and with nobody even to talk about him with.

Until Tuesday night, she would have talked to Sofia, but after she'd come back from the infirmary, everything about her had changed, and even though she kept insisting she was "just fine," Melody knew she wasn't.

She was completely different.

And no longer someone Melody could talk to.

So she'd just do something else—anything to fill the time until tomorrow afternoon when Ryan got back.

She'd do her laundry. And study.

Great.

Sighing heavily, she stood up from the bench and started back to the dorm. The courtyard was almost empty, and the girls' dormitory was bereft of its weekday babble of a hundred girls all trying to get to different places at the same time. Her footsteps sounded oddly loud as she walked down the hall, but when she got to the door to her room, she paused.

There was another sound, even louder than her own footsteps, and it was coming from inside her room.

It was a squeal.

A squeal as if something were in terrible pain.

† † †

Sofia sat on her desk chair. In her lap was the baby rabbit, staring up at her, its eyes wide, too terrified now even to attempt to escape. Not that it could have even if it hadn't been paralyzed by fear, for one or the other of Sofia's hands never let go of it.

Sofia herself was barely aware of what was happening. It was as if she were no longer quite inside her own body, but somewhere else—somewhere in a strange foggy place where she could observe what was happening, could feel the small furry creature in her hands, even feel its heart pounding, but could do nothing about it except watch through the strange mist.

And there was something else, too. Something inside her body and her mind that she could hear and feel, but not control. It was as if something had taken over, controlling her body and her mind, telling her what to do as she herself—the part of her that was the real Sofia—stood aside, reduced to nothing more than an observer.

And now, as she watched, her hands moved from the rabbit's throat to its foreleg.

She held it in both hands, like a long willow twig.

She pressed her thumbs against the bone, and applied pressure.

But the bone didn't bend like a willow twig would have. It snapped like a brittle straw at the end of summer.

It snapped, and the rabbit screamed.

She could put it down now, and it wouldn't run away. How could it, with all four of its legs broken?

But she couldn't put it down, not yet. The voice—the demon—the *thing*—inside her wouldn't let her. No, there was more to be done, more pain to be inflicted on the tiny creature, more—

The door behind her opened, and she heard a gasp. Sofia turned to see Melody Hunt staring at her.

"My god," Melody whispered, her face going ashen as she stared at the whimpering animal in Sofia's hands. "What are you doing?"

Sofia stood up and turned to face Melody, whose own eyes weren't even looking at her, but were fixed instead on the panicked and broken rabbit in her hands. As Melody watched, Sofia gripped one of the bunny's broken rear legs and twisted it hard.

The baby rabbit screamed again, and Melody recoiled from what she was seeing. But then she took a deep breath, and before Sofia could do anything else, she snatched it out of her hands and sank onto her own chair, cradling the rabbit as gently as she could.

An instant later their door opened and they both heard Sister Mary David's voice. "What's going on in here?"

"Look," Melody said, holding out her hands with the grotesquely twisted baby rabbit.

Sister Mary David crossed herself as if to ward off whatever evil had befallen the rabbit. "Where did that come from?"

Before Melody could speak a single word, Sofia spread her hands helplessly. "I just got back from the library," she said. "Melody was torturing it."

"What?" Melody stared up at her roommate, whose face revealed nothing—no shame, no remorse, nothing. "I can't believe you said that," she breathed, then turned back to the nun. "Sister, I came in to get my laundry, and she was the one who had it."

"Give me that poor thing," Sister Mary David said, and took the barely breathing, twitching little body. "You stay right here. Both of you!" She whirled and swept out of the room, closing the door firmly behind her.

"What's the matter with you?" Melody demanded, turning on Sofia. "Why would you even do that? It was just a baby! A sweet little harmless bunny!"

Sofia said nothing, and for several long minutes a terrible silence hung in the room until the door opened again and Sister Mary David reappeared.

The nun took Melody's arm and drew her to her feet. "Father Sebastian wants to see you immediately."

"Me?" Melody protested. "But all I was trying to do was rescue the rabbit. Sofia was the one who—"

"Lying only compounds your sin," the nun said, and began steering her toward the door.

"I'm not lying!" Melody cried, turning toward Sofia. "Tell her, Sofia! Tell her the truth!"

Sofia only looked at her impassively. "I only know what I saw," she said softly.

With Melody still insisting she'd done nothing, Sister Mary David marched her out of the room, leaving Sofia alone once more. As the door closed behind Melody and the nun, she lay down on her bed and gazed up at the ceiling. Her fingers twitched slightly as the thing inside her remembered the feeling of the rabbit's bones breaking beneath their pressure.

The feeling was good.

† † †

Sister Mary David guided Melody down a series of stairs into the labyrinth that was the school's basement.

"Isn't Father Sebastian in his office?" Melody asked, her throat dry.

"No," the nun replied, walking so quickly through the darkened tunnels that Melody had to trot to keep up. "He told me to bring you to the chapel."

"This is stupid. I didn't do anything—it was Sofia!"

"Hush!" Sister Mary David stopped in front of an old wooden door, and a sudden surge of panic gripped Melody as she remembered what Sofia had told her about going to confession in the basement chapel.

A chapel where she'd been forced to pray on her knees for hours on end.

Was she herself going to have to do that now?

Was whatever had happened to Sofia about to happen to her, too?

She did not want to go inside, and took a step back, away from the door.

Sister Mary David pulled the door open, and in spite of herself, Melody looked in.

An enormous, hideous crucifix, with a hollow-eyed, dying Christ loomed over the candlelit altar.

"No," she said, backing away. "I don't want to go in there."

"It's all right, Melody," Father Sebastian said softly as he stepped through the doorway from the vestry.

"It wasn't me, Father," Melody cried as tears of frustration and fear began to choke her. "It was Sofia. I came back to get my laundry, and she had that little thing, and—"

Father Sebastian beckoned to her, inviting her inside. "Come in and let's talk about it."

Melody felt her anxiety begin to melt slightly as she heard the priest's soothing voice. "I—I don't—" she began, but the priest held up a quieting hand.

"Please, Melody," Father Sebastian said. "Talk with me."

Melody swallowed. Something still told her not to go into the strange chapel, but surely Father Sebastian would never hurt her. And he was offering her an opportunity to explain what had just gone on in her room. "All right," she breathed.

Father Sebastian held out his hand. She took it, and stepped across the threshold into the chapel.

CHAPTER 37

JEFFREY HOLMES OPENED his eyes and looked around, but the darkness was so deep that he had to put his fingers to his face to make certain that his eyes were open at all. He winced as he felt the sticky filth that covered him, and he tried to shy away from the fetid odor of his cell.

Why was he here? What had he done?

It had to be some kind of prison, but he couldn't remember—couldn't remember anything, really, except the strange sensation of flickering in and out of consciousness in the blackness, as if something else—some other being—had somehow taken over his body.

Suddenly Jeffrey felt a white-hot fury begin in his solar plexus and boil up through his chest.

It was starting again!

It was as if he was being pushed aside by something deep within himself, and in a moment the wrath burning inside him would consume not just his body, but his mind and soul as well.

"Please, no," he whispered, the words emerging from his lips as nothing but a faint squeal. But he knew it was useless to plead in the face of the rampaging fury, and a moment later the rage erupted in his mind.

Jeffrey Holmes disappeared.

The evil that had conquered the boy's body experimented with it, causing each limb to twitch spasmodically, each finger to clench so hard that its nail sank deep into the flesh of the palms. Relishing the pain, the evil squatted on its haunches and found the powers deep in the body's brain that let it reach far from the cramped cell to probe the grounds of the buildings above the prison.

It detected a change. Something was happening.

It sent out thin tendrils of exploration, creeping through the building above, the grounds, the ancillary buildings, looking for something, something that had changed . . .

There! The place where the girls lived!

A new presence.

A kindred spark.

But wait. He had felt this spark before. But it was stronger now, much stronger. Though it was lying almost dormant at the moment, it was gathering strength, gathering momentum.

If somehow they could meet and their energies merge . . .

They would combine into a force so strong that it could never be conquered.

Yet this was not the spark of change the evil had detected, though it was pleased with this one's progress.

No, there was something else.

Staring into the darkness with all-seeing eyes, the being continued to probe the consciousness of every living creature it could find, until—

There!

Directly above his cell!

A newly emerging larva of evil. Barely discernable, barely detectable, but there.

It concentrated on the fragile thing, and touched it with its awareness.

The other one squirmed within its host, recognizing its own kind, burning a little brighter.

The evil within Jeffrey Holmes fanned the flame for a moment, then retreated, so as not to harm the new host.

It rested against the wall of the prison and smiled. It was happening. Though still locked up, it could feel what was happening. From some nearby portal, more evil was seeping into this world, and soon there would be a release from this cell and the being within Jeffrey Holmes would be able to combine, to merge, to fuse with the others of its kind.

Fuse, and strengthen.

Becoming one, evil would rule.

The being gathered what strength its own host still possessed and prepared to howl in exultation, when suddenly a cloud of danger darkened his awareness.

A priest!

A *priest* was drawing near.

It spat on the ground, its hatred and rage quickly rising.

It could feel the priest just outside, and already knew what it would do: when the priest opened the door, it would fling itself onto the human flesh, tearing his chest open to devour the man's heart even while it still beat.

It tried to stand, to creep toward the door in readiness, but the legs of its host were no longer strong, and instead of readying to spring, the being staggered.

Its fury erupted. It wanted to break the legs, to beat them into submission, but then it remembered its last confrontation with the priest.

His host was not strong, but neither was the priest.

If it was patient, the opportunity would come for it to bond with the fledglings up above, and nothing the priest could do would ever overcome its power.

It sank back onto the floor, concentrating only on controlling its own rage, forcing it down just enough so that Jeffrey Holmes could emerge once more and deal with the priest while the evil rested.

Yet it would still be there, just beneath the surface, watching whatever might happen, just in case an opportunity for escape arose. . . .

CHAPTER 38

RYAN ORDERED THE steak and baked potato, closed his menu, and handed it to the waiter. So far, the day with his mother and Tom Kelly hadn't been as bad as he thought it was going to be; they'd gone to Quincy Market, then had lunch at Legal Seafood, which had always been Ryan's favorite restaurant. Now they were at Ruth's Chris on School Street, just a few blocks from St. Isaac's, and Ryan was wondering why they hadn't gone to some place closer to their house.

Something, he was sure, was going on. In fact, he'd had the feeling all afternoon that there was something his mother wasn't telling him. Now, as the waiter took the last of their order, Tom Kelly stood up and laid his napkin on the table.

"If you'll excuse me for a few minutes," he said, leaning over to kiss Teri's cheek. Then he nodded at Ryan, and walked toward the men's room.

"So," Teri said, leaning in slightly, and both her voice and expression taking on an odd anxiety. "Hasn't this been fun, the three of us together?"

Ryan nodded uncertainly, sensing that his mother was about to tell him something that he wasn't going to like.

"Maybe during Easter week we can go somewhere. Take a trip to-gether."

Ryan frowned. "We?" What did that mean? Just himself and his mother, or was she talking about Tom Kelly, too? "You mean just us?" he asked. "Or are you thinking that guy will go, too?" He tipped his head in the direction in which Tom Kelly had gone, and the flicker in his mother's eyes told him the answer to his question even before she spoke.

"He's not just 'that guy,' Ryan," Teri said, sitting back and crossing her arms over her chest. "He's a good man."

Ryan shrugged. "I'm not saying he's not. Just don't marry him, okay?"

Again the look in his mother's eyes spoke volumes, and for a second he had the horrible feeling that maybe she already *had* married him. But then she shook her head.

"I'm not marrying him," she said.

Ryan started to relax slightly, but then she spoke again.

"But you need to know that Tom may move into the house next week."

Anger and resentment began to boil in Ryan's gut. "Boy, that didn't take long."

Teri did her best to ignore the anger in her son's voice. "He's a good man, Ryan, and he's very good for me. He cares for me, and for you, too. If you'd just get to know him the way I do . . ." Her voice trailed off and she looked down and twisted the napkin in her lap. "And the house is just too empty with you gone."

Ryan glared accusingly at her. "Don't blame it on me."

"Blame?" Teri's head snapped up. "There's nothing to blame. I love Tom, and he loves me, and if he makes me happy, I'd think you'd be happy for me." Out of the corner of her eye she saw Tom coming back, and reached out to take Ryan's hand, but he pulled away from her, his eyes stormy. "Please," she whispered, "let's not ruin the day, all right?"

Tom sat down, smiling. "What did I miss?"

Ryan took a deep breath. "Not much," he finally said. "Just mom telling me that you're moving in on her."

Tom Kelly glanced at Teri, whose face had gone ashen, and raised a placating hand. "Hey, come on. I wouldn't call it moving *in* on—" he began, but Ryan didn't let him finish.

"I think it would be best for me to go back to St. Isaac's tonight," he said.

Tom Kelly looked genuinely surprised. "You're kidding! Why?"

Teri shot Ryan a look, her eyes glistening with tears, and he squelched the angry words in his throat before they burst free. "I've got a lot of catching up to do on classes that I've never taken before," he said, keeping his voice as calm as possible. "I was really looking forward to a weekend at home, but I think I'd better spend it studying, instead." He felt Tom Kelly's eyes on him, and met the man's gaze with his own.

Teri McIntyre sat in frozen silence, praying that neither Ryan nor Tom would push the issue any further.

Finally Tom Kelly nodded. "You're probably right," he said. "At this stage, you'd probably do better to stay at school."

Ryan nodded.

The waiter brought their meals.

Ryan looked at his steak, cooked to perfection, but his appetite had vanished. All he could think about was what Melody had intimated earlier in the day: that many of St. Isaac's students were either trouble-makers or inconveniences.

St. Isaac's had been Tom's idea, and with Ryan out of the house, he was moving right in.

Nor did he seem the least bit disappointed that Ryan wasn't going to be home for the weekend.

"At least we had a good afternoon," Tom said, and lifted his wine-glass.

Teri followed suit, and Ryan lifted his Coke.

"To many more good Saturdays," Tom said.

"Many more," Teri echoed.

Ryan clicked his glass with theirs, but knew that from now on he'd much rather be at school with Melody and Clay Matthews, and the rest of his new friends than be home with Tom Kelly.

For tonight, he'd just get through dinner, and be polite, and not make his mother any more miserable than she already looked. He'd think about Tom Kelly and the rest of it when he was back in his dorm room, alone.

As alone as he already felt, now that he had apparently become just one more of the inconvenient kids stashed away at St. Isaac's.

CHAPTER 39

ABDUL KAHADIJA WALKED slowly down the street. It was twilight, that strange time when the light of Allah is bright enough to illuminate the goal, but faded enough to hide all but the most obvious intruder. And there was nothing obvious about Abdul Kahadija; to anyone glancing out a window, he would have appeared no different from anyone who lived in the neighborhood, and when he casually slipped between two houses and into the backyard of his target, he might as well have been heading for his own garage.

A covered barbecue grill sat like a great humped creature on the wide patio, along with a table and four chairs, minus cushions and the umbrella that surely made this a homey scene, come long summer evenings.

He listened carefully. No sounds from inside the house. No sounds from neighboring houses. Through the glass in the kitchen door, he could see one lamp lighting the living room, as well as the porch light; the rest of the rooms were dark.

He pulled his thin black gloves a little tighter, then took a glass cutter from his pocket. Moving close to the door to muffle the sound, he etched a rough circle in the pane nearest the doorknob, then turned the cutter to rap the glass sharply with its opposite end.

Instead of a single piece of glass falling away, the entire pane shattered.

A dog barked a few houses away. Nothing else.

Abdul Kahadija reached through the broken glass, twisted the knob, and moved silently through the doorway and into the kitchen. Though no one was home, he was loath to make even the smallest of sounds; the tinkle of broken glass had been regrettable, but unavoidable, but there must be no more noise.

Abdul intended to leave nothing of himself in this house, no sound, no print, not even the essence of his spirit.

But where to begin a search for the tiny, easily concealed object he sought?

It could be anywhere.

He stood still in the center of the room and tried to sense the inhabitants of the house. Where might they put such a relic?

But he had no feel for them. They felt foreign—soulless. Surely they had no idea of the treasure that was in their possession.

He checked his watch. He had allowed himself twenty minutes to search, and already four minutes had passed, and he had not even begun.

He started with the small drawers in the kitchen, but it was only a cursory search; surely they wouldn't keep it here. Still, he rummaged quickly through the tangle of rubber bands, receipts, a few screws and broken switch plates that filled the drawers. Not the kitchen.

The living room seemed too austere; what he sought would not be here, not even in the drawers of the breakfront where surely they kept their silver, if this family owned anything of such value.

The bedrooms.

Lightly, making no sound, Abdul glided up the stairs into the master bedroom, where his eyes fell instantly on a lacquered, inlaid jewelry chest that sat squarely on the dresser.

Praise be to Allah.

He unconsciously tugged his thin black gloves once more, then opened the lid of the jewelry box.

A metallic tune began to play, shattering the silence, and setting his heart to jackhammering in his chest.

Abdul quickly found the music box switch and depressed it with a finger while he used his other hand to go through the jewelry.

What he sought was not among the cheap necklaces and bracelets that filled the beautiful box. The box, indeed, was likely worth far more than its contents.

Where else to look? Then he remembered: women sometimes kept their most precious objects hidden with their lingerie.

He opened the top drawer of the dresser and gently ran his hands through the soft silk underwear, probing all the way to the back of the drawer.

Nothing.

Where? *Where?*

The bedside table.

As he opened the nightstand drawer, his elbow caught the edge of a picture frame, which tipped over the edge. He lunged to catch it, missed, and watched as it fell to the wooden floor, the glass shattering.

He looked at the photograph beneath the broken glass. A young boy, holding up a small fish. Should he take the broken photograph with him?

No, better to encourage wrong thoughts.

Abdul let it lay, returned to the jewelry box, grabbed up a handful of earrings and necklaces and stuffed them into one of his pockets. He opened the lingerie drawer and left it open.

Then he left as silently as he had entered, his spirits heavy with disappointment. It was dark now, and in the blackness of the shadows behind the house he stripped off his black gloves, then walked nonchalantly back to the quiet street and around the corner of the next block.

He would dispose of the cheap jewelry in the Dumpster behind the convenience store he had passed on his way here.

As he slipped away into the darkness of the night he told himself that his failure to recover the relic was only a potential problem for his mission. The chances that the stupid people in the house even knew what they owned were slim, and if they truly didn't, then the object's existence would be of no consequence. Though he would feel supremely safer if he had it in hand, his chances of success in his mission were still all but certain.

Victory—*vengeance*—would still be his to claim.

CHAPTER 40

FATHER LAUGHLIN SLOWED as he neared the door to Jeffrey Holmes's tiny room buried deep in the subbasement beneath the old brownstone that had been absorbed by the school nearly a century earlier and now served as its rectory. As he stood alone in the murky depths of the labyrinth beneath the school, what had seemed like an excellent idea in the aftermath of his conversation with the boy's poor grandmother now seemed more like the act of an old fool. Still, if he could recreate what Father Sebastian had achieved with Sofia Capelli a few days ago, and Melody Hunt this very afternoon— and he believed in his heart that he could—what a wonderful thing it would be.

He would bring Jeffrey Holmes back into God's light.

Despite Sebastian Sloane's certainty that the boy was beyond redemption, Laughlin's faith told him that God would not abandon Jeffrey any more than he had Sofia or Melody.

He would not abandon any child.

Laughlin reached to draw the bolt on the door of Jeffrey's cell, but before his pale, soft fingers touched the cold metal, he hesitated. He could still go back upstairs to his rooms, enjoy a cup of hot tea, put his aching legs up on a stool and listen to some Puccini. No one would blame him for leaving the boy solely in the hands of Sebastian Sloane, who was an expert in the ancient rites, far better educated than Laughlin himself.

But if he could manage to save the boy in spite of Sebastian's certainty that he was lost, then he could retire—even die in peace—knowing without the shadow of a doubt that he had done God's work.

God would not let Jeffrey Holmes down, and He would watch over the recitation of the litany as Laughlin remembered it.

Ernest Laughlin looked at the low dark ceiling and whispered a barely audible prayer: "God provide me sufficient faith." Then he crossed himself, kissed his fingertips, and with those same fingertips threw open the bolt on the heavy metal door.

An ice-cold wave of pure evil carrying the fetid stench of rot poured forth from the darkened cell, withering Laughlin's resolve.

Then, in the faint light of the open doorway, he saw Jeffrey's naked body, cowering in the corner.

The boy's pale, veined skin was stretched taut over his protruding ribs, his hair was matted with filth, and his eyes streamed with yellowish pus.

Laughlin's first instinct was to go to the child, hold him, comfort him. Yet the aura of evil surrounding the child held him back, and instead of kneeling next to the starved and fragile body, the old priest concentrated only on the evil that was consuming Jeffrey from within.

Laughlin gripped the crucifix that hung from his belt and began the litany he'd heard Sebastian Sloane recite only a few hours ago, repeating the words as closely as he remembered them, holding the beatific smile of Melody Hunt clearly in his mind. Even now, the girl lay quietly in the infirmary, in the same bed occupied by Sofia Capelli earlier in the week, both of them completely cleansed of all evil, and at peace.

He must do the same for this poor, wretched creature.

But while the words seemed clear in his mind, they didn't sound right as they left his lips. Where Sebastian's robust and vibrant voice had been filled with the authority of his faith, Laughlin's sounded thin and reedy even to himself.

Even the pronunciation of the Latin words sounded wrong, weakened by his own age and infirmity.

He knew now that he should not have come.

Yet the young boy's body began to writhe, and Sebastian had assured him that such movement was certain evidence that the evil residing in the boy was responding. Encouraged slightly, Father Laughlin raised up his crucifix and intoned the passages of the liturgy as best he could remember.

He deepened his voice and filled his lungs as if to command the evil's obedience by sheer volume.

Jeffrey Holmes's limbs began to spasm and anguished moans escaped his lips.

"Thank you, Father," Ernest Laughlin whispered, then raised his voice even further, feeling the power of the Lord welling up inside him to cast out the demon that inhabited the poor boy's body.

"Most cunning serpent," Laughlin found the phrases he'd been trying to remember. They weren't in Sebastian's Latin, but he remembered them from his college texts. "You shall no more dare to deceive the human race, persecute the Church, torment God's elect and sift them as wheat. The Most High God commands you, He with whom, in your great insolence, you still claim to be equal!"

As he bellowed the last words, he saw the wasted muscles of the boy's back and arms bunch as he struggled to a sitting position.

"Begone, Satan, inventor and master of all deceit, enemy of man's salvation." Laughlin fumbled in his pocket for the vial of holy water he had brought with him.

"Father?" The boy's voice was so faint, Father Laughlin wasn't certain he had heard anything at all.

"Father?" It was the tiny voice of a small child.

"Yes, my son?" Laughlin stepped into the cell, closer to Jeffrey, to better minister to the boy. He leaned down and reached out to touch him. "I'm here to help you."

"You!" the evil roared, its foul breath knocking Father Laughlin back. "*You* help *me*? *Never!*"

Laughlin stumbled backward, struggling to maintain his balance, then felt the solid wall behind him and regained his footing.

The boy stood up. Though his body was frail, his face reflected the twisted countenance of Satan himself. "*You will never defeat me!*" Jeffrey stretched out his filthy hands and moved slowly, one step at a time, toward the old priest.

Laughlin, frozen with a terror such as he'd never felt before, could only stare at the snarling, drooling creature that approached him.

Jeffrey spat, and a hot, viscous gob landed on the priest's lips and began to sizzle.

Laughlin cried out as he wiped the stinking mucus from his face. Finally jarred from his paralysis, he bolted for the door, finding it only an instant before the creature would have been on him. He slammed the door shut and threw the bolt, just as Jeffrey's poor body slammed against it. A furious howl erupted from the being trapped beyond the door, and it smashed Jeffrey Holmes's body against it over and over again, the unearthly voice reverberating through the walls of the tunnels and into the very bones of the buildings above them.

Laughlin hobbled away from the cell as quickly as he could, and when he was far enough to be certain he was safe, he leaned against the wall and tried to catch his breath.

He dampened his handkerchief with the holy water that was supposed to have washed the evil from Jeffrey Holmes's body and soul, and used it instead to wipe the spot where the devil's sputum still burned his lips.

When his heart had finally slowed its pounding and he trusted himself to walk, he crossed himself, and hurried back toward his rooms, listening to the unearthly howls that might fade from the walls of the school, but which would follow him all the way to his grave.

† † †

In the infirmary, Melody Hunt's eyes snapped open. She listened to the howling for a moment, and then, as if soothed by a lullaby, closed her eyes and fell back into an easy sleep.

† † †

In her room in the dormitory, Sofia Capelli sat listening to the wailing of a kindred spirit. As its volume rose, it awakened in her a hunger so desperate that it clawed at her insides. She curled up on her bed and held a pillow to her stomach. The time would come when they could be together.

Not yet, but soon.

† † †

Deep in the bowels of the underground, the being inhabiting Jeffrey Holmes fell to the stones in rage and frustration at the weakness of its host. Forcing Jeffrey to his feet, it hurled him against the wall, forcing the boy to smash his own head against the stones, but keeping him conscious. Totally conscious.

The boy must suffer—suffer as the evil itself was suffering.

Using the boy's own long, broken fingernails, the evil began gouging at Jeffrey's face, thrilling at the agony the boy was feeling. As its power and rage built, the thing went after Jeffrey's throat, tearing at the pulsing artery in his neck, ripping and slashing at his skin and muscles and tendons until finally the torn and jagged nails found what they sought and tore into the pulsing artery that pumped blood into the boy's brain.

Blood gushed from the ruined artery, spewing onto the stone floor.

One final rattling laugh bubbled from Jeffrey Holmes's throat as his life drained away, spreading across the floor of the dark cell.

The evil sucked in the last of Jeffrey Holmes's strength, then retreated like a maggot into a chrysalis, waiting for its next host to come. . . .

CHAPTER 41

RYAN MCINTYRE DUMPED his gym bag on his bed, dropped down next to it and swore softly. So much for spending a night back home; now he'd hurt his mother's feelings, Tom Kelly was sure to be pissed off at him, and he had no idea what to do about the whole mess. On the other hand, maybe there wasn't really anything *to* do; it was his mother who'd decided to let Kelly move in, not him, and maybe the best thing to do would be just to stay at school and let his mother do whatever she wanted.

Maybe it wasn't any of his business. Except it *was* his business— anything to do with his mother was his business, and even though he knew Tom Kelly was a perfectly decent guy, there was just something about him that rubbed Ryan the wrong way.

Bullshit, he heard his father's voice whispering inside his head. *You're just pissed off because he's not me, and he never will be. But that's your problem, not your mom's. So grow up and deal with it.*

He took a deep breath, looked up, and saw his roommate look quizzically up from the book he was reading. "Thought you were gone for the weekend," Clay said.

"Change of plans," Ryan said, seeing no point in even going into it with Clay. "Have you seen Melody?"

Clay shook his head. "I've been in here all afternoon."

Ryan fished his cell phone out of the gym bag and punched in Melody's number, but her voice mail came on fast enough to tell him she either didn't have the phone on, or didn't have it with her. So where wouldn't she have taken it? Nowhere very far from her room—probably just the laundry room in her dorm. "Hey," he asked Clay, "can I go into the girls' dorm?"

"No chance," Clay said without looking up from his book. "But maybe you can find someone who'd go knock on her door or something."

† † †

Five minutes later, Ryan opened the door to the foyer of the girls' dormitory. In a small parlor to the right, an elderly nun sat in a wing chair by the fireplace, reading. She peered suspiciously at Ryan over the rims of her glasses. "May I help you?"

"I'm looking for Melody Hunt. Or her roommate. Sofia Capelli?"

"I haven't seen Melody," the old nun said, "but Sofia will be working in the kitchen this evening."

"Thanks," Ryan said. By the time he'd turned back to the foyer, the nun had already disappeared back into her book.

† † †

"Sofia, stop daydreaming and take the garbage out."

Sofia made a face at the cook's back and her fingers tightened on the haft of the carving knife she'd been about to drop back into the drawer under the serving table. She felt a sudden urge to plunge the blade deep into the cook's back.

"Now!" the heavyset nun who had been cooking the same recipes at St. Isaac's for the last thirty years commanded, and the vision of blood spurting from her back vanished from Sofia's mind.

"Okay," she sighed and pulled the heavy black plastic bag from its container by the sink. Half-carrying and half-dragging the bag, she pushed the heavy outside door to the kitchen open, and nosed the wooden doorstop into the jamb with her toe, so she wouldn't be locked out when the door closed behind her.

The stench of rotting meat filled her nostrils as she raised the lid off one of the garbage barrels that stood at the mouth of a narrow passageway leading to the street, but instead of turning away from the stink as she always had before, tonight she found herself breathing it in deeply, sucking the noxious fumes into her lungs as if it were fresh salt air blowing in from the beach.

Releasing her grip on the bag she'd brought from the kitchen, Sofia leaned over the open barrel, peering down at the source of the oddly exciting aroma. At the bottom of the barrel lay a tangled mass of chicken entrails, scraps of beef, and rotting vegetables.

Crawling over the whole mass, making it look as if it were some kind of living thing, were hundreds—thousands—of tiny white squirming things.

Maggots.

The light from the security lamp high above cast a strange yellow-orange glow into the barrel, and as the creatures wriggled and slithered, their skins seemed to glint with millions of tiny diamonds.

She bent closer.

The mass boiled, heaved and swirled, as if all the maggots were but tiny parts of a single living being.

She reached into the barrel and let her fingers brush over them.

Hunger rose in her.

She could feel saliva coming into her mouth, and deep in her gut she felt a strange craving, a craving she knew could only be satisfied by one thing.

Her fingers closing on a fistful of the tiny larvae, she straightened up, then opened her hand to gaze at what she held.

The maggots moved in every direction. One by one they began to drop back into the barrel, instantly burying themselves in the rancid mass at its bottom. But before the last of them could escape, the hunger overcame her and Sofia raised her hand to her face, sucking the last of the maggots into her mouth.

She could feel them on her tongue, feel them writhing against her cheeks.

She began chewing, and as each of the tiny bodies exploded, a burst of sweetness erupted in her mouth.

She reached into the barrel again, scooping out a larger handful of maggots mixed with rotting flesh, and shoved it into her mouth, whimpering softly as she chewed and swallowed.

Another fistful followed, then another.

She could feel them in her belly, as if they were still alive, squirming and twisting, radiating out to fill not only her stomach, but every cell in her body. She was tingling all over, feeling them under her skin, giving her a strength she'd never felt before.

She reached for another handful when suddenly she heard someone behind her speak her name.

Instantly, she brushed the maggots and scraps of rotting meat from her lips and chin, wiped her hands on her apron, and swallowed quickly, emptying her mouth of the last morsels of her feast, then turned to see who had spoken.

Ryan McIntyre was framed in the open door to the kitchen.

"Sofia?" he asked, almost as if he wasn't certain it was really her. "I'm looking for Melody."

"She's not here," Sofia said, her voice rasping oddly as she raised the hem of the apron to wipe her chin.

Ryan cocked his head uncertainly. "Have you seen her?"

Sofia shrugged. "Father Sebastian wanted to see her," she said as she lifted the heavy garbage sack.

"Let me help you with that," Ryan said, stepping forward to take the sack from Sofia. But before he dropped the bag into the barrel his eyes fell on the slimy mass at its bottom, and he instinctively pulled away from the stench that boiled up from it. "Yuck," he muttered as he pressed the bag down on top of the writhing maggots. "That's disgusting."

Sofia only shrugged again, this time saying nothing at all.

"Well, if you see her, have her call me, okay?" Ryan asked as he put the lid onto the barrel.

Sofia just nodded, then turned and disappeared back into the kitchen.

† † †

Ryan watched Sofia go. What was going on? It looked like she'd been eating out of the garbage can. But of course that couldn't be—his own stomach was still churning after only a glance at the roiling mass of maggots squirming like something in the last throes of death. And the stink—

He shuddered just at the memory of it.

He must have been mistaken—she couldn't have done what he thought she'd been doing. It must have been the way the light hit her. But telling himself he must have been wrong wasn't calming his own stomach at all, so he turned his mind away from what he'd seen to what he'd heard.

Father Sebastian had wanted to see Melody.

On a Saturday? Why?

Ryan walked slowly away from the little alcove where the garbage barrels were kept, through the narrow alleyway to the street beyond. When he came to the sidewalk, he paused, gazing unseeingly at the row of bowfront houses across Louisburg Square, his mind filled instead with the memory of Tuesday night, when Father Sebastian had wanted to see Sofia for making out with Darren Bender.

She had to be carried to the infirmary that night, and she'd been . . . He searched his mind for the right word, and only one came to him.

Weird.

Sofia had been just plain weird ever since.

He crossed the street and went into the square, and sat on a bench in the deepening dark as the streetlamps cast strange shadows all around him.

Could the same thing that happened to Sofia have happened to Melody, too?

Could Melody be in the infirmary?

With a bad feeling in his gut, Ryan got up, left the square and crossed the street back to St. Isaac's. He threaded his way through the narrow alley, then headed toward the building whose second floor was occupied by the infirmary.

He didn't see a single person on his way; the whole campus seemed to be deserted.

Once again—just as on the night he and Melody had gone looking for Sofia—the infirmary door was locked. He cupped his hands around his eyes and tried to peer through the frosted glass in the door, but all he saw was a faint light, way in the back.

Had there been a light when he and Melody were looking for Sofia?

No, because Sofia hadn't been taken there yet.

But now someone was inside, and something inside him was telling him it was Melody Hunt.

He jerked at the door handle, praying maybe he'd been mistaken and that it wasn't locked at all, but it wouldn't budge.

The back way!

But even the thought of the maze of dark tunnels beneath the school brought the taste of fear to his mouth.

But Melody was in the infirmary, he knew it in his bones, and if anybody was going to help her before the same thing happened to her that had happened to Sofia Capelli, it was going to have to be him.

He turned away from the locked door and started back the way he'd come.

Would he even be able to find the door to the underground tunnels that Melody had showed him a few nights ago?

And if he could, would he find the courage to go down into the darkness below?

He didn't know, but at least he had to try.

CHAPTER 42

THE MOMENT TERI MCINTYRE opened the front door of her house, she knew that something was wrong. She stopped at the threshold so suddenly that Tom bumped into her from behind.

"What's—" he began, but Teri silenced him with a gesture.

"Something's not right," she whispered. "Someone's been here."

Tom pushed past her into the living room, turning on lights, but nothing looked amiss. "I think you're just upset about Ryan."

Teri shook her head, not moving from the front door, certain that whatever had happened had nothing at all to do with Ryan's going back to St. Isaac's instead of coming home.

This was something else. Something in the house was different. It was as if there was a change in the air, or the smell, or just the feeling of the place. That was it—it just didn't *feel* right. As Tom moved through the living room and dining room into the kitchen, she stepped inside but couldn't quite bring herself to close the door behind her.

"Oh, boy," Tom called from the kitchen. "We'd better call the police."

Terry's blood suddenly ran cold. "What is it? What did you find?"

"Someone's broken in."

Teri picked up the cordless phone on the way to the kitchen and punched in 911. "What if they're still here?" she whispered, rolling her eyes toward the floor above.

Before she could stop him, Tom had taken the baseball bat she'd started keeping in the hall closet after Bill had died, and started up the stairs. "What if there's more than one of them?" she called after him, then shifted her attention to the 911 operator, suddenly blanking on her own address. And not just the number—she couldn't even remember the street.

"It's all right," the operator assured her. "All that information comes up on my screen even before I've answered. I'll send a couple of cars over right away."

"Well, whoever it was, they're gone now," Tom said as he came back down the stairs. "Looks like they took your jewelry, and maybe some other stuff."

Teri's hands trembled as she passed the information on to the 911 operator, then clicked the phone off. Suddenly her knees began to buckle and she leaned on the kitchen counter. "I think I need to sit down," she said as a wave of nausea suddenly rose in her stomach.

Tom guided her into one of the kitchen chairs and she gazed mutely at the broken pane in the kitchen door. Then her eyes shifted to the shattered glass on the floor. One thought kept running through her mind: *Thank God, Ryan wasn't here alone when this happened.*

"You look like you could use a drink," Tom said.

Finally her eyes left the hole in the window and the broken glass on the floor and she shook her head. "No," she said as the threat of nausea passed and her fear began giving way to anger. "At least not right now—certainly not until the police have been here."

"Maybe we'd better go upstairs to see what's missing," Tom suggested. "We should be able to tell the police everything that's gone. Or at least everything you can see right away."

Missing . . . gone . . .

The words echoed in her mind. Someone had come into *her house* and taken *her things.* Just the thought of it was enough to drive away the last tendrils of the near-panic she'd just felt. "You're right," she said, rising to her feet. "Not that there's anything here worth stealing. But let's take a look." She quickly assessed the kitchen, which looked utterly untouched except for the broken glass, then slowly toured the dining room and living room.

Nothing seemed disturbed. Nothing at all.

Tom moved the fireplace poker from where it always leaned against the brick wall and set it in its stand.

Teri folded the afghan and draped it over the arm of the sofa. The house looked neat.

With Tom following close behind, she slowly mounted the stairs. He had turned on every light in every room, and opened all the closet doors.

Or the intruder had.

When they came to the landing, she looked at him questioningly. "Were they in every room?"

"It doesn't look like it," Tom replied. "Just your room, as far as I could see."

Teri saw three things the moment she entered the master bedroom: the broken photograph of Ryan on the floor, her underwear hanging out of a drawer, and the open lid of her jewelry box. As she reached down to pick up the picture, Tom put a gently restraining hand on her arm.

"The police need to see everything exactly as it is," he told her, his voice thick with sympathy.

How dare they come into my home? How dare they touch my things? How dare they—

She glared at the mess with impotent fury, knowing she'd never again be able to wear any of the clothes they had touched, no matter how many times she washed them. And the jewelry box had contained nothing but junk! The only thing she owned of any value was her engagement ring, and it was now on her right hand; she still always wore it.

The rest was worthless!

And the photograph of Ryan . . . its glass and frame broken.

"What else is there besides what we can see?" Tom pressed, pulling her attention from the ruined photograph. "Look around."

Reluctantly—afraid of what she might find at every step—Teri moved through the rest of the upstairs rooms: Ryan's room, the study, the bathrooms.

Nothing else seemed amiss.

She came back into her room and stood looking down into her jewelry box.

"It seems like they just wanted jewelry or money," she finally said. "But it was just junk jewelry. Costume stuff." Unbidden, her lips twisted into a rueful smile. "And I sure don't have enough money to keep cash hidden in my lingerie drawer."

"You should still try to give the police a list of everything that's gone," Tom said, his voice tinged with indignation. "It doesn't matter how much any of it was worth—it was yours!"

Teri chuckled bitterly. "Look at this," she said, pointing. "They took the turquoise necklace—which was nothing but ground turquoise in resin, but left the earrings. And they're at least real! It doesn't make sense."

"Probably junkies," Tom said. "All they'd do is grab whatever looked like it might be easy to sell."

Teri sank down on the bed and put her head in her hands. "First, Ryan is mad at me, and now this." She sighed, then felt the bed depress as Tom sat next to her.

"Not the best of evenings," he agreed.

Nodding tiredly, she laid her head on his shoulder, and he put a comforting arm around her. "Why me?" she asked hollowly. "What could they have been looking for?"

"Cash. And all they need to see is an empty house—doesn't matter which one. It could have been anyone. It's not personal. I'm just glad you weren't home alone when it happened."

Teri looked up at him, emotions swirling so fast she couldn't put words to them.

Tom hugged her close. "You won't ever need to be home alone again. Not if I'm here."

A sob rose up to choke Teri. "Ryan—" was all she could manage to say.

"Ryan's not here, honey. You need someone to be here with you. To protect you." He kissed her temple. "And I need you."

Teri took a ragged breath.

"Shh," he soothed her. "Everything's going to be all right."

With all her heart, Teri wished she could believe him.

Chapter 43

Father Sebastian gazed speechlessly at Father Laughlin, who seemed to have aged at least ten years since the younger man had seen him only a few hours ago. Now the old headmaster sat shrunken and hunched on the couch in Sebastian's small sitting room, his face ashen, his hands trembling as he tried to hold the small glass of whiskey the younger priest had offered him. Only after the old man had taken a sip did Father Sebastian finally find his voice. "You didn't," he breathed. "Please tell me you didn't try to conduct the rite on your own."

"I wish I could," Laughlin said, draining the shot, then setting the glass down and leaning forward to hold his head in his hand. He took a deep breath, then another, and when he looked up, Sebastian saw the shame in his eyes, and the sorrow etched deeply in every wrinkle and crevice of his weathered face. But neither the shame nor the sorrow could change the reality of Laughlin's attempt to exorcise the evil in Jeffrey Holmes.

"What were you thinking?" Sebastian whispered.

Laughlin seemed to become even smaller as he shook his head helplessly. "I'm so sorry."

Sebastian took a deep breath, then laid a gentle hand on the old priest's shoulder. "You understand that the damage you did may well be irreversible?"

Laughlin looked up uncertainly. "But he was already a lost soul, wasn't he?"

"Souls are not ever completely lost," Sebastian replied. "Not while there is life, faith, and hope."

Laughlin sank his head back into his hands.

"We must see how bad he is," Father Sebastian said.

Laughlin's head snapped up again. "You don't mean to go back in there?"

Sebastian spread his hands. "What choice do we have? We must do what we can for the boy."

"I can't. I tell you, it was the most horrible—"

"I know," Sebastian said. "I have seen the demon before. But if there's any chance of saving him, it's going to take both of us."

† † †

The flashlight Ryan had borrowed from Clay needed fresh batteries, but it cast just enough of a weak yellowish beam to illuminate the uneven stones in the floor and enough of the damp walls to keep Ryan's panic at bay. Steeling himself against the terror that had nearly overwhelmed him when he and Melody had come down here a few nights ago, he tried to remember the exact route they had taken to get to the back door of the infirmary.

The staircase in the dining hall had been simple enough to find, and he'd clearly remembered turning right at its foot. But after that he'd been less certain, and now, as the passages seemed to go off in every direction, and he no longer had any real idea of where he might be, it was getting harder and harder to ignore the knot of fear in his belly, and the cold chill that seemed to be coming right up from the floor, through his shoes, and into his legs.

Maybe he should just give it up and try to find his way back.

But how?

He couldn't even remember how many turns he'd made, let alone which way any of them had gone. And if he made a mistake—

The flashlight dimmed slightly, and just the thought of being plunged into darkness elicited a groan from Ryan's throat that echoed off the walls to taunt him over and over. Then, just as he was about to turn and run the other way, he saw it. At the farthest reach of its beam, the flashlight found the edge of a doorway.

A doorway that looked familiar.

A surge of relief ran through Ryan as he stepped through the door a moment later and mounted the stairs.

He paused at the main floor, listened for any sound at all, then went on up to the second floor landing.

There it was—the door to the infirmary, just as Melody had shown him. Carefully, silently, he gripped the cold brass knob on the door and turned it.

The knob turned, but the door didn't open.

Locked.

He turned the weakening flashlight beam on the keyhole beneath the knob—the old-fashioned kind that took a skeleton key. Kneeling down, he flicked the flashlight off and peered into the keyhole. Barely the faintest glimmer of light.

Yet there was light coming through the wide crack beneath the door.

The key must be in the lock!

He thought quickly, then remembered something he'd seen in a movie a long time ago.

He took a pen from his shirt pocket, then unbuttoned his shirt, peeled it off and slid it carefully under the door, pushing enough of it through the crack so, even if it was bunched up, at least three inches of cloth would cover the floor on the other side.

Unscrewing the barrel of the pen, he took the ink cartridge out, and carefully pushed it into the keyhole.

Sure enough, something blocked it when it was no more than half an inch in.

He pushed harder.

Nothing.

In his mind's eye, he tried to picture the key. If it wasn't lined up quite right, he wouldn't be able to push it out.

He probed gently with the point of the pen, poking and prodding until he felt it slip by the blade of the key. Then he levered the blade slightly, felt the vibration of the key moving and suddenly shifting.

He levered it again, but this time, though slightly loose, it wouldn't move. He'd done it! It must be lined up with the slot on the other side. Pulling the pen out, he turned it around so its flat end was away from him, then reinserted it, poking gently until he found the end of the key's shaft.

He pressed gently.

Nothing.

A little harder.

The key moved.

One last time and then he heard a faint sound as the key fell to the floor, and the pen cartridge slid all the way through the lock. When he pulled the pen back out, he could see light through the keyhole.

Carefully, he pulled the shirt back from under the crack beneath the door, and there lay the key.

Ryan put his shirt back on and buttoned it, reassembled his pen and put it in his pocket, and only then inserted the key in the lock and turned it.

The mechanism turned, its soft *thunk* sounding like a sledgehammer in the silence.

Ryan waited a moment, listening.

Nothing.

He turned the knob and opened the door, finding himself in some kind of storeroom, illuminated by the light coming through its frosted pane. Ryan slipped inside and quietly closed the door to the stairwell behind him.

He heard the murmurings of a female voice in the next room, and shoes squeaking on tile.

He stood perfectly still, heart pounding, trying to breathe without making a sound.

A light went out, leaving just a small bluish night-light. Then he heard a door open and close somewhere in the distance.

When he heard nothing else for at least a full minute, Ryan left the storeroom and found Melody, wearing a hospital gown and lying on her back in one of the twelve beds the infirmary's single ward held. Though there was no sign of the nun who tended the ward at night, Ryan was sure she would be back soon.

"Melody," he whispered, gently shaking her shoulder. "Melody, wake up."

Melody opened her eyes, looked at him almost as if she didn't recognize him, frowned slightly, then once more closed her eyes, as if she'd seen him, but wasn't interested enough even to stay awake.

Ryan shook her again, certain the nun would be back any second. "Melody, tell me what they did to you."

Melody's eyes fluttered open again, and this time they focused on Ryan.

Her eyes had changed. They looked darker than he remembered, and had taken on a stormy, angry look. Her pupils were dilated, the whites bloodshot. "Go away," she whispered.

"No," he insisted. "I want to help you."

"Go away," she said again, and closed her eyes. "I don't need any help."

Ryan heard a door open somewhere beyond the front of the ward.

The nun was back.

Touching Melody's cheek, then leaning over to give her a quick kiss, he slipped back into the storage closet, then into the stairwell, barely remembering to replace the key in its slot before closing the door.

It wasn't until he was back in the basement that he suddenly remembered how cold Melody's cheek had felt when he kissed it.

As cold as the stones beneath his feet.

† † †

"Holy Mary, Mother of God," Father Laughlin breathed almost inaudibly as he saw the blood-soaked mass that a little while ago had been Jeffrey Holmes.

"I was afraid of this," Father Sebastian said, laying a steadying hand on the older priest's shoulder. "I've seen it before."

Laughlin crossed himself, then lifted the crucifix that hung from his belt to his lips and kissed it. "This is my fault," he whispered. "My sin. Father Sebastian, will you hear my confession?"

"At the proper time," Sebastian replied, playing the beam of his flashlight around the cell. "I'll have to carry him."

Laughlin's eyes widened in horror. "Carry him?" he echoed. "Carry him where?"

"Someplace where he won't be found, at least until after the Pope's visit." His eyes fixed on Laughlin. "Assuming His Holiness comes at all," he added. "Which he surely won't if this gets out." When Laughlin still hesitated, he spoke again, this time using the headmaster's Christian name. "Ernest, there is nothing we can do to change what has happened. But it isn't only of poor Jeffrey that we must think right now. We also have the school to consider, and all the other children under our care. No matter how we feel, we cannot put our school and the children at risk, and if this gets out, not only will His Holiness not come, but St. Isaac's itself will surely be closed. We must do what is required for the greatest good, and trust in God to forgive us whatever sins we may commit."

Laughlin nodded mutely, still unable to take his eyes off the boy's ruined face, but finally managed to find not only his voice, but his courage as well. "I know a place we can put him," he said. "I shall come back afterward and scrub away the blood. It shall be part of my penance." Tears flooding his eyes, he watched as Father Sebastian lifted the corpse up and put it over his shoulder.

† † †

Ryan stood at the foot of the dark stairs for a long moment before stepping back into the tunnels beneath the school. He hated the whole idea of leaving Melody lying in the infirmary, but what could he do?

Call her parents? But Ryan didn't even have any idea where they were.

The police? And tell them what? That Melody wasn't sick? Why would they believe him? All that would happen was that he'd get in trouble for having snuck in.

Broken in.

He'd better go back to his room, and maybe talk with Clay.

Praying that the flashlight would last until he reached the stairs leading to the dining hall, he stepped out of the shelter of the doorway into the infirmary basement.

Then, before he'd taken more than half a dozen steps, he heard something.

Someone was coming.

Without thinking, he turned around and darted past the doorway from which he'd just emerged, pressing himself into the same alcove in which he and Melody had hidden a few nights ago.

As the footsteps drew closer, he recognized one voice—Father Sebastian—and thought he heard someone else breathing hard.

A few seconds later the beam of a flashlight played along the floor in front of him.

Ryan crouched low and pressed himself against the wall of the alcove, holding his breath.

A figure shuffled quickly past the alcove, immediately followed by another.

The second figure was carrying something slung over his shoulder.

Something that looked like a body.

What was going on in this place?

Only when they were well past him did Ryan finally slip back out into the tunnel, every fiber of his being wanting to run the other way, back toward the dining room.

Instead, his heart pounding, he followed the two figures.

Every few yards they stopped to catch their breath.

Ryan kept as far back as he could without losing track of them, but as they went deeper into the underground, down narrow tunnels and two series of old stone steps, Ryan had to move closer or risk losing sight of them entirely.

Lose sight of them, and lose his own way as well.

At last the two men stopped.

Ryan watched as Father Sebastian fumbled with a key, then pushed open a door so old that it creaked in protest as it swung on its rusted hinges.

In the flickering of the flashlight, Father carried a body that Ryan could now see clearly.

A boy about his own age, naked and covered in what looked like blood.

Ryan's pulse began to hammer in his ears.

A light came on in the chamber beyond the door, and the two men stepped over its threshold.

Ryan moved closer to see what was in the room.

Father Laughlin leaned against the wall, breathing hard, his face shining with perspiration.

Something that looked like a stone coffin stood in the center of the floor. Its rim was ornately carved with garlands, and there was a detailed crucifix on one end. Its lid leaned against the wall.

Father Sebastian laid the body in the sarcophagus.

It took both priests to lift the stone cover and slide it into place.

"Good," Father Sebastian pronounced. "Let's go."

"Oh, Jeffrey," Father Laughlin said, laying a hand on the stone tomb. "I am so sorry."

Jeffrey! The name thundered in Ryan's mind as he slipped back into the darkness, searching for somewhere—anywhere—to hide until the two priests had passed him. *Was that Jeffrey Holmes?* Ryan flattened himself against a small doorway, holding his breath until they passed.

But when he stepped out, he tripped on the uneven flooring, and his shoe hit a rock that ricocheted off the wall.

Father Sebastian whirled around.

The beam of his flashlight caught Ryan square in the face.

CHAPTER 44

THE POPE LEANED in close to the computer screen, unwilling to miss even the slightest nuance of the young blond girl's movements. Though his vision was nearly as sharp as it had been forty years ago when he first came to the Vatican, he wished there were some way of seeing the clip on a larger screen.

As if he'd read the Pontiff's mind, Cardinal Morisco tilted his head toward the large plasma screen that hung incongruously on the wall between a pair of sixteenth-century portraits depicting two of the current Pope's earlier predecessors. "Perhaps if I connected the computer to the big monitor . . . ?" he asked softly.

His Holiness nodded, then waited impatiently as the connection was made and the clip began again.

All too soon, it ended.

"Play it again," he commanded.

Morisco tapped a few keys on the laptop keyboard, and the video began playing for the fourth time, the second time on the big monitor.

The Pope gazed in rapt fascination. The younger priest—the one with the knowledge of the ancient rite—appeared to know exactly what he was doing.

And he appeared to know exactly what proof the Pope needed to see in order to satisfy himself that the young priest truly had full control of the evil in the young girl. As the Pope watched, the priest played the demon like a master puppeteer manipulating a marionette, calling it forth and suppressing it at will, making it flow to the fore then ebb away again like waves on a beach.

But it wasn't a beach upon which the evil played—it was on the soul of the girl in whom it resided, and every one of the demon's tortures were reflected in the child's face as her features twisted from placid in-nocent beauty into the unmistakable snarl of the devil himself, only to return to innocence as the young priest suppressed the evil.

Again and again it happened, taking on an almost hypnotic rhythm.

"Sound!" the Pope whispered. "I want sound!"

"I'm sorry, Holiness," Morisco said as the clip once more came to an end. "There is no sound."

"Play it again."

This time, the Pope watched the faces of those attending the ritual: the old nun, the elderly priest, and the young, dark-haired priest who was conducting the ritual.

They were the same three he'd seen in the previous video—the one with the dark-haired girl—and he was certain their expressions were genuine.

Genuine anticipation as the ritual began.

Genuine terror when the evil showed its face.

Genuine anxiety as the young priest battled for control of the evil.

And, most important of all, genuine relief when the evil had been tamed.

These were not actors. The Pope himself had studied the records of all three of these servants of the Church, and their lifelong devotion to Christ could not be questioned.

Beyond that, there was the face of evil itself. The Pope had seen it be-fore, too many times, and recognized it instantly. There was no mistaking its vileness, nor any way of faking its presence when it was not there.

Yes, this young priest knew what he was doing: he was able to invoke the devil himself from the soul of an innocent.

"I must see this for myself," the Pope finally said, turning to Morisco. "We shall go to Boston."

CHAPTER 45

A LIGHT RAIN BEGAN to fall across the Boston area, but Matt McCain barely noticed it as he slouched against the passenger door of the patrol car, while his partner threaded the vehicle slowly through the late-evening traffic. "Anything about that break-in strike you as odd?" he finally asked as Steve Morgan exited the thruway and braked quickly as they closed on a long, snaking line of red taillights.

"Like what?" Morgan parried, turning on the windshield wipers.

McCain shifted in the passenger seat, sitting up. "Didn't seem like enough was messed up. I mean, usually a break-in like that is some junkie, looking for anything they can sell. And there were things all over that house that a junkie would have taken, starting with the computer sitting right out on the dining room table. How come the perp didn't take it?"

Morgan said nothing, having been McCain's partner long enough to recognize a rhetorical question when he heard one. Sure enough, McCain answered his own question without so much as a pause.

"I think this guy was after something specific."

Morgan shrugged. "Maybe so. But what? Mrs. McIntyre didn't seem to think anything was missing except some jewelry, and she said what was gone wasn't worth much."

"Exactly," McCain said. "And nobody's going to take junk jewelry, except to make it look like a burglary. Most of the junkies know how to spot the good stuff these days." He picked up the report folder, flipped it open and twisted his penlight. "I've just got a funny feeling about this. Something hinkey about the whole thing."

"You want something hinkey, how about this traffic?" Morgan grumbled. "How come people don't just stay home once in a while?"

"Ah, crap," McCain groaned. "You're going to love this."

"What?"

"No signature on the form."

Morgan looked at the clock on the dash. 9:47. Their shift ended at ten. "Christ."

"We gotta go back."

"We're almost at the station," Morgan protested.

"And we can't go in with an unsigned sheet." McCain sighed. "Turn it around."

"Maria's not going to be happy," Morgan said. "I told her I'd be home in time to say good night to the kids—"

"Okay, how about I drop you off at the station and I go back by myself? It was my stupid mistake."

Steve Morgan thought about it for no more than a second. If McCain was alone, and a call came in, either he'd have to respond to it alone, or the department would be short a car. "Forget it," he said, turning on the flashing lights and swerving the cruiser around the gridlocked traffic.

The kids would just have to stay up an extra hour.

CHAPTER 46

RYAN?" FATHER SEBASTIAN asked, his voice sounding slightly puzzled, but keeping his flashlight squarely in Ryan's eyes, making it impossible for him to see the priest's face, let alone read his expression.

Ryan had been caught—there was no escaping that fact—but he had no idea if Father Sebastian knew he'd been following them and had watched them put Jeffrey Holmes's body into the stone sarcophagus. Maybe if he just played dumb . . .

"What are you doing down here?" Father Laughlin asked, giving Ryan an opportunity.

"I don't even know where I am," he said, making his voice as plaintive as he could without overdoing it. "Clay Matthews—my roommate—told me there was a shortcut to the gym, but I got lost." He tried to shield his eyes from the beam of the flashlight. "I was really getting scared 'til I saw your light a minute ago. I didn't think I was ever going to get out of here."

"Well, you're certainly not anywhere near the gymnasium," Father Sebastian said, still holding the blazing light steady. "How long have you been down here?"

Ryan tried for a helpless shrug as his mind worked furiously. "I don't even know. It seems like hours, but I guess it couldn't be. What time is it now? It was about eight-thirty when I left my room."

"And it's almost nine, now," Father Sebastian told him. "So it hasn't actually been hours."

A trickle of perspiration trailed down the side of Ryan's face, but he couldn't tell if the priests noticed it.

"You know, it's against the rules to use the tunnels as a shortcut," Father Sebastian said.

Ryan shook his head. "Nobody told me that, and everyone uses them for shortcuts."

"And too often people get lost," Father Sebastian replied. "Which is exactly why it's against the rules."

"I'm sorry," Ryan said, putting as much conviction into his voice as he could muster. "I really didn't know, and I can tell you after tonight I'll sure never do it again."

He could almost feel the two priests weighing not only his words, but the tone of his voice, and the expression in his eyes as well.

"All right," Father Sebastian finally sighed, lowering the light. Ryan took a deep breath of relief. "Come with us."

As sheepishly as he could—and keeping his head down—Ryan followed close behind the two priests as they walked quickly through the maze of tunnels, up and down various short flights of steps that had been put in where the levels of the various basements didn't quite match. The flashlight beam illuminated only the floor in front of their feet, but Father Laughlin seemed to know exactly where they were and where he was going.

Ryan began rehearsing what he'd do once he was above ground.

The first thing would be to find the nearest door to the streets and get as far away from St. Isaac's as he possibly could.

Then call his mother.

Then call the police.

And then, with his mother and the police, he'd come back and show them where the two priests had put Jeffrey Holmes's body.

And he'd get Melody out of the infirmary and into a real hospital.

Except how was he going to show the police where Jeffrey Holmes was? He'd been trying to keep track of all the turns they'd made, and how many steps they'd gone up and down, but he'd already forgotten some of it, and—

"There's something here you should see," Father Sebastian said, his voice breaking into Ryan's reverie. He put a key in the lock of an old wooden door that was set deep in the wall of the tunnel. "Come and take a look." He pushed the door, and it swung wide, its rusty hinges creaking.

Just the sound was enough to make Ryan's skin crawl. "I—I really need to get back to the dorm," he stammered.

"Just a quick look," Father Sebastian urged. "Given who you're with, I doubt Brother Francis will be too hard on you if you're a little late. And this is part of the school's history. Actually, it's one of the most interesting parts."

Once again Ryan's mind raced. If he insisted on going back to the dorm, they'd figure out he'd seen something. Better to pretend he wasn't worried about anything at all, even though the hairs on the back of his neck were all standing on end, and he was overwhelmed by an urge to turn and run. But there was no choice—he had to maintain his masquerade of innocence.

The sooner he looked at whatever Father Sebastian wanted to show him, the sooner they'd be out of here. Steeling himself against the tide of apprehension that was rapidly rising around him, Ryan stepped in front of Father Laughlin and peered into the dark room.

"Go in," Father Sebastian said. "Light a candle." He shined the flashlight on a candle box in a niche a few feet away and the sand receptacle that stood next to it.

Ryan took two steps into the room.

The light went out.

The door slammed behind him.

Ryan wheeled around and threw his weight against the heavy wooden door, but the unmistakable sound of an old and heavy bolt being thrown echoed in the small room, and Ryan knew his act had failed.

They knew exactly what he'd seen.

The tide of apprehension of a moment ago built into a giant wave of panic, and Ryan turned with his back to the door, pressing himself hard against it as he took deep breaths, willing the panic away. After a moment, his mind cleared enough to remember that there were candles, and certainly matches, and he didn't need to be in absolute darkness.

He felt for the chapel door behind him, trying to remember exactly where the niche with the candles was. To the left, and not very far away. Holding his hands in front of him, he groped slowly and blindly through the darkness. But after he'd taken half a dozen steps he found nothing, and hesitated. Should he try to go back to the door and start over again? But what if he couldn't even find the door? He didn't even know how big the room was—he might wander for hours in the blackness!

That thought alone was enough to bring his panic surging back, and a soft moan of terror rose in his throat. Better to keep going, at least until he found another wall.

He took another step, then another, and suddenly his fingertips touched the hard stone of the wall, and a moment later he found first the niche, then the box of thin wax tapers. Gently, he ran his fingers around the box of candles until he found a box of wooden matches and a striking pad.

He struck a match and held it to a candle, then stuck it in the sand. He lit another and another, until the sand receptacle was ablaze, and the glowing candlelight began to drive the terror from his soul.

At last he saw where the priests had imprisoned him.

A chapel.

A small chapel dominated by a hideous crucifix, which seemed to be suspended in midair over a small altar. An old, ornately carved confessional sat to one side. The walls and floor were cold gray stone.

Ryan picked up one of the candles and walked around behind the altar, where he found a small door, presumably leading to the vestry.

It was as solidly locked as the chapel door.

There was no way out, unless he took the candles and set fire to the chapel door.

But even that probably wouldn't work; he might die of smoke inhalation in this tiny chamber before the door would be compromised enough to attempt an escape.

There was no escape, so he had to wait for them to come back.

But would they come back for him? What if they just left him alone down here? How long would it take for him to die?

And what if he ran out of candles?

With his terror of the darkness already starting to flood back, he blew out all the candles but two—one left standing in the sand in the niche, the other one clutched tight in his own hand.

He sat on the cold stone blocks, his back to the big wooden door.

They'd come back.

They had to come back.

He sat silently, gazing up at the monstrous hollow-eyed Christ who stared unseeingly back at him.

And then he began thinking about his father.

His father would tell him what to do.

† † †

Teri spread a towel across the highly polished surface of the dresser top, then turned the jewelry box upside down to pour out the contents of its lowest compartment, which she'd always used as a catchall for everything from extra earring backs—or single earrings whose mates she'd never given up hope of finding—to spare change, Bill's collar stays, and a few tiny objects she could no longer even identify. "I'll never be able to use this box again," she said, her voice trembling. "And I've loved it since the day Bill gave it to me." She shook her head sadly and looked up at Tom. "And now I hate it. Isn't that sad? Someone I don't even know—probably won't ever meet—has ruined this for me." Now she glanced around the room, but her eyes were seeing far beyond the four walls surrounding her.

Walls that had betrayed her; walls that had failed to protect her.

"Do you think I'll ever feel safe here again?"

"Honey." Tom came up from behind her and put his hands on her shoulders.

"And I'll have to throw away everything in that drawer, too." She nodded her head toward the dresser drawer that was still open, her lingerie still hanging out, just as it had been when she had come home.

Just as it had been when the police had come and taken their report and then gone away again with nothing having changed. "I'll never wear any of it again. Ever. I don't even want to touch it." Now the fear that she would never be safe again began to truly singe into her bones. Suddenly, every window was a doorway and every bed a hiding place.

Every closet could be a refuge for a thief.

A thief, or worse.

Her home, the home she had shared with her husband and son for so many years, the place she had always felt so safe, was no longer a comfort. Her sanctuary had been breached—her very spirit had been violated—and she knew she would never feel safe again.

Not even in Tom's arms.

"I'll always be afraid," she whispered, turning and burying her face in Tom's shoulder. "Always."

Tom hugged her close for a moment, then took a deep breath and Teri felt him stiffen as if he'd just made some kind of momentous decision. "Either you're coming back to my place tonight," he announced, "or I'm going home, packing a few things, and moving in here tonight. It doesn't matter what Ryan says or what he thinks—I don't want you to be here alone."

Teri pulled away slightly, remembering the terrible pain in her son's face when she'd told him Tom was going to be moving in with her. "I don't know," she said. "I don't know if I can do that to Ryan."

Tom tipped her chin up and looked directly into her eyes.

"I do know."

"You can spend the night," she said, drawing away slightly, her eyes pleading for his understanding, "but after the way Ryan reacted, I can't. He's already been hurt so much, and I just can't hurt him any more."

Tom stared at her. "You're kidding! You'd rather be alone in this house, even after it's been broken into?"

"I don't want to," Teri whispered. "But Ryan's my son. Mine and

Bill's. He's already lost his father and now he's afraid he's losing me, too. Please . . . can't you understand?"

"I'll try," he responded, and pulled her closer. "But I'm still not sure it was just a random break-in. They were looking for something—some *thing*." His hand gently caressed her hair. "You must have something here that they wanted."

"There's nothing, I told you," she whispered against his chest. "No money, no drugs, nothing of value. You know how I live, Tom. There's nothing here!"

"There has to be *something*," he insisted, holding her tighter. "Maybe something old—something that might not even be worth anything if it were new. You know, like the stuff people bring from their attics on *Antiques Roadshow* where they don't even know what they have. Could your parents have left you something? Or Bill?"

At the mention of her husband's name the memory of the silver cross that Bill had brought back from Kuwait rose in her mind. "Bill brought something from—" she began, but as she felt his arms suddenly tighten and his body stiffen once again, she cut off her own words.

"What?" Tom asked, his voice tight, almost strangled, the gentleness of a moment ago suddenly gone.

Teri froze in his arms, her mind racing. What was going on? What had changed? All she'd tried to do was think of something that might be of value. And now it felt as if he was angry at her. "What's wrong?" she asked, then tried to step back a little, but his hold on her only tightened. "Let go of me!"

"Tell me where it is," Tom demanded, his voice no longer just tight, but ice cold. "It's a cross isn't it? A silver cross that your husband brought home from Kuwait."

Teri forced her hands against him and shoved him as hard as she could, breaking loose from his grip and backing away.

"It doesn't belong to you," Tom said, his eyes suddenly glittering with fury. "It belongs to us. It's ours." Teri stared at him mutely, the color drained from her face. "You need to get that cross and give it to me, Teri. You need to get it right now."

Teri stared at him, frozen where she stood. Who was this man? Who was this person she'd allowed into her life, who she'd trusted so much she had invited him to move into her home? This man who only a few moments ago had been so loving, so protective?

Now he was a complete stranger—there was not even a trace left of the man she'd fallen in love with. "You did this," she breathed, the truth slashing into her soul like the blade of a knife. "You told them—" Her voice broke, and she began backing away toward the door. What was so important about the cross? Why did this man need it? And how did he know that whoever had broken into the house hadn't found its hiding place in the attic trunk? Suddenly—even though she didn't know why—she knew that whatever happened, she wouldn't help him, wouldn't tell him anything. "I don't know what you're talking about," she said. "All Bill brought was—"

"Don't lie to me," Tom Kelly said, his voice suddenly low and dangerous. "I know what he brought home, and I know it's still here. The fireplace poker hadn't been moved. That was our sign—if he'd found it, he'd have left the poker lying in the middle of the living room floor."

"I don't know what you're talking about," Teri insisted, edging closer to the door.

"You do," Kelly whispered, his eyes dark and menacing. "You know, and you're going to tell me. We've got all night. Trust me on this, Teri. You'll be telling me anything I want to know long before the sun comes up."

Teri turned and fled.

Tom lunged after her, grabbing the back of her dress. She pulled away, feeling the fabric rip, and raced toward the top of the stairs.

He reached for her again, but she twisted away from his grip. He came after her again, but suddenly skidded as a throw rug slipped out from under him on the hardwood floor. He staggered, fell to his knees, but managed to grab one of her ankles.

Now Teri, too, fell, but lashed out with her free leg, kicking at his face, at his chest, at his arms—kicking him anywhere she could, panic giving her a strength she didn't know she had.

"Tell me, damn you!" he roared, finding a grip on her flailing leg.

She grabbed the spindles of the baluster with both hands and wrenched her ankles out of his grasp, then got her feet beneath her and ran down the stairs.

He leaped from the top stair and landed on her, and together they tumbled down the last steps.

Teri's head smashed hard on the bottom step, but somehow she mustered one last burst of energy and started lurching through the living room toward the front door.

Tom Kelly's arm snaked around her neck in a vise grip she couldn't escape. "We don't have to do this," he whispered through gritted teeth. "Just tell me where the cross is."

Suddenly she twisted hard, turning just enough to jerk her knee hard up into his groin. His grip weakened slightly, and for a brief moment she thought she might escape. But then his eyes filled with rage, and a furious howl erupted from his throat. His huge hands closed on her shoulders and he hurled her to the floor.

She reached out, trying to break her fall, but it was too late.

Teri's head crashed on the marble hearth of the fireplace.

She saw a starburst of color.

And then nothing.

† † †

Tom stood still for a long moment, recovering his breath and waiting for the agony in his groin to ease. He glowered furiously at Teri's still form, offering a quick prayer to Allah that she would live long enough to tell him what he had to know. And she would tell him; by the time she awakened, she would be completely restrained, and, if he had to, he would spend the rest of the night getting the information from her.

As the nausea from the agony in his groin passed, he went to her, knelt, and made certain she was still breathing.

She was.

Everything was going to be all right.

But as he rose to his feet to find something with which to bind her, the flare of headlights washed across the living room.

A car pulled up in front.

He stepped to the window and pulled the curtain just far enough aside to peer out.

A police car.

So he wasn't going to have the rest of the night after all.

He ducked into the kitchen, then slipped quietly out the back door.

The one with the broken pane.

CHAPTER 47

RYAN'S HEAD SNAPPED UP.

A sound!

Faint, but definitely there, coming from somewhere in the blackness beyond the chapel's altar.

Both the candle he held as he sat in the confessional and the one in the sand had burned halfway down, yet it didn't feel like nearly enough time could have passed for that much wax to have burned.

Another sound.

This time it was the unmistakable sound of an ancient lock in a heavy door.

Then the squeal of rusty hinges, echoing off the stone walls of the chapel followed by a scraping sound.

Though he could see nothing beyond the faint pools of light cast by the two candles, he was certain the last sound had to be the vestry door sagging on its hinges and dragging on the stone floor as it swung open.

A moment later, the lights came on.

Ryan shielded his eyes against the sudden glare.

"In the confessional, Ryan?" he heard Father Sebastian ask, his voice echoing oddly. "Surely you know your sins have to be confessed to a priest, not merely to an empty booth."

Ryan stood and stepped out of the confessional. "I—I just didn't want to sit on the floor," he stammered, finally dropping his hand from his eyes to look directly into Father Sebastian's face. But the priest's expression was as bland as his voice had been, utterly unreadable.

"I'm glad you're here, Ryan," Father Sebastian said now. "In fact, though you may not have been praying yourself, I think of you as an answer to my own prayers."

A chill ran through Ryan that had nothing to do with the cold stone of the chapel, and his mind began racing. He'd heard the vestry door unlock, but had he heard the priest lock it again? Or even close it?

No! It was still open. If he could shove the priest aside—just knock him off his feet for a moment—

But then what? Where did that door lead to?

More tunnels? How would he ever find his way out? "An answer to your prayers?" Ryan echoed, stalling for time. "What does that mean?"

Father Sebastian's lips formed a smile, but there was a coldness in his eyes that Ryan had never seen before. "I needed help, and God has sent me you. The one person I would have chosen myself. Isn't it wonderful to have been chosen by God?"

Ryan's eyes flicked all over the chapel, searching for a way out, but except for the vestry door behind the altar, there was none. And Father Sebastian's tall figure stood directly between Ryan and that door.

"I—I don't think God chose me for anything," Ryan said.

"Ah, but He did," the priest said, moving closer.

Ryan edged back until he could go no farther, his back pressed against the locked main door.

"The Pope is coming to visit us," Sebastian said, moving closer. "He expects to see a miracle, and you and I, together, are going to show him one."

Once again Ryan's eyes darted around the chamber, coming to rest on the contorted face of Christ that was suspended high above the altar. "I don't know what you're talking about," he said, doing his best to keep his voice from trembling. "I don't know anything about miracles or—"

"You don't need to know anything," Father Sebastian said softly. "I know enough for both of us. I know all about the evil that resides inside you, Ryan. I know all about it, and I know how to draw it forth."

"I'm not ev—" Ryan began, but once again the priest cut him off.

"There is evil inside of every Catholic, Ryan. But I know how to control it. And I know how to exorcise it as well. His Holiness will watch it, Ryan. He'll watch me drive the evil from your soul."

The priest moved closer, and Ryan smelled something acrid emanating from him. Instinctively, he pressed back harder against the chapel door, but when it didn't budge he suddenly ducked his head, twisted to the right, and bolted for the vestry door behind the altar, certain that wherever it led had to be safer than the chapel itself.

But the priest anticipated his move, and grabbed Ryan's arm with far more strength than the boy expected, pulling him off balance. A second later Father Sebastian's free hand was clamping some kind of wet rag over his mouth and nose. Ryan fought to hold his breath against the acrid fumes emanating from the rag, but it was no use.

His own strength seemed to ebb away as the priest's grew. Within a few seconds, Ryan's heart was pounding in his chest, and, despite his own will, his instinct for air overcame his reason and his lungs expanded, sucking in great gulps of the terrible fumes.

It was as if a plug had been pulled inside him, and what little strength was left in his body seemed to leak out of his limbs.

He felt himself slump against the priest, and then drop to his knees on the cold stone.

"It's all right, Ryan," he heard Father Sebastian say. "When you wake up, you'll be a new person."

Ryan gazed up at the priest's smiling, gentle face—marred only by two cold, empty eyes—and then the blackness poured in from all around him.

With no way to escape, Ryan gave himself up to blackness.

Chapter 48

STEVE MORGAN PARKED the patrol car and switched off the headlights. "Let's make this quick, okay? See if you can resist the urge to start thinking up new questions."

"Just a signature," Matt McCain agreed, opening the door to step out into the drizzling rain.

Morgan adjusted his hat, and together the two officers walked up the driveway to the front door. The house was still ablaze with lights; nothing seemed to have changed since they'd left less than an hour ago. Yet even as they mounted the steps to the front porch, McCain's gut began to burn, always a sure sign that, despite appearances, something had, indeed, changed.

Morgan pressed the doorbell and they listened to it ring hollowly inside the house.

They waited, but there were no footsteps, no "I'm coming!" call from inside.

Just silence.

A silence as hollow as the chimes a moment ago.

Morgan pressed the doorbell again. "Maybe she went to her boyfriend's for the night."

Morgan shook his head. "The boyfriend's car's still in the driveway." He opened the screen door and knocked loudly on the wooden door. "Mrs. McIntyre?" he called.

Matt McCain stepped off the front porch into the flower bed and peered through the picture window. Though the curtains were drawn, they were sheers, and he could clearly see into the living room. Probably one of the reasons the house had been hit—anyone watching it for more than a few minutes would have been able to see that no one was home. "Sure doesn't seem like anyone's in there," he said, though the burning in his gut was getting worse, belying his own words. Someone was in there, all right. They just weren't answering the door.

"Crap," Morgan muttered. "Now we'll have to come back in the morning and get this thing signed before we can turn it in." He knocked again, harder.

McCain leaned closer to the window, shading his eyes from the porch light, then he picked his way through the garden to the other side of the picture window.

And he saw something.

Feet.

A pair of women's feet, still wearing high heels. Someone was lying on the floor in front of the fireplace.

Face down.

"Jesus," he whispered, unsnapping the leather safety strap from his .45 and pulling it from its holster. "She's in there, Steve. And it looks like she's hurt. Call for backup and an ambulance."

Morgan keyed the microphone on his shoulder and started talking rapidly even as he drew his own weapon.

"Stay here," McCain said. "I'm going around the back." Moving in absolute silence, he slipped around the corner of the house, shining his flashlight ahead, alert for any movement.

Several houses away a dog's furious barking suddenly exploded the quiet of the night, and McCain knew instantly what had caused it: Teri McIntyre's boyfriend was gone, but not in his car—he was taking an invisible route through the backyards until he got to the park only a few hundred yards away. And just outside the park was a subway station. From there, he could go anywhere.

No longer worried about keeping silent, McCain hurried along the side of the house and through the open gate to the backyard, then crossed the patio and—after a last glance around—went through the kitchen door that was not only unlocked, but stood wide open.

A few seconds later he opened the front door for Steve Morgan, and was crouching by Teri McIntyre, feeling her neck for a pulse.

Though her head was bleeding, and she was unconscious, she was still alive.

"Search the house," McCain told Morgan, even though he was certain that Teri McIntyre's assailant had already vanished into the night.

His weapon still in his hand, Steve Morgan headed upstairs to search as McCain crouched by Teri McIntyre, talking softly to her, telling her that everything was going to be all right.

But even as he spoke the words, he knew everything was not going to be all right. His gut was telling him that this was more than just a simple burglary.

CHAPTER 49

FARROOQ AL-HARBI GENTLY clipped the thread and then inspected the little red pouch he had made. Perfect.

It measured eight inches long by three inches wide. He would fill it from the top and then sew it closed.

He needed to make five more just like it.

He cut the yardage of red fabric into identical pieces, sewed them into pouches, then turned to the three brilliant red cassocks hanging in the closet.

The seam allowances on the inside of the altar server cassocks were generous, fortunately. They were cheaply made, and not well finished, which worked to his advantage. He had plenty of room to sew, but the loaded pouches might bulk up a bit at the sides. Fortunately, the white cotton cotta that each of the children would wear over the cassock would cover any bulges.

Not that anyone would be watching the servers anyway, even in their gaudy high-mass garments.

No, every eye in the entire area would be fixed on only one figure.

The Pope.

His fingers moving swiftly, Al-Harbi pinned the six pouches into the side seams of the three cassocks, then carried the first of the cassocks from the table to the sewing machine. Though he'd failed in one task tonight, he would not fail again.

He felt the spirit of his mother next to him, encouraging his fumbling fingers, as they worked hard to feed the heavy material through the machine. His father used to glower when he watched his mother work at her own machine at home, but he had still watched, though more interested in the machine itself than the use to which his mother had put it. Though the clothes she made fit perfectly well, he'd always preferred the ones his father bought for him at the store.

But who—even Farrooq Al-Harbi himself—would have guessed what good use those hours spent watching his mother sew would come to?

When the six pouches were firmly stitched into the seam allowances of the cassocks, he unlocked the single closet in his tiny apartment and took out the pound of C-4 his brother had given him only yesterday. He held the explosive reverently in his hands, and then held it up as an offering to Allah.

"For the glory of God," he whispered.

Then he returned to his sewing machine and unwrapped the brick of plastique. He marked it into thirds, and then sixths. Very slowly and with well-rehearsed movements, he began pinching off pieces of the gray compound, rolled them into balls that were slightly less than an inch in diameter, and dropped them down into the first pouch. When a sixth of the brick had disappeared into the pouch, Farrooq gently squeezed it to press the plastique into a single mass.

Next went the small blasting cap, along with the batteries to which it was wired, and the firing mechanism, all of which had been fitted together by someone with far more knowledge of such things than he himself possessed.

All he had to do was follow the instructions he'd been given.

Soon, all that was left to do was to feed the trigger wire through the seams to the cuff, where the detonation button would be sewn, easily accessible to the altar servers.

When all three cassocks had been completely wired, each with two sets of explosives, carefully wrapped in tissue paper and packed into their original boxes, he let out a great sigh.

It would be a very dramatic High Mass.

Something that Boston had never seen before.

And Catholics the world over would watch, and know the wrath of Allah.

For him, though, and for his brother, the fate of the Pope would be far more personal. All of the wrongs committed by the Church against his family would at last be avenged. He and his brother would at last be at peace.

Farrooq clicked off the light over his sewing machine and rotated his head to stretch some of the stiffness from his neck. He had worked through the night, but the project was nearly finished. He had yet to deliver the garments and demonstrate how they worked. When that was done, though, all would be left in the hands of Allah.

He opened the refrigerator, and squinted against the bright light in the gloom of the predawn apartment. The shelves were empty but for a shrink-wrapped case of bottled water. He pulled one free, twisted off the top and drained it in a single protracted gulp.

Farrooq stretched out on the floor to ease his aching muscles. The early light of dawn crept in around the closed blinds. He would rest— just for a few moments—before morning prayers. He closed his eyes and gloried in the satisfaction that he had done good work tonight.

He had done Allah's work.

Now the rest was up to his brother, who would see the mission to completion.

CHAPTER 50

RYAN LOOKED INTO the gaping jaws of Hell.

Jagged shards of poisonous multicolored razors surrounded him, growing ever closer. If he could only take a giant leap, he could jump over them to safety, but with each breath, they came nearer. He couldn't get a running start. In fact, they were now slicing into the toes of his shoes, but he couldn't back up, they were all around. He couldn't escape them. In a moment, the greedy, bloodthirsty things would carve away his feet until he fell and let them rip him to shreds.

No, wait, this is a dream!

Like looking up through deep water toward the light, Ryan saw consciousness above, and he began to swim toward it, but it wasn't water, it was some thick, gelatinous stuff that clogged his nose and mouth. He could barely move his arms and legs. As he got closer to the light, he felt colder. He strove to wrap his arms around his chest, to curl up in a cozy position, but he couldn't move his arms or legs. They seemed to be strapped down.

He heard a low, soothing voice intoning.

Break the surface. Take a breath!

He swam hard against the current that sucked him down, the gelatin smelling of sickening, noxious fumes.

Then something tugged hard from the inside of his stomach, pulling on his naval, and he felt his belly rip open.

He paused in his desperate ascent to consciousness and looked down to see what it was.

A gnarled hand reached out of his gut and sank its claws into his flesh, and began to haul itself out of him.

No! No!

Ryan flailed at it with ineffective hands that seemed to move right through the creature. He thrashed desperately in slow motion, but the creature was with him, of course, it was inside him.

Stop! Think! This is just a dream!

But it wasn't just a dream. The creature sank back inside before showing his face. But now Ryan could feel it roaming around inside of him. Then it started to inhabit him. It felt as if it were trying him on, as if Ryan were nothing more than a rubber suit.

He felt the thing squeeze into his legs, then his torso. Ryan felt pinched out of his own chest. The creature commandeered his heartbeat, and then it rammed itself inside Ryan's arms.

But when it started pushing up through Ryan's neck, he began to choke and gag.

And then he was lying on a stone slab, tied down.

His stomach heaved, and he retched.

Sister Mary David held a cloth to his lips to catch the bile.

Father Sebastian raised a bloody heart high in an offering, and when he placed the dripping thing on Ryan's naked chest, Ryan thought he was going to throw up again, and his entire being was seized by a terrible dizziness and disorientation. He lay inert for a moment, cold and confused.

And then his mouth opened and a voice—a voice he'd never before heard, emerged from his lips. As the strange voice uttered words he couldn't even begin to understand, Ryan felt himself slipping into the dark abyss of unconsciousness. He fought against it, struggling against the blackness, but when he opened his eyes, he was faced not with any reality, but a scene from a nightmare that seemed to be suspended directly above him. It was a face, but a face that wavered and changed with every breath Ryan took. One moment it looked like the face of evil incarnate, but the next moment Ryan recognized it as something else.

It was his own face, twisted and contorted into something terrible.

Ryan tried not to look at it, but he couldn't turn away.

"Get away from me!" he whispered.

The thing suspended above him only laughed, but the laughter seemed to emerge from somewhere deep in his own mind.

He was going crazy—right there, right at that moment, and he knew it, and there was nothing he could do about it.

"No!" Ryan screamed, but even as he tried to banish the vision, he felt the demon becoming part of him.

A part of him he would never be rid of again.

"Dad!" he cried, the word emerging as nothing more than a broken sob. But from a long way off, a tiny whisper rose out of the echoing vastness.

It was his father's voice—he was sure of it.

"Dad?" Ryan clung to his own awareness even as it slipped away from him. "Dad?"

Again, he heard the whisper of his father's voice, but could not make out what he was saying.

Suddenly the vision was gone, and above him someone was chanting while someone else smeared blood on Ryan's forehead.

He had lost. The thing—whatever it was—was inside him now. He tried to struggle, tried to protest, tried to cry out, but all that came out of his mouth was a foul-tasting breath.

Then his mouth opened again, stretching wider and wider until his jaws burned with agony and the flesh of his lips threatened to rip apart, and a bellowing roar came forth from deep within him.

All the strength left Ryan. He lost whatever grip he held on himself and slipped quietly under the evil's crushing personality.

The battle was over, and Father Sebastian had won.

CHAPTER 51

OPE INNOCENT XIV sat rigid in his chair for several long moments after the large video screen went black, his eyes still fixed on the monitor, his features frozen.

"Holiness?" Cardinal Morisco said softly, uncertain whether to interrupt the Pontiff's reverie, but equally uncertain that the aging cleric hadn't gone into some strange form of shock as he'd watched the images unfold before his eyes. "Are you all right?"

"Yes," the Pope sighed, sinking back into his chair. He retrieved his handkerchief from some hidden pocket in his cassock and wiped the moisture from his face. "Yes," he said again, his voice slightly stronger. "I'm quite all right. Just give me a moment, please."

"Surely." Morisco busied himself with putting away his computer while the Pope collected his thoughts.

The first time he'd seen this ritual—in the first clip that had been forwarded from Boston—every bit of his intellect had told him to dismiss it as a prank. It had certainly been as badly photographed and ill lit as all the thousands of miracles he'd reviewed over the years, and even if what he'd seen was real, it had to be nothing more than a fluke.

Yet despite what his intellect had told him, his faith—and his guts—had told him something different.

They had told him to keep his mind open.

But the second clip had been far clearer and he'd been certain that the girl Father Sebastian Sloane had put through the ritual could not have faked her reactions.

So it was not a fluke.

But did Sloane really know what he was doing?

The Pope had been interested enough after the second clip to retrieve Sloane's complete file, including the archived copy of his dissertation at Notre Dame.

It appeared that both he and Sloane had become interested in the same ancient Catholic rite, though the man who was now the Pope had begun many years before Sebastian Sloane, put in decades more time in research, and come up with nothing but dead ends.

Sloane, on the other hand, seemed to have had an intuitive sense that led him down pathways the Pope had never considered, even for a moment. The man had made seemingly irrational leaps of logic that, however unlikely, had eventually proved to be correct.

Could it be that the man had been divinely inspired?

Or could he somehow have actually discovered the text of the ancient rite?

Or, even more improbably—and important—had Sloane *re-created* the ancient Rite of Invocation?

The Rite of Invocation that had never, in the Pope's experience, proved to be anything more than rumor.

Old stories handed down from centuries ago, undoubtedly twisted and embellished by every teller of the tale.

The possibility that Sloane had, indeed, either resurrected or re-created the Rite of Invocation had led to a series of sleepless nights for the Pope, as he speculated on the implications of such an event.

If Sloane had done what the Pope was now all but certain he had, this could be the most important event in Catholic history since the loss of the rite hundreds of years ago.

If it had ever existed at all.

Which was why even after witnessing this latest clip, the Pope had his doubts. It wasn't, after all, simply that no one had ever been able to find the Rite of Invocation itself—it was far more than that; scholars had searched for centuries for evidence merely that the rite had ever truly existed. Teams of researchers had scoured every church archive in the world for years, and secular libraries and collections as well.

All to no avail.

So how could a priest from Indiana in the United States have found the answer?

It was beyond improbable.

And yet, in the afterglow of this latest video clip from Boston, the Pope's doubt had all but vanished. He'd watched as Sloane invoked the evil that dwells in every man's soul and done far more than merely banish it from the boy.

This was no simple exorcism as Morisco thought. Indeed, the Pope was quite certain that even Sloane's deputies thought they were assisting at nothing more than an exorcism.

But the Pope knew better.

And so did Sloane. He wasn't merely banishing evil.

He was taming it, controlling it.

Harnessing it to his own will.

And it was clear in the clip that Sloane knew exactly what he was doing.

"Holiness?"

The Pope looked up to see Morisco anxiously awaiting his words.

He trembled with indecision, and then certainty surged through him. "We shall go to Boston right away," he declared, paying no attention at all to Morisco's look of utter horror. "It shall be the first stop on our trip. A brief stop. I want no fanfare at all. A private Mass for the children of this St. Isaac's school, and nothing more."

Morisco's horrified look deepened, but still the Pope ignored it.

"That is all, Guillermo. I shall meet with this priest who performs this ritual. Then we will continue with the tour exactly as it has been planned. Though perhaps we may stop in Boston again on the way back."

"But Your Holiness—" Morisco pleaded.

"Thank you, Guillermo," the Pope said as he rose out of his chair. "You have no idea how important this may be for all of us." Leaving Cardinal Morisco staring at his back, he made his way slowly to the door of his apartment.

As always, the door opened just before his hand touched the knob.

CHAPTER 52

MATT MCCAIN HAD never liked hospitals. He hadn't liked them when his little brother died in one when Matt was only ten years old, and he didn't like this one any better. Just walking down the sickly green corridor with its cracked linoleum floor made him feel gritty and sticky, despite the shower he'd taken less than an hour ago. But his own feelings didn't matter—the job still had to be done. At the third-floor nurse's station, he pulled out his badge and said, "We're here to see Teri McIntyre."

The nurse frowned, punched some keys on her computer, then looked up at him worriedly. "I'm afraid she hasn't regained consciousness yet." Her eyes moved from McCain to Steve Morgan, then back to McCain. "If you're worried she might try to leave, I can tell you that's not going to happen. If she goes anywhere, it'll be to surgery, and as of an hour ago she wasn't even stable enough for that."

"Who's her doctor?" Steve Morgan asked.

"Dr. Conover. Neurosurgeon."

"Is he here?"

"I can page him."

Morgan looked to McCain, who shrugged dismissively. "Who's listed next of kin?"

Again, the nurse consulted her computer screen and tapped at the keyboard. "She was admitted three years ago for pneumonia. At that time, her next of kin was William McIntyre, her husband."

"He's no longer in the picture," Morgan said. "Is there anyone else?"

The nurse looked slightly irked, but went back to her keyboard. "Actually, we recently had a sixteen-year-old named Ryan McIntyre as a patient, whose mother is listed as Teri McIntyre."

"That fits," McCain said. "There's a boy's bedroom in the house."

"And it's the same address," the nurse said, looking up. "But that's all I've got."

"It's a start," McCain sighed, dropping a Police Department card on her desk. "Thanks. And call us when she wakes up, okay?"

"Sure." She took the card and scribbled a note on the back of it. Then, instead of dropping it into one of the desk drawers, she taped it to the monitor, just above the screen so nobody sitting at the computer could miss it.

Knowing there was nothing more to be done at the hospital—at least right now—McCain turned away from the nurse's station, and headed for the elevator.

"So we have a boy named Ryan McIntyre," Morgan said, as he punched the Down button a second time, "who's undoubtedly the vic's kid, but wasn't anywhere around the house. And we have William McIntyre, who might be an ex-husband, and the boyfriend, Tom Kelly. And we liked Kelly for the assault, but if there's an ex out there somewhere, we can't count him out as the perp for either the beating, or the break-in. In fact, he could have done both."

"I'll call it in," McCain said as the elevator finally arrived to carry them down to the main lobby. "Shouldn't be hard to get the story on the ex and the kid. But there's gotta be a million Tom Kellys in Boston."

"There's at least a dozen just in the Department," Morgan said. "And if he was the perp on the beating, I'll give you odds he wasn't using his real name."

McCain nodded. "So let's go back to her house and see if we can find out where the kid and the ex might be. I bet a neighbor knows something."

They pushed out through the main door and McCain inhaled deeply the cool salt air that had blown in off the ocean during the night. It was exactly the kind of spring morning that made you glad to be alive. But even as McCain's lungs sucked in the fresh air, his gut told him not to get too comfortable. Things, he was sure, were about to get strange.

† † †

Archbishop Rand glowered darkly at the telephone on his desk, almost as annoyed by the constant blinking of the line lights as he was by the incessant ringing that began the moment any line became free.

Line one had the local NBC affiliate demanding more information about the Pope's sudden—and utterly unexpected—rescheduling of his tour to include a stop in Boston.

Line two was Arthur Cole, chairman of the Committee for Eucharistic Adoration, offering—actually *demanding*—that his whole organization be put to work for the Pope's visit. Perhaps Rand could put him and his committee to work organizing the volunteers, who already numbered in the hundreds, all of them assuming that their work would be rewarded with a personal introduction to the Holy Father. Not that Rand even knew, at this point, exactly what was going to be needed.

Line three was Mrs. Boothe of the Catholic Women's College Club of Boston wanting to know how she and her group could be of assistance and, of course, to secure a private audience with the Pontiff.

Rand had just hung up line four, a reporter from the *Boston Herald* who said he would wait for the faxed press release, so of course that line was now ringing again.

A soft knock came on his office door.

Rand took off his glasses and squeezed the bridge of his nose for a moment. What he actually needed was a strategy meeting, so everything that needed to be done could be organized in a logical, orderly fashion, but that wasn't going to happen.

There was simply no time.

"Yes?" he called, instantly regretting the note of impatience that had crept into his voice.

His seminarian assistant opened the door. "The mayor to see you," he said, almost apologetically.

Rand nodded, unsurprised that the mayor had simply showed up at his office, where he couldn't be put off as he might have been on the telephone. "Show him in," he sighed. "And ask Mrs. Boothe to bring her volunteers here tomorrow morning to help with logistics."

"Here?" The seminarian's brows rose and his eyes widened, and Rand instantly realized his mistake: there was simply no room for a dozen women to work, not in the cramped space his offices had been reduced to.

"Tell her that her first act will be to find a space for her people to work. Perhaps at the Paulist Center." That, at least, would keep Emerald Boothe well away from him.

The young man nodded his understanding, then opened the door wide.

Rand rose from his chair to greet the mayor as he strode in. George Flowers was one of the few men tall enough for Rand to look straight in the eye, and his handshake was firm and blessedly brief. Then the mayor, as always, went straight to the point.

"Quite a bomb you dropped on my office this morning," he said, lowering himself into one of the two threadbare chairs in Rand's office.

"The same could be said for this office," Rand replied, glancing at the phone where all four lines were still blinking.

"There's no way we can mobilize a security force in time for the Pope's visit," Flowers said. "It's impossible. You're going to have to reschedule."

Rand remembered all too well how he'd gone to the mayor for help when the Archdiocese was drowning in a sea of bad publicity, and Flowers—clearly not a Catholic—had simply shrugged it all off. "The Catholic Church," he'd dryly observed at one point, "can withstand anything. It's its own country, for God's sake, with the Pope as its head, and all you Bishops and Cardinals as his commissioners. You'll all think of something."

Now it was Rand's turn to shrug off Flowers's problems.

"One doesn't simply reschedule His Holiness," Rand replied. "As you pointed out to me not so long ago, he is a head of state." Rand's bland expression betrayed none of the pleasure he felt at the mayor's flinch. "I'm afraid he will neither postpone nor cancel his visit to Boston."

Flowers took a deep breath and ran his hands through his sparse hair. "Then I don't know what we're going to do."

Rand savored the mayor's discomfort for another moment, then relented. "Actually, you don't need to do much at all," he said. "His Holiness will only be here for half a day, and it is to be a very low-key event. The Pope wishes to visit the children at St. Isaac's school, where he will hold a private Mass. That's all."

The mayor stared blankly at him, as if he must have misheard the Archbishop's words. "That's all?" he echoed.

Rand spread his hands in a gesture of magnanimity. "He will need security to and from the airport and around the school. But nothing more."

Now the mayor's face had gone ashen. "Nothing? No public appearances?"

"That is my understanding," Rand said.

The mayor appeared utterly nonplussed, and Rand could practically see the wheels spinning in his mind: having the Pope come to Boston and make no public appearances at all could turn out to be even worse than trying to organize security in the few days they had. Sure enough, Flowers finally found his voice.

"You mean to tell me that the Pope is coming to Boston, and all he's going to do is drive to St. Isaac's and out again? Nothing at the Common? No event? No parade in the Popemobile?"

Archbishop Rand smiled blandly, thoroughly enjoying Flowers's confusion. "All I know is what I've been told, George." Then he decided to make things a little worse for the mayor. "But you never know what he's going to do. He might very well change his mind once he gets here."

"That's what terrifies me," Flowers replied. "If he does, then what am I supposed to do? We have to have some kind of plan, and if he's coming here at all, he has to appear in public." He looked Rand squarely in the eye. "Don't try to tell me you couldn't use an appearance as much as anyone else. So how about a Mass in the Common? We can keep it as small as he wants, but at least it will be something."

Rand shrugged as disinterestedly as Flowers had months ago when he'd so blithely dismissed the Church's problems, and Flowers slumped low in his chair. Only when Rand had decided the mayor had suffered enough did he speak one last time: "But you're right, of course. His Holiness can't come here and simply be invisible, which I'm sure he understands, and you're also right that a Mass in the Common can be put together fairly easily, all things considered. Let's consider it done." He saw no point in telling the mayor that most of the planning for that event was already underway, and the Vatican had already approved it.

CHAPTER 53

RYAN DID HIS best to focus both his eyes and his mind on the math book on the table in the library, but knew it was hopeless.

Something was wrong—with his body, his brain, his soul. His belly kept churning as if he was about to throw up, but every time he'd felt like he'd better bolt from the room and try to make it to the boys' room down the hall before he puked his guts out, the nausea subsided just enough to keep him in his seat.

It wasn't just the nausea, either—it was like his whole body was revolting; when he'd first come into the library, he'd thought someone must have forgotten to turn the heat on, but a couple of minutes later he'd started sweating so bad his shirt was wet. Then, just as he was sure he was going to burn up from the heat, he'd suddenly turned cold again. It was like he had some kind of fever, but at the same time it didn't feel like a fever at all. Besides, if he had a fever, they'd have kept him in the infirmary, wouldn't they?

And how had he gotten to the infirmary in the first place? The last thing he really remembered was following Father Sebastian in the tunnels below the school. After that, it was all like a half-remembered dream: some kind of cross hanging above him, and something on his chest and—

And what? The next thing he remembered was waking up in the infirmary, and being told he'd gotten sick last night. But they'd let him go, and most of the morning he'd felt—

Actually, he'd felt weird. At least half a dozen times he had the sensation that someone was standing behind him—really *close* behind him—but when he turned around to look, nobody was there. Then it had gotten even stranger; it was like somebody was actually inside him. He had a weird feeling like he was being crowded out of his own body. But that was stupid—nothing like that was even possible.

Yet the feeling kept getting stronger, and now he was starting to wonder if maybe he was going crazy. He clamped his eyes shut for a moment as another wave of the strange nausea rose in him. He heard whispering voices all around him, which wasn't surprising considering that as the news had spread through the school that the Pope was coming—not just to Boston, but to St. Isaac's—even the nuns had barely been able to keep order in the classrooms. But as the nausea subsided and Ryan opened his eyes again, he saw that no one was talking at all.

All around him, heads were bent over textbooks, and pens were writing on pads of paper.

No one was talking.

Yet the buzz—like an incomprehensible babble of voices—went on.

And then he felt a new sensation: a pressure in his head, as if some strange force was trying to push him out of his own mind. He grabbed his head with both hands as if holding on to the outside of his skull would help him control the chaos that was suddenly going on inside it.

He concentrated on Melody Hunt, who was sitting at the table behind him. The weird thing was that even though she was behind him, if he closed his eyes, he could actually see her just as clearly as if he'd turned around.

And he could *feel* her, too.

Giving up on trying to study, Ryan put his math book in his backpack and zipped it closed, and when he stood up, he wasn't surprised to find Melody standing next to him.

She reached over and took his hand.

It was as if an electric current surged through him and he reflexively jerked his hand away.

The sensation faded, leaving only an adrenaline rush.

Melody smiled at him—a strange, almost cold smile, as if she knew exactly what had just happened to him—and then she took his hand again.

The electricity shot up his arm like lightning.

"There's something we have to do," Melody said. ·

Except she hadn't said it. She hadn't spoken at all.

Yet he'd *heard* her words—heard them perfectly clearly.

"Come on."

Silently, Ryan followed her out of the library and through the corridors until they came to the empty dining room. When she opened the door that would lead them down to the underground tunnels, Ryan felt no fear at all.

But he felt the strange presence—the peculiar "other" inside him—stir.

He wanted to turn away from the door, but as Melody started down the stairs, he felt himself being drawn to follow her. He took one uncertain step down, and then another.

The door closed behind him, enfolding them in complete darkness, and he felt the first tendrils of panic reaching out to him. But even as the panic rose, that strange "other" within him shrugged it off as if it were nothing, and Ryan found himself following Melody on down the stairs and into the tunnels themselves.

As they started off into the darkness, Melody again took his hand, and once more he felt the stream of energy that seemed to flow from her body into his.

And with her energy came her calm.

Her single-minded purpose.

And suddenly the darkness was no longer his enemy. It was as if there was a bright beacon directing them through the dark tunnels; they needed no flashlight—not even so much as a glowing match.

They needed only to follow the energy that guided them.

Together they walked in silence through the blackness, down more steps, through more tunnels, never hesitating at an intersection, moving confidently through the labyrinth.

Then, from somewhere ahead, Ryan saw a light. A pale, greenish glow emanating from an open door.

When they came to the door, Ryan saw the source of the light, and a memory rose from his subconscious. He was gazing at the sarcophagus that held the corpse of Jeffrey Holmes. Indeed, the strange green light glowed right through the cold stone, and he could see Jeffrey offering him the same cold smile Melody had shown him only a little while ago.

Ryan tried to pull away. He willed his feet to stop, resisted the urge to go into that tiny chamber from which emanated the icy chill of death.

The "other" drew him forward, into the room until he and Melody stood on either side of the glowing tomb.

Against Ryan's own will, his hands reached out and touched the cold stone, and as Melody's hands joined his own on the lid of the sarcophagus, the slab of marble slid aside.

Ryan gazed down upon the bloated, rotting features of the boy he'd never met, and once again nausea threatened to overwhelm him. He struggled to turn away—at least to step back—but found himself watching helplessly as he and Melody joined hands, then reached down and touched Jeffrey Holmes's naked chest.

As their palms came to rest on the boy's bony torso, a new rush of energy gushed into Ryan, and for a moment he thought he must be going crazy. Ice flowed in his veins, and he felt a terrifying power surge through him, chilling first his hands, then his wrists, moving steadily up his arms and into his chest.

Then it reached his heart.

He wasn't going crazy at all—he was dying.

He knew he was dying—knew it with a certainty as strong as the agonizing pain that tore at his body.

Then it was over.

But he wasn't dead.

Instead he was glowing.

The same pale, greenish light that had come from Jeffrey Holmes only a moment ago now seemed to be emanating from the flesh of his own body, and when he looked over at Melody, she, too, was surrounded by the pale aura.

Whatever had been in Jeffrey Holmes's body was now in theirs.

Leaving the stone casket cover askew, Ryan took Melody's hand and together they left the empty body in its stone coffin and began walking back through the darkness, guided only by the cold light that now dwelt within them.

CHAPTER 54

RYAN QUIETLY SAT in the library. The nausea of the morning gone; after he and Melody had come back up from the tunnels he'd felt much better. His mind felt far sharper, too, and even his senses seemed keener than they ever had been. Indeed, as he stared at the neck of the boy who sat at the next table—kind of a geeky guy named Peter Wise—Ryan could almost see right through his skin to the muscles, arteries, and veins that lay beneath the skin. Now he envisioned a blade . . .

A razor blade?

No. The blade of a knife.

A long, thin blade tapering to a point so sharp it would slip through Peter Wise's skin so easily it would be almost as if nothing were happening at all. Maybe a little trickle of blood, but not much.

Not much until the knife sank deeper, cutting through the thick cords of muscle supporting Peter's head, then slashing into the carotid artery.

Then the blood would gush, spurting through the wound as Peter's head pitched forward. As the life began to bleed out of him, Ryan would plunge the blade deeper still, jabbing the point between two of the vertebrae and cutting the spinal cord. Peter would collapse then, but would still be alive, maybe even still conscious. Then—

"Ryan?"

Ryan's face flushed hot and he jerked his gaze away from Peter Wise's neck. *Jesus! What had he just been thinking? What was the matter with him?*

The librarian was glaring at him, almost as if she knew what he'd been thinking about. But then he saw the headmaster's secretary standing near the door.

"You're wanted in Father Laughlin's office, Ryan. Right away."

Ryan felt every eye in the room on him as he gathered up his book, notebook, and pen, and zipped them all into his backpack. *What could Father Laughlin want? Did he know where he and Melody had been a few hours earlier? What had happened in that little room deep in the subbasement?*

"Some people are here to talk to you," Sister Margaret said as they crossed the courtyard.

"People?" Ryan echoed. "Who?"

Sister Margaret shrugged and opened the door to the administration building. "Go on in," she said, nodding toward Father Laughlin's office.

Two men in police uniforms were waiting with Father Laughlin, and they both rose to their feet as Ryan came in, and just the looks on their faces were enough to tell Ryan that whatever they had to say was something he wasn't going to want to hear.

"Ryan McIntyre?" one of the men said. "I'm Officer McCain. This is my partner, Officer Morgan."

Ryan looked uncertainly from one to the other. What was going on?

"Come on in and have a seat," McCain said, indicating an empty chair.

Ryan dropped his backpack to the floor and perched nervously on the edge of a chair.

"Ryan," Father Laughlin began, then nervously cleared his throat.

"Ryan," McCain took over. "We have to tell you that your mother was assaulted last night."

The words seemed to hang in the air, and for a moment Ryan wasn't sure what they were saying. But as the meaning of the words slowly sank in, he finally spoke. "Assaulted? What do you mean assaulted?" His eyes shifted from McCain to the other policeman, then back to McCain. "Is she all right?"

"We hope she will be," McCain said. "She's in the hospital in Newton, and we'll be happy to take you to see her." He glanced at Father Laughlin, who nodded. "But first, we wanted to know if you had any idea who might have done such a thing?"

A single name instantly rose in Ryan's mind. "Tom Kelly," he said. "Her boyfriend."

The two policemen glanced at each other now, and this time it was Morgan who spoke. "Why would you suggest him? Has he ever done anything to her before?"

Ryan hesitated, but then shook his head.

"Then why do you think it might have been him?" McCain pressed.

Ryan shrugged. "I just don't like him, you know?"

"Do you know where we can find him?"

Ryan shook his head. "Is my mom going to be okay? I mean, is anyone making sure he doesn't show up at the hospital?"

"Believe me, we're on that," Morgan assured him. "Now as for this Tom Kelly character—he never mentioned where he lived, or where he worked?"

Ryan tried to think of a single thing he actually *knew* about Tom Kelly, and suddenly realized he couldn't come up with anything. Nothing at all. Had Tom Kelly actually been that secretive about himself, or had Ryan himself just been that uninterested? Or could he just not remember? "Seems like I should know," he finally said. "But I just don't."

"You might remember something later," McCain said. "Hearing about your mom kind of takes away your concentration." He handed Ryan a business card. "Keep this in your wallet, and if you remember anything about him, call me, okay?"

Ryan took the card and nodded.

"Ready to go see her?"

"Yes, please," Ryan said.

† † †

Ryan sat in the backseat of the police car on the short ride to the hospital. He wanted to be afraid for his mom, he wanted to be incensed, furious even, at that jerk Tom Kelly, but something was pressing down on his emotions. He felt like a zombie, just going through the motions of being worried, upset, and angry, without actually feeling any of those things.

Maybe that was the effect of hearing that his mom was in the hospital. Maybe he was in shock.

Or maybe it was something else.

At the hospital, a nurse showed them into a big glass room filled with beeping machines. It wasn't until he looked carefully that he saw the small, pale face of his mother amid all the wires and tubes and flashing lights.

Her head bandaged in white seemed to merge with the pillow behind her. Dark circles hung under her eyes all the way to her hollow cheeks. Her thin body barely made a lump under the blanket.

She didn't look real.

"She's still in a coma," the nurse said. "The doctor will decide tomorrow morning if the swelling in her brain is going to require surgery."

Ryan stood still, unsure of what to do.

"Go ahead, talk to her," the nurse encouraged him. "Sometimes the voice or the touch of a loved one can make a difference."

Ryan felt the eyes of the nurse and the two policemen on him as he approached the bed.

"Mom?" he said quietly, but only the beeping sound of her heartbeat answered him.

Part of him wanted to crawl into bed with her, to hold her the way she had held him so many times when he was sick or hurt. Part of him wanted to sink to the floor and cry, and part of him wanted to rip out all the tubes and wires and smash all the machinery.

But all of that seemed like the thoughts of someone else.

Instead, he just stood there. "Mom?" he said again.

"Hold her hand," the nurse urged.

Ryan took tentative steps closer to the bed. The skin of his mother's face looked like paper. Her hand, just as pale, lay on top of the white blanket.

He reached for her hand, and as he did, the beeping of the heart monitor began to quicken.

"See?" the nurse said. "She could be sensing that you're here."

"Hi, Mom," Ryan said, and then grasped her cool hand with both of his.

"Noooo," Teri McIntyre moaned, and violently ripped her hand from her son's touch, then began thrashing in the bed. All the machines began to beep and flash, and another nurse rushed in.

Ryan backed away as both nurses worked with her. By the time Teri quieted down and the beeps had gone back to normal, she had moved halfway across the bed.

Away from her son.

Chapter 55

THE DARKNESS OF the night surrounded Ryan like a cloak, yet it was a cloak that gave no warmth; his whole body—even his spirit—was suffused with a paralyzing cold. Yet when a shadowy figure emerged from the darkness, passing Ryan without so much as a glance, Ryan followed. He knew who the figure was: Tom Kelly, the man who had beaten up his mother.

The man he was going to kill.

Why? Why not just call the police—they'd take care of Tom Kelly. But even as he asked himself the question, even as he silently stalked his prey, the answer also rose in his mind.

Why not?

The street was empty; a heavy mist hung in the air; the only light came from a single lamp in the middle of the square across the cobbled lane.

Tom Kelly must be an idiot to be walking alone after what he'd done. So he deserved to die.

Ryan's fingers closed on the knife in his pocket and a moment later it was out of his pocket, its glittering blade flicking open with the gentlest touch to the release.

Ryan quickened his step, closing the gap between himself and Tom Kelly. As he neared the man, the knife in Ryan's hand grew warm, its heat spreading quickly through his body. He felt a smile spreading over his lips as he reached out to snake his left arm around Tom Kelly's head, to jerk it backward, exposing the flesh and tendons of the man's neck to the blade clutched tight in Ryan's trembling right hand.

Then with one vicious swipe of the blade—

Ryan awoke, gasping. The street was gone; so too was the icy chill of the night.

He was in his bed in his room at St. Isaac's, and instead of clutching the handle of a bloody knife, his fingers were clenched only on his own sheet and blanket.

The thrill of what he'd been about to do was still tingling in his body.

Ryan lay back on his damp pillow, willing the memories to fade away, but no matter what he did, every time he closed his eyes, the vision hung once more in the darkness. Worse, the thrill he'd felt in anticipation of what he'd been about to do also came flooding back, and he felt his fingers twitching as if the knife were still clutched in them.

Terrified by what dreams might come if he let himself go back to sleep, Ryan sat up and put his bare feet on the cold floor beneath his bed. Clay Matthews breathed rhythmically in his bed on the other side of the room, and Ryan knew he couldn't turn on his reading light without waking him.

Maybe all he needed was to get out of bed for a while, and shake the last remnants of the dream. Silently, he pulled on a pair of jeans and a sweatshirt, and slipped out of the room, closing the door softly behind him. Padding down the hall to the common room, his footfalls were as silent here as they had been in his dream, and when he came to his destination it was as dark and as deserted as the street he'd been wandering in his nightmare, the only illumination coming from the streetlamp in front of the school.

The last thing he wanted to do was to talk with some priest or nun, or even one of his dorm-mates, so he neither turned on the ancient television that crouched in the far corner, nor a light to read by.

Instead, he sat alone in the darkness, still trying to rid his mind of the violence in his nightmare.

Where had it come from?

Even as he posed the question, he knew the answer: the violence had come from inside his own being, from the dark presence that had emerged from deep within him when Father Sebastian had taken him to the small chapel hidden in the depth of St. Isaac's School.

He could feel that presence spreading through him, its tendrils twisting around him, tightening their grip on him with every minute that crept by.

He paced the room nervously, as if by sheer movement he could rid himself of the thing that was growing inside him. His eyes flicked from the glass-fronted cases filled with old books to the dark oil paintings depicting St. Isaac himself, all of them framed in fading gilt, then to the worn furniture that seemed to have been collected from a half dozen different times and places. He moved to the window flanked by threadbare brocade draperies with torn and dingy lace curtains covering the glass. Ryan pulled back the curtain and gazed out. A light mist hung over the cobbled street, exactly as it had in his dream, and the sidewalks and the park were equally as deserted, but from somewhere far away he heard the faint moan of a siren.

An ambulance? Ryan leaned his forehead against the cool glass, wondering if it might be going to the same hospital where his mother still lay unconscious.

The same hospital where he, himself, ought to be, sitting next to her and holding her hand instead of standing here looking out over Boston and worrying about a nightmare.

Except that when he had seen her—when he'd touched her—she'd screamed.

Screamed, and jerked away from him, as if she knew about the thing that was inside him, growing steadily, threatening to utterly overwhelm him. And if it did—

If only he could see her, and talk to her, and tell her what was happening. But of course he couldn't, not now.

Not tonight.

Not until she woke up.

If she woke up.

Ryan shuddered in the darkness as he thought once more of the nightmare. Of it turning into reality, of finding himself actually clutching a knife and holding it against someone's throat, of feeling the blade sink into the flesh and slash at the tendons, ripping open the aorta to let human blood flow.

A movement beyond the window distracted him from the vision in his mind, and he peered into the darkness to see a silver car creeping down the street to come to a silent stop in front of the steps of St. Isaac's. A moment later, a man clad in jeans, a black T-shirt, and a dark jacket ran down the steps and got into the car. Just before pulling the car door closed, the man glanced upward, seeming to look directly at the window from which Ryan was gazing.

Father Sebastian Sloane!

Ryan looked at the clock that hung on the wall above the television.

Almost 3:30.

Was there some sort of emergency? But what kind of emergency would make Father Sebastian leave in such a hurry in the middle of the night?

And not dressed in the cassock he had always worn before?

The car made a U-turn in front of the building, and as it did, the streetlight caught the face of the driver.

Ryan gasped and stepped back.

It couldn't be! Surely it had only been a trick of the light!

Too late, Ryan peered out the window once more, but by now the car was gone.

The street was empty.

CHAPTER 56

ABDUL WATCHED AS Farrooq unwrapped one of the scarlet cassocks and laid it carefully in his lap. "I have made three," Farrooq said, then showed Abdul the carefully sewn inserts that held the explosives, the detonation wires that had been snaked through the seam allowances, running first up to the right sleeve, then down the sleeve to the cuff.

Abdul nodded in appreciation of his older brother's intricate work. "Beautiful," he murmured, his fingers gently caressing the silken material of the cassock, only to come to rest on the hidden explosives. He could almost feel the energy compressed within the packets hidden in the seams.

"The triggers are here," Farrooq said, interrupting his brother's reverie. Abdul ran his fingers lightly over a tiny button in the hem of the sleeve, made all but invisible by the lace trim of the sleeve's cuff. "It will be for you to decide when they are to be activated," Farrooq said softly.

Abdul's eyes met those of his brother. "The altar servers will carry the tall candles, placing them into the holders on the altar. At that moment they will be as close to the Pope as it is possible to be. As soon as they have placed the candles, they will all take a single step back from the altar, at which point each of them will activate a trigger."

"Praise Allah," Abdul sighed.

"There are bombs," Farrooq continued. "Two for each of the servers. *Insha-Allah,* all six will detonate." He paused, then smiled. "But we only need one."

"Fail safe," Abdul said.

"Fail safe," Farrooq agreed, "assuming the servers follow through." He gently lifted the garment, repackaged it, and set it carefully with the others. "Now," he went on as he took two bottles of water from the small refrigerator, handing one to his brother. "What of our father's cross?"

Abdul shrugged. "You worry too much. Even if it were to surface, we don't know that it would mean anything. Nor are we counting on a single server—that is why we have two backups." Now it was Abdul's lips that spread into a dark and joyless smile. "What one might call an Unholy Trinity."

"Fail safe." Farrooq raised his bottle to his brother, then drained it of water. "We will not meet again until it is done," Farrooq said.

Abdul nodded. "For too many centuries we have been persecuted by the Infidels, but at last they will pay for what they have done to our family and our tribe."

"I do not deserve the honor of this sacred errand," Farrooq breathed.

"We were chosen," Abdul said. "Allah knew we would find the strength or He would not have led us to the hiding place." He hesitated, then looked deeply into his brother's eyes. "These past years I have finally started to understand what our families went through, pretending to be Christian and renouncing Allah. They were strong men, our fathers, to have separated themselves from all they believed in, in order to save themselves and their children and their children's children from the Inquisitors."

"Your sacrifice has been no less than theirs, *Paquito,*" Farrooq said softly, laying a gentle hand on his younger brother's shoulder.

"It is nothing," Abdul murmured, but the glistening in his eyes told his brother how difficult it had been. A moment later, though, his eyes cleared, and he breathed deeply. "Soon the world shall know the wrath of Allah, and the Church will be no more."

"*Insha-Allah,*" Farrooq intoned. "God willing."

"*Insha-Allah,*" Abdul echoed. He stood and grasped his brother in a fierce embrace. "Now," he went on as he wiped moisture from his eyes. "Let us pray together, for the last time until this deed is done."

"And then?" Farrooq asked.

"And then I will go put on my priest's costume and continue the charade for a few more hours."

"I think this is the happiest day of my life," said Tom Kelly.

"Mine will be the day the Pope is blown to bits," replied Father Sebastian Sloane.

† † †

Sebastian Sloane twisted the key in the lock of the lowest drawer of his old oaken bureau, then slid the drawer open on the hardware he himself had installed when he'd decided the contents of the drawer were too important even to trust to a bank vault. The drawer itself on the outside looked no different from the other four the old chest held. But while the others were all made of nothing more than their original dovetailed oak, the bottom drawer was different: perfectly constructed to fit exactly within the dimensions of the drawer were several boxes, each nested in another. Each box served a special purpose: one was fireproof, another waterproof; others provided absolute protection against anything Sloane had been able to imagine: microbes, radiation, nearly anything short of a nuclear explosion. After working the combination locks set into each of the first three lids, he opened the others until he was finally able to lift out the treasure that was both hidden and protected in the drawer's center. Wrapped in a scrap of an ancient prayer rug was the rosewood box he and his brother had unearthed in the courtyard when he was a child.

For several long moments he gazed silently at the box, barely able to believe that the time had finally come. Everything he had done since the moment he and his older brother had dug the grave for the pet iguana, and found the box with the missing cross and the scroll, was finally culminating in an act of justice that was nearly six centuries over-due.

Since that day, his resolve to avenge the terrible wrong that had been done to his family had steadily grown until it was a furiously burning rage so strong that no force in the world could stop it.

But now, nearly three decades after that first fateful discovery, it would soon be finished.

The gravity of the moment pulled him first to his knees, then fully down until he was prone on the floor for a moment, his arms stretched toward Mecca, offering a prayer of thanks to Allah, who had guided him. Allah, who had heard his prayers and had given the Catholic Church a Pope who was familiar with the ancient rituals. Allah, who had made certain that this Pope understood what he had seen in the video the priest known as Sebastian Sloane had sent through the fool-ish—but highly malleable—Cardinal Morisco.

Now it was Allah who was about to deliver the Pope to him, to Abdul Kahadija, the name the man called Father Sebastian Sloane had taken when he discovered the truth about his family's history and had returned to his forefather's true Islamic faith, throwing off the heresies of the Roman Church as he'd thrown off the Spanish name he'd grown up with.

Paquito, his brother had called him a little while ago. But never again.

Soon their vengeance would be complete, and their hated Christian names would never cross either of their lips again. But even in his fury, in his lust for the vengeance the Church had so richly earned, he would see that the Pope received a good death.

A righteous death, at the hands of the very ritual the Catholic Church used to exterminate Muslims from Spain so long ago.

Used to exterminate his family, to tear them from the faith that had sustained them for a hundred generations!

What could be more righteous than that?

Fresh strength flowed through Abdul Kahadija, setting his whole being aquiver with energy, and he raised his hands to Allah in praise and worship. Then, when his trembling ceased, he stood, gathered his materials into a cloth bag, and left the room that was little more than a monastic cell, clad once more in the black cassock that belonged to Father Sebastian Sloane.

† † †

It was no more than a quarter-hour later that Sebastian Sloane placed his cloth bag on the cold floor next to the stone sarcophagus that held Jeffrey Holmes's corpse. Removing a handful of candles from his bag, he placed them in a wide circle around the sarcophagus, and lit them slowly, whispering a prayer from the ancient ritual before igniting each wick. Only when all the candles were lit did he turn off his flashlight and put it back in the bag. Then he withdrew the precious scroll, wrapped now in a large square of emerald green silk.

Next came the single piece of chalk he would need.

By the flickering light of the unsteady candles, Sebastian carefully surveyed the uneven stone floor, visualizing how best he could expand the drawing of the labyrinth contained within the ancient scroll to fit the floor around the sarcophagus. Yet even as he gazed at the space around the stone coffin, he knew it couldn't be "best." No, "best" wouldn't do.

The labyrinth had to be perfect.

Yet from one angle, the room didn't seem big enough to hold the complexity of the pattern, while from another angle, the space seemed far too big.

Yet it had to be done, and it had to be perfect.

The labyrinth had three entrances and three paths, and though all three paths found the same destination, all moved in different directions, twisting and turning as they led toward their goal, yet never connecting, never intersecting.

Where even to begin?

Trust in Allah, he told himself. *Let the hand of Allah be your guide.*

The chalk began to vibrate in his fingers, and a moment later he was on his hands and knees. As if of its own volition, the chalk began making marks on the floor. The lines encircling Jeffrey Holmes's tomb were all evenly curved; those that radiated out were perfectly straight. As he worked, the man in the priest's garb found himself moving first one way around the sarcophagus, then the other, moving out a little with the completion of each circle. At first he saw nothing but a jumble of lines, but slowly a pattern began to emerge.

He worked faster, not feeling the cold hardness of the stone floor beneath his hands and knees, utterly unaware of how much time might be passing.

As the labyrinth took shape, the entire room grew darker as if filling with a shadow, though the shadow had no visible source. The candles burned steadily, but it seemed as if their light was being swallowed by the gathering shadow. The cavernous, high-ceilinged chamber grew close, the air thin and difficult to breathe.

Yet Sebastian's arm raced over the stones, detailing the path the servers would tread to complete the ritual he'd begun with each of them in the preceding days. His arm moved faster and faster, jerked this way and that by an invisible force. Though the stick of chalk had worn away, the drawing continued, as he tore off the skin and meat of his knuckles until it was completed in his own blood.

Still, the room filled with the strange shadow, and the atmosphere grew heavier and heavier until finally Sebastian Sloane lay prostrate on the floor.

The weight in the chamber grew so heavy that his very breath rasped, and the pressure on his lungs threatened to collapse them inside his body.

What if he did not survive the preparation?

Please. Without me, this cannot be completed.

And then it was finished.

After seven complete revolutions had been made around the coffin, the pressure in the room eased, and the deep shadow suddenly vanished.

As if startled out of a reverie, Sebastian hesitated for a moment, then rose slowly to his feet and looked down at the diagram that had been traced on the floor.

Though he knew it was perfect, he still compared it to the labyrinth laid out in the ancient scroll.

They were alike in every detail. But beyond that, he could feel something—some presence—in the chamber that had not been there before.

All was ready.

Only the children were missing. . . .

Chapter 57

The flickering light glowing at the end of the long tunnel drew Ryan through the darkness like bait in a trap, and even though he knew that very soon the jaws of the trap would close in on him, he could no more turn away from the light than a wolf can turn away from fresh meat.

Moments ago, he'd been sitting in the cafeteria eating dinner with Melody and Sofia, and trying to figure out the easiest way to get to the hospital to see his mother. But then a strange feeling had washed over him, a feeling that he was wanted—that he was *needed.* He'd looked around, half-expecting to see one of the priests or nuns beckoning to him from the doorway, but even as he saw no one he realized that the feeling hadn't come from outside himself at all. It had risen from somewhere deep within himself, and he had stood up from the table and walked toward the door.

He'd wanted to stop, wanted to bus his dishes, but there was no time.

He had to follow the summons.

Melody and Sofia had risen at exactly the same moment as Ryan, and he followed them out of the dining room and through the door at the top of the stairs. This time, though, there was no hesitation as he gazed into the darkness below and no fear of the confusion of tunnels through which he must pass.

As he drew close to the soft, pulsing light he found himself gazing into the dank chamber in the very center of which stood Jeffrey Holmes's carved marble sarcophagus. But unlike the last time he'd been here, when the chamber had been filled with darkness, now there was a circle of candles around the room's perimeter, and a strange diagram—like a maze—was inscribed on the floor.

Inscribed in chalk, and in blood.

To the depths of his soul, Ryan did not want to go into that room and though his feet threatened to disobey him—though he felt an almost irresistible force drawing him into the chamber—he stopped at the doorway.

Sofia and Melody were already inside, standing quietly at two of the three entrance points to the labyrinth that had been drawn on the stone floor.

The third entrance point was vacant, and Ryan knew they were waiting for him.

The strange force inside him urged him on, but still he resisted. He could smell the stench of death mixing with the smoke of the candles, and the stink of the rotting corpse that lay inside the coffin.

Now the power of the candlelight itself combined with the force within Ryan, and he gripped the edge of the doorway to keep himself from crossing over the threshold.

A black figure emerged from the shadows of the far corner of the room and stepped into the glow of the candlelight. "Come in, Ryan," Father Sebastian said, his voice soft, soothing. "A gift awaits you."

Beads of perspiration erupted on Ryan's face as he struggled against the forces that were compelling him to step into that room.

"It is through my blood that you exist and you are bound to my bidding," the black-clad priest intoned.

The words reached out to Ryan, combining with the force inside him and the power that seemed to fill the room itself, and he knew he was not going to be able to deny Father Sebastian.

He felt his fingers slipping from the doorjamb.

"I command you to submit," the priest said, the words belying the softness of his voice.

Ryan felt his feet move, inching closer to the threshold.

"Submit," Father Sebastian instructed, a little more forcefully.

Ryan's left foot slipped over into the room, and instantly an eerie calm washed over him.

Suddenly he felt as if he had come home.

He looked at Melody and Sofia. Both of them were smiling at him.

Smiling in welcome, as if a family—a family of just the four of them, three children and a father—were now complete.

But that wasn't true.

The priest wasn't Ryan's father, and Sofia and Melody weren't his sisters. Something was wrong—something was very, very wrong.

"Excellent," Father Sebastian crooned. "Please take your place."

Ryan's whole body trembled as he struggled to resist each step that led him to the third entrance of the intricate maze that had been drawn on the stone floor, but his mind seemed to have lost control over his body, which seemed now to be obeying only the commands of the strange presence—the *thing*—inside him.

The *thing*, and Father Sebastian's hypnotic voice.

As if he had somehow been forced out of his own body, Ryan watched himself move to the third entrance to the labyrinth.

Father Sebastian laid a small bundle on the lid of the sarcophagus, then ceremoniously untied the scarlet ribbon and folded back the black velvet. A glint of silver flashed from the dark material, and then the priest picked up a large silver crucifix, holding it almost as if he were offering it to Ryan. But then he turned it upside down and Ryan saw that it was more than simply a crucifix.

It was also a dagger, and as the priest closed his right hand around the head of Christ, he pressed the stiletto-sharp point of the cross's base to his lips, kissing it.

Candlelight glinted off the blade, and cold sweat began to trickle down the side of Ryan's face.

The priest laid the holy weapon on the cold marble of the coffin's lid, and turned again to the black velvet, opening its last fold. Now he lifted up an ancient scroll, its edges tattered, its dowel worn. Father Sebastian carefully unrolled it and began to read in Latin.

After a few words, first Sofia and then Melody began to recite along with him.

And then, even though Ryan had never heard the words before in his life, the verses began to emanate from his lips as well.

He not only spoke them, but he understood them.

They were uttering a prayer for unity.

A prayer for power.

Their voices began to rise into a chant, and though the candles seemed to grow brighter, Ryan felt the room beginning to fill with something else.

Something dark.

Something evil.

All the resistance he'd felt as he entered the room melted away, and as their chanting continued to rise, he and Melody and Sofia began moving slowly through the chalked labyrinth, weaving first one direction, then another, approaching close to one another, only to turn away at the last moment.

Back and forth Ryan walked, one slow step at a time, as if in a dream. Melody and Sofia kept passing him, each treading her own path, never touching him or each other, their courses never crossing. The strange ballet went on, the chanting rising ever higher as the three of them drew inexorably closer to the center of the maze.

Closer to Jeffrey Holmes's cold tomb.

Their voices rose together into the howling crescendo, as if all the demons in hell had unloosed their bonds, and as the last note sounded all three of them stood at the center of the maze, separated only by the marble coffin. With the echo of their voices still reverberating in the chamber, Father Sebastian raised the heavy silver crucifix once more. He held it high, the stiletto's point aimed at the ceiling. His voice rumbled as a new invocation rose from his lips.

He handed the desecrated cross to Sofia.

Without hesitation, Sofia drew the point of the blade across her palm, then let the blood from her wound drip onto the white marble as she passed the crucifix to Melody.

Melody repeated what Sofia had just done, and her blood, too, fell onto the sarcophagus.

The blade was passed to Ryan.

Against his own volition, he took the blade from Melody, and the instant their eyes met, Ryan saw that the light in her eyes—the light that had first drawn him to her—had completely gone out.

Something in Melody had died, and as he took the crucifix from her hands, Ryan knew that something was about to die in him, too.

But he was powerless to stop it.

He held the point steady above his wrist. Then, just as he was about to plunge it into his own flesh, a vision flashed before his eyes.

It was his father. His father clad in his full-dress uniform. A silver crucifix hung around his neck, and he was looking Ryan squarely—lovingly—in the eye. "Do not be afraid," he heard his father say. "I have a gift—"

His father's words were suddenly cut off as the blade bit into his flesh.

The vision vanished.

His blood flowed from the wound onto the stone lid of the coffin, and as the blood of the three of them mixed together, the white marble turned to mist, then vanished completely.

Now their blood was pooling on the rotting flesh of Jeffrey Holmes's corpse, and as Ryan watched, the flesh itself began to bubble.

"This is my body," Father Sebastian whispered, his voice low and raspy. "And this is my blood."

"Eat of my body," Father Sebastian commanded, but now it was no longer Father Sebastian at all, but only a face—a face that Ryan recognized at once.

It was the face of the darkness that had filled the room, the face of the thing inside him, the face of the thing that had come to inhabit Melody and Sofia as well.

It was the face of pure evil.

The face of the Devil himself.

"Drink of my blood," the voice commanded.

Silently, unable to summon any resistance at all, Ryan McIntyre and Melody Hunt and Sofia Capelli obeyed the commands.

They dipped their fingers into the bubbling putrefaction that had once been Jeffrey Holmes, and completed the blasphemous communion.

"It is finished," Father Sebastian said. "Now sleep. Sleep, and forget until you're summoned."

† † †

Ryan awoke in his bed, in his darkened dorm. Clay Matthews stirred in his bed on the other side of the room, then was still.

A nightmare . . . it had to have been a nightmare!

But a moment later, as every detail of the dream came flooding back to him, a great wave of nausea rose over him. He scrambled out of bed and raced toward the bathroom, the vomit spewing from his mouth even as he dropped down in front of the toilet. When it was over he found himself gazing down into a vile mess of what looked like entrails mixed with fresh blood.

A mess that smelled not like vomit, but exactly like the rotting corpse he'd beheld in the dream.

His gaze shifted from the toilet to the palms of his trembling hands, and as he stared at the blood-red marks where the stiletto had cut into his flesh, he knew the truth.

It had not been a dream at all.

Ryan rested his heated cheek on the cold porcelain floor.

It had not been a dream, and he had not forgotten it, despite Father Sebastian's final command.

What was happening to him?

† † †

Even though his stomach had calmed—and the marks on his palms were invisible in the darkness—he still couldn't bring himself to go back to bed. The memories, or fragments of dreams, or whatever they'd been, were still too fresh in his mind to risk going back to sleep.

All he really wanted to do was get out. Out of his room, out of the dorm, out of St. Isaac's. But where could he go?

It didn't matter—all that mattered was that he get out. Pulling on his clothes, Ryan slipped out of his room into the silent hallway, grabbing his jacket just before he closed the door silently behind him. But even as he made his way quietly through the dorm, the question of where he was going still hung in his mind. He couldn't go home—no one was there. But where else was there?

The police?

Even if he found a police station, what was he going to tell them? What had happened—or at least what he thought had happened—sounded crazy even to him, and there was no way the police were going to believe him.

His father.

That's who he really wanted to talk to. If his father were here, he'd know what to do.

But his father was dead, and his mother was in the hospital.

The hospital! That was it—he'd go to the hospital, and maybe his mother would be awake.

Awake, and able to touch him, and smooth his hair and tell him everything was going to be all right, even though he knew that nothing would ever be right again. Even if she wasn't awake, at least he'd be able to touch her.

He shuddered slightly as he remembered the last time he'd touched her, and she'd screamed, recoiling away from him even though she was unconscious.

Something was wrong with him. Something was very, very wrong, and it had all started when he'd come to St. Isaac's, and tonight—right now—he was going to get away. And there was no place to go except the hospital. He moved quickly and quietly through the hallways of the ancient school until he came to a door that led outside into night.

The courtyard was filled with shadows and in every one of them

Ryan could feel something sinister hidden, something evil waiting for him. Threading his way quickly through the courtyard, terrified of being seen in the dim moonlight but even more terrified of what might lie in the shadows, Ryan slipped through a narrow passageway between two buildings and emerged out onto the street.

Somewhere in the distance, a clock tolled eleven.

Could it really be that early? If felt more like three in the morning. But his watch agreed with the tolling bell.

He hurried down Willow and Spruce, glancing back over his shoulder every few seconds, half expecting to see Father Sebastian coming after him. But when he got to Beacon and started cutting across the end of the Common to the Park Street station, he began to relax just a little. At the subway entrance, he ran down the stairs, scanned his Link Pass at the turnstile, and headed down to the platform. According to the map, the green line would take him to within a block or so of the hospital, just three stops after the one he'd have gotten off at if he were actually going home. For a moment he wondered if there might be another route, but even if he could figure it out, it might take the rest of the night. Better to just go the way he knew.

A security camera caught his eye, and Ryan found himself stepping back until a pillar concealed him from its lens. But even if it caught him, what did it matter? He wasn't really doing anything wrong—sneaking out of the school wasn't like mugging someone. And yet, even as he tried to step away from the pillar, something—that *thing*—inside him held back, unwilling to step out of the shadows.

Was that it? Was it not he, himself, that was afraid of being seen, but rather that *thing* he could feel inside himself, trying to take over?

The D train pulled into the station, and Ryan boarded quickly, wishing there were more people on the car than the bum dozing in a seat in the far corner, and a woman about his mother's age dressed in some kind of waitress's uniform, who glanced at him for a second or two then went back to the magazine she was reading.

Yet even though the bum was asleep and the waitress was reading, he still had the feeling that someone was watching him.

What was wrong with him? Why was he feeling so paranoid? All he was doing was going to see his mother. It wasn't like he was going to do something wrong.

Was he?

Now the dream he had last night about stalking Tom Kelly rose up in his mind. But that had been only a dream—it wasn't as if he was actually stalking anybody. And he sure wasn't going to kill anybody—he was just going to go visit his mother.

Then why was he afraid someone was going to see him?

Half an hour later, Ryan left the train and ran up the steps to the street two at a time. The hospital was just a couple of blocks to the left, and as he started walking, a vague sense of relief began to replace the paranoia he'd been feeling since he'd awakened only a little over an hour ago.

Ten minutes later he was outside his mother's room in the ICU, gazing in through the glass at her thin, pale body. There were tubes and wires everywhere, and half a dozen glowing screens flashing graphs and numbers. His mother lay absolutely still in the confusion of equipment, and as he gazed at her, a terrible question rose in Ryan's mind.

What if she doesn't wake up?

What if she dies?

The cold fingers of terror began to close around his throat. He swallowed hard, then swallowed again, fighting not only against the fear that suddenly threatened to overwhelm him, but the tears that were welling in his eyes. His fingertips turned white as he gripped the metal window casing.

Every time his father had been sent away, he'd left Ryan in charge of taking care of his mother. But back then—back when his father was still alive—nothing terrible had ever happened. And besides, he'd always known, despite his father's words, that his mother would take care of him.

But now everything was different. Something terrible had happened, and he had failed.

He hadn't taken care of her. He had let her down, and he had let his dad down, and he had let himself down.

He needed his father. He needed to tell his father that he couldn't take care of his mother, that it was too great a responsibility, that he was too young, and he wasn't up to it, and he had failed.

A sob broke through the choking in his throat and reverberated through the silent hospital hallway and his eyes blurred with tears. But as he wiped the tears away with his sleeve, he suddenly saw something else in his mother's room.

Something that hadn't been there before.

A figure.

A figure standing at his mother's bedside. But a second ago there hadn't been anyone in there but his mother! He rubbed his sleeve across his eyes and looked again.

It was his father! His father standing at his mother's side. Standing straight and tall, in his full-dress uniform.

Ryan rubbed his eyes—it was impossible!

Was he having another dream?

His father's eyes met his, and Ryan sobbed again. "I'm so sorry," he whispered. "So—"

"My gift."

The two words struck Ryan as clearly as if he'd been standing right next to his father, not fifteen feet away on the other side of a heavy glass door. And now, as he watched, he saw his father touch the silver crucifix that hung around his neck.

Ryan stared at it. The crucifix! The one his mother had tried to give him, but that he'd refused. He rubbed the last of the tears from his cheeks and eyes, and looked again.

His father was gone.

But Ryan knew what he had to do.

† † †

The thing inside Ryan began to stir as soon as he rose to his feet to get off the subway train at the stop nearest his house. It was as if it understood that he was going home, and it didn't want him there, and even as the train slowed and he moved toward the door, he felt an urge to stay on the train, ride it all the way back in to the city, and go back to St. Isaac's.

Back to where whatever evil or madness that was growing inside him had begun. As the train came to a stop, Ryan knew that if he gave in to the desires of the being inside him, he would never be himself again. Slowly, inexorably, the person that was Ryan McIntyre would disappear, leaving only the strange dark force that seemed to be steadily invading his mind and body. Focusing his mind only on the vision of his father standing quietly next to the hospital bed, and the silver crucifix around his father's neck, Ryan forced himself to move toward the opening doors of the subway train.

"*You're dreaming,*" the thing inside him whispered. "*Your father is dead.*"

Ryan knew his father was dead, but he also knew what he'd seen.

"*You saw nothing,*" the evil being insisted. "*You wanted to see him, but he's dead.*"

Ignoring the voice, Ryan focused all his attention on putting one foot in front of the other and stepped off the train onto the platform. As he climbed the steps to the street and started toward home, the voice kept whispering.

"*You're hallucinating.*"

"*You're out of your mind.*"

"*They'll lock you up!*"

Doubt began to creep into his resolve, and the evil knew it. Its power reached from his mind into his body, and suddenly he was turning away, starting back toward the subway.

The subway, and St. Isaac's.

Concentrating hard, deafening himself to the insistent voice, Ryan forced himself to turn back again toward home. His whole body was twitching now, and he balled his hands into fists and stuck them into the pockets of his jacket. His arms jerked spasmodically, but he held them still against his sides. His head began bobbing and his legs seemed about to betray him, but he stiffened his neck, and forced himself to keep going.

He was doing the right thing—doing what his father wanted him to do—and he would not be stopped.

He would not be distracted by the voices in his head or the betrayal of his body or anything else.

The fury inside him suddenly surged, its wailing and howling built until Ryan could hear nothing else. It felt as if his head were about to explode, and then, as he stepped from the street onto the front lawn of his house, it was as if something had kicked his legs out from under him. He crashed to the pavement, his hip smashing against the curb as the asphalt of the street tore through his pants and into his skin.

Ignoring the pain, he got up again, and closed his mind not only to the demonic rage in his head but to the pain in his body. He walked up the front steps to the darkened house.

Yellow police tape was still stretched across the front door, but he tore it down. He picked up the little ceramic duck from the porch and retrieved the key that had been hidden inside it for as long as he could remember, then opened the front door.

The voice in his head screamed louder, but Ryan shut it out, his own rage growing as he stared at the dark blood on the hearth and carpet.

His mother's blood.

His own anger drowning out the fury of the being inside him, he charged up the stairs, tugged open the attic door, and turned on the single light bulb that was suspended from the main beam of the roof.

His mother had brought him up here, had shown him the cross that was hidden in his father's footlocker, and above the cacophony of the raging being inside him, he heard the echo of the words she'd spoken: "*Your father said this always helped him do the right thing.*"

Struggling to control legs that were no longer under his own control, Ryan stumbled over to the old trunk and lifted the lid. On top, wrapped in tissue, was his father's dress uniform—the one he'd been wearing when Ryan had seen him in the hospital only a short while ago. He wanted to pick it up, wanted to press his cheek to it, just to feel the closeness to his father, but he didn't dare. If he paused even for a moment, he might never regain control of himself.

He lifted the upper tray out of the trunk and set it aside.

The screaming voices residing within him rose, and as he reached inside the trunk to open the lid of the secret compartment hidden in its depths, first his fingers, then his hands, then his whole body began trembling as every nerve seemed to catch on fire. Ignoring the pain, he found the lid, and lifted it.

The rosewood box lay exactly where it had before, and as he reached down to touch it, he began to feel the evil within him weakening.

Power flowed into his hands, up his arms and into his heart as he lifted the box from the trunk and opened it.

The thing inside his head lost its grip on his body and its howling rage faded into whimpered obscenities.

Ryan, still kneeling on the floor, opened the box and closed his fingers around the silver crucifix that lay within. "What's happening to me?" he whispered. "Dad? Tell me what's happening to me. Tell me what to do." He closed his eyes, certain he would hear his father's voice, but all he could hear were muttered curses in his head; all he could feel was something still struggling to control his body.

He held the silver cross with both hands and curled up against the trunk, breathing in the scent of the wool uniform. Tears fell from his eyes and ran down his cheeks as the battle continued to rage inside his mind and his body and his soul, and it wasn't until the darkest hour of the night that he finally emerged from the house and started back to St. Isaac's.

But the battle inside him was not yet over.

Chapter 58

FATHER LAUGHLIN STOOD at the foot of Spruce Street. Across Beacon Street, the Common was a beehive of activity. Aside from the hundreds of people sprawled on the lawn to soak up the sunshine of the perfect spring afternoon, there were workmen everywhere. A platform was being built, upon which would stand the altar where His Holiness would celebrate the Mass that would be his only public appearance in the city. Even though the stage itself was as yet far from complete, sound technicians were untangling what looked to Laughlin like a hopeless snarl of cables, while a second crew was unloading and setting up truckload after truckload of folding chairs, which would be claimed by the earliest arrivals. Only a small section in front would be reserved for himself, the mayor, Archbishop Rand and the faculty of St. Isaac's school. The Vatican had been very clear on that: even the governor would have to find his own seat, should he choose to attend. Faced with no reserved seat, that dignitary had already pleaded an immutable scheduling conflict, as had nearly everyone else who felt they deserved special treatment. And that, Father Laughlin was certain, was the whole idea. This Pope was far more interested in the common people and the welfare of their souls than in their leaders and the salving of their egos. It also meant, of course, that security could be far less intrusive, given that so few public figures would be in attendance at all, and the Pope himself would be protected only by a Plexiglas shield that would make him totally visible, but utterly safe from anyone not on the stage. The chief of police had still insisted on a fence around the seating area for crowd control, and as he watched, Father Laughlin could understand why.

Even today, with the actual crowd who would see the Pope not even starting to gather, there were people everywhere. Besides the enormous crew that was doing the actual work of setting up for the open-air Mass, the mayor's staff seemed to be everywhere, wandering aimlessly with clipboards and cell phones, while the media was even more ubiquitous, cornering any priest wearing a collar for an on-camera interview. And all around the perimeter, policemen on horses stood sentry.

What had started out to be a small, personal visit by the Pope had turned into a circus, and even now Father Laughlin wasn't quite sure how it had happened. Perhaps, when it was over, and the Pope had come and gone, it really would be time for him to retire. But for today, all he could do, really, was try to look out for the students of St. Isaac's Academy as they rehearsed their part in tomorrow's event.

Sister Mary David was trying to keep them in some semblance of order as they walked down Spruce and started across Beacon, but just as the intermediate classes were starting across, another flatbed truck pulled up carrying a dozen Porta Potties, which seemed destined to stand precisely where the senior class was intended to gather.

Brother Francis handed Father Laughlin a bullhorn. "I think you'd better move everyone to the front of the stage, Father," he said, leaning close to Laughlin's ear and raising his voice enough to be heard over the din of the sound testing.

Having never actually used a bullhorn before, Laughlin experimentally squeezed its trigger a couple of times, before actually speaking into it, but even then found himself jumping at the sound of his own voice. "If everyone from St. Isaac's will please gather at the front of the stage," he began, and found no need to repeat himself. The faculty quickly herded the nearly two hundred students into the area between the stage and the first row of chairs, and when there was a sudden lull in the sound testing, Laughlin seized the opportunity to quickly explain what would happen tomorrow. "The youngest children will be in the front row," Father Laughlin instructed. "You will walk down from the school in classes, starting with first grade. Sister Mary David will lead you, and it's really quite simple. Ours are the front rows of the center section, and as each row fills, a faculty member will lead you into the next row. The seniors will be last, except for the faculty." He let his eyes wander over the students, focusing on those most likely to misbehave. "Keep in mind that the entire staff will be behind you, and we're all quite good at recognizing the backs of your heads. So, shall we try it?" He dropped the bullhorn to his side as the classes began sorting themselves out and filing into the rows in their designated order. Over to the side, Father Sebastian stood with the three students—Sofia Capelli, Melody Hunt, and Ryan McIntyre—who had been specifically requested by the Vatican to assist the Pope at the altar during the Mass. "Tomorrow morning," he told the rest of the students as they began settling themselves onto their chairs, "you will all receive new uniforms, and you will not get them either dirty or wrinkled on the walk down from the school. Is that clear?" He saw the woman from Channel 5 listening and taking notes, and suddenly wished he had something more important to say than cautionary words about school uniforms, but nothing came to mind. "When the Mass is over, we will all walk together back the way we came, and when we are back at the school we will have a private blessing from His Holiness." As the younger children started to whisper excitedly among themselves, while the older ones did their best to appear utterly blasé about a private audience with the Pope, Father Laughlin turned to the three students gathered around Father Sebastian.

Though it was not up to him to question the choice of the Vatican, Father Laughlin still wondered how wise that choice had been. Of course, these were the three students the Pope was most interested in—the three from whom evil had been totally exorcised by Father Sebastian—and certainly none of them had given Father Laughlin any cause for concern; all of them had been utterly cooperative in every way, paying complete attention to Father Sebastian as he'd instructed them in their duties as altar servers, rehearsing them in the school's chapel all morning. They'd stood uncomplainingly holding the heavy candlesticks for a full hour, none of them seeming even slightly stiff after the ordeal. The two girls had carried the trays, holding the wafers and the wine in hands that never trembled at all, while Ryan McIntyre had supported the full weight of the large Bible that would be used during the ceremony tomorrow as if it were no heavier than a single sheet of paper.

And all of it had been done without a single word of complaint or a muttered grumble, or even the impatient glancing at the clock that is endemic among students everywhere. Deciding that the Vatican had, after all, known what it was doing, Laughlin turned to Father Sebastian. "You have their cassocks and their cottas?"

Father Sebastian nodded.

"And the lighters?" the older priest fretted.

"Everything is ready," Father Sebastian assured him. "They all know their duties, and exactly how to perform them. And I'll rehearse them at least five more times before tomorrow."

Mollified, Laughlin turned his attention back to the rest of the student body, but as he raised his bullhorn to begin instructing them on their exit from the Common, he was interrupted by Sister Margaret, who was hurrying toward him, holding a cell phone.

"Ryan McIntyre's mother is waking up," she said, whispering directly into Laughlin's best ear. "They want him at the hospital immediately."

Father Laughlin signaled to Ryan, who stepped forward and listened quietly as the priest told him what had happened. "Brother Francis will drive you to the hospital." He hesitated, then turned to Father Sebastian. "Perhaps we should replace Ryan with one of the other students for tomorrow—" he began, but Father Sebastian shook his head.

"Cardinal Morisco was very clear," he said. "It is these three His Holiness wants."

"Still, given that he might not be able to finish rehearsing—"

"What do you think, Ryan?" Father Sebastian asked, once again cutting off the elder priest's words.

Ryan gazed steadily at Father Sebastian. "I can do it," he said softly. "I can do whatever you need me to do."

"Good boy," Father Sebastian said. He turned back to Father Laughlin. "Everything's going to be fine. And I'll take Ryan to the hospital. You'll need Brother Francis to help get everyone back to school, and Sofia and Melody can help."

Before Father Laughlin could object, Father Sebastian Sloane and Ryan McIntyre were gone.

CHAPTER 59

POUNDING.

Someone was pounding on the door.

Or the wall.

It had been going on a long time, growing louder with every beat, and now every time the sledgehammer struck, Teri McIntyre could feel it.

But it wasn't coming from the door or the wall. It was coming from inside herself; she could feel it in her chest. Her heart? Was that it? Was it her own heart pounding?

But it was in her head, too, pounding away at her like the worst throbbing migraine she'd ever experienced. "Stop . . ." she whimpered, barely aware of her own voice. "Make it stop . . ."

Something touched her arm . . . her wrist. Something warm.

Teri's lips moved, but no more sound came out.

"Teri?" a female voice asked, seeming to thunder in her ear. "Can you hear me?"

"Don't . . ." Teri pleaded, but even as she whispered the word, the pounding eased slightly, and her mind cleared just enough to let her re-alize that it was, indeed, her own heartbeat, and that it was timed perfectly to the throbbing pain in her head. Without opening her eyes, she whispered yet another word.

"Headache."

Her mind cleared even more, and with consciousness came even more pain. She whimpered again, this time the exquisite agony in her head rendering the sound of nothing more than a faint groan.

Once again she felt the warm touch, and this time recognized it as human fingers. And the fingers were putting something in her hand. "This is the button that controls your pain medicine," the voice said. "When it hurts too much, just press the button." The voice spoke again as Teri's thumb instantly reacted to the words. "Can you tell me your name?"

Why is she asking my name? Teri wondered. *She just called me by my name.*

"Can you tell me what year it is?"

Teri wished the woman would leave her alone so she could sink back into whatever place she'd come from, that place where there had been no pain and no pounding. But it was too late. She was awake.

She opened an eye.

The light made the pain worse, so she closed her eye again, but now her mind was clear enough so she knew where she was.

A hospital.

A hospital? How could that be? She was at home and—

"Mom?"

Ryan? Teri struggled to open her eyes again, and sit up, but even the tiny amount of movement she managed sent such a jolt of pain through her that she dropped back onto the pillow.

"Mom? Can you wake up?"

"Try to open your eyes," the female voice urged, but it seemed softer this time, and the warm hand that rested once again on her arm felt slightly comforting. "You're safe now. You're in a hospital. You've had a head injury."

Safe? Head injury? What was going on?

"Your son is here to see you."

"R-Ryan?" Teri stammered. Her mouth felt sticky and her voice sounded thick, and then she felt a straw touch her lips. She grasped at it, and eagerly sucked in a little water. She opened her eyes again to see a young nurse next to the bed, with Ryan standing next to her.

"Do you want more water?" Ryan asked.

Teri nodded, the headache easing slightly as the pain medication kicked in. She took the straw between her lips and sucked in a little more of the water.

"Do you think you could talk to the police?" the nurse asked.

"Police?" Teri repeated.

"They need you to tell them what happened, Mom."

A movement near the door caught Teri's eye and then she saw that there was someone else in the room. A priest—Father Sebastian, from St. Isaac's—who smiled at her as their eyes met.

And she remembered. She remembered everything. "Tom," she breathed. "It was Tom Kelly. He pushed me down the stairs!"

"Let me get the police," the nurse said. She stepped quickly through the door and was back a moment later with two men that Teri recognized, but couldn't quite place.

"Remember us?" the older of them asked, stepping forward and smiling down at Teri. "Matt McCain and Steve Morgan? We were at your house the night of the break-in. We're the ones who found you."

"But you left," Teri said uncertainly. "And Tom—"

"We came back," McCain explained. "It seems I forgot to get your signature on the report. But it also seems we were a little too late getting back. Can you tell us what happened?"

As Father Sebastian joined the little group surrounding the bed, Teri began to recount what had happened after the police had left that night, how Tom had suddenly turned into a stranger—someone she'd never met before. Someone who was nothing at all like the man she'd known for half a year. Someone who wanted something from her.

"What was it he wanted?" McCain asked as Teri finished.

Teri looked from one of the faces around her to another. Both of the officers were looking at her intently, but Ryan's face was almost impassive, as if whatever Tom had wanted meant nothing to him.

But Father Sebastian's eyes were boring into her, as if he wanted to hear her answer even more than the two detectives.

"He kept yelling at me about some kind of crucifix," she finally said. "Something he seemed to think my husband had. But I didn't know what he was talking about." She looked helplessly up at the group around the bed. "I wish I did know," she said. "But how could I give him something I didn't even know about?" Her eyes flicked from Matt McCain to Steve Morgan, then back to McCain. "Do you think maybe he thought I was someone else? Or my husband was someone else?" Her gaze shifted to her son. "Ryan?" she asked. "Do you know what he might have been talking about?"

Ryan shook his head, his face still utterly blank, almost as if he didn't even remember who his father was, let alone what he might have had that Tom Kelly wanted.

But out of the corner of her eye, Teri was watching Father Sebastian Sloane, too. And she saw something else in the priest's expression as Ryan shook his head.

Something that looked exactly like relief.

She took Ryan's hand and squeezed it. "Don't forget him," she said softly. "Don't ever forget your father—he'll always take care of you."

Ryan said nothing, and the look in his eyes—the strange blankness—didn't change at all.

Chapter 60

THE MAYOR OF Boston stood on the stage and surveyed the activity taking place on the Common. Tomorrow was forecast to be as perfect as today, and with no rain for tonight, there were already a few people preparing to spend the night in the park, eating from picnic hampers and sleeping wrapped in blankets. If any parallels could be made between rock concerts and papal appearances, enough people to fill every available seat will have gathered in the Common before sunrise. By the time of the Mass, the trees to the left would be full of hundreds of people as well, each of them risking broken arms and legs for a better vantage point. So the Pontiff would be gazing out over a sea of people with a turquoise sky above and a background of swans swimming lazily in the lake behind.

But that was tomorrow; right now the mayor needed to focus on the present. And the present seemed to be going very well, all things considered: four speaker towers were up and fully functional, the fence around the perimeter of the seating area was in place, and workmen on the stage were assembling the backdrop—a curtain of deep purple, in front of which would stand the altar at which the Pope would celebrate the Mass. As the mayor watched, half a dozen more workmen appeared from somewhere behind the stage, dressed in uniforms he'd never seen before, but a moment later the chief of police appeared at the mayor's elbow.

"Vatican security," he said, nodding toward the uniformed workmen and perfectly reading the mayor's puzzled expression. "They're in charge of the Plexiglas, and they're the only ones allowed to set it up. Grimaldi told me they can do the whole job in half an hour if they have to."

"Grimaldi?" the mayor repeated, cocking his head slightly as he shifted his gaze to the chief.

"Roberto Grimaldi," the chief explained. "Head of Vatican security whenever the Pope is traveling." He paused to survey the activity, which seemed to be increasing with every minute that passed. "We're cutting it a little closer than I like, but we'll make it. Grimaldi knows what he's doing."

"I hope so," the mayor replied dourly. "And I trust you let him know that if anything goes wrong, it's going to be more on them than us. I still don't think we should have agreed to this at all. Just not enough time to get ready."

The chief shrugged. "And if we hadn't agreed, we'd have every Catholic in Boston on our backs, and you could forget about running next time, let alone serving another term."

"I know," the mayor sighed. "But I still don't have to like it." Just then a young man with an athletic build, intense dark eyes and an official looking clipboard in his hand stepped through the curtain, spotted the chief and came over.

"Well, speak of the Devil," the chief said, then introduced Roberto Grimaldi to the mayor.

"My apologies for the short notice, Your Honor," Grimaldi said. "I must tell you, I think I was probably as upset over the lack of planning as you, but as it happens you have an excellent venue here, and your people have made it very easy for us."

"I wish that made me feel better." Flowers sighed. "But I'm afraid I'm not going to get much sleep until this is all over."

"Nor will I," Grimaldi agreed. "But for us this is actually a very small event, comparatively speaking. If you block vehicular access to the

Common tomorrow morning in time to have the streets cleared by ten-thirty, that should do it. Since we began using the plexi shield, we no longer have to worry about snipers or people in the audience, and if the streets are blocked, it eliminates the possibility of a car bomb. His Holiness will arrive in his armored car, and our security along with your own will be in place when he moves from the car to the stage." Grimaldi offered the mayor and the police chief a thin smile. "I should think that between us we can keep him safe while he walks ten feet, don't you?" Grimaldi flipped a couple of sheets over on his clipboard. "The three students from St. Isaac's Preparatory Academy who will be servers for the Mass will follow His Holiness in a second limousine, escorted by Father Sebastian Sloane." Seeing the mayor and police chief exchange a nervous glance, Grimaldi smiled. "Believe me, the Vatican has been watching Father Sebastian for years, and both he and the three children are here at the direct request of His Holiness." He pointed toward the foot of Spruce Street. "They'll enter from that street, and the cars will pull up directly behind the stage. His Holiness will not be visible to anyone in the Common until he appears on the stage, and then he will be protected by the plexi shield. Keep the streets clear until thirty minutes after he's gone, and that will be it."

The mayor fumbled in his pocket for his antacids, and glanced questioningly at the police chief.

"We'll have security at the school and all along the three blocks of the route to the Common." When the mayor looked no happier, he spread his hands helplessly. "It's the Vatican's show, and they want to do it their way. And I've got to say that from what I've seen and heard, they run a very tight ship. Frankly, short of spending three days trying to put everyone who comes in through a metal detector, I can't think of anything else we'd do."

"Okay," the mayor sighed. "So there's nothing else to do but sit back and enjoy the show?"

"Exactly," Grimaldi said, finally smiling. "And you'll enjoy it—there's something quite magical about His Holiness. Everywhere he goes, it's the same—everyone who sees him adores him." He glanced at his watch. "And since His Holiness lands in about ten minutes, I need to go."

The mayor shook Grimaldi's hand, as did the chief, then Grimaldi flipped open his phone, punched a couple of buttons, and headed off in the direction of the back gate, where a chauffeured black sedan waited.

"Tums?" The mayor held the open package out to Chief Warner.

"Don't mind if I do," the chief replied, and helped himself to two.

CHAPTER 61

I T WAS THE dank cold that woke Ryan.

He'd gone to bed early, leaving Clay Matthews in the common room with José Alvaréz and Darren Bender. He'd opened the window to let the cool spring air into the dorm room, but it hadn't been cold enough to add an extra blanket to the bed. But now the cold had permeated his whole body, and he felt like he'd never be warm again.

He groped for the covers, but all he touched was something cold and hard and damp, and as the last vestiges of sleep fell away he realized he wasn't in bed at all.

He wasn't even in his dorm room.

He was somewhere deep in the tunnels beneath the school, and he was by himself, and he had no memory of how he'd gotten here. But even as he tried to figure out what might have happened, he realized he was moving. As if of their own volition, his legs were carrying him through the tunnel, moving slowly, but deliberately. And when he tried to stop, to pause for a moment to figure out where he was, nothing happened.

He simply kept walking, moving through the dark passage like a zombie, unable to stop, unable even to choose which direction to take when he reached a spot where two passages intersected. But finally, after the third turn, he knew.

Ahead was a door, standing open, yellow light spilling through. A moment later he was gazing into the small chapel hidden deep in the bowels of St. Isaac's.

And on the floor was the strange labyrinth that had been inscribed around Jeffery Holmes's coffin.

"Come in, Ryan," Father Sebastian said, his voice soft.

Ryan didn't want to go in. All he wanted to do was turn away and run back through the tunnels until he found his way out, found his way back to his room. But even as he struggled to make himself turn away from the open doorway, the two candles flickering on the altar drew him in.

Father Sebastian was standing in the center of the labyrinth, and directly above him hung the enormous crucifix, suspended upside down, the face of Christ seeming to leer at Ryan. Half a dozen candles set around the periphery of the chapel made shadows dance everywhere, and it was a moment or two before Ryan realized the shadows were cast by Sofia Capelli and Melody Hunt, who were standing at two of the entrances to the labyrinth.

Melody turned and smiled at him and held out her hand.

And though he still wanted to turn away—wanted it more than anything else in the world—his legs refused to obey his mind. He took three steps into the room, and found himself at the third entrance to the labyrinth.

A strange tune began, a slow pavane that seemed to come from inside his own head. The beat grew more insistent, throbbing through his body, and Ryan found himself beginning the dance that would end only when he, along with Melody and Sofia, were at the center of the maze.

At last they stood in a triangle around Father Sebastian, and Ryan felt his right arm rise, reaching out until the tips of his fingers touched Melody Hunt's. A current almost like electricity flowed through him at Melody's touch, and he felt a dark energy begin gathering around him, flowing into the room as if emanating from the walls themselves.

It was if the very stones in the building had begun to vibrate.

Father Sebastian gazed up at the twisted face of the Christ suspended above him, his eyes glowing as if from some inner flame. "Tonight we combine this trinity into a single being," he intoned. "A being whose power is far greater than yours—a being who answers only to me."

His voice dropped, and he whispered a few more words. Sofia Capelli reached out to Ryan, and once again he found himself powerless to resist the impulse to reach back to her. As their fingers touched, the energy in the room redoubled and Ryan's skin began to tingle, he felt unsteady, and then a wave of nausea washed over him.

As quickly as it came, it was gone, and when it had passed, so too had the unsteadiness and the tingling on his skin.

All that was left was a feeling of power.

That, and an eagerness to hear whatever Father Sebastian was about to tell him.

Father Sebastian took an ancient scroll from the sleeve of his cassock, unrolled the yellowed parchment and began to read. Though he'd never heard the words before, Ryan's lips, along with those of Melody and Sofia, were forming the phrases in unison with Father Sebastian, and soon their voices began to rise filling the chapel with a hypnotic chant. As their voices rose, the darkness began to swirl around them until the three of them formed a vortex around Father Sebastian.

Their voices continued to rise, and now the chapel itself seemed to be spinning around them. Still their voices soared higher until the walls themselves began to tremble.

Then, as they howled out the last syllable of the chant, a wailing scream erupted from directly above Father Sebastian, and when he looked up, Ryan once again saw the figure of Christ hanging upside down on the suspended cross. The Savior's mouth was open, and his entire body was writhing in agony. From the wound in his side, blood was streaming, and as Ryan stared upward a few drops hit his face.

His skin burned as if the blood were glowing embers.

Now Ryan's own hands were bleeding again, his blood once more mixing with Melody's and Sofia's.

Father Sebastian's voice fell silent, and he rolled up the parchment and slipped it back in the sleeve of his cassock. He approached Sofia. His hands, too, were bleeding now, and he held them out to Sofia, laying them on each of her cheeks. "It is through my blood that you live and you are bound to my bidding," he said.

"I will obey," Sofia whispered.

Father Sebastian turned to Melody and placed his hands on her face, repeating the words as blood flowed from his palms down Melody's cheeks.

"I will obey," Melody said quietly.

Now Father Sebastian was facing Ryan, gazing directly into his eyes, and when his bleeding palms came up to press against the flesh of Ryan's face, a great exaltation flooded into Ryan, and, as he listened to the priest's words, he knew what his answer would be.

"It is through my blood that you exist and you are bound to my bidding," Father Sebastian intoned, his eyes still locked on Ryan.

Ryan stood perfectly still, and his voice rose from his throat, confident and strong: "I will obey."

Father Sebastian broke the circle and moved to the altar, where three packages lay neatly wrapped. "Here, then, are your vestments for tomorrow," Father Sebastian said as Ryan and Melody and Sofia followed him from the labyrinth. "Put them on, and then I will instruct you as to exactly what you will do tomorrow."

Ryan opened his package and took out the crimson cassock, slipping it on over the pajamas that were all he wore. It felt heavy and bulky under the arms, but he ignored the weight and put on the surplice, whose lacy cuffs concealed those of the cassock itself.

Not a single drop of blood from either his hands or his face stained the white surplice when he was finished.

"May Allah be pleased with you all," Father Sebastian said softly when all three of them were fully clad in their vestments. "*Radiya 'Llahu 'anhum*. Glory be to God, the one God, the true God!" He closed his eyes and swayed back and forth, then whispered, "Tomorrow it will end, and my ancestors will be avenged. *Subhana wa ta'ala*."

As Ryan and Melody and Sofia watched and listened, the priest showed them how to arm the bombs concealed within the cassocks, and where the trigger buttons were concealed in their sleeves.

Finally, he told them the exact moment during tomorrow's public Mass at which they would press the triggers, ending not only the life of the Pope of Rome, but of themselves as well.

"*Subhana wa ta'ala,*" Father Sebastian repeated. "Allah is exalted above weakness and indignity."

Chapter 62

ALONE FIGURE stood on the hill far off to Ryan's right, silhou-etted against the clear, scarlet light of early dawn.

As he gazed at the figure, he wasn't quite certain what it was.

A man?

A scarecrow?

The figure came slightly more into focus, and now he could see that it was a man. A man on a cross! He was at the foot of Calvary, gazing up at the crucified Savior! He took a step closer, and then another. Yes, it was a cross, but as he drew nearer, he could see that the man wasn't hanging on it after all.

Rather, he was standing in front of the cross, and though he was bound to it with chains wrapped tight around his body, his eyes were serene.

Serene, and fixed steadily on Ryan.

Now, as the sky began to brighten, Ryan could see the man's face more clearly, and his breath caught in his throat. "Dad?" he breathed so softly that the word was instantly lost on the morning breeze.

"Come here, Ryan," his father called. "Come back to me."

But now another voice was calling to him from somewhere off to the left, and Ryan turned away from the figure bound to the base of the cross.

"No, Ryan," his father said. "Don't look anywhere but here. I am your salvation."

Ryan hesitated, but the other voice called again, and there was a note of command he couldn't ignore: "You will stay with me. It is by my blood that you live, and you will do as I bid."

Ryan moved farther away from his father.

"No, Ryan," his father whispered, his voice low but his words distinct. "Come to me, Ryan. Come back to me. Only I can save you."

As his father's voice called out to him, Ryan tried to turn back, tried to begin the climb up the hill to where his salvation stood bound to the cross. But his body was no longer his own, and slowly he turned once more in the other direction, turned once more away from his father. And there, on another hill, a hill much lower and much closer than Calvary, he beheld another figure: Father Sebastian Sloane standing at the headwaters of a river of blood that seemed to flow out of nowhere.

"It is through my blood that you live and you are bound to my bidding," Father Sebastian repeated, quietly and with no emotion whatsoever.

His words struck a chord deep within Ryan, and he started toward the dark figure that was the priest. "I come, Father. I obey. I will always obey."

"Ryan!" his father called, his voice already fading as Ryan drew farther and farther away from him. "Do not forget my gift. Do not forget the gift I left to you."

As if he hadn't heard his father's words at all, Ryan kept walking toward the dark priest. But as he drew near, he suddenly saw that Father Sebastian was not alone. Melody was with him and she was smiling at Ryan and beckoning to him. He quickened his step, reaching out to her as she was reaching out to him, but just before their fingers touched, Father Sebastian's right hand rose high in the air, clutching a silver crucifix that was as long as his arm. His hand was clutched around the face of Christ, and as he raised it high, the light of the rising sun glinted off the keenly honed blade to which the feet of the Savior were bound.

Then the crucifix flashed downward in a great arc, and in the instant his fingers touched Melody's, the glittering blade slashed through the flesh and tendons and bones of her neck.

As Father Sebastian let Melody Hunt's body fall to the ground, her blood gushed from her neck to join the river that flowed from beneath the priest's feet. Her head dropped next to Ryan's own feet.

She looked up at him, her agony clouding her perfect blue eyes and twisting her face into a mask of pain. Her lips worked, and he could see her trying to form a word. She struggled, her eyes tearing, and then—

Ryan awoke, gasping and sitting straight up in bed, his heart pounding, his skin clammy, and a vision of Melody's tortured features still hanging in the fading darkness before dawn.

Clay Matthews slept peacefully on the other side of the room.

Ryan lay still, waiting for the terror of the dream to pass. And soon it would pass and he would go back to sleep and when he awoke again he would be ready for the day.

The day that was to be the most important day of his life.

The most important, and the last.

The Pope was coming today, and by the end of the day, Allah would have three new martyrs, who would live in eternal glory for the deed of their martyrdom.

Now, as he lay in the brightening light of the dawn, Ryan knew what the dream had meant. It had been a temptation from the Infidels who would turn him away from the true faith. But he would deny temptation today. He, and Melody, and Sofia would obey.

Yet even as he made his silent vow, his gaze shifted from the window shade to the seam in the wainscoting next to his bed. The source of his temptation lay inside the secret compartment; he had placed it there himself after bringing it from the attic of his father's house.

Tonight it had spoken to him.

It had come to him in the nightmare, and it had tempted him.

It must be destroyed.

Ryan slipped out of bed and quietly worked the piece of wood loose from the wainscoting. When it came free, he laid it on his bed and reached into the hole behind the plaster.

His fingers closed around the cold silver and instantly a tingling ran up his arm.

He brought the crucifix out and gazed at it in the dawn light.

A voice inside him whispered. "You know what you must do. You must do as you are commanded."

The crucifix glowed as if with a light from within.

His fingers closed on it, so that his eyes would not succumb to its temptation.

He would not let this trinket stand in the way of his obeying the command of the Father.

He carefully replaced the wainscoting, then slipped back into bed. He gazed at the ceiling—ignoring the temptation of the object clutched in his fist—waiting.

Waiting until morning.

Waiting for the fulfillment of his destiny.

Chapter 63

From the moment he awoke in the dark hours before dawn until the moment his limousine arrived at St. Isaac's Preparatory Academy, Pope Innocent XIV had been feeling his excitement grow. The rediscovery of the ancient Rite of Invocation—a rite lost so long ago that its very existence was regarded by all but a handful of Vatican scholars as nothing more than a myth—would be the crowning achievement of his Pontificate. Ever since he'd viewed the first file, the ramifications of the ritual's rediscovery had never been far from the forefront of his mind, and the longer he'd considered the matter, the more he understood that the importance of the ritual could not be overestimated.

To be able to exorcize evil so ill-concealed as to be easily banished by the simplest of parish priests was one thing; to be able to summon forth and wash away the most deeply hidden and firmly rooted evil that stains every human soul was quite another.

This was something that would forever change the current of human endeavor.

It would eradicate war.

It would be the dawn of true peace on earth, just as the Savior had promised. And today, he, Innocent XIV—a simple man who finally understood the reason why God had chosen him to wear the shoes of the Fisherman—was about to confirm that the ancient lost rite had truly reemerged.

He felt a light touch on his elbow, then heard Cardinal Morisco's soft voice. "Holiness?"

Startled from his reverie, the Pope looked up, and then out the car window at the crowds that lined the street despite his orders that the route from the airport to St. Isaac's not be publicized. Still, the faithful always found him; he smiled and waved.

The car pulled to a stop, and his security detail emerged from the limousine directly ahead, scanned the crowd that was being held back from the front door of St. Isaac's by the local police, then quickly surrounded his own car. A moment later he was out of his car, up the steps, and through the front door of the school.

And there they were—he recognized them in an instant, not only because of the familiarity of their faces from the video clips he'd seen, or the fact that they were wearing the red vestments of their service at the Mass this morning, but by the very air around them.

They were smiling at him, all three of them, their faces utterly devoid of any expression except adoration, their eyes wide and clear. Yes, these were souls who were free of any impurity at all, clearly guided by a single spirit.

Father Sebastian Sloane had indeed performed the miracle.

The Pope tried to match their own serenity as each of them stepped forward in their turn.

First, the lovely dark-haired child. "Sofia Capelli, Your Holiness," she whispered, dropping to her knees and kissing his ring. He laid a hand gently atop her head and listened to his heart.

He could sense no evil in this child at all. He took her hand and drew her to her feet; as she rose, her deep brown eyes met his, a serene smile giving her full lips a tiny curve. Here, he sensed, was a child who knew she stood in perfect grace in the eyes of God. He touched her cheek. She was as a newborn.

It was the same with the angelic fair-haired girl, Melody Hunt, whose perfect complexion, and eyes the color of flawless sapphires, gave unchallengeable testament to the glory of God.

And finally the young man, Ryan McIntyre, who introduced himself as humbly as the two girls. As the boy looked up into his eyes, the Supreme Pontiff saw the same clarity in his eyes that he had seen in theirs, sensed the utter purity of his spirit. Again, this was a child whose soul wanted nothing more than to glorify the perfection of its Maker.

It was true. It was all true, and Pope Innocent XIV's heart and soul swelled with joy at what he beheld.

At last he turned to Father Sebastian Sloane, the young priest who had somehow wrought this miracle. He offered his hand, and the young priest instantly dropped to his knees, leaned forward, and reverently kissed the ring of his Office. "It is truly a pleasure to meet you, my son," the Pope said so softly that only Father Sebastian could hear. "I have followed your career, and your work shall be rewarded."

Father Sebastian looked up, and once more the Pope beheld that perfect clarity he'd seen in the three children. Here before him was a man who understood his destiny. "As you, also, shall be rewarded, Holiness," Sloane murmured.

"I look forward to the afternoon," the Pope said, "when we shall have time to discuss not only your work, but your future as well."

"You are my future," the priest replied. "Today my destiny is fulfilled."

"Holiness, it is time," Cardinal Morisco said, and a moment later the three students and their teacher were being escorted to the third limousine in the motorcade, while the Pope resumed his seat in the center car. As soon as they were once more underway, the crowd pressed in, and the Pope smiled and waved.

He had much to smile about. This was a glorious day. This was a day that would be remembered forever.

This would be a Mass that no one would ever forget.

CHAPTER 64

TERI McINTYRE LAY in bed staring at the ceiling, idly fingering the morphine pump that allowed her to control her own pain. Not that she was in that much physical pain anymore—she'd awakened with the residual aches and pains consistent with a fall down the stairs several days ago, but the pounding in her head had finally receded.

The emotional pain was another matter, and she'd discovered last night that the morphine did a pretty good job with that as well.

Tom Kelly.

How could she have been so trusting? And how could he have been so deceitful? She'd taken him into her life, into her bed—the bed she'd once shared with Bill.

Worst of all, she'd brought him into *Ryan's* life, and stood up in Tom's defense every time Ryan had voiced any objection at all. She'd stood up for Tom Kelly against her own son, and all the time he was some kind of a—a—

A what?

She didn't even know. All she knew was that he'd wanted the crucifix that Bill had brought home from Kuwait after the war there. He'd never loved her at all—hadn't even been interested in her. All he'd wanted was

to use her, and the pain of that knowledge made her finger the morphine button; she could already feel the relief the drug would bring.

No! she told herself. *Don't drug it away. That was last night. Today, you
have to face it. You did the wrong thing, and drugging yourself against the
pain is not going to make things right.*

She reached over and dropped the button on her tray table. She had
to figure it out—it wasn't just Tom Kelly. There was something else—
something that had happened yesterday, when the room had suddenly
been filled with people, and the police were asking her questions, and
Father Sebastian—

Father Sebastian!

Tom Kelly had known Father Sebastian—it was Father Sebastian
who had helped them get Ryan into St. Isaac's so quickly. And then yesterday, even in the haze of pain and drugs that had fogged her mind,
she'd seen something.

Something in the priest's eyes.

Something that had made her very careful when she'd told the police
about the crucifix, made her deny that she knew anything about it at
all.

Something was going on—something to do with that crucifix. Was
that why Tom Kelly had wanted to get Ryan into St. Isaac's?

Her mind swam.

As soon as she got out of the hospital—which would be either today
or tomorrow—she would go directly to St. Isaac's, get Ryan and go
away.

Go away where?

Somewhere—anywhere—just so Tom Kelly, or whoever he was,
would never find them again.

Teri let out a long sigh and sank back into her pillows.

On the television pinned to the wall high up in the corner of her
room, one of the news shows was playing a tape from yesterday, when
the Pope's plane had landed at Logan Airport and immediately taxied
to a far corner of the field where it was cordoned off.

Now they cut to this morning at dawn, when the Pope had finally
appeared at the top of the stairs leading to the tarmac and a waiting mo-

torcade, stepping through the plane's door at the exact moment the first rays of the rising sun bathed the plane—and the Pope—in a golden aura.

The image changed again, and a "Live From The Boston Common" message began scrolling across the bottom of the screen. Teri reached for the volume control.

"We're standing by at the Common right now," the announcer, a petite brunette, said. "Pope Innocent Fourteenth is expected to arrive at any moment." The camera panned to the left, and behind her were shoulder-to-shoulder crowds of people packing the park in front of a big stage, completely surrounded and roofed with Plexiglas, with what looked like the entire Boston police force acting as crowd control. "His Holiness will come down from St. Isaac's Preparatory Academy, along with three of the school's students whom the Pope has asked to serve with him at this morning's Mass. In a major break with tradition, we are told that two of the students are girls."

Teri's pulse suddenly quickened, and she raised the head of the bed a little higher and brought the small handheld speaker closer to her ear, dialing up the volume as she did so.

"Here comes the motorcade, now," the announcer said, as three black limousines moved slowly down Spruce Street. "The stage has been set up so that the first glimpse the crowd will get of His Holiness will be when he steps through the backdrop behind the altar onto the stage itself. We're told this is primarily a security precaution, though it certainly heightens the drama, too. Doesn't it, Cliff?" she added, turning to a blond man standing next to her.

"It certainly does, Annette," Cliff Whoever-he-might-be picked up. "From our vantage point, though, we'll be able to see the Pope disembark from his car, which should happen in just a moment or two." There was a slight pause, and just as Annette was opening her mouth to fill the silence, Cliff spoke again. "Yes, here are the cars now."

The door of the first limo opened and a man in a black suit got out, quickly surveyed the area around the small motorcade, and went to the second car.

Holding open its back door, he stood respectfully as the Pope, clad in a white cassock and a brilliantly jeweled surplice, stepped out.

Then the doors of the third limousine opened, and Teri saw Father Sebastian Sloane step out.

He was followed by two girls, one of whom Teri recognized as the girl Ryan had introduced Tom and her to.

Her heart was racing now, and when Ryan himself finally stepped out of the limousine, Teri knew she'd been expecting it. But why?

What was he doing with the Pope?

He hadn't even been at St. Isaac's two weeks! Why would they have chosen him to serve at the altar with the Pope? He barely even knew the sequence of the Mass!

She struggled against the pain of her sore muscles and cracked ribs and sat up straight, staring at the television screen in numb disbelief as the three teenagers, all of them dressed in bright red cassocks with white surplices over them, moved toward the Pope, who took their hands and greeted each one warmly.

The camera pulled back to reveal the Pope, a Cardinal, and the three students moving toward the stairs at the back of the stage.

But what about Father Sebastian Sloane?

There! As the camera pulled even farther back, Teri saw the priest at the top of the screen. But he wasn't moving toward the Pope; instead he had turned the other way, away from the stage, away from the limousines and was now hurrying across Beacon Street, where another man was waiting.

Teri stared at the other man, unable to believe her eyes.

It couldn't be.

It was impossible.

But it was true.

Tom Kelly greeted Father Sebastian Sloane with a quick pat on the back, then both he and Sloane ducked under the cordon that blocked both Beacon Street and the sidewalk, and vanished into the crowd.

And at the moment they disappeared, Teri knew:

Something horrible was about to happen.

"Call the police!" she shouted. "For God's sake, someone call the police!" Ignoring the pain wracking her body, she swung her legs off the bed and put her feet on the floor, but her knees buckled when she tried to stand.

She grabbed at the table, which rolled away from her and banged into the wall, then flailed at the IV stand, catching her hand on a tube as she lost her balance.

Both she and the stand crashed to the floor, and white hot pain shot through her elbow. "Help!" she screamed, fighting against the pain that threatened to knock her out. "Somebody—please! Call the police!"

Two nurses rushed in, saw what had happened, and began trying to disentangle her, but Teri brushed them away. "Leave me alone," she wailed, pointing at the television. "Call the police! Something terrible is going to happen to the Pope!"

As the nurses stared at her uncomprehendingly, Teri curled up on the floor, the pain in her body and her soul too enormous to handle.

It was her fault—whatever was about to happen was all her fault. And not only was it going to happen to the Pope, it was going to happen to Ryan, too.

With a terrible certainty, Teri McIntyre knew that she was about to watch her son die.

Chapter 65

Ryan McIntyre stepped through the curtain onto the stage. Sofia Capelli was two steps ahead of him, Melody Hunt two behind. Once all three of them were in place, the Pope himself would step through the curtain, but even before the appearance of the Supreme Pontiff of the Roman Catholic Church, the roar of the crowd was already setting not only the Plexiglas shields to vibrating, but the stage as well. The trembling of the floor beneath his feet, combined with the steadily building wave of noise rising over him, made Ryan step reflexively back; he might have fallen off the stage had Melody not instantly offered her support, steadying him so smoothly that he regained his balance before he'd completely lost it.

He looked out over the sea of people—more people than he'd thought the Common could even hold—all of them on their feet, cheering and clapping and waving signs offering the Pope a welcome in half a dozen languages. Some were even standing on their chairs, while the limbs of every tree sagged under the weight of even more people.

Yet even as Ryan gazed out at them, the roar began to fade from his consciousness, and a quiet serenity fell over him. Soon all of this would end, and the man in the cassock and miter—the man who led these misguided followers—would die for the glory of Allah. So, too, would Ryan and he would secure an eternity filled with Allah's rewards for his martyrdom.

The roar of the crowd swelled as Ryan sensed that the Pope had joined them on the stage, and the man whose ring he had kissed only a little while ago stepped between himself and Melody to the front of the stage to acknowledge the welcome he was being given.

Now Ryan stood behind the Pope, Sofia to his right, Melody to his left.

The Pope raised his arms in benediction to the assembled, and the roar grew even greater. Then the Pope spoke his first words into the tiny microphone clipped to his vestments, and as his voice boomed out through the massive speaker system the crowd instantly quieted.

"In the name of the Father, and of the Son and of the Holy Spirit," he intoned, his voice carrying easily to every corner of the Common.

In unison, every person Ryan could see crossed themselves exactly the way Ryan and Melody and Sofia were crossing themselves. But the throng beyond the shield was following the lead of their Pope, while the three young people behind it were obeying the instructions of Father Sebastian Sloane.

"You must be perfect in every detail," he'd whispered to the dark force he had harnessed within each of them. *"Until the moment comes, perform the infidel rite, but think only of Allah. Allah, and me."*

"Amen," the combined voice of the multitude intoned.

"The grace of our Lord Jesus Christ and the love of God and the fellowship of the Holy Spirit be with you all," the Pope proclaimed.

"And also with you," the crowd responded.

Obeying the instructions of the dark force within him, Ryan turned to light the candles on the altar, Melody and Sofia flanking him, the Pope still facing the crowd. As they stepped toward the altar, they turned to smile at each other in anticipation of the moment so soon to come. Then, in unison, they lit the candles. Ryan felt the same serenity in the two girls that imbued his own soul. They—as he himself—were ready.

"Let us pray to the Lord."

As one, the multitude bowed their heads and stood so silently that when a flock of pigeons suddenly rose into the air, Ryan could hear the flutter of their wings. As the birds vanished beyond the treetops, the Pope began to pray, his voice full and rich.

Before bowing his own head, Ryan looked out to the front row of seats, where Father Sebastian would be sitting with the rest of the school. But the chair the priest had been assigned was empty. Father Laughlin was there, and Sister Mary David, and Brother Francis, and all the other priests and nuns Ryan had come to know over the last two weeks, but Father Sebastian seemed to have vanished.

He couldn't have, of course—he had to be there somewhere.

Ryan scanned the side sections, searching for the priest, and at the far end of the second row he saw a single man whose head wasn't bowed. It was him! It was Father—

But it wasn't! It wasn't Father Sebastian at all.

Instead, Ryan found himself staring into the face of his own father. His father, in his uniform, his hat on his head!

No! It was impossible—it had to be a trick of the light!

Ryan looked away, but almost instantly his eye was caught by the glint of sunlight reflecting off some kind of polished metal, and when he looked to see what it was, he saw another unbowed head, this one halfway back in the seats, on the opposite side.

And again, Ryan would have sworn he was looking at his father.

The man, the sun still glinting off the medals on his chest, smiled at Ryan, and nodded slightly.

What was wrong? What was happening? He shouldn't be seeing his father at all. He should be seeing Father Sebastian!

A burning sensation grew in his chest.

The Pope finished his prayer, then turned toward the enormous Bible on the altar as the Boston Children's Choir, dressed in blue robes with gold trim, began to sing *Ave Maria.*

The moment was approaching.

Ryan's heart quickened as Father Sebastian's voice whispered in his memory, repeating the instructions over and over.

The timing had to be perfect. One slip, and it could all go wrong. He eased slightly toward Melody, drawn to her now as he had been since the moment he'd first seen her.

The moment was very close now; the "amen" from the crowd that would mark the end of the next prayer would also mark the moment when he and Melody and Sofia would press the buttons that had been sewn into the sleeves of their cassocks.

The moment when they would greet Allah and receive his gifts.

The choir finished, and the crowd stood silent, muted by the beauty not only of the song, but of the voices that had sung it.

The Pope turned to the altar, and the waiting Eucharist. "Blessed art thou, O Lord our God, Creator of the fruit of the Earth. The Earth is the Lord's and the fullness thereof," he said. He picked up the small silver pitcher and poured a drop of water into the chalice of wine.

"Lord wash away my iniquity, cleanse me from my sins." The Pope washed his hands in the basin set upon the altar for that purpose, then dried them on a linen towel.

"Let us pray."

Ryan looked beyond the edge of the stage.

Once more his father was smiling at him, and once more he felt the burning in his chest. *It wasn't possible—it couldn't be his father—*and yet it *was,* and he was looking directly into Ryan's eyes, and he was raising his hand to his chest as if he were feeling the same burning that was now searing Ryan's heart.

Without thinking, Ryan raised his right hand, and slipped it beneath the surplice and between the buttons on the cassock.

His fingers closed on the silver crucifix.

The crucifix his father had promised would protect him.

The crucifix he had intended to leave hidden in the wall.

Now, with his father's eyes fixed on him, with his father smiling at him, and with his father's gift clutched in his hand, a new energy flooded through him, bursting from his heart and his soul to flow through his body.

And he realized what he and Melody and Sofia were about to do.

Ryan stared at his father, who was now standing at the very edge of the stage. He was reaching out to Ryan, as if to put his hand right through the Plexiglas, to touch him.

Ryan's gaze shifted to Sofia. Her fingers were twitching, and he saw them disappear into the sleeves of her cassock.

The sleeves where the triggers were hidden.

He turned the other way; Melody, too, was slipping her fingers into her sleeves.

He heard the Pope begin the doxology. The last four lines of the prayer had begun.

"I will praise Thee, O Lord my God, with all my heart."

Ryan's gaze flashed back to his father, and everything inside him changed. His right hand still clutching his father's crucifix, he reached over with his left and grabbed Melody's hand, feeling the energy of the silver cross flow through his arm and hand into her own. Melody's eyes widened, and she looked at him in terror as comprehension suddenly dawned in her mind.

"And I will glorify Thy name forevermore."

Ryan and Melody lunged toward the Pope. As his lips formed the final word, they threw themselves on him, toppling him near the end of the altar and onto the floor, all of them falling just as Sofia, still heeding only the instructions Father Sebastian had planted in her mind, pressed the buttons in the cuffs of her cassock.

The concussion of the twin bombs exploding knocked the breath from Ryan, and for an instant he lay paralyzed, certain he was dead. But a moment later he felt the crucifix in his right hand; felt Melody stir beside him. Beneath them, the Pope struggled, and Melody began to pull away from him, trying to free herself from Ryan's grip so the fallen Pope could recover himself. But if he let go of her hand—

Still holding Melody with his left hand, Ryan released his grip on the silver crucifix and tore her cassock away with his right. Flinging it to the far end of the stage, he ripped off his own and a moment later it fell onto Melody's, both the cassocks lying in a crumpled heap, the full Mass on the altar itself standing between them and the Pontiff.

"Bombs," Ryan whispered, his voice nearly failing him. He clutched at the crucifix once more, and again it lent him the energy he needed.

"We were supposed to kill you," he whispered to the Pope, who was now on his knees, steadying himself against the altar with his right arm as he reached out to Melody with his left. "Father Sebastian—"

His voice broke, and suddenly all he wanted was to see his father again. He turned away from the kneeling Pontiff, but when he tried to search for the man who only a moment ago had been reaching out to him, all he saw was the Plexiglas shield, smeared with the flesh and blood of Sofia Capelli.

Beyond the shield, the crowd was screaming and backing away, crushing against the temporary fencing, but Ryan barely saw any of it. Then there were security men in black suits swarming everywhere, and someone was helping Ryan to his feet and someone else was tending to Melody and a dozen people seemed to be crowded around the Pope and the altar was dripping with blood and bits of Sofia's flesh and hair and clothing clung to the purple curtain behind the altar and—

Ryan was going to faint.

He knew it; knew it as certainly as he'd ever known anything in his life. He was going to faint, and there was nothing he could do about it.

And then, as the darkness began to close in around him, it happened again.

His father was right there, standing at the end of the stage, watching him.

Making certain he was all right.

And then, as his father looked down on him one last time, the faintness drained away from Ryan, and he nodded to his father.

Everything, he knew, was finally going to be all right.

Epilogue

RYAN PRESSED HIS back against the cold stone wall of the cat-acomb and tried to control his rising panic, but the same bit-ter taste at the back of his tongue, the same hammering heart and the same cold sweat he remembered from being in the tunnels under St. Isaac's Academy were starting to overwhelm him.

But he wasn't at St. Isaac's anymore—all that was over, and half a year had passed, and until an hour ago he'd thought Rome was the most beautiful place he'd ever seen. For almost a week he and his mother had been touring the city, seeing not only the fountains and piazzas and ruins everyone else saw, but things no one else ever saw: rooms in the Vatican to which the public was never invited, but which the Pope had led them through, explaining everything they were seeing, taking a whole day simply to show Ryan and his mother the heart of the Eternal City. "And you must see the catacombs," he'd told them at the end of that day. "No visit to Rome is complete without it. It is only there that you will truly understand what our earliest believers suffered for the true faith."

So they came to the catacombs today, and now everything that had happened at St. Isaac's was flooding back to him as he tried to walk with his mother and their guide sixty feet beneath the streets of the ancient city.

Dim light bulbs were strung every twenty feet or so, but they emitted no more light than had their counterparts in the maze of tunnels beneath the school, and he could barely see anything except the next bulb. Between those small beacons, the darkness closed around Ryan with a cold fist.

It was as if he was caught once again in one of the horrible nightmares he'd had at school. Once again he was lost in the dark, trying to navigate dark tunnels, feeling eyes everywhere, watching him from somewhere beyond the reach of his own eyes.

He gulped at the musty air, trying to rid himself of the rising panic, and looked around for his mother and their guide. Faint tendrils of their voices echoed from somewhere in the distance, but they had vanished into the darkness ahead.

He needed to catch up.

But just like in a nightmare, he couldn't make his feet move; it was as if they were mired in thick mud.

He leaned against the wall for a moment, the cold stone on his back settling his nerves slightly, and he tried again.

Touching both sides of the narrow tunnel, he took one step, and then another, finally making his way through the ancient passage that the early Christians had carved by hand out of the stone beneath the city.

I can do this.

He closed his eyes and wiped the sleeve of his shirt over his sweating face.

And heard footsteps.

He whirled, but saw nothing.

He heard the footsteps again, and once more spun around to gaze into the darkness. The footsteps stopped, and now the tunnel was filled with nothing but a terrible silence that was as suffocating as the musty air.

Settle down! Just walk.

With the sheer force of his will he tamped the rising panic down.

Now he could hear the sound of voices again.

But was it his mother and the guide? Or was it something else, something close behind him, something that would vanish if he turned to look.

He forced the dark thoughts from his mind, concentrating only on putting one foot in front of the other, praying he was going in the right direction, and hadn't somehow gotten turned around in the dark.

On both sides of the tunnel, small crypts—barely more than shelves—had been carved out of the stone, and each of the shelves still held the bones where the dead had been laid so many centuries ago. Ryan began counting them as he passed, trying to keep his mind on something other than the phantom footsteps he still heard behind him.

And ahead of him.

And all around him.

Footsteps exactly like those he had heard in the tunnels beneath St. Isaac's the night he had followed the two priests to the dark crypt far below the school.

The crypts here were different, though. Many of them had carvings on their stone walls, and he tried to focus his mind on them and ignore the phantom presence he felt all around.

Then, illuminated by one single lightbulb that seemed to be brighter than the others, he saw a familiar symbol carved into the back of one of the niches.

It was a circular pattern that he recognized in an instant.

The same symbol that had been drawn in chalk on the floor around Jeffrey Holmes's coffin was etched here in the eternal stone!

The labyrinth.

Ryan's whole body trembled. This had to be a nightmare— it couldn't possibly be real. He heard the footsteps behind him again, but they were much closer this time. He steeled himself to spin around and face whatever lurked in the darkness, but before he could turn, something reached out of the blackness.

It was an arm that slipped around his neck and held him utterly immobile.

A rough hand groped at his chest, tearing open his shirt, and then he felt a fist close around the crucifix—his father's crucifix—that had hung around his neck since that morning six months ago when he had been sent by Sebastian Sloane to kill the Pope.

He felt a terrible jerk.

The silver chain broke.

And a soft voice spoke in his ear: "*For the salvation of Christ.*"

Ryan dropped to the floor of the tunnel as his assailant fled, and a moment later even the footsteps faded away.

The tunnels were silent for a moment, and then a single word floated out of the darkness: "Ryan?"

It was his mother's voice that made Ryan realize he must have cried out loud as the arm slid around his neck.

Now, emerging from the darkness ahead, he could see his mother and the guide coming back for him.

He touched his chest and felt the empty place where his father's crucifix had lain heavily since that morning on the Boston Common.

And all he felt was a profound relief.

It was over. The whole thing was finally over.

Wherever that cross had come from, he was certain that it was now going back where it truly belonged.

And wherever it was going, it no longer had anything to do with him, and it had nothing to do with his father's love for him.

That love, he knew, would always be with him.

"Ryan?" his mother called out again.

Ryan got to his feet and brushed the dust from his pants, and by the time his mother reached him, it was as if nothing had happened at all. "Let's go home," he whispered. "I just want to go home."

ABOUT THE AUTHOR

The Devil's Labyrinth is JOHN SAUL's thirty-fourth novel. His first novel, *Suffer the Children,* published in 1977, was an immediate million-copy bestseller. His other bestselling suspense novels include *In the Dark of the Night, Perfect Nightmare, Black Creek Crossing, Midnight Voices, The Manhattan Hunt Club, Nightshade, The Right Hand of Evil, The Presence, Black Lightning, The Homing,* and *Guardian.* He is also the author of *The New York Times* bestselling serial thriller *The Blackstone Chronicles,* initially published in six installments but now available in one complete volume. Saul divides his time between Seattle, Washington, and Hawaii. Join John Saul's fan club at www.johnsaul.com.

About the Type

This book was set in Garamond, a typeface originally designed by the Parisian typecutter Claude Garamond (1480–1561). This version of Garamond was modeled on a 1592 specimen sheet from the Egenolff-Berner foundry, which was produced from types assumed to have been brought to Frankfurt by the punchcutter Jacques Sabon.

Claude Garamond's distinguished romans and italics first appeared in *Opera Ciceronis* in 1543–44. The Garamond types are clear, open, and elegant.